WORLD OF WARCRAFT®

VOL'JIN
SHADOWS OF THE HORDE

MICHAEL A. STACKPOLE

POCKET BOOKS

New York London Toronto Sydney New Delhi

Pocket Books
A Division of Simon & Schuster, Inc.
1230 Avenue of the Americas
New York, NY 10020

This book is a work of fiction. Any references to historical events, real people, or real places are used fictitiously. Other names, characters, places, and events are products of the author's imagination, and any resemblance to actual events or places or persons, living or dead, is entirely coincidental.

First Pocket Books paperback edition May 2014

POCKET and colophon are registered trademarks of Simon & Schuster, Inc.

For information about special discounts for bulk purchases, please contact Simon & Schuster Special Sales at 1-866-506-1949 or business@simonandschuster.com.

The Simon & Schuster Speakers Bureau can bring authors to your live event. For more information or to book an event, contact the Simon & Schuster Speakers Bureau at 1-866-248-3049 or visit our website at www.simonspeakers.com.

Manufactured in the United States of America

10 9 8 7 6 5 4 3 2 1

ISBN 978-1-4767-0297-1
ISBN 978-1-4767-0298-8 (ebook)

That night, visions mocked Vol'jin. He found himself in the midst of fighters, each of whom he recognized. He'd gathered them for that final assault on Zalazane, to end his madness and free the Echo Isles for the Darkspears. Each of the combatants took on aspects of a jihui cube, faced to be at their maximum power. Not a fireship among them, but this did not surprise Vol'jin.

He was the fireship, but not yet turned to display his maximum power. This was not a fight, though desperate, in which he would destroy himself. Aided by Bwonsamdi, they would slay Zalazane and reclaim the Echo Isles.

Who be you, this troll, who be having memories of a heroic effort?

Vol'jin turned, hearing the click of a cube snapping to a new facing. He felt trapped inside that cube, translucent though it was, and shocked that it had no values on any face. "I be Vol'jin."

Bwonsamdi materialized in a gray world of swirling mists. "And who be this Vol'jin?"

The question shook him. The Vol'jin of the vision had been the leader of the Darkspears, but was no longer. Reports of his death would just now be reaching the Horde. Perhaps they had not yet gotten there. In his heart, Vol'jin hoped his allies had been delayed, just so Garrosh could dwell one more day wondering if his plan had succeeded.

That did not answer the question. He was no longer the leader of the Darkspears, not in any real sense. They might still acknowledge him, but he could give them no orders. They would resist Garrosh and any Horde attempt to conquer them; but in his absence, they might listen to envoys who offered them protection. They could be lost to him.

Who do I be?

Vol'jin shivered. Though he thought himself superior to Tyrathan Khort, at least the man was mobile and not wearing sick-robes. The man hadn't been betrayed by a rival and assassinated. The man had clearly embraced some of the pandaren way.

And yet, Tyrathan hesitated when he should not have. Some of it was a game to make the pandaren underestimate him, but Vol'jin had seen through that. The other bits, though, such as when he'd hesitated after Vol'jin complimented a move, those were genuine. *And not something a man be allowing in himself.*

Vol'jin looked up at Bwonsamdi. "I be Vol'jin. I know who I was. Who I gonna be? That answer only Vol'jin could be finding. And for now, Bwonsamdi, that be enough."

To all the World of Warcraft *players, who have taken a fascinating world and made it that much more fun.*

(Especially those who, through random acts of buffery, have saved me more than once.)

Brewmaster Chen Stormstout couldn't think of anything he didn't like. There certainly were some things he liked less than others. For example, he wasn't terribly fond of waiting for his latest brew to ferment and mature to the point where he could sample it. That wasn't because he was anxious to know how it tasted. He had that figured out already—it would be fantastic. What he liked less about waiting was that it gave him all sorts of time to think of new brews, with new ingredients, and he wanted to dive right in and work on them.

But brewing took time and care. With the equipment at the brewery fully involved in the last batch, waiting to develop a new batch was his only option. That meant he had to find something to do by way of distraction, otherwise waiting and planning and brewing things up in his mind would drive him crazy.

Out in the world, in the lands of Azeroth, finding distraction had been easy. There was always someone who didn't like you, or a hungry creature that wanted to eat you—and discouraging both did wonders to occupy an idle mind. And then there were places that had once been, or were becoming, something else that might be again what they were. On his travels he'd seen many of those places and more, and had even helped make some into something.

Chen sighed and looked toward the center of the sleepy fishing village. There his niece, Li Li, was entertaining a dozen of Binan Village's cubs—most of them residents, some of them refugees. Chen was pretty sure she had intended to tell them stories of her travels on Shen-zin Su, the Great Turtle, but this plan had gone awry. Or maybe she was still telling a story but had enlisted their aid in acting out a scene. Clearly the story of a fight, and one that apparently involved her being swarmed over by a pack of young pandaren.

"Is everything going well, Li Li?"

The slender girl somehow surfaced from amid a boiling sea of black and white fur. "Perfectly well, Uncle Chen!" The frustration in her eyes belied her words. She reached down, plucked one scrawny boy from the pack, and tossed him aside, then disappeared beneath a wave of shrieking cubs.

Chen thought to step in but hesitated. Li Li was in no real danger and she was a strong-willed girl. If she needed help, she'd ask for it eventually. To intervene before that would make her think he doubted she could take care of herself. She'd sulk for a bit, and he just hated when she did that. She'd also be outraged and then would go do something to prove she could take care of herself, and that might land her in even greater trouble.

Though that was his primary line of reasoning, the whispers and tutting from the two Chiang sisters gave him further cause to hold back. The two of them were old enough to remember when Liu Lang had first departed Pandaria—or so they said. Though their fur ran much more to white than black, save where they darkened it around their eyes, Chen assumed they weren't quite that old. They'd spent all their lives in Pandaria, and very little of them in the company of those who had lived on the Wandering Isle. They'd developed opinions of those who "chased the turtle," and Chen had taken a delight in confounding them by acting against type.

Li Li, in their eyes, was purely one of the turtle's wild dogs. Impulsive and practical, quick to action and a bit prone to overestimation of her own abilities, Li Li was a fine example of a pandaren accepting the philosophy of Huojin. It was people of such an adventurous spirit who had departed on the turtle or adventured in Outland. Such conduct, in the minds of the Chiang sisters, simply was not to be condoned or given any credit.

Nor were those who did such things.

Chen, were he of a nature to dislike things, certainly would dislike the Chiang sisters. He'd actually taken a liking to them. In addition to fixing up the Stormstout Brewery and concocting fantastic beverages, he'd wandered Pandaria to learn more about the place he'd determined would be his home. He'd seen them, two maiden sisters, struggling with a small garden patch that had gone untended during the yaungol siege, and had offered to help.

They'd not so much as replied to him, but he'd pitched in anyway. He repaired fences and weeded. He laid down new stones for the path to their door. He entertained their great-grandcubs by breathing fire. He swept, hauled water, and piled up firewood. He did that under their disapproving stares and only because, beneath it all, he read disbelief in their eyes.

He'd worked long and hard without their speaking a word to him before he first heard their voices. They didn't speak to him or with him or even really at him. They spoke toward him while speaking to each other. The elder had said, "It is the sort of day that tiger gourami would be nice." The younger merely nodded.

Chen knew it was a command, and he complied. He did so carefully. He fished three gourami out of the ocean. The first fish he threw back. The last one he kept for the sisters, and the largest he gave to a refugee fishwife and her five cubs because her husband was still one of the missing.

He'd known that giving the sisters the first fish would have been seen as a sign of his being hasty. To give them all three would show he was prone to proud displays of excess. To give them the biggest, which was more than they could eat, would show a lack of discretion and calculation. But in doing what he did, he demonstrated reason, consideration, and charity.

Chen did understand that his exercise of dealing with the sisters wasn't likely to win him friends or patronage. Many others he'd known in his travels would have considered them ungrateful and ignored them. For Chen, however, they were a means through which he could learn about Pandaria and the people who would become his neighbors.

Maybe even my family.

If Li Li was an exemplar of the Huojin philosophy, then the Chiang sisters represented believers in the Tushui. They were given to far more contemplation. They measured acts against the ideals of justice and morality—though both could easily be a narrow, parochial, small-village version of those grander notions. In fact, grand notions of justice and morality might seem far too ostentatious for the likes of the Chiang sisters.

Chen liked to think of himself as being firmly in the middle. He mixed and matched both Huojin and Tushui, or so he told himself. More realistically, he tended toward Huojin when adventuring in the wider world. Here, in Pandaria, with the verdant valleys and tall mountains, with most people enjoying a simple lifestyle, Tushui seemed just the thing.

Deep down, that was what Chen needed distraction from. It wasn't about new brewing projects but the knowledge that someday, at some point, he would have to choose one philosophy or the other. If he did make Pandaria his home, if he found a wife and started a family, the days of adventuring would vanish. He'd just become a roly-poly brewmaster, armored with an apron, haggling with farmers over the price of grain and with customers over the price of a mug.

That wouldn't be a bad life. Not bad at all. Chen neatly stacked firewood for the sisters. *But would it be enough?*

Cub shrieks again attracted his attention. Li Li was down and wasn't getting up. Something sparked inside him—that ancient call to battle. He had so many stories of great conflicts. He'd fought alongside Rexxar and Vol'jin and Thrall. Rescuing his niece would be nothing compared to those battles (and recounting those tales would make his brewery very popular), but taking action fed something within him.

Something that defied Tushui.

Chen jogged over and waded into the roiling pile of bodies. He grabbed cubs by the scruff of their necks and tossed them to one side and the other. Being mostly muscle and fur, they bounced and rolled and twisted around. A few bumped against one another, with parts pointing up that should have pointed down. They untangled themselves and scrambled to their feet, ready to dive back in.

Chen growled with just that right mix of gentle warning and true menace.

The cubs froze.

The elder pandaren straightened up, and by instinct, so did most of the cubs. "What exactly was going on here?"

One of the bolder cubs, Keng-na, pointed toward a recumbent Li Li. "Mistress Li Li was teaching us to fight."

"What I witnessed wasn't fighting. It was brawling!" Chen shook his head, exaggerating the action. "That will not do, not at all, not if the yaungol return. You are to have proper training. Now, look smart!" Chen snapped to attention as he gave the command, and the cubs mimicked him perfectly.

Chen fought to hide a smile as he dispatched the cubs, singly and in groups, to fetch more wood, to haul water, and to get sand for the sisters' pathway and brooms to smooth it down. He clapped his paws sharply, and they sprung to their tasks like arrows loosed from taut bows. He waited until they'd all disappeared before he offered Li Li a paw.

She looked at it, her nose wrinkled with disgust. "I would have won."

"Of course, but that wasn't the point, was it?"

"It wasn't?"

"No, you were teaching them a sense of camaraderie. They're a little squad now." Chen smiled. "A bit of discipline, some division of labor, and they might be useful."

He added volume to the last phrase for the sisters, since they'd seen that initial benefit.

Li Li looked at his paw suspiciously, then took it and used it to steady herself as she stood. She tugged her robe into place and reknotted the sash. "Worse than swarming kobolds."

"Of course. They are pandaren." This, too, he said loudly so the Chiang sisters could take it in. He lowered his voice again. "I admire your restraint."

"You aren't kidding." She rubbed her left forearm. "Someone was biting in there."

"As well you know, someone is *always* biting in a fight."

Li Li thought for a moment, then smiled. "No escaping that. And thank you."

"For?"

"Unburying me."

"Oh, that was me being selfish. I was done hauling for the day. No grummle here to help, so that's a detail for your little army."

Li Li cocked an eyebrow. "You're not fooling me."

Chen pulled his head high and looked down at her. "You can't imagine that I might think a niece of mine, who is a well-trained martial artist in her own right, would need my help with cubs. I mean, if I thought that, I'd simply not help you. You'd be no niece of mine."

She paused, her face scrunching up. Chen could see in the quick movement of her eyes the way she was working through that logic. "Okay, yes, Uncle Chen. Thank you."

Chen laughed and draped an arm over her shoulder. "It is tiring work, dealing with cubs."

"True."

"In my case, of course, I had only one to deal with, but she was a pawful."

Li Li dug an elbow into his ribs. "Still am."

"And I could not be prouder."

"I think you could." She spun from beneath his arm.

"Are you disappointed that I haven't asked if I can work with you at the brewery?"

"Whatever would have given you that idea?"

She shrugged uneasily and glanced off toward the Valley of the Four Winds, where the Stormstout Brewery was. "When you're there, you are happy. I see that. You love it so."

Chen smiled wryly. "I do. And do you want to know why I haven't asked you to cease wandering and join me there?"

Her face brightened. "Yes, I want to know."

"It is because, my dearest niece, I need a partner who will still adventure. If I need Durotarian mosses from deep inside caves, who will fetch them? And at a good price? The brewery means I have responsibilities. I can't be gone for months or years at a time. So I need someone I can trust, and someone who, someday, can come back and take over for me."

"But I'm not cut out to be that sort of brewmaster."

Chen waved away that objection. "Sedentary brewmasters I can hire. Only a Stormstout can run the brewery. Maybe I will hire a cute brewmaster, though, and you can marry him and . . ."

". . . and my cubs will inherit?" Li Li shook her head. "You'll have a brood of cubs next time I see you, I'm sure."

"But I'll always be happy to see you, Li Li. Always."

Chen suspected Li Li would have given him a hug, and he'd have gladly returned it, save for two things. First, the sisters were watching, and displays of emotion would make them uncomfortable. More important, however, was that Keng-na came dashing through their vegetable garden, howling, eyes wide.

"Master Chen, Master Chen, there's a monster in the

river! A big monster! He's blue and has red hair and he's awful cut up. He's clinging to the bank. He has claws!"

"Li Li, gather the cubs. Keep them away from the water. Don't follow me."

She stared at him. "But what if . . . ?"

"If I need your help, I'll shout. Go, quickly." He glanced at the sisters. "It looks as if it might storm. You might consider going inside. And locking the door."

They stared defiantly at him for a moment but uttered not a word. He sprinted off, cutting around the garden, and oriented himself on the wooden bucket Keng-na had abandoned. Tracing the boy's path through flattened weeds to the riverbank wasn't hard, and Chen was halfway down the embankment when he saw the monster.

And recognized it immediately. *A troll!*

Keng-na had been right. The troll had been hacked badly. His clothing hung in tatters, and the flesh beneath was not in much better shape. The troll had halfpulled himself out of the river; clawed hands and a tusk thrust into the clay bank were the only things that anchored him.

Chen dropped to a knee and turned the troll onto his back.

"Vol'jin!"

Chen stared at him and the ruin of his throat. If not for the rasp of breath through the hole in his neck, and the bloody red seepage from the wounds, the pandaren would have imagined his old friend to be dead. *And he might still die.*

Chen grabbed Vol'jin's arms and pulled him from the river. It wasn't easy. Scrabbling came from higher up the bank, and then Li Li was at Vol'jin's left shoulder, helping her uncle.

The pandaren's eyes met. "I thought I heard you yell."

"Maybe I did." Chen bent low to the ground, then lifted the troll in his arms. "My friend Vol'jin is badly hurt. Maybe poisoned. I don't know what he's doing here. I don't know if he will live."

"That's Vol'jin, from all your stories." Li Li stared wide-eyed at the mangled creature. "What are you going to do?"

"I'll do what we can for him here." Chen looked up toward Kun-Lai Summit and the Shado-pan Monastery built high upon it. "Then I guess I'll take him there and see if the monks have room for another of my foundlings."

2

Vol'jin, shadow hunter of the Darkspear tribe, could not imagine a worse nightmare. He could not move. Not a muscle, not even to open his eyes. His limbs remained stiff. Whatever bound them felt as heavy as ship's cable and stouter than steel chain. It hurt to breathe, and he could not do so deeply. He would have abandoned the effort, but the pain and weary fear that he might stop kept him going. As long as he could dread not breathing, he was alive.

But do I be so?

For now, my son, for now.

Vol'jin recognized his father's voice in an instant yet knew he'd not actually heard it with his ears. He tried to turn his head in the direction from which the words seemed to come. He couldn't, but his awareness did shift. He saw his father, Sen'jin, keeping pace with him, but not walking. They both moved, but Vol'jin knew not how or toward where.

If I not be dead, then I must be alive.

A voice, strong and low, came from the other side, from his left. *That decision be still hanging in the balance, Vol'jin.*

The troll dragged his consciousness around to look toward that voice. A fearsome figure, troll in general aspect, with a face that looked to Vol'jin like a rush'kah mask, studied him with pitiless eyes. Bwonsamdi, the loa who served the trolls as the guardian of the dead, slowly shook his head.

What be I making of you, Vol'jin? You Darkspears be not offering me the sacrifices you should, yet I help you free your home from Zalazane. And now, you be clinging to life when you should be giving yourself to my care. Have I treated you badly? Be I unworthy of your worship?

Vol'jin desperately wished his hands would curl into fists, but they remained weak and limp at the ends of dead arms. *There be things I must do.*

The loa laughed, the sound scourging Vol'jin's soul. *Listen to your son, Sen'jin. Were I telling him it be his time, he would be telling me his needs are paramount. How be it you raised such a rebellious son?*

Sen'jin's laughter fell as a soothing, cool mist to bathe Vol'jin's tortured flesh. *I taught him that the loa respect strength. You be complaining he did not offer sufficient sacrifices. Now you be complaining that he wishes more time to offer greater sacrifices. Be I boring you so that you need my son to entertain you?*

Think you, Sen'jin, that his clinging to life is so he can be serving me?

Vol'jin could feel his father smile. *My son may have many reasons, Bwonsamdi; but that one be serving your purposes should suffice for you.*

You would be telling me my business, Sen'jin?

I be reminding you, great spirit, only of what you have long taught us to do in your service.

Other laughter, distant laughter, rippled gently through

Vol'jin. Other loa. The high keening tones of one laugh and the low rumble of another suggested Hir'eek and Shirvallah were enjoying the exchange. Vol'jin took some pleasure in this yet knew he would pay for that liberty.

A growl rolled from Bwonsamdi's throat. *Were you so easily convinced to surrender, Vol'jin, I should be rejecting you. You be no true child of mine. But, Shadow Hunter, know this: the battle you face be more terrible than any you have known before. You gonna be wishing you had surrendered, for the burden your victory earns gonna be one that will grind you into dust.*

In a heartbeat Bwonsamdi's presence evaporated. Vol'jin sought his father's spirit. He found it close by, yet fading. *Be I losing you again, Father?*

You cannot lose me, Vol'jin, for I be part of you. As long as you be true to yourself, I gonna be with you always. Vol'jin sensed his father's smile again. *And a father being as proud of his son as I be of you gonna never let that son get away.*

His father's words, though demanding contemplation, provided enough comfort that Vol'jin did not fear for his life. He would live. He would continue to make his father proud.

He would march straight into the terrible fate Bwonsamdi foresaw and deal with it in defiance of all predictions. With that conviction held firmly in mind, his breathing eased, his pain dulled, and he dropped into a black well of peace.

When awareness came to him again, Vol'jin found himself whole and hale, strong of limb and standing tall. A fierce sun beat down on him as he stood in a courtyard with thousands of other trolls. They had nearly a head's height on him, yet none of them made an issue of it. In fact, none of them seemed to notice him at all.

Another dream. A vision.

He did not immediately recognize the place, though he had a sense that he'd been there before. Or, rather, *later*, for this city had not surrendered to the surrounding jungle's invasion. The stone carvings on walls remained crisp and clear. Arches had not been shattered. Cobbles had not been broken or scavenged. And the stepped pyramid, before which they all stood, had not been humbled by time's ravages.

He stood amid a crowd of Zandalari, members of the troll tribe from which all other tribes had descended. They had become, over the years, taller than most and exalted. In the vision they seemed less a tribe than a caste of priests, powerful and educated, quite apt for leading.

But in Vol'jin's time, their ability to lead had degraded. *It is because their dreams all be trapped here.*

This was the Zandalar empire at the height of its power. It dominated Azeroth but would fall victim to its own might. Greed and avarice would spark intrigues. Factions would split. New empires would rise, like the Gurubashi empire, which would drive Vol'jin's Darkspear trolls into exile. Then it would fall too.

The Zandalari hungered for a return to the time when they were ascendant. It was a time when trolls were a most noble race. The trolls, united, had risen to heights which someone like Garrosh Hellscream could not possibly dream existed.

A sense of magic ancient and powerful flooded through Vol'jin, providing him the key to why he was seeing the Zandalari. Titan magic predated even the Zandalari. It was more powerful than they were. As high as the Zandalari had been above things that slithered and stung, so were the titans above them—likewise their magic.

Vol'jin moved through the crowd as might a specter. The Zandalari faces glowed with fearsome smiles—the sort he'd seen on trolls when trumpets blared and drums pounded, inviting them to battle. Trolls were built to rend and slay—Azeroth was their world, and all in it were subject to their dominion. Though Vol'jin might differ with other trolls as to the identity of their enemies, he was no less fierce in battle, and vastly proud of how the Darkspears had conquered their foes and liberated the Echo Isles.

So Bwonsamdi be mocking me with this vision. The Zandalari dreamed of empire, and Vol'jin wished the best for his people. Vol'jin knew the difference. It was simple enough to plan for slaughter and far more complex to create a future. For a loa who liked his sacrifices bloody and battle-torn, Vol'jin's vision held little appeal.

Vol'jin ascended the pyramid. As he moved up, things became more substantial. Whereas before he had been in a silent world, he could now feel drums thrumming up through the stone. The breeze brushed over his light fur, tousled his hair. It brought with it the sweet scent of flowers—a scent just slightly sharper than that of spilled blood.

The drumming pounded into him. His heart beat in time. Voices came to him. Shouts from below. Commands from above. He refused to retreat but stopped climbing higher. It seemed he might be rising through time as he would be rising through lake water. If he reached the top, he would be there with the Zandalari and feel what they felt. He would know their pride. He would breathe in their dreams.

He would become one with them.

He would not allow himself that luxury.

His dream for the Darkspear tribe might not have excited Bwonsamdi, but it provided life for the Darkspears. The Azeroth the Zandalari had known had been utterly and irrevocably changed. Portals had been opened. New peoples had come through. Lands had been shattered, races warped, and more power released than the Zandalari knew existed. The disparate races—elves, humans, trolls, orcs, and even goblins, among others— had united to defeat Deathwing, creating a power structure that revolted and offended the Zandalari. The Zandalari hungered to reestablish rule over a world that had so changed that their dreams could never come true.

Vol'jin caught himself. *"Never" be a powerful word.*

In an eyeblink the vision shifted. He now stood at the pyramid's apex, looking down into the faces of the Darkspears. His Darkspears. They trusted his knowledge of the world. If he told them they could recapture the glory that was once theirs, they would follow him. If he commanded them to take Stranglethorn or Durotar, they would. The Darkspears would boil out of the islands, subjugating all in their path, simply because he wished it done.

He could do it. He could see a way. He'd had Thrall's ear, and the orc had trusted him in military matters. He could spend the months of recuperation plotting out the campaigns and organizing strategies. Within a year or two of his return from Pandaria—if that was still where he was—the Darkspear banner would be anointed with blood and more feared than it already was.

And what be that gaining me?

I would be pleased.

Vol'jin spun. Bwonsamdi stood above him, a titanic figure, ears forward and straining to gather the pulsed shouts from below. *It would gain you peace, Vol'jin, for you be doing what your troll nature demands.*

Is that all we be meant for?

The loa do not require you to be more. What purpose be there in your bein' more?

Vol'jin looked for an answer to that question. His search left him staring at a void. Its darkness reached and engulfed him, leaving him with no answer and certainly no peace.

Vol'jin finally awakened. His eyes opened, so he knew it was not a dream. Faint light came to them, filtered through gauze. He wished to see, but that would require removing the bandages. In turn, that would require him to lift a hand. He found this task impossible. He had so little connection with his body that he didn't know if it was because his hand was tied down or had simply been struck off at the wrist.

Finding himself alive gave him impetus to remember how he had been hurt. Until he'd been certain he would live, the effort had seemed a waste.

Unbidden by anyone, and in gleeful defiance of what Garrosh's wishes would have been, Vol'jin had chosen to travel to the new land of Pandaria to see what Garrosh had the Horde doing. Vol'jin had known of the pandaren because of Chen Stormstout and wished to see their home before the Horde and Alliance war laid waste to it. He'd not arrived with any plan to stop Garrosh, but Vol'jin had once threatened to shoot an arrow through him, and he packed a bow just in case.

Garrosh, though in his usual foul mood, offered Vol'jin a chance to contribute to the Horde's effort. He agreed, less for the Horde's benefit than to be a brake on Garrosh's ambition. Along with one of Garrosh's trusted orcs, Rak'gor Bloodrazor, and a number of other adventurers assembled for the mission to Pandaria's heart, Vol'jin set off.

The shadow hunter enjoyed the journey, comparing this land to those he had visited previously. He'd seen rounded mountains that were weathered and defeated, but in Pandaria they merely seemed gentled. Or jagged, angry mountains that here, though no less sharp, just appeared eager. Jungles and groves abounded with life yet never seemed to hide lethal menaces as they did, say, in Stranglethorn. Ruins existed, but only because they were abandoned, not broken and buried. While the rest of the world had been scourged by hatred and violence, Pandaria had not felt their lash.

Yet.

All too quickly for Vol'jin, the troop reached its objective. Rak'gor and two aides had taken to wing on wyverns to scout ahead, but Vol'jin saw no sign of them when the group reached the mouth of a cave. Large, vaguely humanoid lizard-beasts warded the entrance. The adventurers cut through them and prepared to plunge into the cave's darkened depths.

Black bats shrieked and exploded from the cave's hidden recesses. Vol'jin only faintly caught their cries—he doubted the others heard anything other than the flapping of leathery wings. One of the loa, Hir'eek, wore a bat's shape. *Be this a warning from the gods that no good gonna come going farther?*

The loa gave him no answer, so the Darkspear led the way. A cold sense of corruption strengthened as they pressed forward. Vol'jin stopped and squatted, removing a glove. He scooped up a handful of moist earth and raised it to his nose. The faintly sweet rot of vegetation mixed with the sour stink of bat guano, but he caught hints of something else. Saurok, certainly, but undeniably containing something else.

He closed off his nose and shut his eyes. His hand closed halfway; then his thumb sifted the earth through his fingers. When it was gone, he opened his hand again and extended it. As light as a spiderweb, with the wayward, twisting aspect of a snuffed candle's smoke, residual magic brushed over his palm.

And raked it with nettles.

This be a truly fel place.

Vol'jin opened his eyes again and headed along the ancient passage deeper into the caves. As they came to forks, the adventurers secured both. The troll, his right hand open and naked, didn't even need to sweep through air to find clues. What had been spider silk had become a thread, then yarn, and threatened to grow to cord and rope. Each bit came with tiny needles. The pain grew no worse, but the stripe of it across his palm became wider.

By the time the magic grew to the width of a stout ship's cable, they found a large chamber overseen by the most massive saurok they'd yet encountered. A steaming subterranean lake dominated the chamber's heart. Hundreds of saurok eggs—perhaps even thousands—lay nestled about, warming as they gestated.

Vol'jin held up a hand to stop the others. *A rookery at the heart of the magic.*

Before Vol'jin had a chance to take in the full import of that realization, the saurok discovered them and attacked. The troll and his allies fought back hard. The saurok fought hard as well, and though Vol'jin's company prevailed, everyone ended up cut and bloodied. Yet while his companions saw after their own wounds, Vol'jin felt compelled to investigate.

Silently he waded into the shallow lake and flung his arms wide. Closing his eyes, the troll slowly turned a circle. The invisible magic cables caught like jungle vines over his arms and twisted around his body. Wrapped in them, feeling their burning caress, he understood the place as only a shadow hunter could.

Spirits screamed in agonies ages old. The saurok essence blasted into him, slithering through his belly like the adder that had once writhed across the cold, stone floor aeons before. That snake was true to itself in nature and spirit.

Then magic had hit it. Fearsome magic. Magic that was a volcano to the ember that most magi could command. It flooded through the snake, piercing its golden spirit with a thousand black thorns. Those thorns then pulled apart, this way and that, up from down, inside from outside, even past from future and truth from lie.

In his mind's eye, Vol'jin watched as the thorns pulled and pulled, stretching the gold into taut bowstrings. All at once the thorns shot back toward the center. The thorns dragged the golden lines with them, weaving them through an arcane tangle. Threads twisted and knotted. Some snapped. Others were spliced back with new ends. All the while the adder shrieked. What it once was had been transformed into a new creature, a creature half-mad from the experience, yet malleable and pliant in the hands of its creators.

It was far from alone.

The name "saurok" came to him—it had not existed before that first savage act of creation. Names had power, and that name defined the new creatures. It also defined their masters and pulled aside the veil on the magic used. The mogu had created the saurok. The mogu Vol'jin knew as faint shadows in dim legends. They were dead and gone.

The magic, however, was not. Magic that could re-make a thing so completely came from the dawn of time, from the beginning of everything. The titans, the shapers of Azeroth, had used such magic in their acts of creation. The incredible power of such sorceries could not be un-derstood by a sound mind, let alone mastered. Yet dreams of it fueled insane flights of fancy.

In experiencing the making of the saurok, Vol'jin grasped a core truth of the magic. He could see a way— just the glimmer of a path—he could pursue its study. The same magic that had made a saurok could unmake the murlocs that had killed his father, or cause men to regress back to the vrykul they clearly had been crafted from. Doing either of those would be a worthy use of such power and would justify the decades of study its mastery would require.

The shadow hunter caught himself. There, in think-ing just that, he was falling prey to the trap that had doubtlessly ensnared the mogu. Immortal magic would corrupt a mortal. There was no escaping it. That corrup-tion would destroy the wielder. And, likely, his people.

Vol'jin reopened his eyes and found Rak'gor stand-ing there with the group's survivors. "Be about time you caught up."

"The warchief says there is a connection between these creatures and the mogu."

"Dese mogu, dey be da creators. Dey workin' wicked, dark magic here." Vol'jin's flesh crawled as the orc saun-tered forward. "Dis be the blackest of magics."

The orc offered a quick, feral grin. "Yes, the power to shape flesh and build incredible warriors. This is what the warchief wants."

Vol'jin's guts knotted. "Garrosh playing god? Dis ain't what the Horde be about."

"He didn't think you'd approve."

The orc struck viciously and without mercy. The dagger caught Vol'jin in the throat, spinning him away and to the ground. All around him his companions leaped into battle. Rak'gor and his allies fought with a reckless abandon, heedless of their own safety and dying for their efforts. *Perhaps Garrosh be convincing them that his new magic gonna bring them back and make them better.*

Vol'jin rose to a knee and waved his companions back. He pressed a hand to his throat, closing the wound. "Garrosh betrays himself. He gotta believe we be dead. It be the only way to get time to stop him. Go. Watch him. Find others like me. Swear a blood oath. For the Horde. Be ready when I return."

He'd honestly thought, as they abandoned him there, that what he'd told them was true. But as he tried to stand, black agonies shot through him. Garrosh had planned in depth. Rak'gor's blade had been steeped in some noxious poison. Vol'jin wasn't healing as he should be, and he could feel his strength ebbing. He fought against it, against the fog that drifted through his mind.

And he might have made it had more saurok not found him. He dimly recalled fighting them, blades flashing in the darkness. Pain from cuts that refused to close. Cold seeping into his limbs. He ran blindly, smashing into walls, tumbling down passages, but always forced himself up and to keep moving.

How he'd gotten out of the cave, and how he'd gotten

to wherever he was now, he couldn't say. It certainly didn't smell like a cave. He did catch something hauntingly familiar in the air, but it hid beneath the scent of poultices and unguents. He wouldn't go so far as to assume he was among friends. His being cared for suggested it. Or his enemies could be treating him well in hopes of ransoming him back to the Horde.

They gonna be disappointed with Garrosh's offer.

That thought almost made him laugh. He couldn't quite muster one, though. His stomach muscles tightened but relented from fatigue and pain. Still, that his body could react involuntarily reassured him. Laughter was something for the living, not the dying.

Just like remembering.

Not to be dying, that was enough for the moment. Vol'jin drew in as deep a breath as he could manage, then slowly exhaled. And was asleep before he finished.

3

Chen Stormstout, overlooking a courtyard of the Shado-pan Monastery, felt the cold but didn't dare give any sign of it. Below where he'd been sweeping a light dusting of snow off steps, a dozen of the monks, all barefooted and some stripped to the waist, exercised. In unison, with a discipline he'd not seen in even the world's finest troops, they went through a series of forms. Punches flashed by, blurry, and crisp kicks crackled through chilly mountain air. The monks moved both fluidly and strongly, with the power of rivers raging through canyons.

Except they didn't rage.

Through these most martial of exercises, the monks somehow drew peace. It made them content. Though he'd watched them often, and hadn't heard too many laughs among them, Chen had not detected anger. That certainly wasn't what he expected from troops finishing training, but then he'd never seen anyone quite like the Shado-pan before.

"If I might, Brewmaster, have a word?"

Chen turned and went to lean the broom against the wall but then stopped. That wasn't really the place for it, but Lord Taran Zhu's request wasn't really a question, so he couldn't go to put the broom where it should go. Instead, he just pulled it behind himself and bowed to the monastery's lord.

Taran Zhu's face remained impassive. Chen couldn't tell how old the monk was, but he'd believe the pandaren had been born well before the Chiang sisters. That wasn't because he looked old. He didn't, not really. He had the powerful vitality of someone Chen's age, or even Li Li's. It was something else about him, and something he shared with the monastery.

Something he shares with all Pandaria.

Pandaria had an elusive sense of antiquity. The Great Turtle had been old, and the structures on him were old, but none of them felt as venerable as the monastery. Chen had grown up among buildings that harkened back to Pandaria's architecture but were to the original what a cub's sand castle might be to its inspiration. Not that they weren't wonderful; they just weren't the same.

Chen, having held the bow a respectfully long time, straightened up again. "What can I do for you?"

"A missive has arrived from your niece. She has, as you requested, visited the brewery and made sure they know you will be away for a short while. She is proceeding to the Temple of the White Tiger." The monk inclined his head slightly. "For this latter thing I am grateful. Your niece's strong spirit is . . . irrepressible. Her last visit . . ."

Chen nodded quickly. "Will be her last. It's good to see that Brother Huon-kai is no longer limping."

"He has recovered, both in body and spirit." Taran Zhu's eyes tightened. "Half as much can be said of your latest refugee. There are signs that the troll has regained his senses, though he still heals slowly."

"Oh, that's wonderful. I mean, not that he is healing slowly, but that he is awake." Chen made to transfer the broom to Taran Zhu, then hesitated. "I'll just put this away on my way to the infirmary."

The elder monk raised a paw. "He sleeps at the moment. It is concerning him, and the man you brought previously, that prompts my desire to speak with you."

"Yes, Lord."

Taran Zhu turned and, in an eyeblink, had progressed along a windswept walkway that Chen had not gotten around to clearing. The monk moved so gracefully that his silken robes didn't even whisper. Chen couldn't see the least little sign of his spoor in the snow. Hurrying after him made Chen feel like a stone-footed thunder lizard.

The monk led him downstairs through dark, heavy doors, into dim corridors paved with carved stone. The stones had been fitted together in interesting patterns that united both each block and the designs carved on them. The few times Chen had volunteered to sweep them, he had spent far more time being lost inside the lines and their weavings than actually using his broom.

Their journey ended in a large room lit by four lamps. The center of the floor had been given over to a circular construction, fitted with a reed mat. At its heart sat a small table with a terra-cotta teapot, three cups, a whisk, a bamboo ladle, a tea caddy, and a tiny cast-iron pot.

And beside it knelt Yalia Sagewhisper, her eyes closed, her paws in her lap.

Chen couldn't hold back a smile when he saw her, and had a sneaking suspicion Taran Zhu knew he was smiling and how broadly. Yalia had caught his eye immediately upon his first visit to the monastery, and not just because she was beautiful. The pandaren monk had a hint of the outsider to her that Chen noticed, then noticed her doing her best to suppress. They'd had a few brief conversations, of which he could remember every word. He wondered if she remembered them too.

Yalia stood and bowed first to Taran Zhu, then Chen. Her first bow lasted a long time. The second, not as much, but Chen marked it and matched it when he bowed to her. Taran Zhu pointed him to the narrow end of the rectangular table, nearest the cast-iron pot. Chen and Yalia knelt and sat back, and then Taran Zhu did likewise.

"You will forgive me, Master Stormstout, for two things. First, I would ask that you make us tea."

"Deeply honored, Lord Taran Zhu." Chen looked up. "Now?"

"If it will not disturb you to work and listen at the same time."

"No, Lord."

"And, second, you will forgive my inviting Sister Yalia here. I felt her perspective would be most illuminative."

Yalia bowed her head—and Chen felt a little thrill at seeing the exposed nape of her neck—but she said nothing, so Chen remained silent as well. He started to make tea and immediately noticed something to which he'd not quite become accustomed, despite having spent a great deal of time at the monastery during his stay in Pandaria.

The cast-iron pot's lid had an ocean wave motif worked onto it. The terra-cotta teapot had been shaped like a ship. The handle had been formed out of an anchor. Those choices had not been randomly made, though what sort of message they foreshadowed, Chen couldn't begin to guess.

"Sister Yalia, there is a ship in the bay. It is stable. What is it that makes it so?"

Chen carefully drew one ladle of hot water from the pot and noiselessly replaced the lid so he'd not distract her while she thought. He poured the water into the teapot, then gently teased powdered green tea from the caddy. Red birds and fishes had been painted on a black background on the caddy's lid, and a band of symbols running round the middle represented each of Pandaria's districts.

Yalia looked up, her voice as soft as the first petals of a cherry tree's blossoms. "I would say, Lord, that it is water that makes the ship stable. It is the ship's foundation. It is the ship's very reason for being. Without water, without an ocean, there would be no ship."

"Very good, Sister. So you would say that water is of Tushui—to use the term common on Shen-zin Su—the foundation, the meditation and contemplation. As you say, without water, there is no reason for the ship to exist."

"Yes, Lord."

Chen watched her face but saw no sign of her seeking approval. He couldn't have done that. He'd want to know if he was right. But Yalia, it occurred to him, already knew she was right. Lord Taran Zhu had asked her opinion; therefore her answer couldn't be wrong.

With the tip of his tongue just barely visible at the corner of his mouth, Chen applied the whisk to the water and tea within the pot. He did so vigorously, but also gently. The object was not to smash the tea into the water but to mix it all thoroughly. He had to clear the sides, pulling everything to the middle, and then work it out again. He worked briskly, turning the two disparate elements into a green froth that thickly sloshed in the clay ship's hold.

Taran Zhu pointed to the teapot. "There are others, of course, who would maintain that the anchor is the source of the ship's stability. Without the anchor rooting the ship in place, it would be ground against shore by wind and wave. The anchor gouging the bay's floor is what saves the ship, and without it, the ship would be nothing."

Yalia bowed her head. "If I may, Lord, then you are saying that the anchor is like Huojin. It is the impulsive, decisive act. It is what stands between the ship and disaster."

"Very good." The elder monk looked over as Chen added the last ladle of steaming water and clamped the lid back on the teapot. "Do you understand what we have been discussing, Chen Stormstout?"

Chen nodded, patting the teapot. "All shipshape now."

"The tea, or your understanding?"

"The tea. Just a couple of minutes." Chen smiled. "But about the water and the anchor and the ship. I've been thinking here."

"Yes?"

"I would say it's the crew. Because even if there was an ocean, if there was no crew who wanted to see what was on the other side of that ocean, there would be no ship. And the crew chooses the anchorage and when to sail. So the water is important, and the anchor is important, since they are the start and stop, but it's the crew who does the discovery."

Chen, who had been waving his paws through the air to aid in his explanation, stopped. "This was never really about ships, was it?"

"No. Yes." Taran Zhu closed his eyes for a moment. "Master Stormstout, you have sailed two ships into my harbor. They are at anchor here. But I can have no more ships."

Chen looked at him. "Okay. Shall I pour?"

"Have you no interest in knowing why I can have no more ships?"

"You are the harbormaster, so you must make those decisions." Chen poured tea for Taran Zhu, then for Yalia and himself. "Mind, it's still hot, and best to let the leaves settle to the bottom first."

Taran Zhu lifted his small earthenware cup and breathed in the steam. It seemed to relax him. Chen had seen that a lot. One of the great joys of his life and of practicing the brewmaster's art was how what he did affected people. Granted, most of them preferred his alcoholic offerings to tea, but good tea, well brewed, had a unique charm and no hangover.

The monastery's leader sipped, then lowered his cup. He gave Chen a nod. This allowed Chen and Yalia to sip also. Chen caught just the hint of a smile tugging at the corners of Yalia's mouth. For his own part, he thought he'd done a pretty good job.

Taran Zhu regarded him through heavily lidded eyes. "Let me begin again, Master Stormstout. Do you wish to know why I am willing to have your two ships anchored in my harbor?"

Chen barely had to think on his answer. "Yes, Lord. Why?"

"Because they are of a balance. Your troll, from what little you have mentioned and the fact that he is a shadow hunter, doubtless is of Tushui. This other, the man who every day goes up the mountain a bit farther, then returns, he is of Huojin. One is Horde; the other is Alliance. They would, by nature, oppose each other, and yet it is this opposition that unites them and gives them meaning."

Yalia set her cup down. "Forgive me, Lord, but is it not possible, given their opposition, that they might try to kill each other?"

"This is not a possibility I have any cause to discount, Sister. Enmity between Horde and Alliance runs deep. These two bear many scars—the man bears them in his mind as well, and so might your troll, Master Stormstout. And someone well and truly tried to murder your troll. Whether Alliance forces ambushed him, or the Horde has turned on its own, I cannot guess. However, we cannot have them murdering each other here."

"I don't think Tyrathan would do that, and Vol'jin, well, I know . . ." Chen hesitated for a moment, memories burbling up in his mind. "I'll just have a talk with Vol'jin. Explain the no-murdering thing to him?"

A frown darkened Yalia's expression. "Do not think me cruel, Master Stormstout, but I must ask if harboring the two of them here does not embroil us in foreign politics and strife. Could we not turn them out, or turn them back to their own people?"

Taran Zhu slowly shook his head. "We are already embroiled, and they have not proved to be without value. Alliance and Horde have helped us deal with the sha in the Townlong Steppes. You know how great an evil they are, and how thinly spread are we. As has been long said, the enemy of my enemy is my friend—no matter the havoc they might wreak—and the sha have ever been the enemy of Pandaria."

Chen almost chimed in with, "If you lie down with dogs, you wake up with fleas," but he refrained. Not that it wasn't on point, but it wasn't terribly helpful, especially when so many pandaren thought of wanderers like Li Li and himself as wild dogs. He hoped Yalia didn't see him that way, and wasn't about to introduce the concept.

Chen lowered his head just a bit. "I am not certain, Lord, that you can ever get the two of them—my ships or the Horde and Alliance—to work together permanently, no matter how unfriendly the mutual enemy might be."

Taran Zhu chuckled, almost silently, definitely without echo and with nothing more than a ghost of a smile. "That is not my purpose for keeping your ships in harbor, Chen. It is so that by being here, troll and man can learn from us, and as they learn from us, so we can learn from them. For as you wisely suggest, when there is no more enemy to unite them, they will once again be at each other's throats, and then we will have to choose whom we will befriend."

4

Vol'jin of the Darkspear trolls chose not to move. He did this because he found making that choice preferable to acknowledging that he felt too weak to move. Though the hands dealing with him were gentle, their touch respectful, he could not have thrown them off were it his greatest desire.

Unseen aides plumped pillows, then thrust them behind him to prop him up. He would have protested, but the pain in his throat made anything more than harshly growled words—and very short words—impossible. The obvious choice—"stop"—no matter how sharply barked, would have mocked his inability to stop them. Though he accepted his silence as a concession to vanity, he found the roots of his discomfort running deeper.

The soft bed and softer pillows were not comforts in which trolls luxuriated. A thin sleeping mat over a wooden floor was the height of opulence in the Echo Isles. Many trolls slept on stretches of ground, occasionally seeking shelter if a storm blew in. Yielding sand made for a better bed than the hard stone of Durotar, but trolls were not given to complaining about harsh accommodations.

The insistence on softness and comfort irritated him because it emphasized his weakness. The thinking part of him couldn't deny that a soft bed made shifting his wounded body much easier. He doubtless slept a bit better. But in calling attention to his weakness, it somehow denied the nature of his being a troll. Trolls were to hardship and harsh reality what sharks were to the open ocean.

To remove me from that be killing me.

The clunk of a chair or stool at his right surprised him. He'd not heard whoever carried it approach. Vol'jin sniffed, and the maddening scent underlying everything came back with the force of a punch. Pandaren. Not just pandaren, but one in particular.

Chen Stormstout's voice, low but warm, came to him in a whisper. "I would have been to see you before, but Lord Taran Zhu did not think it wise."

Vol'jin struggled to reply. He had a million things he wished to say, but few came wrapped in words his throat was willing to utter. "Friend. Chen." Somehow Chen came more easily, being softer.

"No playing blindfold guessing games with you. You're too good." Robes rustled. "If you would close your eyes, I'll remove the bandages. The healers say your eyes were not hurt, but they did not want you overly alarmed."

Vol'jin nodded, knowing Chen was half right. Had he a foreigner brought to him in the Echo Isles, he'd also have blindfolded him until he decided whether the captive could be trusted. Doubtless that was Taran Zhu's reasoning, and for some further reason, he had decided that Vol'jin could be trusted.

Chen's doing, I be suspecting.

The pandaren carefully unwound the bandages. "I

have my paw over your eyes. Open them, and I will slowly draw it away."

Vol'jin did as commanded, voicing a grunt meant to be a signal. Chen apparently took it as such, for he pulled back his paw. The troll's eyes watered in the bright light; then Chen's image swam into focus. The pandaren was much as Vol'jin remembered—stoutly built with a jovial sense about him, and an intelligence in his golden eyes. He was a very welcome sight.

Then Vol'jin looked down at his own body and almost closed his eyes again. Sheets covered him to the waist, and bandages covered almost the rest of him. He noted that he did have both hands and all fingers. The long lumps beneath the sheets told him his lower extremities were likewise intact. He could feel bandages constricting around his throat, and itching suggested that at least a portion of one ear had been sewed back into place.

He stared at his right hand and willed the fingers to move. They did, to his eye, but the sense of their moving took time to reach him. They seemed impossibly far away, but unlike when he'd first wakened, he could actually feel them. *It be progress.*

Chen smiled. "I know there are many things you want to know. Shall I start at the beginning or the end? The middle would not be so good a place, but I could start there. But that would make the middle the beginning, wouldn't it?"

Chen's voice rose with his explanation and its flight into folly. Other pandaren turned away, their interest in the conversation waning with their anticipation of tedium. In noticing them, Vol'jin also noticed the dark, ancient stone walls. As he had seen elsewhere in Pandaria, the place reeked of age, and yet, here, of strength as well.

Vol'jin wanted to say "beginning," but his throat refused. "Not end."

Chen looked back and apparently noted that the other pandaren had chosen to ignore them. "The beginning, then. I fished you out of a small watercourse far from here, at Binan Village. We did for you there what we could. You were not dying, but you were not healing either. Seems there was poison on the knife that did your throat. I brought you here, to the Shado-pan Monastery, at Kun-Lai Summit. If anyone could help you, the monks could."

He took a moment and surveyed Vol'jin's wounds, shaking his head. The troll noticed no pity in his assessment, and this pleased him. Chen had ever been sensible when he wasn't clowning, and Vol'jin knew Chen cast himself as a clown so others would forever underestimate how clever he truly could be.

"I cannot imagine it was Alliance troops who did this to you."

Vol'jin's eyes tightened. "My. Head. Gone."

The pandaren gave a short laugh. "Someone would be supping with the king in Stormwind, with your head the centerpiece, no doubt. But I figured you'd never let the Alliance catch you where they could hurt you so much."

"Horde." Vol'jin's stomach tightened. It wasn't really the Horde; it was Garrosh. Vol'jin's throat constricted before he could speak the name. The bitterness of the attempt lingered on his tongue regardless.

Chen sat back and scratched at his chin. "That's why I brought you here. There wasn't any other choice for your care anyway, but your safekeeping . . ." The brewmaster sat forward, lowering his voice. "Garrosh leads the Horde now that Thrall is away, yes? He's eliminating his rivals."

Vol'jin let himself sink back on the pillows. "Not. Without. Reason."

Chen chuckled, and try as he might, Vol'jin could detect no hint of reproof. "There's not an Alliance head that's touched a pillow that's not had a nightmare of meeting you. Not surprising the same is true of a few in the Horde."

Vol'jin tried to smile and hoped he succeeded. "Never. You?"

"Me? No, never. People like me, like Rexxar, we've seen you in battle being fierce and terrible. We've also seen you mourning your father. You've been loyal to Thrall and the Horde and the Darkspear tribe. Thing is, those who can't be loyal never believe when others are. I trust in your loyalty. Someone like Garrosh figures it's a mask over treachery."

Vol'jin nodded. He wished his voice worked enough that he could tell Chen of his threatening to kill Garrosh. It wouldn't have mattered to the pandaren; of this the troll was certain. Chen's loyalty would have led him to rationalize a dozen justifications for the threat. Vol'jin's current state would prove each of them true.

Only thing proved by that be the depth of Chen's friendship.

"How. Long?"

"Long enough for me to do a spring ale and be halfway into a late spring shandy. Or early summer. Pandaren are a bit looser about time, and those from Pandaria looser still. A month since we found you, two and a half weeks here. The healers poured a draught down your throat to make you sleep." Chen raised his voice for the benefit of those who had begun to come closer. "I told them that I could brew you up a hot black tea with some kelp and berries that would have you up and about in no time, but they don't think a brewmaster knows enough about healing or you. Still, they did pour nourishment into you, so they're not completely without hope."

Vol'jin made the effort to lick his lips, but even that seemed to exhaust him. *Two and a half weeks and this be all I have mended. Bwonsamdi released me, but I be not progressing as I should.*

Chen leaned in again, his voice dropping. "Lord Taran Zhu leads the Shado-pan. He has agreed to allow you to remain here to recuperate. There are conditions. Given that both the Alliance and Horde would be quite happy to see to your further care, each in its own ways . . ."

Vol'jin shrugged as much as he was able. "Helpless."

". . . and given that you're on the mend, listening won't hurt." Chen nodded, holding a paw palm out in a calming gesture. "Lord Taran Zhu wishes you to learn of us. Well, not us really. Most pandaren from here see pandaren who grew up on Shen-zin Su as 'wild dogs.' We look like them, sound like them, smell like them, but we're different. They aren't sure what we are. Puzzled me, at first, all that, until it struck me that a lot of the other trolls might see the Darkspears the same way."

"Not. Untrue." Vol'jin closed his eyes for a moment. *If Taran Zhu wishes me to learn of the pandaren and their ways, then he gonna study me. As I would be doing with him.*

"He thinks you're Tushui—more thoughtful and stable. I've told him a lot about you, and I think that, too. Tushui's not a trait he's seen in the Horde. He wants to understand why you're different. But this means he wants you to learn the pandaren way. Some of our words, our customs. It's not like he wants you to be one of those trolls who go to Thunder Bluff and become blue tauren. He wants you to understand."

Vol'jin opened his eyes again and nodded. Then he caught a moment's hesitation in Chen's recitation. "What?"

Chen looked up and away, nervously tapping his fingertips together. "Well, see, Tushui is balanced by Huojin. That's more impulsive, kind of kill them first, sort the hides out later. Like Garrosh deciding to kill you. Very Hordish thing to do these days. Not what the Alliance normally does."

"And?"

"These things are in balance now. Taran Zhu talked to me about water and anchors and ships and everything. Very complicated, even without mentioning crews. But the important thing is balance. He really likes his balance, and, you see, until you got here, they were out of balance."

Vol'jin, though the effort cost him mightily, arched an eyebrow.

"Well . . ." Chen glanced over his shoulder toward an empty bed. "About a month before I found you, I found a man wandering, hurt badly, his leg broken. And I brought him here too. He's a bit further along than you are, but trolls heal faster. And the thing is that Lord Taran Zhu is putting you in his care."

A jolt ran through Vol'jin's mind, and though he was weak, he attempted to rise. "No!"

Chen reached out, pressing the troll down with both paws. "No, no, you don't understand. He's here under the same restrictions you are. He won't—I know you're not afraid of a man, Vol'jin. Lord Taran Zhu hopes that in helping you heal, this man will help heal himself. That is part of our way, my friend. Restore the balance and you encourage healing."

Even though Chen kept his paws soft and strength gentle, Vol'jin could not struggle against him. For a heartbeat he imagined that the monks had made certain that whatever potion they'd poured down his throat would leave him this weak. That, however, would have required Chen to be part of the deception, and he never would have agreed to that.

Vol'jin forced his anger away and let frustration go with it. Lord Taran Zhu wanted to study not only him but also his dealings with a man. Vol'jin could have easily given him a long history of troll-human relations and why they pulsed with hatred. Vol'jin had killed more men than he cared to think about. Far from losing sleep over it, he slept better for it. And he was willing to bet the man in the monastery felt much the same way.

The troll realized that while Taran Zhu might have had access to all that history, those accounts would be tainted by the nature of the tellers. By putting troll and man together, he would watch, learn, and make his own judgments.

A wise course, I be thinking. Vol'jin reminded himself that no matter how much Chen had told Lord Taran Zhu about him, to the pandaren monk, Vol'jin was nothing more than a troll. Doubtless the man's pedigree mattered little either. Who they were had nothing to do with how they reacted to each other. That was the information the pandaren wanted. Knowing that, and realizing he could control the information, gave Vol'jin power.

He looked up at Chen. "You. Approve?"

Surprise widened Chen's eyes; then he smiled. "It is best for you and for him, for Tyrathan. The mists have hidden Pandaria for a long time. You and he share common bonds that the pandaren never will. You will heal better together."

"To. Later. Kill."

Chen's brows arrowed down. "Likely enough. He is no more happy about this than you are, but he will abide so he can abide here."

Vol'jin cocked his head. "Name?"

"Tyrathan Khort. You won't know him. He's not risen as high in the Alliance as you have in the Horde. But he was an important man. He was a leader among the Alliance forces here. And his wounds were not from the king's assassins. I only know he was hurt in a battle that helped Pandaria. This is why Lord Taran Zhu agreed to tend to him. He has great sadness, which nothing seems to cure."

"Not. Even. Brew?"

The pandaren shook his head, his eyes focusing distantly. "He drinks and holds his liquor well. But he's not a boisterous drunk. Introspective and quiet. Another trait you two share."

"Tushui, no?"

Chen threw his head back and roared with laughter. "They cut your body but could not hurt your mind. Yes, that would seem to be Tushui, which would cause the balance to be off. But every day, every day since he has been able to stand with crutches, he heads out to climb the mountain. Very Huojin. And then he stops. A hundred yards, two hundred, and returns, spent. Not physically, but in will. Very Huojin."

Very curious. I wonder why— Vol'jin caught himself, then gave Chen a tiny nod. "Very. Good. Friend."

"Maybe you can find the answer."

Which means I have to abide the man, being exactly what everyone wants. Vol'jin slowly exhaled and let his head rest on the pillows. *And, for the moment, I be including myself in that group.*

5

The monks did not require that Vol'jin allow the man to see to his bodily care, for the troll would not have tolerated that. Vol'jin could sense no malice in the firm efficiency with which the pandaren washed him, dressed his wounds, changed his bedding, and fed him. He did note that the monks on the team, in turn, would deal with him for a full day, then not return for two days before repeating their term of duty. After three days spent caring for him, they left the rotation and did not attend him again.

He caught sight of Taran Zhu only now and again. He felt certain the old monk watched him far more often than Vol'jin noticed, and Vol'jin noticed only when the old monk wished to be seen. It seemed to Vol'jin that the people of Pandaria were much like their world—shrouded in a mist that allowed only glimpses. While Chen had bits and pieces of that, he was a clear and sunny day compared to the elusive complexity of the monks.

So Vol'jin spent much of his time watching and determining what he would reveal of himself. His throat did heal, but scar tissue made speaking difficult and somewhat painful. Though it might not have seemed so to the pandaren, the troll tongue always had a melodious flow, but the scars had stolen that. *If the ability to communicate be a mark of life, then the assassins may have succeeded in murderin' me.* He hoped the loa—who had been quiet and distant as he recovered—would still recognize his voice.

He did manage to learn some words in the Pandaren language. The fact that the pandaren seemed to have a half dozen words for almost everything meant he could pick one that he could pronounce with minimal discomfort. The fact that the pandaren had so many words to begin with fed back into the difficulty of knowing their race. The language had nuances an outsider would never understand, and the pandaren could use them to mask their true intent.

Vol'jin wished he could have overplayed his physical weakness when dealing with the man, but it would have mattered little. Though tall by human standards, Tyrathan didn't have the physical bulk of human warriors. More lithe, with faint scars on his left forearm and calluses on the fingers of his right hand, which marked him as a hunter. He wore his white hair short and unbound. The man maintained a mustache and goatee, also white and begun recently. He had donned the simple clothing of a novitiate—homespun and brown, cut for a pandaren, so it hung on him. Yet it was not so large—Vol'jin suspected it had actually been sewn for a pandaren female.

Though the monks did not have the man tend Vol'jin's body, they did require he launder the troll's clothes and bedding. The man did so without comment or complaint, and was efficient. Everything came back spotless and sometimes scented with medicinal herbs and flowers.

Vol'jin noted two things that marked the man as dangerous. Most would have taken what he'd already seen—the calluses, the fact that the man had survived with not too many scars—to prove that much. But for Vol'jin, the man's quick green eyes, the way he turned his head at sounds, and the way he paused for a heartbeat before answering even the simplest of questions—all of these marked the man as being incredibly observant. Not a trait unknown among those of his avocation, but only so pronounced in those who would be very good at it.

The other aspect the man displayed was patience. Vol'jin, until he realized his attempts were fruitless, repeatedly made simple mistakes that would cause the man to do more work. Dropping a spoon and smearing food over his clothes to create a stain did not perturb the man. Vol'jin had even managed to conceal a stain so it set, but the robe returned spotless.

This patience manifested in how the man dealt with his own wound. Though his clothes hid scars, the man walked with a limp—stiffness in the left hip. Each step had to be incredibly painful. He couldn't conceal all of the grimaces, though his effort to do so would have done Taran Zhu credit. And yet each day, as the sun slowly crept over the horizon, the man would head out and up the trail toward the mountain summit above them.

After Vol'jin had been fed, he sat up in his bed and nodded as the man approached. Tyrathan bore with him a flat, gridded game board and two cylindrical canisters—one red and one black—each with a round hole in the middle of the lid. The man set them on the side table, then retrieved a chair from next to the wall and sat.

"Are you ready for jihui?"

Vol'jin nodded. Though each knew the other's name, they never used them. Both Chen and Taran Zhu had told him the man was Tyrathan Khort. Vol'jin assumed they'd informed the man of his identity. If the man bore him any enmity, he gave no sign. *He must know who I be.*

Tyrathan picked up the black cylinder, twisted off the lid, then poured the contents onto the board. Twenty-four cubes rattled and danced on the tan bamboo surface. Each had symbols inscribed in red on a black background, including dots to indicate movement and an arrow to indicate facing. The man nudged them into four groups of six to prove the count, then made to sweep them back into the canister.

Vol'jin tapped one piece. "This face."

The man nodded, then turned and called a monk over in halting pandaren. They spoke quickly—the man hesitantly, and the monk as if indulging a child. Tyrathan bowed his head and thanked her.

He turned back to Vol'jin. "The piece is the ship. The face is the fireship." Tyrathan placed it so the pandaren glyph was sitting the right way for Vol'jin to see it. The man then repeated the word "fireship" in perfect Zandali.

And his eyes flicked up just fast enough to catch Vol'jin's reaction.

"Stranglethorn. Your accent."

The man pointed to the playing piece, ignoring his comment. "The fireship is a very important piece to the pandaren. It can destroy anything but is consumed in the destruction. It is removed from play. I am told some players burn the piece. Of the six ships in your navy, only one can become a fireship."

"Thank you."

Jihui encapsulated much of pandaren philosophy. Each piece had six sides. A player could move as indicated by the uppermost face and attack, or could change the face by one side, then either move or attack. It was also possible to pick the piece up and roll it, randomly selecting a new side, then return it to its facing and play. This was the only way the fireship face could come up for a ship.

Most interesting, a player could also decide not to move at all, but instead could draw a new piece from the canister by chance. It would be shaken and up-ended. The first piece to fall out would be put into play. If two fell out, the second would be removed from play, and the opposition would be allowed to draw a new piece without penalty.

At once jihui was a game that encouraged thoughtfulness yet incorporated impulsiveness. It balanced deliberation with chance, and yet chance could be punished. For a player to lose to a foe who had more pieces on the board was not a great loss. To yield to a superior position, regardless of the pieces in play, was not considered a loss without honor. While the game's aim was to eliminate all of these opposition pieces, to play to that point was considered ill-mannered and even barbaric. Usually one player found himself out-maneuvered and surrendered, though some relied on chance to shift their fortunes and go on to victory.

And to play to a standstill, to have forces balanced, this was the greatest victory.

Tyrathan handed Vol'jin the red canister. Each shook out a half dozen cubes, centering them on the last row of the twelve-by-twelve grid. They oriented them to their lowest value and faced them toward the opposition. Then each shook out one more cube and compared the highest side. Tyrathan's beat Vol'jin's, so he would move first. Those cubes returned to the canister, and they began playing.

Vol'jin nudged a piece forward. "Your Pandaren. Good. Better than they be knowing."

The man raised an eyebrow without lifting his gaze from the board. "Taran Zhu knows."

Vol'jin studied the board, watching the man's flanking maneuver develop. "You hunt. His track?"

"Elusive but strong where he means you to see it." The man nibbled at a thumbnail. "Interesting choice in refacing your archer."

"Your kite move too." Vol'jin had seen no hesitation in making the move, but his praise of it caused Tyrathan's glance to flick toward that piece again. He stared hard, searching for something, then glanced at the canister.

The troll anticipated him. He shook out a cube, which spun and clattered to a stop. The fireship. He placed it contiguous to the archer, strengthening that flank. The game's balance shifted—not in either player's favor, but away from that side of the board.

Tyrathan added another piece—a warrior that did not fall on its strongest side, but strong enough. Knights, which could move far, came up quickly on that other flank. Tyrathan played his moves swiftly, but not in haste.

Vol'jin picked up the canister again, but the man grabbed his hand. "Don't."

"Remove. Your. Hand." Vol'jin's grip tightened. One twitch of his hand and the canister would shatter. Game pieces and splinters would fly everywhere. He wanted to shout at the man, asking how he dared touch a shadow hunter, the leader of the Darkspears. *Do you know who I be?*

But he didn't twitch. Because his hand couldn't tighten any more than it had. In fact, that brief exertion was enough to fatigue his muscles. Already his grip was failing, and only the man's hand kept the canister from crashing onto the board.

Tyrathan opened his other hand, dispelling any hint of malice. "I am given to teaching you this game. You do not need to draw another piece. Were I to allow you to draw, I would win and your draw would inflate the value of my victory."

Vol'jin surveyed the pieces. Black's warrior, with the change of a face, could crush his warlord. The fireship would have to come back to counter that threat, but in doing so would come into range of Tyrathan's kite. Both pieces would be destroyed, leaving the warrior and the cavalry on the right to crumple that flank. Even the best draw out of the canister, even if it fell well, could not save things. If he reinforced the right, the man would renew his assault on the left. If he reinforced the left, the right would go.

Vol'jin let the canister drop into Tyrathan's hand. "For my honor. Thank you."

The man set the canister down on the table. "I know what you were doing. I would win, but I would have defeated a student whom I allowed to make a frightful mistake. So you would have won. And you have won, because you forced me to act at your whim."

And should it not be so, manthing? Vol'jin's eyes narrowed. "You win. You read me. I lose."

Tyrathan shook his head and sat back. "Then we both lose. No, this is not a semantic game. They are watching. I read you. You read me. They read the both of us. They read how we played the game and how we played each other. Taran Zhu reads them all and how they read us."

A chill ran down Vol'jin's spine. He nodded once. He'd hoped it was all but imperceptible, but Taran Zhu would know. It was enough, however, that the man caught it, and, for the moment, the two outsiders were united.

Tyrathan's voice shrank as he scooped pieces back into the canisters. "The pandaren are used to the mists. They see through them and are unseen within them. They would be a terrible force unleashed were they not so balanced and concerned with balance. In it they find peace and, with reason, are reluctant to surrender that peace."

"They be watching. Looking at how we balance."

"They would like us to balance." Tyrathan shook his head. "On the other hand, perhaps Taran Zhu wants to know how to unbalance us so much that we destroy ourselves. It is my fear that this is something he'll learn all too easily."

That night, visions mocked Vol'jin. He found himself in the midst of fighters, each of whom he recognized. He'd gathered them for that final assault on Zalazane, to end his madness and free the Echo Isles for the Darkspears. Each of the combatants took on aspects of a jihui cube, faced to be at their maximum power. Not a fireship among them, but this did not surprise Vol'jin.

He was the fireship, but not yet turned to display his maximum power. This was not a fight, though desperate, in which he would destroy himself. Aided by Bwonsamdi, they would slay Zalazane and reclaim the Echo Isles.

Who be you, this troll, who be having memories of a heroic effort?

Vol'jin turned, hearing the click of a cube snapping to a new facing. He felt trapped inside that cube, translucent though it was, and shocked that it had no values on any face. "I be Vol'jin."

Bwonsamdi materialized in a gray world of swirling mists. "And who be this Vol'jin?"

The question shook him. The Vol'jin of the vision had been the leader of the Darkspears but was no longer. Reports of his death would just now be reaching the Horde. Perhaps they had not yet gotten there. In his heart, Vol'jin hoped his allies had been delayed, just so Garrosh could dwell one more day wondering if his plan had succeeded.

That did not answer the question. He was no longer the leader of the Darkspears, not in any real sense. They might still acknowledge him, but he could give them no orders. They would resist Garrosh and any Horde attempt to conquer them, but in his absence, they might listen to envoys who offered them protection. They could be lost to him.

Who do I be?

Vol'jin shivered. Though he thought himself superior to Tyrathan Khort, at least the man was mobile and not wearing sick-robes. The man hadn't been betrayed by a rival and assassinated. The man had clearly embraced some of the pandaren way.

And yet, Tyrathan hesitated when he should not have. Some of it was a game to make the pandaren underestimate him, but Vol'jin had seen through that. The other bits, though, such as when he'd hesitated after Vol'jin complimented a move, those were genuine. *And not something a man be allowing in himself.*

Vol'jin looked up at Bwonsamdi. "I be Vol'jin. I know who I was. Who I gonna be? That answer only Vol'jin could be finding. And for now, Bwonsamdi, that be enough."

6

Vol'jin might not have been wholly clear about who he was, but he certainly knew who he was not. He forced himself out of his sickbed by degrees. He would ease back the covers, deliberately folding them neatly when he desperately wanted to throw them off, and then he'd swing his legs out.

The first touch of cool stone on his feet surprised him, but he drew strength from the sensation. He let it override the pain in his legs and the tight tugging of scars and stitching. Holding on to the bedpost, he pulled himself upright.

On the sixth attempt he made it. The fourth had popped stitches on his stomach. He refused to acknowledge that fact and waved away the monks attracted by the darkening stain on his tunic. He thought he would have to apologize to Tyrathan for making him work harder, but he asked the monks to set the tunic aside.

He did that after lying down again. He'd gotten to his feet and stood for what seemed like forever. Sunlight through the window had not shifted a bug's width along the floor, providing him a true measure of time, but he had been upright. That was a victory.

Once the monks had closed the wound again and re-bandaged it, Vol'jin asked for a basin of water and a brush. He took the tunic and, as best as he was able, scrubbed at the bloodstain. It proved tenacious, but he was determined to get it out even though his muscles burned with exertion.

Tyrathan waited until Vol'jin's motions had slowed enough that the water had stilled, and then the man took the tunic from him. "You are most kind, Vol'jin, for accepting my burden. I shall hang this out to dry."

Vol'jin wished to protest, since he could still see the stain's dark outline, but he remained silent. In an instant he saw the balance of Huojin and Tushui reestablished. He had been impulsive, and Tyrathan had been thoughtful, intervening at a time and in a way that cost neither of them dignity. It silently acknowledged effort and intent, achieving the desired end without ego or a need for victory.

The next day, Vol'jin made it to his feet by the third attempt and refused to lie back down until the sunbeam's edge had moved a thumb's length past a seam in the block floor. The day after, it took him that long to walk from one end of the bed to the other and back. By week's end he actually walked to the window and peered down into a courtyard.

Pandaren monks arrayed in straight ranks dominated the center. They worked through exercises, shadow-boxing with blinding speed. Trolls were not strangers to unarmed combat, but since they were ganglier, their techniques did not match the discipline and control the monks displayed. Around the edges, at various points, other monks fought with swords and spears, polearms and bows. A single blow with just a stick would have humbled a Stormwind warrior shut up in a steel carapace. Were it not for the flash of sunlight off razored edges, Vol'jin doubted he would have followed much of the blurred weapons' work.

And then there, on the steps, Chen Stormstout swept snow. Two steps above, Lord Taran Zhu did the same.

Vol'jin leaned on the window's casement. *What be the odds that I would see the monastery's lord doing a menial task?* He considered that he had become a creature of habit, always getting up at the same time. *That be changing.*

But this meant that Taran Zhu not only knew what Vol'jin had been doing but also had anticipated the time he would reach the window. Vol'jin had no doubt that were he to ask Chen how often Taran Zhu swept snow, he would discover it was only that day, only at that time. The troll glanced to the side to see a number of monks ignoring him, which meant they were watching his reaction but did not want to be detected.

Not five minutes after he lay back down did Chen come to visit, bearing a small bowl of a frothy liquid. "It was good to see you up, my friend. I've wanted to bring you this for days, but Lord Taran Zhu had prohibited it. He thought it would be too strong for you. I told him it would take a lot more than that to kill you. I mean, you are here, right? So you get first taste. Well, aside from me." Chen smiled. "I had to make sure it actually wouldn't kill you, after all."

"Most kind."

Vol'jin lifted the bowl and sniffed. The brew had a tang to it, and a woody sense. He sipped and found it neither sweet nor bitter, but full and rich. It tasted the way the jungle smelled after a rain as steam rose from vegetation and brought everything together. It reminded him of the Echo Isles, and that realization almost closed his throat.

He forced himself to swallow, then nodded as it burned down to his belly. "Very good."

"Thank you." Chen glanced toward the floor. "The day we got here you were not looking very good. The journey had been hard. We were told we'd bury you on the mountain. But I whispered in your ear—the good one, not the one Li Li helped sew up—that if you made it, I'd have something special waiting for you. I'd tucked into the corner of a satchel some spices, a few flowers, from your home. To remember it all by. And so I used them to make you an ale. I call it 'Get Well.'"

"Your credit, my recovery."

The pandaren looked up. "It was a small batch, Vol'jin. Your recovery will take longer."

"I will recover."

"Which is why I've begun a new brew called 'Celebration.'"

Whether it was Chen's brew or Vol'jin's troll constitution, the clean mountain air or the therapies to which the monks subjected him—or all of them combined—within a handful of weeks Vol'jin progressed admirably. Each day, when standing in rank with the monks, he would bow to their teacher, then glance up at the window from which he'd watched them. Scarcely would he have believed he would join them, and yet now he felt so much better that he could scarcely remember who he'd been at the window.

The monks, who accepted him without comment or great solicitude, referred to him as Vol'jian. Somehow that rolled more easily off their tongues, but he knew it was not that alone. Chen explained that "jian" had a number of meanings, all centered around greatness. At first, the monks used it to describe his clumsy oafishness, but then it came to mark the speed with which he learned.

Were they not eager teachers, he would have been contemptuous of their disrespect. He was a shadow hunter. Great though the monks' skills were, not a single one of them could imagine what it had taken for him to become a shadow hunter. The monks fought to embody balance, but to be a shadow hunter was to master chaos.

His hunger for knowledge and his quick competence at little things prompted them to throw more and more complex techniques at him. As his strength increased and his body slowly regained its ability to heal from cuts and bruises, the only thing that limited him was his lack of endurance. Vol'jin wanted to put it down to the thin mountain air, but shortness of breath was not limiting the man.

Other things did limit Tyrathan. He still limped, though not nearly as much as he had before. He used a cane and often trained with monks who fought with sticks. Vol'jin noticed that in the midst of sparring, the limp would disappear. Only at the end, after Tyrathan had caught his breath and became aware of himself again, would it return.

The man also watched the monks training at archery. One would have to be blind to not see how much he wished to be shooting. He would measure the monks, watch them shoot, his head dipping when one failed, a smile sparking when one split an arrow already embedded in the target.

Now that he was well enough to be training, Vol'jin moved to a small, austere cell on the monastery's eastern side. Its simplicity of appointments—a sleeping mat, a low table, a basin and pitcher, as well as two pegs for the hanging of clothes—was doubtless meant to discourage distraction. Its bareness would make it easier for the monks to gather themselves and find peace.

Vol'jin found it reminiscent of Durotar—though considerably colder. Dwelling in it provided no real hardship. He placed his bed where the first light of dawn would waken him. He'd go off to do chores as the others did, then have a simple breakfast before the morning's exercises. He noted that his rations included more meat than the monks consumed, which made sense considering the status of his recovery.

Morning, midday, and evening all fell into that same pattern: chores, food, and exercises. For Vol'jin, the exercises revolved around strength and flexibility, learning about combat and his physical limitations. In the afternoon, he got more individual instruction, again with a rotating band of monks because the majority of them attended classes. They rejoined the physical exercise in the evening, though this consisted mostly of stretching, preparatory to getting a good night's rest.

The monks taught him well. He'd watched them shatter up to a dozen boards with a single punch. Vol'jin had looked forward to trying that because he knew he could do it. But when it came time for him to try the exercise, Lord Taran Zhu took over. In place of boards had been arranged an inch-thick slab of stone.

Do you mock me? Vol'jin studied the monk's face but read no deception. That didn't mean there wasn't any there, but the pandaren's impassive expression could have masked anything. "You be wanting me to break stone. Others break wood."

"Others do not believe they can shatter wood. You do." Taran Zhu pointed to a spot a finger's length beyond the stone slab. "Place your doubt here. Strike through to it."

Doubt? Vol'jin forced away the thought because it was a distraction. He wanted to ignore it, but instead, he did as the monk had instructed. He visualized doubt as a shimmering blue-black ball spitting sparks. He let it float through the stone to hover behind it.

Then Vol'jin set himself, drew in a deep breath, and exhaled sharply. He drove his fist forward, pulverizing the stone. He continued through, smashing that ball of doubt. He could have sworn that he'd not felt the impact until he'd hit the ball. The stone had been as nothing, even though he brushed its dust from his pelt.

Taran Zhu bowed to him respectfully.

Vol'jin returned the gesture, holding it longer than before.

The other monks bowed as their lord withdrew, then bowed to Vol'jin. Vol'jin returned their bows and noticed, thereafter, that their emphasis on "jian" had changed again.

It was not until later that evening, as he sat alone in his cell, the stone cool against his back, that Vol'jin allowed himself to understand at least some of what he had learned. His hand had not swollen or stiffened, yet he could still feel his fist crushing doubt. He flexed his hand, watching it work, happy he was fully reconnected to it.

Taran Zhu was right to make doubt a target. Doubt destroyed souls. What thinking creature, when entertaining doubt about success, could undertake any action? To doubt that he could punch through stone was to acknowledge that his hand could break, his bones could splinter, his flesh could tear, and his blood could flow. And if he dwelt on that outcome, could there be any but that outcome? That ending would be his target; therefore he would succeed and hit that target. Whereas, if his target was to destroy doubt and he hit that target, then would anything be impossible?

Zalazane returned to his mind, not as a vision but as a series of memories. Doubt had destroyed his soul. The two of them had grown up together, best friends. Because Sen'jin, the Darkspear leader, was his father, Vol'jin had always been considered first between them, but not in his own mind. And Zalazane had known that; they'd spoken of it often, laughing at the ignorance of those who thought of one as hero and the other as benighted companion. Even as Vol'jin concentrated on becoming a shadow hunter, Zalazane became a witch doctor under Master Gadrin. Sen'jin himself had encouraged Zalazane, and there had been those among the Darkspears who thought Zalazane was being trained to lead after Sen'jin, while Vol'jin was destined for greater things.

But even in that people were fooled, for the both of them believed in Sen'jin's dream of a homeland for the Darkspears. A place where they could thrive without fear, without enemies preying upon them. And even Sen'jin's death at the webbed hands of murlocs could not kill that dream.

Somewhere, at some time, doubt wormed its way into Zalazane's soul. Perhaps it was knowing that Sen'jin, a powerful witch doctor, could die so easily. It could have been hearing just one too many times that Vol'jin was the hero and he was the companion. It could have been something that Vol'jin couldn't even guess at, but whatever it was, it caused Zalazane to savagely lunge for power.

That power made him insane. Zalazane enslaved most of the Darkspears, turning them into mindless minions. Vol'jin escaped with some, then returned with his Horde allies to free the Echo Isles. He'd led the forces that killed Zalazane, felt his blood splash, heard him breathe his last. He liked to think, in that last moment, in the last spark he'd seen in Zalazane's eyes, that his old friend had returned to sanity and was pleased to be free.

So, I think, it be with Garrosh. Exalted because he was his father's son but hardly revered for himself or his actions, Garrosh was feared by many. He had learned that fear was an effective lash with which to keep subordinates in line. But not all of them cringed at the whipcrack.

Not me.

Because Garrosh felt his position was due as much to his father's memory as it was to his own worthiness, he doubted his standing. If he could see himself as unworthy, clearly others could. *I did, and I told him so.* Doubt could be hidden, so anyone could be a potential enemy. The only way to eliminate them would be to conquer them.

Yet all the conquests in the world would not silence that voice in his head that said, *"Yes, but you are not your father."*

Vol'jin stretched out on his sleeping mat. *My father had a dream. He shared it with me. He made it my legacy, and I was fortunate enough to be understanding it. Because of that, I can make it come true. Because of that, I can know peace.*

He spoke into the emptiness. "But Garrosh gonna never know peace. That means no one else will."

7

Astorm blew in from the south, with howling winds, dark clouds, and snow flying sideways so hard it stung the flesh. The blizzard hit very fast. Vol'jin had awakened to sunshine, but before he had finished his chores—in this case dusting the tops of shelves in which many ancient scrolls were kept—the temperature dropped, the air darkened, and the storm shrieked as if the monastery were under assault by demons.

Vol'jin knew little enough about blizzards that he didn't panic. Senior monks combed through the monastery, bringing everyone together in the massive dining hall. Everyone went to their mess area. Being taller than anyone else, Vol'jin could easily see the monks counting heads. It occurred to him that such a savage storm might blind someone and confuse him. To be lost in the storm would be to die in it.

To his shame, Vol'jin did not notice what Chen pointed out even before the head count was completed. "Tyrathan's not here."

Vol'jin glanced toward the mountaintop. "He wouldn't head out when a storm gonna be blowing up big like this."

Taran Zhu stood on a raised dais. "There is a hollow

where he often stops to rest. It faces north and is sheltered. He never would have known the storm was coming. Master Stormstout, you will fill a cask with your Get Well brew. First and second houses will organize themselves to search."

Vol'jin lifted his head. "What you be having me do?"

"Return to your chores, Vol'jin." There was no "jian" in Taran Zhu's use of his name. "There is nothing for you to do."

"That storm will be killing him."

"It will kill you, too. Faster than it will him." The elder pandaren clapped his paws once and his charges scattered. "You know little of snowstorms like this. Shatter stone you might, but the storm will shatter you. It will suck out your warmth and your strength. We would carry you back here before we ever found him."

"I cannot be standing by . . ."

". . . and do nothing? Good, then I shall give you a task, a question to contemplate." The pandaren's nostrils flared, but his voice remained even and unemotional. "Is it to save the man that you wish to act, or to preserve your self-conception as hero? I expect much dusting to be done before you have reached the truth."

Fury roared through Vol'jin's soul, but he did not give it voice. The master monk had hit the truth twice, perfectly on target like the archers under his command. The storm would kill Vol'jin. It might even kill him were he fully healthy. A tolerance for cold had never been much in demand among the Darkspear trolls.

More important, and the shot that sunk home the deepest, was Taran Zhu's reading of why Vol'jin wished to be part of the rescue. It was less out of concern for Tyrathan Khort's welfare than it was for himself. He did not want to be sidelined when danger demanded action. That spoke of weakness, which he did not want to acknowledge. And were he able to rescue Tyrathan, then Vol'jin and his condition would be ascendant over that of the man. The man had witnessed his weakness, and this rankled.

As he returned to his dusting, Vol'jin realized that he felt beholden to the man, and this did not sit well with him. Trolls and men had never been true to each other except through hatred. Vol'jin had killed more men than he cared to count. The way Tyrathan had studied him said the hunter had killed his share of trolls. They had been born enemies. Even here, the pandaren kept them because they were so opposite that they balanced each other.

And yet, what have I been having from this man but kindness? Part of Vol'jin wanted to dismiss that as weakness. It was supplication based in fear. Tyrathan hoped that when Vol'jin was well, he would not kill the man. While it was easy to imagine this was true, and countless were the trolls who would believe it as if it were a message delivered by the loa, Vol'jin could not accept it. Tyrathan might have been tasked with his care, but the kindness with the tunic, that was not a servant fulfilling a duty.

It was more. *It deserves respect.*

Vol'jin had finished the high shelves and begun the lowest before the search parties returned. Excited voices suggested they'd been successful. At the noon meal, Vol'jin looked for Tyrathan first, then Chen and Taran Zhu. When he failed to see them, he looked for the healers. He saw one or two but for only as long as it took them to grab some food and disappear again.

The storm's occupation of the mountain meant a grim dark day, the end of which was heralded by greater darkness and more cold. As monks gathered for the evening meal, a young female monk found him and brought him back to the infirmary. Chen and Taran Zhu awaited him, neither looking happy.

Tyrathan Khort lay in bed, his flesh gray yet with sweat dappling his brows. Several thick blankets covered him to the throat. He thrashed against them, but so weakly they imprisoned him. Sympathy flashed through Vol'jin.

The monastery's lord pointed at Vol'jin. "There is a task you will perform. If you do not do it, he shall die. And before an ignoble thought can root itself in your mind, I tell you this: if you refuse, surely you shall die. Not by my action or by that of any of the monks here. Because that thing you shattered beyond the stone will be allowed back into your soul, and it will kill you."

Vol'jin dropped to a knee and watched Tyrathan's face. Fear, hatred, shame—these emotions and more passed over his features. "He sleeps. He dreams. What can I do?"

"It is not what you can do, troll; it is what you *must* do." Taran Zhu exhaled slowly. "Away from here, to the south and the east, there is a temple. It is one of many in Pandaria, but it and its companions are special. At each the emperor Shaohao, in his wisdom, trapped one of the sha. The sha are of a similar nature to your loa. They embody aspects of intelligent nature—the darker ones. At the Temple of the Jade Serpent the emperor trapped the Sha of Doubt."

Vol'jin frowned. "There be no spirit of doubt."

"No? Then what was it you destroyed with that punch?" Taran Zhu gathered his paws at the small of his back. "You have doubt; we all have doubts, and the sha uses them. It makes them resonate within, paralyzing us, killing the soul. We, the Shado-pan, are trained, as you now understand, to deal with the sha. Unfortunately, Tyrathan Khort encountered them before he was prepared."

Vol'jin stood again. "What can I be doing? What must I be doing?"

"You are of his world. You understand it." Taran Zhu nodded to Chen. "Master Stormstout has prepared a draught from our apothecary. We call it memory wine. Both you and the man will drink, and then you will be guided into his dreams. As the loa sometimes work through you, so you shall work through him. You have destroyed doubt, Vol'jin, but doubt still infects him. You must find it and drive it out."

The troll's eyes narrowed. "You cannot?"

"If I could, do you not think I would do it rather than entrust it to someone who is barely a novitiate?"

Vol'jin bowed his head. "Of course."

"One caution for you, troll. Understand that what you see and experience is not reality. It is his memory of what happened. Were you to speak with every survivor of that battle, none would tell the same tale. Do not strive to understand his memories. Find his doubt and uproot it."

"I be knowin' what to do."

The female monk and Chen dragged over another bed, but Vol'jin waved it away. He stretched out on the stone floor next to Tyrathan. "Better to remember I be a troll."

He accepted the wooden bowl from Chen's paw. The dark liquid tasted greasy and stung as if laced with nettles. It soured quickly on the tongue save where the tannic bite numbed him. He swallowed twice to get the memory wine all down, then lay back and closed his eyes.

He projected his senses as he would when reaching out to the loa, but found the landscape distinctly

Pandaren—all green and warm gray, though flecks of snow flashed through it. Taran Zhu stood there, a silent ghost. His right paw pointed toward a dark cave. Pandaren footprints also pointed the way but stopped at the stone mouth.

Vol'jin twisted sideways and ducked to get through. The stone walls squeezed. For a heartbeat he feared he wouldn't make it. Then, with what felt like a tearing of his flesh, he made it.

And almost screamed.

He looked out at the world through Tyrathan Khort's eyes and found it too bright and too green. He raised a hand to shield his eyes. Surprise raced through him. The arms were too short, the body broader and yet weaker. He could take only tiny steps. Everywhere he looked, men and women, wearing the blue tabards trimmed in gold of Stormwind, sharpened weapons and adjusted armor while jinyu conscripts gaped in awe.

A young soldier appeared in front of him and saluted. "The war leader requests your presence on the hill, sir."

"Thank you." Vol'jin rode along with the memory, getting used to the sensation of being in a human body. Tyrathan wore his bow over his back. A quiver slapped against his right thigh. A few bits of mail rustled, but otherwise leather encased him. He'd taken every part from beasts he'd killed. He'd tanned it and sewn it, trusting in nothing others had prepared.

Vol'jin smiled, for he recognized that sentiment.

Tyrathan ran up the hill easily—leaving Vol'jin little doubt why he enjoyed time on the mountain here. He stopped before a massive hulk of a man with a thick beard. The war leader's armor gleamed blindingly, and the white of his tabard had no hints of blood.

"You asked to see me, sir?"

The man, Bolten Vanyst, pointed to the valley below. "That's our objective. The Serpent's Heart. Seems peaceful enough, but I know better than to trust that. I've culled a dozen skirmishers from my force—the best of the hunters. I want you to scout and report. I won't have us ambushed."

"Understood, sir." Tyrathan saluted smartly. "You'll have my report in an hour, two at most."

"Three if it's complete." The war leader dismissed him with a salute.

Tyrathan sped off and Vol'jin cataloged every sensation. As they descended a rocky hill trail, the troll noticed the leaps that the man refused. He sought a sense of doubt in those choices but instead found confidence. Tyrathan knew himself well, and to make those leaps, which would not have concerned a troll, would snap a leg or twist an ankle.

The sheer fragility of being human surprised Vol'jin. He'd always rejoiced in it. It made breaking them so very easy, but now it made him wonder about them. They knew death could come quickly, yet they fought and explored and showed no lack of courage. It was as if mortality was so well-known a companion that they could embrace it easily.

As Tyrathan arrived amid a squad of twelve hunters like himself, Vol'jin noticed that the man had no companion animal with him. The others did, marking their travels throughout the world. Raptors and turtles, giant spiders and bloodseeker bats—the humans chose their companions through a logic that escaped Vol'jin.

With concise hand signals, Tyrathan gave his soldiers their orders, then split them into small groups. *Just as he splits the cubes in jihui.* His own group he took around to the south, to the farthest objective. They moved quickly and quietly—equal in stealth to the velvet-footed pandaren monks. Tyrathan had an arrow nocked but not yet drawn.

When the scream came from the west, the reality of things changed. Vol'jin would have been lost save that he understood battle and how it shifted perception. Time slowed as he watched disaster unfold; then it sprinted as disaster erupted. It would take forever to watch an arrow fly toward a friend and yet only an instant for her life to pump out in a great crimson spurt.

Where there had been no enemies, now a legion beset his people. Odd spirit creatures raced among them, touching, rending, ripping shrieks from them before opening those same throats. Companion animals roared and snarled, biting and clawing, only to be swarmed over and ripped apart.

And Tyrathan, for his part, tried to remain calm. He loosed arrow after arrow with smooth, strong draws. *Oh, da monks, they would be so shamed were he to touch a bow.* Vol'jin did not doubt that Tyrathan could shoot so quickly and accurately that he could split a monk's arrow before it ever hit the target, and then drive its head straight through.

Then a woman went down. Dark haired and sleek like the cat accompanying her. Tyrathan shouted, darted toward her. He sped arrows at the sha attacking her. He killed one, then a second, but a stone rolled beneath his foot. He missed the third.

From his vantage point, Vol'jin knew that shot would not have mattered. She stared at the both of them with glassy eyes in a red mask. Blood spurted, her tabard drinking it all in. If there was anything to be remembered at all of her death, it was the way her hand lay easily on her dead companion's broad head.

Tyrathan went down to a knee; then something hit him hard in the flank. His bow flew from his hand as he sailed through the air. He smashed into a stone serpent, hitting just below his left hip. The leg snapped, arcing argent agony through him. He bounced once, then rolled to a stop. He faced the dead woman.

If not for me, you would be alive.

There it was, the root of doubt. Vol'jin looked down and caught a black thread stuck to a thorn. It pierced him once, just missing his heart, then burst out his back. It came around again, poised like a viper to strike once more.

But Vol'jin reached out with a spirit hand and caught it beneath the thorn as he might grab a snake. With the caress of a thumb, he decapitated it, then reached down and broke off the longer thread.

The middle section slithered quickly and deep into Tyrathan. It wrapped tight round his heart and began to squeeze. The man's body tightened, his back bowed, but the broken thread could not squeeze hard enough. It twisted down and away, threading itself into his spine, and rode his pain up into his brain.

There it struck and wrung from the man a soul-rending howl. Vol'jin's image of Tyrathan vanished like a reflection swallowed in a vortex. All light drained into a black hole, and then silver suffering burst back out, shocking man and troll alike.

Vol'jin jerked, face wet with sweat, his hands searching his body for wounds. He grabbed his thigh, feeling the pain of its breaking fade. He gasped, then looked at Tyrathan.

Hints of color had returned to the man's flesh. He breathed more easily. He no longer struggled beneath the blankets.

Vol'jin studied him. Still so weak and far more frail than the troll could have imagined before walking in his skin, the man had steel in him that would allow him to recover. Part of Vol'jin hated that, since he recognized it as a trait that many humans shared. It was trouble for trolls. And yet, at the same time, he admired it because of the spirit it took to fight hard against death.

The troll looked up at Lord Taran Zhu. "Some escaped me. I be not able to get it all."

"You got enough." The pandaren monk nodded solemnly. "And for now, that will have to suffice."

8

The storm broke along with Tyrathan's fever, causing Chen to wonder if the weather wasn't somehow supernatural in nature. It certainly was a sinister notion, but it didn't stay with him too long. It really found no purchase in his heart, for even as the last snowflake fell, Chen saw signs of snow lilies fighting their way up toward sunshine. Surely something evil never would have allowed that to happen.

Taran Zhu did not pass judgment on the nature of the storm's origin but dispatched monks south, west, and east to assess damage. Chen volunteered to head east, since that would take him toward the Temple of the White Tiger. He'd be able to see his niece and learn how she'd fared. Taran Zhu had agreed to allow him to go and promised that Tyrathan would have the best of care in his absence.

For Chen, it felt good to be out of the monastery. Traveling fed his wanderlust. He was certain most of the monks put his willingness to descend the mountain down to that and that alone. It fit with their sense of the world and their idea that those who dwelt on Shen-zin Su were, by their very nature, out of balance and tilted toward Huojin.

Chen wasn't going to deny that he liked travel and exploration. Others might have itchy feet because they feared being trapped, but not Chen. He turned to his traveling companion and smiled. "I just feel that every time I move on, I'm making room for someone else to rest and enjoy for a while."

Yalia Sagewhisper graced him with a quizzical expression, yet not one devoid of mirth. "Master Stormstout, are we having another conversation of which I've not been part of the first half?"

"My apologies, Sister. Sometimes thoughts rattle around in my head and just tumble out like jihui cubes. Never know which face will be up." He pointed back toward the monastery hidden beneath a cloak of clouds. "I like the monastery perfectly well."

"But you could not dwell there forever?"

"No, I don't think so." Chen frowned. "Have we had this conversation before?"

She shook her head. "There are times, Master Stormstout, when you pause while sweeping, or when you watch the man head off for his trek up the mountain, and you get lost. You focus elsewhere, just as you focus when you are preparing a concoction."

"You've noticed that?" Chen's heart beat a bit faster. "You've been watching me?"

"It is difficult not to pay attention when the love of enterprise shines so brightly in one." A sidelong glance lingered, and a smile joined it. "Do you wish to know what I see when you work?"

"I would be honored to hear your thoughts."

"You become a lens, Master Stormstout. You have the experience of the world—the world beyond Pandaria—and you focus it on what you do. Take, for example, the Get Well brew you created for the troll. There are pandaren brewmasters who could have executed the brewing with your same skill. Perhaps even more. However, their lack of experience means they would not know what to add to it to infuse it with well-being for the troll." She glanced down. "I fear I do not express myself well."

"No, I understand, thank you." Chen smiled. "It's humbling to see yourself through someone else's eyes. You're right, of course. It's just that I've never seen it as focus. I see it as fun, as a gift I am giving others. When I made tea for you and Lord Taran Zhu, I wanted to show my appreciation and to share some of me. By your reckoning, that meant I was sharing part of the world."

"You did. Thank you." She nodded as they slowly descended into a valley surrounded by a patchwork of distant villages and cultivated fields. "Your earlier statement suggests motivation for this journey beyond chasing the turtle or the desire to see your niece. Am I correct?"

"Yes." Chen's brow furrowed. "If I could identify it, I would not run from it. I'm not really running now. I just need . . ."

". . . perspective."

"That's it." He nodded quickly, liking that she'd pulled the word from his mind. "I have been seeing to the physical recovery of Vol'jin and Tyrathan Khort. They are healing. Bodily, anyway. But each still carries wounds. I cannot see . . ."

Yalia turned and laid a paw on his shoulder. "It is not your fault that you cannot see. What they hide, they hide well. And even if you could see, you could not make them see. Healing of that sort can be encouraged but not compelled, and sometimes it hurts the healer to have to wait."

"You speak from experience?" Chen leaped over a small brook.

Yalia spritely picked her way over rocks. "An experience, yes. A very rare one. Most of our initiates are chosen through a series of trials, but this is not always so. Do you know how the other cubs, the very special cubs, come to be chosen, Master Stormstout?"

The brewmaster shook his head. "I never thought about it."

"Legend has it that some cubs are not meant to undergo the Trial of the Red Blossoms. Their fates are decided in a very different way."

As she spoke, her stare grew distant and her soft voice became even softer. "These cubs, wise beyond their years, some suggest, arrive as toddlers in form but ancient in spirit. Kind travelers give them aid, and legends suggest those travelers are the gods themselves. These cubs are accepted by the Shado-pan lord. They're spoken of as the Guided Cubs.

"I was a Guided Cub. My home village, Zouchin, is there on the north coast. My father was a fisher. He owned his own boat and was prosperous. In our village, there were many proud families. As I grew up, I understood that I would be given in marriage to the son of another fisher. The difficulty was that there were two candidates, each a half dozen years older than I. They competed for my attention and for the whole village's attention. The choice would guarantee the fortunes of one family, and sides were chosen quickly."

Yalia glanced at him for a heartbeat. "You must understand, Master Stormstout, that I understood the way of the world. I understood that I was a prize and that this was my role in life. Perhaps, were I older, I would have resented being reduced to chattel. The reality I saw made that unimportant."

"What did you see?"

"Yenki and Chinwa's rivalry had begun with a benign nature. They are pandaren. Many antics, much noise and bustle, but no real hurts. Yet each did things that progressed. Their actions escalated, each egging the other on to do more. And, in their voices, hints of acrimony."

She opened her paws. "I could see what others could not. This rivalry between friends would become enmity. And while it might never get to the point where one would strike another in anger, they would each do something to prove themselves worthier of winning me. They would take undue risks, silly risks. This would not stop after I had been won, but would continue until one or the other died. The survivor would live forever with guilt. Thus two lives would be destroyed."

"Three, counting your own."

"This I understand after many years. Then, not yet a half dozen years old, I knew only that they would die because of me. So one morning I packed some rice balls and a change of clothes, and headed out. My mother's mother saw me. She helped. She wrapped me up in her favorite scarf. She whispered, 'I wish I had known your courage, Yalia.' And then I made my way to the monastery."

Chen waited for more, but Yalia remained silent. Her story made him want to smile, for she'd been a very brave cub, and wise, to make the choice and the journey. At the same time, it was a terrible choice for a cub to make. In the echoes of her words, he caught notes of pain and sorrow.

Yalia shook her head. "It is not lost on me the irony of my being in charge of the Trial of the Red Blossoms' traditions. I, who never had to endure those tests, now am a gatekeeper to decide who among the hopeful can join us. Had I been judged by the same harsh standards I must now employ, I would not be here."

"And having to be a harsh taskmistress chafes against your true nature." Chen bent and deftly plucked a pawful of yellow flowers with little red runners. He snapped the blossoms off and rubbed them together between his palms. They released a wonderful scent. He held his paws out to her.

She accepted the crushed flowers in her cupped paws and breathed deeply. "Spring's promise."

"There's a similar flower in Durotar, which grows up after rain. They call it heart's ease." Chen rubbed his paws over his neck and cheeks. "Not the trolls, mind. They have noble hearts but do not believe they should be at ease. I think they think there was a time when they were at ease, but that ease is what led them to fall."

"They let bitterness drive them?"

"Some do. Many, in fact. But not Vol'jin."

Yalia poured the yellow petals into a small linen pouch and pulled the drawstring tight. "You know the content of his heart that well?"

"I thought I did." Chen shrugged. "I think I do."

"Then believe, Master Chen, that your friend will come to know himself as well as you do. That will be the first signpost on his road to healing."

Their initial intent had been to head roughly toward dawn, then cut down along the road to the Temple of the White Tiger. However, before they'd gone even a league along the road, they found two young male pandaren tending a turnip crop, but neither moving very quickly. In fact, they were using their hoes and rakes more as crutches than as farm tools. They had the bruised appearance and defeated demeanor of the recently thrashed.

"It was not our fault," one protested as he shared a boiled turnip porridge. "We had virmen infesting our field, after digging out from the storm. We asked a wanderer to help us. Before the dust settled from the first fight, she'd finished the lot and expected a reward. I offered her a kiss, and my brother offered two. We are handsome, you know, under these bandages."

The other nodded quickly, then raised paws to his head as if the nod threatened to dislodge his skull. "She was a pretty young thing, for a wild dog."

Chen's eyes narrowed. "Li Li Stormstout?"

"You've run afoul of her too?"

Chen let a low growl roll from his throat and bared his teeth, since that was what an uncle must do under such circumstances. "She is my niece. And I am a much wilder dog. She must have had some reason for leaving you alive. Tell us which way she went, and I won't have to decide if it was a good enough reason."

The two of them quailed and fell all over themselves to point north. "People been coming south since the snows, looking for help. We've sent food. We'll pack up some for you to bring."

"Before you find a cart and bring it yourself?"

"Yes, yes."

"That will be good."

Chen remained silent, as did the brothers. Yalia was silent as well, but her silence had a different quality to it. After the porridge, Chen made tea and added a few things that would aid the brothers' recovery. "Strain the tea leaves into cloth and use it as a poultice. Good for what ails you."

"Yes, Master Stormstout." The brothers, of the Stoneraker family, bowed deeply and often as the two travelers took their leave. "Thank you, Master Stormstout. All blessings to your niece and on your travels."

Yalia broke her silence as they passed down a hill, putting the crest between them and the croft. "You would not have inflicted a beating on them."

Chen smiled. "You know me well enough that it's not a question."

"But you did frighten them."

He opened his arms to take in the vista of the narrow valley with steep mountainsides. Below, a stream snaked along, blue where the sun could not touch it, silver where it did. Green, so much green and very deep, along with the rich brown of cultivated fields, screamed fertility. Even the way the buildings had been constructed into the landscape, adding to it without exploiting it, felt incredibly right.

"I grew up on Shen-zin Su. I love my home. As I look out here, however, it is as if I had been living in a picture. A beautiful picture, yes, but a picture of Pandaria. This land calls to me. It fills an emptiness that I'd never known I had. Maybe that is why I have wandered so much. I was looking, but didn't know what for."

He frowned. "I growled less for Li Li than for them calling her a 'wild dog.' For her, for me, Pandaria is home. It is a place where I could be at home."

"And yet those two are like others who would forever point out why you are not of Pandaria."

"You understand."

She passed him the sachet of heart's ease. "Better than you know."

• • •

They marked their travel north to Zouchin not by days or hours but by the tales of Li Li's passing before them. She'd been helpful but irascible. More than one person referred to her as a wild dog, but they quoted her as calling herself that. Proudly, too, as it turned out. Chen could not help but smile, and he easily imagined the legend of a wild dog spreading throughout Pandaria.

At Zouchin, nestled between cliffs and the sea, they found Li Li working hard in the midst of the village. The storm had wrecked one boat, collapsed some houses, and ripped a dock from its pilings. Li Li had pitched right in, and by the time they arrived, she was supervising a salvage crew and barking orders at carpenters to speed up work on the houses.

Chen caught Li Li, hugged her, and spun her around as he had when she was a cub. She squealed, but this time in protest at the destruction of dignity. He set her down, then bowed deeply and respectfully. That gesture silenced clucking tongues, though her returning the bow just a bit deeper and holding it a second longer started their clucking again.

Chen introduced Yalia to his niece. "Sister Yalia Sagewhisper has traveled from the monastery here with me."

Li Li raised an eyebrow. "I bet that was a long journey. How did you get him out of taverns and not drinking beer all the way here?"

Yalia smiled. "Our journey was sped because we were chasing stories of Li Li the Wild Dog and her exploits."

Li Li smiled broadly and dug an elbow into her uncle's ribs. "She's a sharp one, Uncle Chen." Li Li scratched her chin. "Sagewhisper? There's a Sageflower family here—name's almost the same. They survived pretty well, just bumps and bruises."

"This is good to know, Li Li." Yalia nodded respectfully. "If there is time, I might pay them a visit; our names are so close."

"I'm sure they will marvel at the coincidence." Li Li looked around the village. "I'll get back to work, then. The villagers are great on the water, I'm sure, but need some driving on the land."

Li Li hugged her uncle again, then ran back to her work crews—whose pace quickened with her increasing proximity.

Chen cocked his head. "You've not been back here since you joined the monastery, after Taran Zhu changed your name. Does your family know you are alive?"

She shook her head. "Some of us are wild dogs by birth, Master Chen. Others by choice. It is for the best."

Chen nodded and returned to her the packet of heart's ease.

9

It surprised Vol'jin that Tyrathan was already up and out of bed by the time he arrived with a jihui board and pieces. The man had made it all the way over to the window and leaned against it, much as Vol'jin himself had done. The troll noticed that the man's cane remained at the foot of the bed.

Tyrathan looked back over his shoulder. "Can barely see any signs of the storm now. They say you never see the arrow that will kill you. I didn't see that storm. Not at all."

"Taran Zhu said such storms be unusual but not rare." Vol'jin set the board down on the side table. "The later they come, the more savage they be."

The man nodded. "Can't see anything, but can still feel it. There is a chill in the air."

"You should not be barefoot."

"Nor you." Tyrathan turned, a bit unsteadily, then hooked his elbows on the casement. "You've taken to adapting yourself to the cold. Up before dawn, standing in the snows on the south side, the snows sheltered in shadow during the day. Admirable but foolish. I do not recommend it."

Vol'jin snorted. "Calling a troll foolish be most unwise."

"I hope you will learn from my folly." The man levered himself away from the wall and staggered toward the bed. The limp had almost vanished, despite his weakness. Vol'jin turned toward him but made no move to aid him. Tyrathan smiled, catching himself on the footboard for a rest. It was part of the game they played.

The man lowered himself to the edge of the bed. "You're late. Do they have you doing my chores?"

Vol'jin waved the question away as he dragged the side table over, then fetched a chair. "It speeds my recovery."

"Now you come to take care of me."

The troll's head came up. "Trolls be not without a sense of obligation."

Tyrathan laughed. "I know trolls well enough to know that."

Vol'jin centered the board on the table. "Do you?"

"Do you remember when you commented on my troll accent? You said Stranglethorn."

"You ignored me."

"I chose not to respond." Tyrathan accepted a canister, poured out the black pieces, and arranged them in sets of six. "Do you want to know how I learned?"

Vol'jin shrugged, not because he didn't want to know but because he knew the man would tell him regardless.

"You're right. It was Stranglethorn. I found a troll. I paid him very well for a year. He told himself he was my guide. He performed his duties well. I picked up his language—at first without him knowing I was listening, then in conversation. I have a facility for that."

"I be believing that."

"Tracking is a language. I would track him. Every day I would go back to a patch of ground to watch how his footprints deteriorated. In the hot season, after the rain.

I learned the language that told me how long before he had passed, how quickly he'd gone, how tall he was."

"Did you kill him after?"

Tyrathan scooped the black troops back into the canister. "Not him. I've killed other trolls."

"I be not fearing you."

"I know. And I have killed men, as have you." The man set his canister on the table. "This troll, Keren'dal he called himself, would pray. That's what I thought, and I mentioned it. He said he was speaking to the spirits. I forget what he called them."

Vol'jin shook his head. "There would be no forgetting. He never told you. Secrets be secrets."

"Times he would be irritable, like you. Those were times when he spoke to them but got no answers."

"Does your Holy Light answer you, manthing?"

"I've long since stopped believing in it."

"Which be why it abandoned you."

Tyrathan laughed. "I know why I am abandoned. For the same reason as you."

Vol'jin locked his face into a neutral mask but knew that by that very act, he had betrayed himself. The fact was that since he had tracked through Tyrathan's memories, since he had seen the world through the man's eyes, the loa had been distant and quiet. It felt as if the storm that had raged around the monastery still raged in the spirit realm. He could see Bwonsamdi and Hir'eek and Shirvallah, but only in dim, gray silhouettes that vanished in waves of white.

Vol'jin still believed in the loa, in their leadership and gifts, in the necessity of their worship. He was a shadow hunter. He could read tracks with the same facility as Tyrathan, and just as easily he could commune with the loa. Yet in the storm, tracks vanished and swirling winds stole words.

He'd tried to reach them. His latest attempt had been, in fact, what made him late to meet Tyrathan. Vol'jin had composed himself in his cell, had moved beyond awareness of his surroundings, but could not breach the storm's barrier. It seemed as if the cold and the distance from his home and even his having walked inside the human's flesh had distracted him. He could not focus to punch through and bridge the distance between himself and the loa.

It was as if once Bwonsamdi had relinquished his claim on Vol'jin, the loa had lost interest.

The troll's head came up. "Why be you abandoned?"

"Fear."

"I be not afraid."

"But you are." Tyrathan tapped his own temple with a finger. "I can still feel you in my mind, Vol'jin. Being inside my skin terrified you. Not because you found it repulsive— not just because you find it repulsive—but because you found me so fragile. Oh, yes, that sense remains with me. Bitter, oily, it will never go away. It's an insight I shall value, I am sure, but you miss its import to you."

Vol'jin nodded once, though he did not want to.

"My being so easily breakable reminded you how close you were to death. There I was, leg broken, trapped, unable to escape, knowing I would die. And you knew the same thing when they tried to kill you. Can you remember what happened after?"

"Chen found me. Brought me here."

"No, no, that you've been told." The man shook his head. "What do you remember, Vol'jin?"

"When I be walking in your skin, be you living in mine?"

"No. Nor would I do that on a bet. Worse than you knowing how vulnerable I am would be my knowing how invulnerable you feel. But to the point. Do you remember what happened after? Do you know how you got to where Chen found you? Do you even know why you're alive now?"

"I live, manthing, because I refused to die."

The little bug of a man laughed arrogantly. "So you tell yourself. But this is what you're afraid of. You don't know. The link in the chain of experiences between who you were and who you are now has been severed. You can look back at who you were, and you can wonder if that's still you, but there's a void. You can't be sure."

Vol'jin growled. "And you be sure?"

"Who I am?" Tyrathan laughed again, but the timbre shifted. Melancholy and a hint of madness ran through it. "You saw what you saw. Do you wish to know the rest of it? What you didn't see?"

Vol'jin again agreed with a nod, wanting to avoid assessing the man's words.

"I stopped being Tyrathan Khort. I crawled from that place. Not a man, a beast. Perhaps I saw myself as a troll would see me. Wounded, pathetic, driven by thirst, by hunger. I, a man who had dined with lords and princes, eating the finest flesh that I had placed on the table, I was reduced to prying grubs from dying wood. I ate roots I hoped would finish me or heal me but often found those that just made me sicker. I covered myself with mud to keep vermin away. I wove twigs and leaves into my hair so I could hide from hunters on both sides. I shied from anything and anyone until happened upon by a pandaren gathering herbs, humming happily to himself."

"Why hadn't you summoned your companion?"

That stopped Tyrathan. He looked down, remaining

silent. He swallowed hard and his voice grew tighter and small. "My companion had bound himself to the man I had been. I would not dishonor him by having him see me as I was."

"And now?"

The man shook his head. "I am no longer Tyrathan Khort. My companion no longer answers me."

"Be this because you fear death?"

"No, I fear other things." The man looked up, his eyes glistening emerald. "You fear death."

"Dying not be scaring me."

"It was more than your death to which I referred."

The man's comment sank a blade to the hilt in Vol'jin's breast. He had seen the wisdom of the chain analogy, though he hated it. Clearly the Vol'jin he had been had made mistakes that resulted in his almost being murdered. Yet he lived and had learned, so he would not make the same mistake again. But something in his mind twisted that notion such that it made who he had once been somehow wrong, inferior. While Vol'jin rejected that concept and accepted that he was capable of error, he could not reject the idea that his changed circumstances meant he could not be the troll he had been.

The chain be severed. The links be gone.

With that loss, however, came new perspective on the greater picture. Vol'jin was not just a troll. He was a shadow hunter. He was the leader of the Darkspears. He was a leader within the Horde. The troll nearly had died. Did the distance from the loa signal the death of the shadow hunter? And did his death mean the Darkspears would die and the Horde would die?

Does this mean my father's dream be dying? If his dream died, would it then mock the battle to free the Echo Isles from Zalazane? All the blood that had been shed would be for nought, all the pain meaningless. Event after event, everything in his life and beyond it, trailing back into troll history, all of it crumbled.

Do I fear that my failure, my death, be leading to the deaths of the Darkspears, of the Horde, of trolls themselves? He visualized the black chasm between lying in a pool of blood in a dark cave and waking up in the monastery. *Will that void be swallowing everything?*

The man's voice barely rose above a whisper. "Do you want to know the truly cruel thing, Vol'jin?"

"Tell me."

"You and I, we have died. We are not who we were." Tyrathan looked down at his empty hands. "What we must do now is create ourselves—not re-create, but create. This is why it is cruel. When we first did this, we had all the energy of youth. We did not know that attaining our dreams would be impossible—we just went out and got them. Innocence shielded us. Enthusiasm and unflagging confidence got us through. But now we have none of that. Now we are old, wiser, tired."

"Our burden be lighter."

The man smirked. "True. I think this is why the simplicity of the monastery appeals to me. It is spare. Duties are defined. The chance to excel is present."

The troll's eyes tightened. "You shoot well. You watch the archers. Why don't you shoot?"

"I haven't decided if that is part of me." Tyrathan looked up and opened his mouth, then shut it abruptly.

Vol'jin cocked his head. "You had a question."

"Having a question doesn't mean it deserves an answer."

"Ask."

"Will we get past our fear?"

"I be not knowing." Vol'jin's lips pressed together in a grim line. "If I find an answer, it be yours."

That night, as Vol'jin lay down and sleep swept the waking world away, the loa proved they had not completely abandoned him. He found himself one of thousands of bats, flapping through the night. He was not with Hir'eek, but he certainly was a bat by the loa's grace. So he flew with the others, reading the echoes of their screams piercing the darkness in a world rendered colorless in sound.

It made sense to Vol'jin that he could contact the loa, because being a shadow hunter had been so much of himself. That void, though he could not see into it, could only have been breached by a shadow hunter. All he had learned, all he had endured, surely those were what had kept him alive long enough to escape the cave.

And the bats in that cave, they witnessed the void, the time I be forgetting. Vol'jin hoped that perhaps this vision, even rendered in the bat's sound-sight, would show him the void. He hoped the chain could be reforged, yet deep down knew it could not be reforged easily.

Hir'eek instead, in his wisdom, brought Vol'jin to another place and another time. Crisp edges on stone buildings marked these as new construction, not ruins. He guessed he'd been taken back to when the Zandalari had spawned many troll tribes, and trolls were at the height of their power. The bats circled, then roosted high in towers surrounding a central courtyard, where legions of trolls hemmed in a jostling crowd of insectoid aqiri captives.

Amani, forest trolls, fresh from their wars with the aqir. Vol'jin knew the history well, but suspected Hir'eek wished to remind him of more than the glory days of the Amani empire.

The vision did just that. Trolls drove aqir up stone steps at spearpoint, to where priests waited. Acolytes would hoist the aqir onto stone altars slick with ichor, bellies exposed; then the celebrant would raise a knife. The blade and the hilt were worked with symbols, one for each loa. Sound-sight let him image the pommel and see Hir'eek's face there, a heartbeat before the blade plunged down and ripped the sacrifice open.

Then, there, above the altar, Hir'eek himself manifested. The aqir's spirit rose as ethereal steam from the corpse, and the bat god breathed it in. With subtle motions of gentle wings he pulled more of it to himself, glowing brightly, becoming more sharply defined.

Sound-sight did not communicate that to Vol'jin. That he saw with his own inner sight—something he'd refined and learned to trust as a shadow hunter. Hir'eek showed him the proper way to worship, the true glory and honor the loa were due.

A voice sounded in Vol'jin's head—a high, piping voice. *You have labored to preserve the Darkspears so there be trolls to worship us. This labor, it be withdrawing you from us. Your body heals but your soul cannot. Won't heal, unless you be returning to the true ways. Abandon your history, and the chasm grows.*

"But will returning make the chasm shrink, Hir'eek?" Vol'jin sat upright, speaking to darkness. He waited. He listened.

No reply came, and he took that as a fel omen.

10

Khal'ak refused to huddle beneath the tiger-fur cloak, though she was glad for its warmth. The storm had long since shrieked away its fury in battering the wooden ramparts surrounding the harbor on the Isle of Thunder, sharp breezes and brisk gusts still cutting at her exposed flesh. She'd hoped she'd actually consumed enough ice troll flesh that their comfort with the cold would have been transferred to her, but this was not the case.

Little matter. I be preferrin' Sandfury flesh. The desert environment gave it more flavor. It did not do her much good here, north of Pandaria, but there would come a time. *When we retake Kalimdor.*

That time would come. She knew it. All of the Zandalari did. All troll tribes had descended from their noble lineage, corrupting themselves as they pulled away. One needed to look no further than physiology to prove it: she stood taller than any other troll she'd met who was not pureblood Zandalari. Their worship of the loa was a game compared to the devotion she showed the spirits. And while some trolls might reach back and honor those traditions—the shadow hunters a rare example among them—they did not possess the traditions as the Zandalari did.

There were times, in her travels through the world, doing the bidding of Vilnak'dor, that she thought she had found a hint, perhaps a spark of the ancient ways amid the corrupted ones. She sought those who were throwbacks to the old days, searching often in vain. Many were the pretenders to a mantle they claimed to have inherited from the Zandalari, as if she and her tribe no longer existed. All too often—always, in fact—these self-anointed saviors of trollkind were the pathetic product of a degraded society.

That they failed so often no longer surprised her.

Vilnak'dor had risen from among the Zandalari, from a long line of trolls steeped in the lore and traditions that had faithfully been maintained and practiced for millennia. He had not allowed himself the distractions that others had. He did not look upon the Amani and Gurubashi empires as things to be reestablished and then elevated. He accepted that their failure marked their inherent instability. To reestablish them was to court failure, so he reached further back into history, to resurrect an alliance that had borne fruit.

A mogu captain approached her, respectful despite her standing on the walls of his city. A head and a half taller than she, ebon skinned, strongly built, he possessed a leonine aspect that was uniquely suited to Pandaria. His brows, beard, and hair were as white as his flesh was black. When she'd first seen statuary depicting the mogu, she had thought it highly stylized. Meeting them in the flesh dispelled that notion, and seeing them in action suggested that any round softness of form hid only a sharpness of purpose and courage.

"We have, my lady, completed all but the last of the loading. When the tide begins to go out, we will sail south."

Khal'ak looked down at the black fleet bobbing in dark waters. Her troops, including her own elite legion, had boarded in good order. The assault force, save for mogu scouts, consisted primarily of Zandalari. None of the lesser races—though she would have entertained the notion of goblin artillery or a handful of their war engines.

Only two ships remained on the quay. Her flagship, which would be last off but would lead the way, and a smaller ship. It should already have been anchored near the breakwater. "What be the delay?"

"Concerns have been expressed, of signs and portents." The mogu captain stood up straight, hiding massive fists behind his back. "The storm, they do not understand."

Her eyes tightened. "Da shaman. Of course. I gonna attend to it personally."

"The tide runs in six hours."

"It gonna be takin' but six minutes once I be down there."

The mogu bowed sincerely enough that Khal'ak almost accepted the sentiment as genuine. It was not that she thought he or any of the other mogu hated or resented the Zandalari. They regretted needing Zandalari help and, secretly, wondered why it had taken so long for it to be offered.

Many millennia past, back when there were only the Zandalari, back before the mists hid Pandaria, the mogu and trolls met. It was a time when only a quarter of all there was to know even existed. Lion recognized lion. They should have destroyed each other, that first mogu and first troll, but they did not. They understood that in a war, pitting strength against strength, the survivor would be weakened. The survivor might even succumb to creatures far weaker than it. That would be a tragedy that neither race wanted.

With back firmly set against back, mogu and trolls carved out their positions in the world. Yet as events took place, as each race faced challenges, its ally became forgotten. The mogu disappeared along with Pandaria. Trolls found their own world sundered. And as it was with storied races pressed with immediate problems, the distant past dimmed in recollection, and more recent outrages burned blindingly bright.

Khal'ak descended the switchback steps. The steps numbered at seventeen. She did not understand the significance of this for the mogu, but then she did not have to understand. Her job was simply to carry out her master's orders. He, in turn, sought to accommodate his ally, the Thunder King. Power would drive power until both possessed enough to return to their positions of glory and set the world to rights again.

She walked through a settlement that had been humbled by age yet now awakened to a new youth. The mogu, more and more of them appearing each day, bowed quietly in their way. They understood her significance and acknowledged it because her actions had brought them joy and would bring them more.

Even though they did bow and show her honor, enough reserve remained in their behavior to reveal how much superior to her, and to trolls, the mogu felt. Khal'ak suppressed a laugh, since her training would make it child's play to kill any of them. The mogu had no understanding of how precarious their position in this alliance was or how vulnerable they could be if the Zandalari decided to destroy them.

Cold waves slapped against pilings, splashing the quay. Gulls wheeled and screamed above. The scent of salt air and rotting fish struck her as remarkably exotic. Cables groaned and planking creaked as the ships rode the harbor's dark green surface.

She quickly boarded the smaller ship and found a dozen shaman circled in the center of the main deck. A third of them squatted, poking at bones and feathers, pebbles and odd bits of metal. The others stood by, sage and silent—conditions that intensified when they saw her come aboard.

"Why be you not weighin' anchor?"

"The loa, they be not pleased." One of the squatting shaman looked up at her, pointing at two bones crossed above a feather. "The storm be not natural."

She opened her hands and resisted the urge to kick him over the side. "Did you expect it to be? What manner of fool be you? The loa were pleased enough when we set sail for Pandaria. You yourselves said as much. You said you be readin' the thing same in your bones and bits. Sheer idiocy for the loa to bless our undertaking then, yet protest now because of a blizzard."

Khal'ak pointed back toward the palace hidden in the island's interior. "You know what we have done. The Thunder King walks again. Dat storm, it be honoring him. The world rejoices at his return. Of all seasons, he loved winter best. Of all weather, he felt most alive when snow be stingin' and blindin' the world. You may not have remembered him, but the world did, and it welcomed him. And now you cast bones to determine what the loa think? If they protested, how could that storm ever have happened?"

Gyran'zul, the youngest of the shaman and the one

most given to reason, turned toward her. She favored him for his shock of red hair and the strong thrust of his tusks. He knew that and trusted in it to give him time to speak.

"Honored Khal'ak, what you say be reasonable. The loa could have stopped the storm. They could have stopped our armada sailin' long ago. While my colleagues may be seeking clarity where none exists, that dey need to seek clarity means confusion exists."

The fur began to rise at the nape of her neck. "You speak sense. More of it, please."

"Da loa be demanding and deserving of our worship—the worship of all trolls. They value strength. While we have offered each other as sacrifices, and these sacrifices be accepted and revered, they be not preferred. Da loa, as we reach them, speak to us less because they also speak to others. We be not alone in comin' to Pandaria. Alliance and Horde be here as well."

She looked from one to the other of the shaman, taking in the full dozen. "An' this be what gives you pause? Perhaps you do not fully understand. Perhaps it be not your place to understand. My master has long anticipated others arriving in Pandaria. Vermin always be finding a way to spoil things. To assume we would escape dem here be folly. Contingent plans been made. Opposition will not stand."

Another shaman with short tusks rose. "This be well for dealin' with the Alliance, but what of the Horde?"

"What of dem?"

"Trolls be among them."

"Vermin choosin' to run in packs does not make them noble. They still be vermin. And if trolls believe joining such a pack benefits them rather than degrading them, more fools they. We be welcomin' those trolls who come to see the wisdom of our actions and wish ta join us. We always be needing garrison troops and subalterns to organize various details. If the loa be distracted by reachin' those trolls and tellin' them to come to us, dis I favor. Perhaps this be what you should entreat da loa to do."

She snorted. "From dis ship. Out at the breakwater."

The short-tusked shaman shook his head. "We will be needing time to prepare. A sacrifice."

"You have six hours. Less. Moonrise."

"That be not enough time."

She stabbed a finger at the shaman's chest. "Den I gonna give the loa a sacrifice. I gonna tie your left ankle and wrist to the dock, and the right ankle and wrist to this ship. I will order the captain to haul anchor an' sail. Be this how you wish to serve da loa, your fleet, and your people?"

Gyran'zul intervened. "The purity of your faith, Honored Khal'ak, be reflectin' great esteem upon your master and your family. No doubt your fidelity to the loa be accounting for our great initial success. We gonna communicate that to the loa, and we gonna be prepared to set sail immediately."

"You be pleasing our master."

The young troll raised a finger. "Dere be one other thing."

"Yes?"

The shaman pressed his hands together. Slender and delicate, too much so. His eyes narrowed. "The loa speak to us, and they speak to some among the Horde, but this does not occupy the whole of their attention."

"What else be there?"

"This be the point. We do not know. The reason the

storm concerns us be because when we seek whatever else there be, it be hiding behind a curtain. It could be a ghost. It could be a troll in the distance. It could herald da birth of a troll destined to greatness. We do not know, and we must tell you of it because you seek certainty where doubt exists."

A shiver ran the full length of her spine. Somehow the presence of this unknown troll concerned her more than learning Horde and Alliance had come to Pandaria. They were known quantities. The Zandalari could deal with them. *But how does one lay contingency plans for an unknown?* The mogu assured them that the pandaren were, effectively, defenseless. *What else could dere be?*

Khal'ak looked past the shaman toward the south, where mists gathered just beyond the harbor. Their fleet would sail into the night and through another night. She'd been to Pandaria. She'd chosen the landing zone. A small fishing village with nothing of substance or value save a decent harbor. Once they'd landed and secured the harbor, they'd plunge inland. Troll scouts indicated there was nothing that could stop them. Nothing even to slow the Zandalari down.

Other than succumbin' to the suspicions of those who stand to lose the most if we succeed. She glanced at Gyran'zul again and felt certain he wasn't playing a game. If he wanted power, she would give it to him. The both of them knew that. Therefore his concerns were real.

Khal'ak nodded. "You gonna prepare to sail. You gonna bend your will to determining what be hidden in da void, in that pale shadow. All of you. If you do not be satisfyin' me on this point, I gonna feed you to the loa until they be satisfied. No thwarting us, something that does not exist."

• • •

That night, far to the south, Vol'jin found his sleep disturbed by a vision. This surprised him. After Hir'eek's visit, the loa had ignored him, and he had affected to ignore them in turn. He'd realized that to reach out to them before he knew who he was would only be an attempt to mimic who he had been. As Tyrathan's companion would not come to a summons from someone he did not recognize, it would not do for Vol'jin to reestablish a bond with the loa if he was not going to be the troll who had created it in the beginning.

He couldn't identify the loa sending him the vision. He soared through the air effortlessly, so it could be Akil'darah. Still, he flew at night, and the eagle would not. Then he realized he was actually floating and seeing through many eyes. He decided that Elortha no Shadra, the Silk Dancer, had made him into one of her children. He floated high, suspended from spider-silk threads carried by the wind.

Below him clouds parted. Ships under full sail made haste south. It had to be ancient times, for the broad, square sails carried Zandalari crests. He couldn't call to mind any time in history when the Zandalari had launched such a powerful fleet.

He looked up at the night sky, expecting to see the constellations arranged in different ways. That he recognized them shocked him.

And he laughed.

Very good, Mother of Venom. You be showing me a vision of a now where I could assemble such a fleet. You be showing me the glory I could win for you and the loa. So generous a vision. I could even be believing it would further my father's dream. The problem be, am I still Sen'jin's son?

The breeze failed.

The spider fell.

And Vol'jin brushed it and its web away from his face, before turning onto his side and sinking back into a dreamless sleep.

11

Even though Lord Taran Zhu's uncharacteristic revelation of emotion—seen in a pinched expression that mixed disapproval with serious reservation—hinted at trouble, Chen could not help but smile. His heart was fit to bursting with pride and happiness, both being redoubled with Taran Zhu's agreement with his plan.

A great chunk of his happiness came from his knowing that Yalia Sagewhisper's intercession had changed the old monk's mind. Chen had managed, while working at Zouchin and then on the way back, to mash together ingredients for a wonderful brew. He was certain it would be for Pandaria what the Get Well brew had been for Vol'jin. He wanted to share it when he got back, and his sheer enthusiasm, he realized now, had probably been what made Taran Zhu dubious of the effort.

That Yalia had spoken with the monk on his behalf had touched him deeply. Chen liked her. He always had. On the journey, however, he found even more to like. He also found reason to hope that she might return some of his affection. How much, he wasn't sure, but anything was good, because from small eggs grew mighty turtles.

No one at Zouchin had recognized her, and it struck

Chen as odd that she did not immediately seek out her family. She certainly learned about them, from Li Li and others, and learned that they prospered. Even her grandmother still lived. Yalia held herself apart, and a piece of that withdrawal had her pulling away from him as well.

Chen had a hard time understanding her desire for distance—from her family, not so much from him. In Pandaria, Chen found pieces of home he'd been missing. Zouchin felt like another one. It had readily available resources that made it perfect for a small brewery. The moment he saw it, he was determined to build one there because it was the perfect location, and it would bring him closer to Yalia.

That first night, after he'd brewed tea, he broached the subject of her family.

Yalia stared into the depths of her tea bowl. "They have their lives, Master Chen. I left so they would have peace. I would not bring havoc here."

"Don't you think knowing you are well and respected would bring them more peace?" He shrugged and forced a smile. "I worry whenever Li Li is out of sight. Your family must have worries or . . ." He fell silent as a thought occurred to him.

She looked up. "Or?"

"It wasn't a worthy thought, Sister Yalia. Not of you."

"I would have you share it. Even if we decide it is an error, I would have honesty between us." She laid a paw on his forearm. "Please, Master Chen."

He let the snap and pop of the little campfire they shared fill the silence for a moment, then nodded. "I wondered, only because I wonder it of myself sometimes, if it is your peace you wish to protect instead of theirs."

Her paw came back to her cup. She held it so still Chen

could see stars reflected in the tea. "The monastery has provided me much peace."

"One can never tell how others will react. I would think your family would be happy to see you. Maybe a little sister will resent having had to do your chores, or your mother will mourn the cubs you never gave her to spoil. It seems to me that even if these things are true, they are minor upsets compared to the joy of knowing you live and are happy."

"Does a quiet night and warm tea make difficult wisdom more palatable?"

"I don't know. I don't get many quiet nights and am not that often accused of committing acts of wisdom." He drank tea and let a little drip from his muzzle, just to make her smile.

She reached out and brushed a droplet away. "You are wise enough to play the clown at times when it needs playing. It makes entertaining your idea much easier. And to see the truth of it."

Chen couldn't hide his smile, but he shrank it enough that it did not appear prideful. "You will see your family."

"Yes, but tomorrow. I should really like to enjoy another peaceful night, with warm tea and a thoughtful friend. I shall remind myself who I am so I can share that with them, instead of trying to explain why I am not who they think I should be."

The next day had dawned bright and warm, which Chen took as a good omen. He traveled with Yalia to meet her family. They deflected some of their shock at Yalia's return into an enthusiastic welcome for him, since he was Wild Dog Li Li's famed uncle. Apparently, in motivating workers, she'd invoked his name and suggested dire consequences were they such slack laborers and he were in command.

Yalia's father, Tswen-luo, recognized the truth behind the story almost immediately, because he, as the master of a fishing fleet, had to hide behind a similar mask. The two of them had also discovered a mutual love of beer and, as males would do, proceeded to try to drink each other under a bug's belly. Somewhere in all of that, Tswen-luo agreed that the Stormstout Brewery should open an operation in Zouchin and that he would finance it in return for a modest share of profits and a bottomless mug.

Though he spent his time with her father, Chen did watch Yalia interact with her family. She won immediate acceptance from nieces and nephews by shattering boards with a punch or a kick. They ran through the village with broken bits of wood, collecting a pack of cubs for another demonstration. Several of them were offspring of the pandaren who had been rivals for her favors. Chen caught a hint of melancholy on her face when they were introduced. Clearly they had no clue as to who she had been.

Her mother and sisters tutted and scolded—at least, did so after shrieking and hugging and crying. Her brothers hugged her solemnly, then stole away back to work or for a mug or two with Chen. Yalia retained her composure and peace in dealing with all of them.

And then she got to her grandmother. The old pandaren had grown frail with years, hunched, her flesh hanging loosely. She walked with a cane, better than Tyrathan on his worst days, but not by much. Age had clouded her dark eyes, so she lifted a paw to Yalia's face and let it linger.

"Are you the granddaughter I lent my scarf to?"

"Yes, Ama."

"Have you brought it back?"

Yalia looked down. "No, Ama."

"On your next visit you will, Granddaughter. I have been missing it."

Then the old pandaren smiled, gap-toothed, and embraced Yalia. Silence reigned as the elder female disappeared in the circle of Yalia's arms. Their bodies shook with sobs that went unheard, which everyone affected not to notice.

Which was why Tswen-luo burped loudly and inappropriately to divert attention to himself. Chen, being a good guest, and protective of his reputation as a prodigious belcher himself, rattled the rafters quickly thereafter. That way the women could not vent their emotions in scolding the patriarch too much, and Yalia and her grandmother were granted a bit more privacy amid utter chaos.

Over the next two days, reconstruction work finished in the village and preparations for building the brewery commenced. Chen designated Li Li as his agent and enlisted the Stoneraker brothers—who happened to arrive with the food they'd promised—as masons. They clearly weren't cut out to be farmers, since their fields had grown more stones than turnips, and they'd spent enough time hauling rocks from their fields that a mason's work suited them.

Chen took some time to gather herbs from the area and prepare a test mix in a wooden keg, which he strapped to the small of his back. It sloshed as he and Yalia slogged their way back to the monastery. He burped it every so often, and watered it, and fed bits of this and that to the mix.

On the road Chen frowned as Yalia paused at the base of a switchback. "I realize I may need to apologize, Sister Yalia."

"Whatever for?"

"For inserting myself into Zouchin."

She shook her head. "You have been seeking a home, and you found that Zouchin felt like home. Why would you apologize for that?"

"It is your home, and I would not intrude on your privacy."

Yalia laughed, and Chen enjoyed the sound of it immensely. "Dear Chen, the monastery is my home. I am fond of Zouchin—and fonder now that you like it as well. But you, as a wanderer, must know that a true sense of home must be carried within. If one cannot spend a silent evening sipping tea and feel at peace, there is no geographical place that will confer that peace. We seek a place because it amplifies that peace. It shows us another face of it and reflects it back on us."

She pointed back down in the distance. "By seeing Zouchin through your eyes, and by reuniting with my family at your suggestion, I now have another place that will amplify peace. But you should know that on a quiet night, sipping tea with a friend, I feel even more peaceful."

Chen felt that had she suddenly become a tree and rooted herself in that spot, he would never wander farther than the shade she provided. He couldn't say that, of course, and his smile couldn't convey it. So he climbed up to where she stood, wishing the brew would not slosh so loudly, and nodded.

"Quiet night, or loud, with tea or beer or just cool water, I would also feel at peace with my friend."

She shyly turned her face from his, but could not hide a smile. "Then let us return to our home away from our homes, and enjoy that peace as well."

• • •

Only after Yalia had made a case to allow it did Taran Zhu agree to permit Chen to share his new concoction with a select few of the monks in the monastery. Yalia was not among them—Taran Zhu had chosen five of the eldest. Chen wasn't sure if the master monk felt things would turn into a drunken debauch, or if he just felt these monks might appreciate the new experience. He was betting more on the former than the latter.

Vol'jin and Tyrathan also joined the group, though they arrived separately. Chen couldn't help but notice a stiffness and formality between them. It probably wasn't that vast a gulf, but compared to the closeness he felt with Yalia, the two of them appeared to be continents drifting apart.

Chen poured for each guest a modest portion of his concoction. "Please understand this is not a final formula. I mixed many things together, including some of the spring beer I brewed a while ago and left forgotten in the storerooms. I won't tell you what I mean this to be. What I wish from each of you is to know not what it tastes like but what it feels like. You'll taste and smell, but those sensations will link back to memories."

He raised his own bowl. "To home and friends." He bowed his head first to Taran Zhu, then Vol'jin, then all the others in order around the table. As one, save for Taran Zhu, they drank.

Chen let the brew linger on his tongue. He easily picked out berries and hints of heart's ease, but other ingredients had mixed and mingled into a sometimes sweet and sometimes sharp taste, with just a bit of bite. He swallowed, relishing the scratch running down his throat, then set his cup down.

"This reminds me of a time, in lands beyond the mists, when I found myself the dinner guest of three ravenous ogres. Well, not their dinner guest really, but their dinner. They argued among themselves what I was going to taste most like. One said I'd taste like rabbit, since I was a bit mottled, and I said, 'Very close.' Another suggested bear, for obvious reasons, and I said, 'Very close again.' And the third said crow—he had a rather odd dent in his skull—so I said, 'Very close for you as well.' Which left them arguing."

A monk smiled. "So you chanced to escape."

"Very close." Chen grinned and drank a bit more. "I offered to settle the argument by way of a contest, with a prize. I told them to fetch rabbit, bear, and crow, and to cook each up, for they must have the taste in their mouths if they were to know what I truly tasted like. And I offered to brew something for each meat and then to make a brew they could enjoy with me. So they set off, each to fetch his meat. They cooked them all up, and I brewed. Then they ate. And I chanced to ask which brew tasted best with which meat, which set them arguing again. So they swapped meals and drinks around. And I, after a night's revel, being the only sober one, walked away free in the morning.

"This brew reminds me of how freedom felt in the dawn's light."

The monks laughed and applauded—even Tyrathan chuckled. Only Taran Zhu and Vol'jin remained untouched by the story. But Vol'jin drank, then nodded and set his cup down. "This be reminding me of the peace one knows from crushing his enemies. Their dreams be dying with them, leaving your future clear, like a morning after rain. Its crispness be echoing the snap of their bones. The sweetness be the joy of hearing their dying sighs. And I be tasting the freedom there, as well."

The troll's story left everyone quiet and the monks wide-eyed. Tyrathan drank, then smiled. "For me it is autumn, as the leaves turn crimson and gold. It's gathering the last of the crops, finding the last of the berries, everyone working together to lie in stores for the coming winter. It is a time of unity and joy in preparation for the uncertainty of winter—yet with the knowledge that hard work will be rewarded. So, it is freedom for me too."

Chen nodded. "Yes, both of you, you found the freedom. Good." He looked over to where Taran Zhu sat, his bowl yet untouched. "And you, Lord Taran Zhu?"

The eldest monk stared at the bowl, then lifted it carefully in two paws. He sniffed, then sipped. He sniffed again, then drank a little more before setting his bowl down.

"This is not for me a memory. It is a portrait of now. Of a state of being of the world." He slowly bowed his head. "And of freedom, for change. It portends coming change. Crushing of enemies, perhaps; a coming winter, most like. But as you will never brew exactly this brew again, so the world will never again know this time or, alas, this peace."

12

With some bitterness lingering on his tongue from Chen's offering, Vol'jin took himself out and away from the monastery. Taran Zhu's remark echoed in his head and found resonance with Tyrathan's tale of harvest time among men. Autumn, the time the world died, death being the line drawn between old and new, another definition for change. Cycles like that implied new, and creatures with an awareness of self and of time often chose a season or other arbitrary chronological point to mark the end or herald the beginning.

End of what? Beginning of what?

He had not lied when he shared the emotions and memories triggered by Chen's brew—though he did realize they were harsh and counter to what the pandaren brewmaster had expected. But they were a troll's memories, and no less valid because they were not those of a pandaren. Any troll would have felt the same thing, for that was the nature of what it was to be a troll. *Trolls be masters of the world.*

Vol'jin shivered as he worked his way up the mountain and toward the north. His feet found snow and he squatted there in shadow. He drank in the cold, wanting it to toughen him, but having it remind him of the chill of the grave. Trolls once were masters of the world.

His father, Sen'jin, had looked at other trolls and had seen the folly of their desires to rise again. Those trolls sought to bend the world to their will. They wanted to subjugate everything and everyone. But why?

So they could feel the freedom Chen's brew invoked?

In an instant, he caught the flash of insight that his father must have had, yet had never shared. If the goal was to feel that freedom, the question was whether conquest was the only path to that goal. Freedom from fear, from want, freedom to see a future, none of those things demanded dead enemies. They might require that some enemies die, but dead enemies were not a sacrifice that would secure those things.

The troll thought of the tauren at Thunder Bluff. They lived there in relative peace and isolation. While many of them joined and fought for the Horde, they did not appear to be driven to do so. They joined because it was the right and honorable thing, to aid their comrades in fighting the Alliance, not because it sanctified some millennia-old traditions.

It wasn't as if his father had advocated abandoning the old ways. Vol'jin had seen the occasional troll—blue tauren, as Chen had called them—who had gone to live with the tauren and adopted their ways. He couldn't recall if they seemed more or less at peace with themselves, but their disjointed relationship with their traditions left them a half step out of sync with others. It was as if they had traded one tradition for another, and functioned within neither terribly well.

Sen'jin had great respect for troll traditions. Had he not, had he wished to break with them completely, Vol'jin never would have headed down the path to becoming a shadow hunter. His father had always encouraged him in his pursuit, and had done so by looking forward. He always stressed lessons in leadership, not traditions to copy blindly.

A comment Chen had made and had attributed to Taran Zhu, about ships and anchors and water, came back to Vol'jin as the troll rose and headed for higher ground and colder shadows. Traditions could be the water that permitted the ship to travel, or they could anchor it and prevent all movement. The loa, and what they demanded of trolls, could be seen as an anchor. The loa and their needs were born in an earlier time. For their demands, and for their glory, trolls had raised great empires and razed civilizations.

Cutting himself off from them could free him from the anchor, but it would leave him to be tossed about on unfriendly seas. It was the sort of rash and radical decision that his father would have counseled against. It occurred to Vol'jin that the loa could be the tide and waves to propel the ship forward.

Which makes our history an anchor, ever trapping us in the same bay.

Before he could explore that thought, however, he came around a corner on the path and found Tyrathan Khort facing northeast, staring off into the misty distance. He hesitated, wishing only to escape into his own solitude, and not wishing to disturb the man's.

"You're more quiet than most trolls, Vol'jin, but I'd have long since died a thousand times over if I couldn't hear one sneaking up on me."

Vol'jin raised his head. "Trolls do not sneak. And you did not hear me." He watched the way the mountain wind molded a red woolen cloak to the man's body. "Chen's brew, or my scent."

Tyrathan turned slowly, smiling. "I spent many hours getting your scent out of bedding."

"I would not be disturbing you."

The man shook his head. "I mean to apologize to you."

"You have done me no slight." Vol'jin squatted, his feet buried in snow. He meant to say that any slight a man might do him would be beneath his notice, but he contented himself with the words as spoken.

"When I said you were afraid, it was to strike out at you. That sense of you in my head remained. It haunts me still. Less and less, but you are there. I thought I could drive you out by driving you away, by hurting you." Tyrathan glanced down, his brow furrowed. "That's unbecoming the man I was, and not part of the man I hope to become."

Vol'jin's eyes narrowed. "Who be it you wish to become?"

The man shook his head. "I know better who I cannot be than who I will be. Do you know why I was stopped here the day the storm came? Do you know why I was so lost I did not see it coming? You, above all the others, must be aware that such a storm could not steal upon me."

"Your body was here. Your mind was not."

"Yes." Tyrathan half-turned, sweeping a hand out over the distant green valleys. "I swore, when undertaking Stormwind's call to action here, that I would not die before I saw the green valleys of my home once more. It was my pledge to my . . . family. I have always kept my word. They knew I would return. But the person I was, the person who made that pledge, isn't here anymore. Am I still bound by it?"

Something in Vol'jin's stomach tightened. *Be I bound by traditions and promises made by trolls long dead? Do their dreams and desires hold me still?*

The troll flicked at the snow with a finger, scraping through the crust. "If you be assuming the mantle of the man you once were, you be him again. If you are a new man, this be your home valley."

"So shadow hunters are philosophers, then." Tyrathan Khort smiled. "I had seen you before, before the monastery. I was with the forces from Kul Tiras—I'd been lent to Daelin Proudmoore. I was much younger then, darker of hair and smoother of skin. You've not changed, really, save for some scars. Another hunter wanted to bet ten gold he could kill you. I heard later on that he died hunting trolls."

"You did not take that bet."

"No. Fix on a target, you lose track of the others." The man sighed, his breath jetting in white vapor. "Had I been commanded to kill you, on the other hand . . ."

"You be doing your best in the hunting."

"Hunting men or trolls—any thinking creature— reminds me that we're all animals. I've killed men and trolls, too many of each. I don't have a count." Tyrathan shivered. "I know hunters who do. Disrespectful, I think, morbid. It reduces people to quantities. I'd like to think I'd be more than a scratch in someone's journal."

"*You* think that, or the old you?"

The man bowed his head. "Both of us. More now. There is something about the way the monks live and conduct themselves that is more respectful of life. That idea of balance, and seeking harmony. Do you wonder, Vol'jin, if the new you can balance the old?"

"You wonder."

"I do."

"I be knowing."

"For me or for you?"

The troll opened his hands and stood. "Both. You said it. The child be hauling no burden. The child be knowing no limits. But the child be lacking experience, so cannot choose balance. We can."

"We can't escape our pasts."

"No? I be Vol'jin, leader of the Darkspears. You be a man, a troll killer. Why be we not dead or bleeding from a fight between us?"

"Fair point." Tyrathan scratched at his goatee. "Here, we are not enemies."

Again the image of ships came to Vol'jin. He smiled. "You see your past as burden. You wish to drop it. If you do that, you are free, but you do not know who you be. Think of it as a shipwreck. You can never be making it whole again. Be salvaging from it. This place here, now, may be your home. But it be feeling like home because of the memory you salvage."

"Run aground, that was certainly me."

Vol'jin nodded. "The hunter who died. Who was she?"

Tyrathan shook his head, a gloved hand rising to cover his mouth. "I don't really know."

"Your sense of her be very strong."

"Her name was Larsi. I met her before sailing. Never seen her before. But she thanked me and said that when she heard I was traveling to an uncharted island, she knew it would be an adventure she would not miss." He hugged his arms around himself. "She— If I needed a volunteer, she was there. She made sure I had hot food, that my tent had been erected. We weren't lovers. We didn't talk much. I just got the sense that she felt she owed me something. And since she was there because I was there, and . . ."

"You plunder the pain. You be dishonoring her." The troll nodded solemnly. "You would honor her by salvaging her belief in you."

"That belief got her dead."

"No. Her death be not yours to possess. It was her choice. Happy she be to know you still survive."

"That would be one." The man turned to face northeast and the jagged coastline. "My old life, so much debris scattered up and down the beaches. Salvage will take a long time."

"Consider it child's play." Vol'jin stepped forward and joined the man at the mountain's edge. Sunlight shimmered silver off the distant sea. They were too high up to see anything but the play of light on the water, but Vol'jin allowed himself to imagine his own life broken and scattered. *What be I salvaging?*

Something brushed over his face, light and ethereal. It felt like a spider's web. He went to scrape it away but found nothing. Instead, he remembered being a spider, floating, and looked seaward again.

His vision changed, sharpened by a lens that bent time. Out there, riding the waves, came the black fleet he'd seen in his vision. But he'd been wrong. The vision had showed him another time but not a distant one. What he saw now, what he had seen in the dream, was bare days away, and not in the past but in the future.

"Come quickly; we have to be seeing Taran Zhu."

Alarm opened Tyrathan's expression. He stared out at the ocean, then looked at Vol'jin with a lack of comprehension. "Your eyes aren't that much better than mine. What did you see?"

"Trouble, great trouble." The troll shook his head. "Trouble I be not certain we can limit, much less prevent."

They raced back down the mountain as best as they were able. Vol'jin's longer legs made for strides that ate more ground, but much too soon pain stitched his side. He dropped to a knee to catch his breath, which enabled Tyrathan to reach him. Vol'jin waved him on, and the man went, his limp barely noticeable.

One of the monks on the walls must have seen them coming, because Taran Zhu met them in the courtyard. "What is it?"

"Charts. Do you have charts? Maps?" Vol'jin sought the Pandaren word but wasn't sure if he'd ever learned it.

Taran Zhu snapped a quick order, then took Vol'jin by the arm and led him inside. Tyrathan Khort followed. The elder monk guided them to the chamber where they'd shared Chen's brew, though the table had long since been cleared. Another monk arrived with a rice paper scroll.

Taran Zhu took the scroll and unrolled it across the table. Vol'jin had to come around so he could face north. He couldn't read the symbols, but there was no missing the monastery or the mountain peak to the east. He looked a bit farther east, then tapped a spot on the northern coast.

"There, what be there?"

Chen Stormstout bounced his way down the stairs. "That's Zouchin. That's where I'm building a new brewery."

Vol'jin studied the map to the north and northeast. "Why be the island not on the map?"

Chen raised an eyebrow. "What island? There's nothing out there."

Taran Zhu looked at the monk who had brought the map and gave him a command in Pandaren. Chen started to turn away and follow. "No, Master Stormstout, stay. Brother Kwan-ji will gather the others."

Chen nodded, returning to the table. The smile with which he'd accompanied his announcement about Zouchin had completely vanished. "What island?"

The Shado-pan monk clasped his paws at the small of his back. "Pandaria is home to more than the pandaren. There was a time when another race, a powerful race, the mogu, ruled this island."

Vol'jin straightened up. "I be aware of the mogu."

Tyrathan blinked, taken by surprise. Chen's eyes tightened.

"Then you know their time is past. That you know it, however, does not mean they know it." Taran Zhu touched the map near the northeast corner. An irregular island slowly appeared, as if the mists that hid it had evaporated. "The Isle of Thunder. Many believe it a legend. Few know it is real. And if you know of it, Vol'jin, then others who know could cause great mischief."

"I did not know until I had a vision." The troll pointed at Zouchin. "I had another. A fleet has sailed from that island. It be a Zandalari fleet. Their only purpose can be great evil. And if we are to stop them, we have to be moving fast."

13

Foreboding slithered into Vol'jin's guts as Taran Zhu stood as still as one of the stout stone pillars supporting the roof. "What would you suppose us to do, Vol'jin?"

The troll shared a disbelieving glance with the man, then opened his hands. "Send messengers to the village. Call up the militias. Prepare defenses. Call up your elite troops. Deploy them to Zouchin. Summon your fleet. Deny the Zandalari landfall."

He looked at the map. "I be needing other maps. Tactical maps. More detail."

Tyrathan stepped up. "The valleys make for choke points. We can— What is it?"

The old monk lifted his chin. "In your islands, Vol'jin, what resources have you prepared to deal with a blizzard such as the one we had here?"

"There are none. Blizzards do not happen in the Echo Isles." The sense of disaster constricted his stomach. "Bad weather be not the same as an invasion."

The monk shrugged stiffly. "If night never came, no one would maintain lanterns. The mists have been our defenses since before history began."

"But you're not defenseless." Tyrathan pointed out toward the courtyard. "Your monks can shatter wood with their bare hands. They fight with swords. I watch them shoot arrows. They are among the world's elite fighters."

"Fighters, but not an army." Taran Zhu pressed his paws together at his breastbone. "We are few and spread across the continent. We are Pandaria's only line of defense, but we are more than that as well. Our training in the martial arts imparts to us more than just the ability to kill. For example, we study archery not for its martial aspect—we study it for balance. It is a means by which we can connect two points through an intervening space, having to manage and balance distance and momentum, arc and the breeze, and the arrow's nature. We defend Pandaria and defend the balance."

Vol'jin tapped the map. "You talk philosophy. This be war."

"Can you tell me, troll, that war exists only on a material plane? That it is only steel and blood and bone?" Taran Zhu's eyes became dark slits. "The two of you have physical scars. And deeper scars. War has thrown you out of balance, or your hunger for it has."

The troll snarled. "War be imbalance. If it destroys your balance, your balance was false."

Chen stepped between them. "I have just come from there. Li Li will be returning there. Yalia's family is there. The Zandalari will unbalance everything for those people. We have to do what we can to tip the balance back."

The man agreed with a nod. "If nothing else, we have to warn the people. Evacuate."

Taran Zhu closed his eyes and composed his face. "You three are of the world beyond the mists. Your experience makes you value urgency above ways that are comfortable here. Where you demand haste, you will see sloth as resistance. Where you are skilled at tactics, you will think me blind. My charge, as the leader of the Shado-pan, is to deal with larger things."

Vol'jin crooked an eyebrow. "Maintaining the balance?"

"War will not always exist. War only wins if the world cannot recover from it. You look to stop war. I look to re-conquer it."

Vol'jin almost snapped off a harsh retort, but something in Taran Zhu's words pierced his heart. They echoed something his father had shared, in a private moment, after a predawn rain had left the world clean. He'd said, "I be loving the world like this. No blood, no pain, the world wet with happy tears and the hopes for sunshine."

The troll squatted and bowed his head. "Your monks' skills still apply."

"They do. You shall have resources. Not enough to win your war, but enough to dull their war." Taran Zhu exhaled slowly as he opened his eyes. "I will give you eighteen monks. They will not be the biggest or fastest, but they will be those best able to accomplish your ends."

Tyrathan's open-mouthed expression revealed his heart. "Eighteen monks and the three of us." He looked at Vol'jin. "In your vision, the fleet, that's, what, two ships apiece?"

"Three. One be small."

"That's not going to dull the invasion; it will just knock some rust off it." The man shook his head. "We have to have more."

"I would give you more were I able." The Shado-pan leader opened empty paws. "Alas, only twenty-one of you can reach Zouchin in enough time to be any help at all."

• • •

Vol'jin had expected that girding himself for war might be familiar enough a ritual that it would reforge a link with his past. Pandaren armor, however, frustrated him. Too short and too large at the same time, the quilted silk felt too light to be effective. The strip scale metal—all bound together with bright cords, along with a lacquered leather breastplate—flopped in places it shouldn't and made him round in places he shouldn't have been. A monk worked quickly to extend the armor skirting from the breastplate, and Vol'jin vowed that the first thing he'd do was strip the armor off a Zandalari and use that.

Then he laughed. He was too tall for pandaren armor but too short for Zandalari. He'd dealt with them before. They stood at least a head taller than he did, and twice that if one measured arrogance. Though he disliked the way they viewed all other trolls as their inferiors, he could not deny that their clean limbs and ennobled features made them pleasing to look upon. He'd once heard that they'd been referred to—by a man—as the "elves of trolls." The Zandalari had found that a great insult, and their discomfort amused him.

While he was fitted for his armor, much banging and clanging heralded the preparations for battle. Chen proudly presented him with a dual-bladed sword. "I had the swordsmiths knock the grips off two of the curved swords, then rivet the tangs together and wrap them in shark's skin over bamboo. It's not quite your glaive, but it's scary-looking."

"Scarier yet when it drinks Zandalari blood." Vol'jin took the blade by the central grip and twirled it around. He snapped the weapon so it was still, but the blades quivered and hummed curiously. Though it wasn't his glaive, the balance matched favorably. "You be possessing more skills than just brewing."

"No. Brother Xiao was one of those who drank with us." Chen smiled. "I told him to make a weapon that was what you remembered from the brew."

"He has done well."

Tyrathan gave a low whistle as he entered the hallway. He wore a long leather surcoat with metal plates riveted onto it. His helmet came to a point and had a mail skirt to protect his neck. He carried two bows and a half dozen quivers of arrows. "Nice glaive. It'll get lots of work."

The man tossed Vol'jin a bow. "These are the best out of their armory. I scoured it and have the best of their arrows too. All field points—the combat arrows have been sent to monks elsewhere. These'll fly true but won't punch through armor."

Vol'jin nodded. "You be needing careful shooting, then."

"With trolls, I draw a line connecting the bottom of the ears, drop it three inches, and split it in half. Easy shot at the spine, and you get the tongue as you're going."

Chen looked aghast. "I think, Vol'jin, what he meant—"

"I be knowing what he meant." The troll looked at Tyrathan. "These be Zandalari. Four inches. Their ears be set high."

Chen and Tyrathan followed Vol'jin into the monastery courtyard. The monks who were part of the force most closely resembled the man in attire, save that each of them had the monastery's tiger crest emblazoned on chest and back. They had a single strip of cloth—half of them red, half of them blue—dangling from their helmet's point. Taran Zhu had not lied. These were not the monks Vol'jin would have chosen, but he accepted that the master monk knew his people best. It did surprise Vol'jin to see Yalia Sagewhisper among the eighteen, but then he recalled that they were going to defend her home and that her knowledge of the surrounding area would be invaluable.

Vol'jin also realized, as he came up the steps to the plane between monastery and mountain, why Taran Zhu could only send so limited a force. Eleven flying beasts, sinuous and languid, had been hitched up with double saddles and laden with some meager supplies in leather satchels. He'd seen smaller versions of the beasts carved into walls or as statues in niches throughout the monastery. He'd somehow assumed they were a pandaren artistic representation of dragons.

Yalia beckoned them forward and pointed each monk to a beast. "These are cloud serpents. In days past, they were feared, before a brave young woman befriended them. She taught us what they could do. They are not common these days. The monastery has access to a flock."

Vol'jin glanced back at the monastery and caught sight of Taran Zhu at a balcony. The monk gave no sign of noticing Vol'jin, but that did not fool the troll. Though Taran Zhu professed ignorance of the ways of war, he understood well enough that information was power and that access to information had to be limited by necessity. Vol'jin should have been told immediately of the cloud serpents but hadn't been.

I been told nothing that would benefit the Zandalari were they to capture me.

Irritation flashed through the troll; then he caught himself. He was going to war, but it was not his war. The

Zandalari were invading Pandaria, not the Echo Isles. *And yet, if it be not my war, why be I going off to fight it? That Chen may have a brewery on the north coast? Or to frustrate the Zandalari?*

A thought echoed up through his mind, coming in a deep, distant voice. Bwonsamdi's voice. Coming up from the void. *Or be it to prove that Vol'jin be not dead?*

Vol'jin had no answer, so he formulated one as he slid into the saddle behind a monk. *I go to war, Bwonsamdi, to be giving you guests to welcome to eternity. You may be believing you no longer know me, but I be knowing you. It be time you are reminded of that fact.*

At a sign from the monk acting as flight master, the cloud serpents slithered toward the edge of the mountain and hurled themselves from the heights. The beasts plunged toward the earth below. Vol'jin, who wore no helmet since nothing at the monastery had fit, felt the air tug at his red hair, and he howled exultantly.

Then the cold mountain wind flooded his lungs and reawakened the aching in his throat. He coughed and felt a sympathetic stitch tug at his side. The troll snarled, breathing in through his nose, resenting the pains from his last fight.

The cloud serpents coiled and sprang into flight. Their scaled bodies twisted and danced, playful and gleeful. Vol'jin might have taken pleasure in that another time, but the contrast of their flight with the grim nature of his mission knotted his stomach. What they were racing to prevent was the antithesis of pleasure, and he wasn't at all certain they would make it before disaster unfolded.

• • •

They arrived in the mountains near Zouchin just in the nick of time. Vol'jin wished they had been much faster or more greatly delayed. Five ships had already entered the harbor. Out on the ocean a fishing boat was merrily burning to the waterline. Siege machines—although the smaller kind suitable to ships—hurled stones to bounce through the village. Their tumbling runs splintered houses and yet, somehow, left no crushed bodies in their wake.

Vol'jin studied the unfolding battle, then tapped his monk on the shoulder. He circled with a finger, then pointed toward the south, where a single goat track snaked out of the village. Already pandaren had begun to head that way.

Information be power. The Zandalari cannot allow alarm to be spread.

Tyrathan whistled loudly and pointed. He'd seen it too. Whether his eyes were really that good, or he'd just known where the Zandalari would lay their ambush because he'd have chosen the same location, did not matter. Vol'jin pointed as well, and the first two cloud serpents dropped from the sky.

The flight master soared down before them and brought his beast around in a long curve. It ducked below a line of hills, then landed on a small flat spot a hundred and a half yards west of the road. Without a word the monks alighted. Tyrathan had his bow strung already, and Vol'jin did the same a heartbeat later. The two of them moved to the fore and the monks followed.

This land might not belong to troll or man, but they knew the landscape of war better than the others. Chen, himself no stranger to war, took the blue squad and cut directly toward the path. The red monks, behind Vol'jin and the human hunter, drove north and pushed hard.

Up ahead, on a hillside, a Zandalari archer rose and drew back an arrow. Tyrathan saw him and fluidly nocked his own arrow. He measured the distance, drew, and loosed his arrow with well-practiced economy of motion. The bowstring hummed. The arrow ripped and popped through broad leaves. It angled up and transfixed the troll's neck. It entered below the jaw on one side and jutted out beneath the opposite ear.

The Zandalari's arrow hopped from the bow, its flaccid flight ending even before the troll had raised a hand to the shaft protruding from his neck. The troll tried to look down at the arrow—an act made impossible because the more he turned his head, the more the end hid from him. Then it caught on his shoulder and his eyes widened. His mouth opened, but blood gushed instead of words. He collapsed and rolled loose-limbed down the hill.

Then war unbalanced the world.

14

Shouted orders heralded chaos, yet they were issued without panic. The Zandalari did not know panic. One squad was to head south, toward the attack; the other two were to cut the road. Arrows flew at targets unseen, not in hopes of hitting anything, but in hopes of flushing quarry.

An arrow flashed past Vol'jin's ear within a hair-breadth of undoing the work that had sewed it back on. He shot back, not expecting a kill. The arrow hit but didn't penetrate armor. A shout of surprise became a grunt of good fortune. The Zandalari must have thought luck was with him.

Which be not the same as having the loa favor you.

Vol'jin judged the eager lack of discipline with which the Zandalari harshly crashed through the brush. The Zandalari had, so far, met no serious opposition and had seen no organized defenses. The arrow that had hit Vol'jin's target was little more than a toy. It was clearly not meant for war and was equally clearly of pandaren manufacture. All of the Zandalari's experience of the enemy pointed to a serious lack of dangerous opposition.

He acknowledges no threat. His mistake.

Vol'jin, who had crouched as the troll raced down a small hill, rose and whipped the glaive up and around. The Zandalari blocked with his own sword, but late and slow. Vol'jin shifted his grip. He levered the upper blade forward, then shoved and twisted. As the Zandalari's momentum sent him farther down the hill, the curved blade tip sunk deep into the troll's neck. Vol'jin wrenched the tip free, opening the carotid artery in a bright fountain of blood.

The Zandalari stared at him as he fell. "Why?"

"Bwonsamdi hungers." Vol'jin kicked the troll away. He stalked up the hill, slashing low to open another troll's leg. In one motion he came up, whirling the blade around, then snapped it down, crushing the back of the troll's skull.

That troll grunted, his eyes glassy before he fell and tumbled through the brush.

Vol'jin smiled in spite of himself. The tang of hot blood filled the air. Grunts and groans, screams and the clang of weapons, locked him into combat. He felt more at home there, stalking foes, than he ever would in the monastery's peace. That realization would have horrified Taran Zhu but made the Darkspear feel more alive than he had at any time in Pandaria.

Off to Vol'jin's right, the human hunter shot. A Zandalari spun to the ground, a black shaft with red fletching quivering his breastbone. The hunter finished the troll by stroking a knife across his throat. Tyrathan appropriated more Zandalari arrows from this kill and moved silently through the brush. He was death on tiger paws, stalking, slaying.

The monks ranged to the left and right, moving curiously with the landscape and yet apart from it. Save for the armor he wore, the one closest to Vol'jin could have been out gathering herbs. He moved outside the rhythms of battle, not yet engaged and not long to be allowed that detachment.

A Zandalari warrior charged him, sword raised for a murderous slash. The monk twisted left. The blade whistled past. It returned in a crosscut. The monk grabbed the troll's wrist and spun so they faced the same direction. The troll's sword arm straightened and locked against the pandaren's stomach. The monk twisted his right wrist and the troll's knees buckled. Before he could go down, however, the monk's elbow blurred upward. The troll gurgled as the blow shattered his jaw and crushed his throat.

The little monk skipped forward, unconcerned. Vol'jin darted toward him, the bloody blade coming up and around. Unaware of a troll's ability to recover quickly from nonlethal wounds, the monk had taken the thrashing behind him as the sounds of death. Instead, they were the harbinger of an angry troll gathering himself to strike.

Then Vol'jin's glaive cut cleanly from front to back. The troll's head popped free, hanging in the air as the body dropped bonelessly beneath it. Then the head fell, bouncing off the dead troll's chest. Vol'jin continued forward, and behind him the true death thrashing began.

Vol'jin and the monks plunged deeper into the undergrowth and down into a small grassy bowl that paralleled the escape route. Without conscious thought, Vol'jin raced down into it and the midst of the Zandalari-led force. Even if he had paused to think, it would not have slowed him. He already knew they were lightly armored skirmishers, sent ahead to slaughter refugees. He attacked swiftly not out of any sense of outrage, but simply because such troops were beneath his contempt. They had no honor—they were not warriors but butchers, and clumsy ones at that.

A Gurubashi, sword raised high, charged at Vol'jin. The Darkspear gestured, lip curled with contempt. Shadow magic staggered the other troll, eating away at his soul. It paralyzed him for a moment. Before Vol'jin could get to him, a Shado-pan monk flew through the air with a kick that snapped the troll's head back, dropping him dead.

Vol'jin's double blades whirred as battle thickened. Razored metal slashed open exposed flesh. The blades clanked against swords raised to block. They hissed free of parries. The impact that stopped one blade would drive the other in reverse, hooking behind a knee or up through an armpit. Hot blood splashed. Bodies crumpled, limbs awry, breath bubbling from gaping chest wounds.

Something struck Vol'jin heavily between his shoulder blades. He spilled forward, rolled, then spun, rising. Vol'jin wanted to roar a challenge filled with fury and pride, but his aching throat defied him. He whipped the glaive around, spraying blood in a broad arc, then crouched, the blade held back, ready.

He faced a Zandalari even taller than most and decidedly wider. He carried a longsword—relic of some battle elsewhere. He came in quickly—a bit more than Vol'jin expected—and brought the blade around and down in an overhand cut. The shadow hunter blocked with his glaive, but the force of the blow ripped it from his hands.

The Zandalari lunged forward, smashing his forehead into Vol'jin's face, knocking the Darkspear back a step.

He tossed the longsword aside and swept in, grabbing the shadow hunter by the chest. The Zandalari lifted him high, thumbs driving in at the center of Vol'jin's chest. He squeezed, hard, then shook Vol'jin.

Iron fingers dug into ribs, reigniting aches. The troll's thumbs even punched through the breastplate and tore at the silk beneath. The Zandalari roared, defiant and angry. He shook Vol'jin even harder, teeth bared, and looked up.

Their gazes met.

That moment of time stretched forever. The Zandalari's widening eyes betrayed his disbelief at having found a troll fighting against him. Doubt creased his brows. Vol'jin read it easily and clearly.

He knew what to do.

As Taran Zhu had instructed, Vol'jin cocked his fist. His eyes narrowed. He visualized the Zandalari's doubt as a shimmering ball. It sank beneath the troll's face, lodging right behind his eyes. Nostrils flaring, Vol'jin drove his fist through the Zandalari's face, smashing bone shards through the doubt.

The Zandalari's grip broke. Vol'jin fell to his knees. He caught himself with one hand. The other snaked around his chest, hugging ribs. He tried to draw a full breath, but something ground in his side, stabbing sharply. He pressed a hand over the hurt, but couldn't concentrate enough to invoke healing.

Tyrathan hooked a hand under his arm. "Come on. We need you."

"Did any escape?"

"I don't know."

Vol'jin rose slowly, stooping only to recover his weapon and wipe his bloody hand off on a body. Straightening up, he surveyed the bowl. The battle signs read easily enough. The blues had sped along the goat path and come up the hill, engaging the Zandalari waiting in ambush. The reds had blown through the troops set to guard the southern approach. Vol'jin and the others had hit the Zandalari in the flank, rolling them up.

Vol'jin freed his arm from the man's grasp and hurried after him as best as he was able. They descended the hill to the road and found Chen talking with a young female pandaren leading a group of refugees.

"These are the first ones, Uncle Chen. There are more to fetch. Trolls have hit them before, so they're desperate to get away."

Chen, whose fur already dripped with Zandalari blood, firmly shook his head. "You're not going back, Li Li. You're not."

"I must."

Vol'jin reached out, resting a hand on her shoulder. "You must listen."

She leaped back into a defensive crouch. "He's one of them."

"No, he's my friend. Vol'jin. You remember him."

Li Li took a closer look. "You look better with your ear back on."

The troll stood tall, arching his back. "You must be taking these people south."

"But there are more trolls coming, and more people need rescuing."

Chen pointed toward the sea. "And most of them have never been outside their village. Take them to the Temple of the White Tiger, Li Li."

"Will they be safe there?"

"More easily defended." Vol'jin waved the flight

master over. "You need to ferry people. Slow people. The blues gonna gather them."

"Good plan." Tyrathan looked over at the reds. "I'll use the other monks to harry the Zandalari."

"You?"

The man nodded. "You're hurt."

"You limp and I heal fast."

"Vol'jin, what has to be done here is my kind of war. Slow them down. Delay them. Sting them. Hurt them. We will buy you the time to get these people clear." Tyrathan patted a quiver of Zandalari arrows. "A number of the skirmishers dropped these and I mean to return lost property."

"Very kind." Vol'jin smiled. "I be helping you."

"What?"

"Many arrows, and the refugees, they be trusting everyone else. We be providing them cover." Vol'jin nodded to both squads of monks. "Gather people, arrows, and bows. We gonna retreat south and east. We gonna draw them off."

Tyrathan smiled. "Use their pride to deflect them?"

"Zandalari always need to be learning humility."

"Right." He addressed the monks. "Look, stash arrows and bows at standing stones, like those, all the way up into the mountains." The man gave Vol'jin a half smile. "I'm ready to die when you are."

"Then it gonna be a long time." Vol'jin turned to Chen. "You command the blues."

"You'll have the left; he'll have the right. I should have the center."

"Ours gonna be thirsty work, Chen Stormstout." The troll rested both hands on the pandaren's shoulders. "Only you can brew what gonna slake it."

"You will be terribly alone."

"What he's trying to say, Chen, is that we're not going to be fighting out there so you can die with us."

The pandaren looked at Tyrathan. "What about the two of you?"

The man laughed. "We're fighting to spite each other. He'd be mortified if he died before I did, and I feel the same way. And we will be thirsty. Very thirsty."

Vol'jin nodded toward the refugees. "And they, Chen, be needing leadership of a pandaren."

The brewmaster paused for a moment, then sighed. "I find a place I wish to call home, and yet it's the two of you who fight for it."

The troll accepted a Zandalari war bow and quiver from a monk. "When one be without a home himself, then fighting for a friend's home be the most noble act."

"Ships have dropped anchor. They're lowering boats."

"Let us go."

Vol'jin for a moment found it curious to be stalking down a cobbled road with pandaren monks fanned out before him on both sides and a man apace with him. All he had known in his life had not prepared him for this. Hunted and hurting, homeless and believed dead by many, yet he felt completely alive.

He glanced at Tyrathan. "We should be shooting the tallest first."

"Any special reason?"

"Bigger targets."

The man smiled. "And it's four and a half inches."

"You know I not gonna wait on you."

"Just get the one that gets me." Tyrathan tossed him a salute and cut east, following the blues as they moved into the village.

Vol'jin kept on straight as reds hustled shocked pandaren from shadows and doorways. They'd clearly seen trolls before and, given how they cringed from him, it had been commonly in nightmares. Even though they might understand he had come to help, they could not help but fear.

Vol'jin liked that. He realized it wasn't because, as with the Zandalari, he wanted to rule by fear, or felt that his inferiors should fear him. It was because he had earned their fear. He was a shadow hunter. He was the slayer of men and trolls and Zandalari. He had liberated his home. He led his tribe. He had advised the warchief of the Horde.

Garrosh so feared me that he had me murdered.

For a heartbeat, he considered marching straight to the quay that several longboats of Zandalari were approaching, and revealing himself. He'd fought against them before but doubted his presence would surprise them. Worse, it might alert them to the fact that their understanding of their enemy was incomplete.

Part of him realized that, in the past, he might have done just that. The same way he confronted Garrosh and threatened him while taking the Darkspears out of Orgrimmar, he would have roared his name and dared them to come after him. He would let them know that he wasn't afraid and that his lack of fear should inspire fear deep in their hearts.

He nocked an arrow. *This be what they need deep in their hearts.* He drew and let fly. The arrow, with a barbed, flesh-rending head, arced out. His target, the troll hunched at the bow, waited to jump out as soon as keel scraped sand. He never had a chance of seeing the shaft. It flew straight out at him, a lethal flyspeck. It caught him in the shoulder, nicking the backside of his collarbone. It slid into him, running parallel to his spine, burying itself to the feathers in his body.

He collapsed, crashing into the gunwale. He bounced up, then slid over the side, his feet the last thing going under. The boat, unbalanced, listed to starboard, then righted itself again.

Just in time for Vol'jin's second arrow to pin the tiller troll to the rudder.

Vol'jin ducked back and turned away. As much as he might like to watch confused soldiers in an unsteady boat, that luxury would have cost him his life. Four arrows thudded into the wall against which he'd stood and two more overshot him.

Vol'jin pulled back to the ruins of the next building. He arrived as a monk helped a pandaren with a crushed shoulder crawl from beneath rubble. Farther out in the bay, where the last boat was coming in, an arrow slammed into the pilot's ear. It twisted him around and flung him from the boat.

The lead boat grounded. A few Zandalari sprinted for cover. Others tipped the boat up and huddled behind it. The middle two boats backed water quickly in an attempt to stop. The last had a hardy soul take the pilot's place at the rudder. An arrow transfixed him through the guts. He sat hard but kept his hand on the tiller, guiding the boat shoreward as the other trolls pulled on the oars.

The troll commanding the invasion from a ship farther at sea signaled furiously. The ships in the harbor renewed their assault with siege engines. Stones arced out, slamming into the beach in a great spray of sand. Vol'jin thought the half-buried stone a waste of effort, but one of the Zandalari sprinted toward it and threw himself down behind it.

And then another stone hit, and another.

So the game began. As Zandalari advanced, Vol'jin moved to the flank and shot. Spotters aboard ship would then turn the siege engines on his hiding place, smashing it to flinders. Off to the east they did the same with Tyrathan's hidey-holes, though how they saw him Vol'jin had no idea. He couldn't.

Each wave of stones drove Vol'jin back and let more trolls advance. The ships lowered more boats. Some of the Zandalari even stripped off their armor and dove into the bay with bows and arrows tightly wrapped in oilskins. The ships lay waste to a wide arc in the center of Zouchin, and troops moved ashore to occupy it.

The shadow hunter made every arrow count. He didn't always kill. Armor blunted some shots. Occasionally a target provided him only the glimpse of a foot, or a patch of blue skin through a tangle of fallen timbers. The simple fact was, however, that for every arrow he possessed, the ships had a dozen ballista stones and half that many soldiers.

So Vol'jin pulled back. He found only one monk's body as he went. She'd been struck through by two arrows. From the tracks leading south, she'd shielded two cubs from the shots that had killed her.

He paced after those cubs, trailing them back through the village. Just when their trail broke into the open behind a home collapsed on splintered pilings, Vol'jin heard scrabbling. He turned, quickly, as a Zandalari warrior slid into view. Vol'jin reached back for an arrow, but his enemy shot first.

The arrow caught him in the flank and punched out his back. Pain pulsed from his ribs, staggering him. Vol'jin dropped to a knee and reached for his glaive as the other troll nocked another arrow.

The Zandalari smiled broadly in triumph, flashing teeth proudly.

A heartbeat later, an arrow arced down between those teeth. For a half second, it appeared as if the troll was vomiting feathers. Then eyes rolled up in his skull and he pitched backward.

Vol'jin turned slowly, looking back along the arrow's line of flight. Long grasses closed at the crest of a hill. *Shot through the mouth. Four and a half inches. And he was wanting me to get the one who got him.*

Dust still slowly settled over the twitching troll. Vol'jin reached back and snapped off the arrow's head, then slid the shaft from his chest. He smiled as the wound closed; then he pilfered the troll's quiver and continued the fighting withdrawal.

15

It should be rainin'. The bright sun mocked Khal'ak while failing to warm her. She stood tall on the bow of her barge, not because of the commanding image it made but because it was the best vantage point from which to survey the shore.

The barge nudged a floating longboat aside. It bobbed there in the slight swell. The pilot had died with his hand on the tiller, an arrow through his bowels. It had to have been painful, but his expression betrayed nothing. He stared forward, eyes now dulling as flies explored them.

Sand hissed beneath the barge's hull as it came gently to shore. She leaped down, her dark cloak flapping. Two warriors awaited her—Captain Nir'zan, and a larger hulking troll carrying a massive shield. They immediately snapped to attention and saluted crisply.

She returned the salute, fueling it with her displeasure. "You determined what happened?"

"With as much certainty as be possible, my lady." Nir'zan faced inland. "Owing to previous infiltration an' study, we inserted scouts through a cove to the west. A pair swam ashore, killed two pandaren fishing dere, and secured the heights. They remained on station as per their orders and been interrogated. At that point the scouts proceeded inland, and all was as planned."

She swept a hand out, taking in the broken landscape. "The plan deteriorated."

"Yes, my lady."

"Why?"

The Zandalari warrior's eyes tightened. "The why be less important than the how, my lady. Come."

She followed him into the village, to the wreckage of a house nearly fifty yards from the beach. At their approach, another warrior dropped to a knee and peeled back a reedy sleeping mat. It had preserved a single footprint.

Ice water trickled through her insides. "Not one of ours?"

"No. Definitely a troll, but too small for Zandalari."

Khal'ak turned and looked back down to the shore. "Dis archer killed the pilot?"

"And another warrior on that boat."

"A very good shot."

Nir'zan pointed to the east. "Over there, where you be seein' your lieutenant, there be another track. Human, using our arrows. He killed another pilot."

She measured from where the far soldier stood to the bay. "And one of our bows, yes? A lucky shot?"

Nir'zan lifted his chin, exposing his throat. "I be liking to believe that, but can't. Neither luck nor bow leaves a track."

"Honesty. Good." She slowly nodded. "What else?"

The warrior headed off out of the village and south along the road. "We be finding a few more bodies in town. The archers shot and moved quickly. They were buyin' time for others to evacuate. Many tracks leading south. You'll want to see this."

Nir'zan brought her to where one of the pandaren lay, transfixed with two arrows. Even in death, even wearing armor emblazoned with a snarling tiger's face, the creature looked ridiculously benign. Khal'ak dropped to a knee beside the body and prodded the thigh with her fingers. Despite the body's stiffening from death, she could tell the pandaren was well muscled and quite compact.

She looked up. "I see no weapon. No belt."

"The paws, my lady."

She grasped a paw and ran her thumb over the pandaren's knuckles. The fur had been worn away. The dark skin had callused over. The palm felt similarly rough. "These be not fisherfolk."

"We found four more. Some had weapons." The warrior hesitated. "All had killed."

"Show me."

They continued south and then veered east to the grassy bowl beside the road. Khal'ak had chosen that spot for the ambush. She'd meant the scouts to kill a few refugees and drive the rest back into the village. Once her troops had secured it, the pandaren would serve as bearers and haulers.

She surveyed the carnage. Her troops, albeit clad in light armor, with light weapons, meant to move fast, lay scattered and broken. Three dozen of them dead, and only a handful of pandaren to account for that destruction? That she could see two bodies here indicated that they'd made no attempt to remove their dead. And even if two or three had been wounded for every abandoned corpse . . .

"Have you any accounting for the number of pandaren?"

"South and a bit more east be where they staged. We

found da man's and troll's footprints too, as well as tracks of other beasts."

"The whole of the force, Nir'zan!"

"Twenty-one, near as we be making it."

Khal'ak stood and strode to the center of the bowl where an exceptionally large body lay. It was Lieutenant Trag'kal. At least she thought it was. His face had been destroyed, but there was no mistaking his height. She'd handpicked him to lead the scouts.

And he failed me.

She kicked his corpse, then turned to Captain Nir'zan. "I want it all cataloged. I want to know their positions, their wounds, everything. I want all you know, not guesses or estimates. And I be wanting to know who dese pandaren are. We been told they have no army. They have no militia. They have no defenses. Our sources appear to be woefully misinformed."

"Yes, my lady."

"And I want to be knowing where the villagers have gone."

The Zandalari warrior nodded. "We be deployin' a screening force forward. We tracked the archers, the man and the troll, heading east, away from da road, but all indications be that the refugees have withdrawn south. We found signs that dese beasts have returned to carry the old and wounded."

"Yes, I need to know more about dem as well." She stooped and pulled a bloody arrow from a dead troll's neck. The slender shaft ended in a simple point. "This be not even suited to varminting. We brought an army, and they faced us with toys?"

"Dey took our supplies as quickly as they could, my lady."

"And organized a retreat in good order." Khal'ak pointed the arrow at the scouts' bodies. "After you have cataloged everything, I be wantin' them stripped an' skinned. Fill their skins with straw and post dem on either side of the road. Throw their bodies in the sea."

"Yes, my lady, but you realize there are no pandaren that sight gonna frighten."

"I be not wanting to frighten pandaren. It be meant for the rest of us." Khal'ak flung the arrow down. It bounced off armor and settled in the grasses. "Any Zandalari who believes empire be his birthright needs to remember that births be seldom easy and often are inclined to be bloody. Dis will not happen again, Nir'zan. See to it."

Vol'jin woke with a start. It wasn't because of his dream of being chased by Zandalari. He'd enjoyed that. To be hunted meant he was someone. They hunted him out of anger and fear, and to be able to inspire that gave him pleasure. Being able to inspire dread in his enemies had ever been a part of him, and it was a part he wanted to salvage.

His body ached, especially his thighs. He could still feel the stitch in his side, and his throat remained raw. His wounds had all closed, but permanent healing would take longer. He resented the lingering pains, not because of what they were but because they reminded him of how close his enemies had come to killing him.

He and the man had pulled back as planned. They found stores of arrows and bows where they'd told the monks to leave them. They also found food, which they consumed hurriedly, and lines of stones pointing them to the next cache. They scattered those before they moved on; without those indicators, they'd have been lost and doubtlessly killed.

The Zandalari had come after them, but both man and troll had known their business. They killed the archers first, which gave them the advantage in ranged combat. The Zandalari archers had not been bad—a bloodied rag tied around Vol'jin's left thigh attested to that. Vol'jin and Tyrathan had just been better. The troll grudgingly admitted Tyrathan was much better. He'd killed one pesky Zandalari archer by arcing one arrow into a narrow crack between rocks, and had the second in the air—aimed at where the troll would draw himself back—even before the first had struck. Vol'jin told himself he'd seen equivalent displays of skill before, but never at a time when targets shot back.

The troll awoke with a start because of his surroundings. The Temple of the White Tiger, while by no means posh or opulent by any standard, was warm and filled with light. Vol'jin had been given a cell not much larger than the one he had at the Shado-pan Monastery, but the lighter color, and flashes of greenery through the windows, made it seem huge.

He arose, washed, and, when he returned to his cell, found a white robe laid out for him. He pulled it on, then followed the elusive piping of a flute to a courtyard away from the temple's main precincts. Chen and Tyrathan stood there, along with the rest of the red and blue monks. Taran Zhu had appeared—undoubtedly flown in on a cloud serpent—and all of them wore white. Some of the monks, like Vol'jin, had been wounded in the fighting. They leaned on crutches or had arms in slings.

Five small white statues, no more than a handbreadth in height, carved of a soft stone, stood on a table to the side.

Beside them were a small gong, a blue bottle, and five tiny blue cups. Taran Zhu bowed to the statues, then to the assembled crowd. They returned the bows. Then the master monk looked toward Chen, Tyrathan, and Vol'jin.

"When a pandaren becomes fully Shado-pan, the monk travels with one of our master artisans to the heart of Kun-Lai. They travel deep beneath the earth. They find the bones of the mountain and they mark out a little piece of it. The artisan then carves it into their likeness, leaving it connected to the bone. And when the wheel turns, and when that monk passes, the statue breaks free. The statues are gathered, and we store them in the monastery, so all may remember who have come before."

Yalia Sagewhisper moved from the ranks of the monks and struck the gong. Lord Taran Zhu called out the name of the first monk. Everyone bowed until after the echoes of his voice had died. They straightened up again, the gong sounded, and Taran Zhu called out another name.

It surprised Vol'jin that he recognized the names and could easily call the faces to mind. Not as the monks were when they went to war, but before, during the time of his recovery. One had fed him strong broth. Another had changed his bandages. A third had whispered advice at playing jihui. He remembered each of them as they lived, and that both sharpened the pain he felt at their loss and closed the wound just a bit faster.

He realized that Garrosh, were they to have somehow changed places, would not recognize these five monks. He would understand them. He would have assessed them and measured them for their martial prowess. For their ability to project his power and will upon others. But that was all they would be to him, five or five thousand.

His hunger for war did not permit him to know soldiers, just armies.

This be not how I wish to be. This was why, whenever he was home in the Echo Isles, he spoke with the trolls who had done well in their training. He made an effort to remember them and their names. He valued them and wanted them to know that. Not just so they would feel proud that he had taken notice of them, but so that he would not think of them as numbers to be pitched into the maw of war.

Once the last monk's name had been spoken and everyone had straightened up, Yalia replaced the gong. She returned to the ranks and Chen stepped forward. He took up the cups—so very tiny in his paws—and placed one before each statue. Then he picked up the bottle.

"My gifts are not much. I do not have much to give. I have not given as much as they have. But my friends said that fighting the Zandalari would be thirsty work. This I intended to slake their thirst. While I am happy to share it with all of you, it's these five who should drink first."

He poured out a golden liquid in five equal measures into each cup. He bowed after each cup was filled, then set the bottle down on the table when he was done. Taran Zhu bowed to honor him, then the statues, and everyone else followed his lead.

The master monk looked at the others. "Our fallen brothers and sisters are pleased that you survived. You have honored them in doing this and in saving so many. That this may have required from you acts that you never thought you might have to commit is regrettable, but not insurmountable. Contemplate, grieve, pray, but know that what you have done has preserved the balance for many, and this is, after all, our purpose."

After another round of bowing, Taran Zhu approached the three outsiders. "If you would favor me with consultation in these matters."

Taran Zhu led them to a small room. A number of maps had been laid out in a detailed mosaic of Pandaria. Jihui pieces had been placed strategically. Vol'jin hoped against hope that the relative strengths were not meant to be reflective of reality. If they were, Pandaria was lost.

Taran Zhu's sober expression suggested the pieces represented worse: optimistic estimates.

"I must confess, I am at a loss." The monk swept a paw out at the map. "The Alliance and Horde incursions did not involve wholesale slaughter. They balance each other, and both sides have been useful in dealing with difficulties."

Tyrathan's eyes hooded. "Like the Serpent's Heart."

"The release of the Sha of Doubt, yes." The pandaren hid his paws behind his back. "Either force is better suited to opposing this invasion than we are."

Vol'jin shook his head. "Bad blood between everyone. No trust. They'd be slow to move. No telling where they would move to. Can't be moving without secure supplies and flanks."

Taran Zhu's head came up. "Could neither of you influence your old allies?"

"My people tried to murder me."

"It would be best for mine if I truly was dead."

"Then Pandaria is lost."

Vol'jin smiled, flashing teeth. "We be without a voice. We can be telling you how to speak to them. They gonna listen to reason. We be needing information to convince them, and I know how we be getting it."

16

Chen Stormstout did a last check of his pack. He was pretty sure he had everything he needed. Physically, anyway. But there, at the temple gate, he lingered just a little longer.

And smiled.

Back in the courtyard, Li Li was organizing an oxcart. That meant she was commanding the Stoneraker brothers to load and shift things. They suffered less because of her tongue's lash, Chen thought, than because they were afraid of her, and because they'd been growing to like her. Yalia's father, Tswen-luo, helped with the loading, and his presence did dull Li Li's commentary.

Yalia left off supervising Li Li and approached Chen. Were it not for a quick glance down as she came, he might have thought her all business. But that one little break, it made his heart soar. "We will soon be ready to go, Master Chen."

"I can see that. I'm only sorry our paths will diverge so quickly."

She looked back at where her family gathered in the first group of refugees. "It is a very good suggestion you have to send people to the Stormstout Brewery in the

Valley of the Four Winds. It is a hard trip but worth it for their safety. I am very happy my family is among those chosen."

"That just makes sense. There they can learn all they need to learn for the Zouchin brewery. I should have thought of it before."

She laid a paw on his forearm. "I know you send my family because only by giving Li Li the mission of getting them there safely will she leave your side."

"And I am pleased that you are going to see to her safety." Chen busied himself tying his pack shut again. "It was not an easy thing, there on the road, to have to go away while you fetched others. It won't be easy leaving now."

She brought her paw up and caressed his cheek. "You honor me by entrusting Li Li to me, and my family to her."

He turned and wanted to gather her into a hug, but he could feel all eyes upon them. He didn't care what anyone thought, but he would not besmirch her dignity. He lowered his voice. "Were you not Shado-pan—"

"Hush, Chen. Were I not Shado-pan, we would never have met. I would have been a fishwife with a half dozen cubs. Had you come to Zouchin, you would have given me a smile and a nod. You would have breathed fire to make my cubs laugh, and that would have been the end of that."

He smiled. "Your wisdom makes you even more attractive, you know."

"So does your honesty." Yalia looked him in the eyes and smiled. "Having chased the turtle, you are not hidebound as we are. Tradition promotes stability but also inflexibility. Circumstances threaten stability and demand flexibility. I like that you can share your heart."

"I like sharing it with you."

"And I look forward to more time to share."

"Chen, are you read— Oh, forgive me, Sister Yalia." Tyrathan, his pack already slung on his back, stopped just inside the gate and bowed.

"I'll be with you in just a moment." Chen bowed to him and to Yalia, then jogged over to his niece. "Li Li."

"Yes, Uncle Chen?" Her words came edged with frost, unhappy as she was to be doing "delivery service."

"Less wild dog, Li Li, more Stormstout."

She stiffened, then bowed her head. "Yes, Uncle Chen."

He drew her into his arms and held on tight. She resisted at first, then clung to him. "Li Li, you will be saving lives, very important lives. Not just to me, or to Sister Yalia, but to all Pandaria. Great change has come to this place. Violent, horrible change. The Sageflowers and the Stonerakers and others will show such change can be survived."

"I know, Uncle Chen." She squeezed a grunt out of him. "Once we get them to the brewery, Sister Yalia and I can—"

"No."

"You don't think . . ."

He pulled back and tipped her face up so she could look at him. "Li Li, you have heard my many stories. The stories about the ogres, and tricking murlocs into making themselves into a stew and . . ."

". . . teaching ice avatars and frost giants to dance . . ."

"Yes. You've heard many stories but not all my stories. There are some I could not share with anyone."

"You would share them with Vol'jin or Tyrathan?"

Chen glanced over at where the man and Yalia were talking. "Vol'jin, because he was there for many of them.

But those stories are terrible, Li Li, because there is no fun to them, there is no chance to laugh. The people of Zouchin have sad stories, but survival makes them good stories. In what we have seen, in what Tyrathan and Vol'jin and Yalia will see, there are no smiles."

Li Li nodded slowly. "I've noticed Tyrathan does not smile much."

Chen shivered, because he remembered Tyrathan grinning broadly at Zouchin. "I can't save you from those stories, Li Li. But what I want you to do is to prepare the people at the brewery so those stories don't happen to them. The Stonerakers may be lousy farmers, but put a scythe or a flail in their paws and they will give a Zandalari nightmares. If Taran Zhu and Vol'jin are going to have a chance of saving Pandaria, they'll need as many reconstructed farmers and fishers as you can create."

"You're trusting me with the future."

"Who better?"

Li Li threw herself into his arms and held on as tightly as she had when she was a cub and he'd head off on his adventures. He returned the hug and stroked her back. Then they parted and bowed, deeply and long, before returning to their appointed duties.

The refugee caravan shared the road with Chen and Tyrathan Khort for only a short time. Li Li and Yalia headed south, while the others went north. Tyrathan called for a halt at the top of a hill, ostensibly to make notes about the topography. Chen watched until the refugees had disappeared around a far bend in the road—at about which time Tyrathan finished his note-taking.

Chen's heart ached, but he couldn't bring himself to

feel glum. As he and the man worked their way north, always traveling through the countryside and not on the road itself, Chen saw things that made him think of Yalia. He plucked some heart's ease and crushed it up, just to have the scent. He memorized the shape of a stone, which looked like a big-bottomed ogre bent over to stare down a virmen hole. She'd have found that funny, and perhaps funnier still his embarrassment had he got halfway into his explanation and realized it wasn't appropriate.

Within an hour, Tyrathan called for another stop, in a grassy bowl a half mile east of the road. To the west lay Kun-Lai, shrouded in clouds. Vol'jin and Taran Zhu would have returned with any monks who, unlike Yalia, were not guarding refugee caravans. There the Shado-pan would prepare what defenses they could and then deploy them based on the scouts' reports.

Tyrathan unwrapped a ball of sticky rice. "Sister Yalia is worth mooncalfing about, Chen, but going forward we need to focus. So, get it out now."

The pandaren stared at him. "I have the utmost respect for Yalia Sagewhisper, my friend. Mooncalfing—whatever that is—is hardly dignified enough of a term . . ."

"Yes, Chen, of course, my mistake." The man's eyes glittered. "That each of you has feelings for the other is pretty plain. And she seems very special."

"She is. She makes me feel . . . home." There, he'd said it. Pandaria may have been the place he'd been searching for all his life, but she was the reason he'd been searching for it. "Yes, she makes me feel home."

"So, marriage, cubs, a life growing old together in the shade of your brewery? Breweries?"

"I would like that." Chen smiled, then stopped. "Can Shado-pan monks get married? Do they have cubs?"

"I'm sure they can." The man chuckled easily. "And your cubs will be a handful, I'm sure."

"Well, you'll always be welcome, you know. I will offer you the same privilege I gave Yalia's father. Your mug will never run dry at one of my breweries. You can bring your family. Your cubs can play with mine." Chen frowned. "Do you have a family?"

Tyrathan looked at the half-eaten rice ball in his hand, then rewrapped it. "That's an interesting question."

The pandaren's stomach twisted in on itself. "You haven't lost them, have you? A war didn't—"

The man shook his head. "They're alive, best I know. Lost is another thing entirely, Chen. Whatever you do, don't lose Yalia."

"How could I lose her?"

"The fact that you ask that question means you probably don't have it in you to lose her." Tyrathan flopped over onto his belly and studied the road. "I'd give my right arm for one of those gnomish spyglasses. Or the goblin equivalent. Better yet, a battery of their cannons. That was the funny thing about the Zandalari ships: no cannon. Didn't see anything but trolls either."

"Vol'jin would know why that was." Chen nodded as he sank down beside the man and watched the road. "He wanted to be here, but you were right. Taran Zhu needs him more than we do."

"As I told him, this is my kind of war." Tyrathan slid down beneath the lip of the bowl. "I'm all tactical, not a strategic thinker. He's done that with the Horde. I mean, he could be doing this, but neither you nor I could do that. That will be what saves Pandaria."

• • •

For the next three days, pandaren and man crisscrossed the road, working north with painstaking attention to detail and a pace that would have made a snail seem faster than a gryphon in flight. Tyrathan made many notes and sketched numerous diagrams. Chen suspected that not since the court of the last mogu emperor had anyone done so thorough a survey.

They made cold camps in the heights. Given his fur and ample size, this didn't bother Chen very much. The cold mornings clearly got to Tyrathan, however, and it might be midmorning and a mile or two before the traces of his limp finally disappeared. The man went to great efforts to erase all sign of their passage. Even though they'd not seen much of anyone, he insisted on doubling back and setting ambushes along their back trail just in case.

Through watching and helping Tyrathan, Chen got a better understanding of Vol'jin and why he did the things he did. The man pointed out that the lack of Zandalari foragers and skirmishers meant that the invasion force had come prepared with ample supplies. He guessed that two-thirds of the ships had contained supplies and support personnel. Since no one had headed south yet, it meant they were building up for a sustained campaign. While this gave pandaren forces a chance to rally, it meant their task would be that much harder.

And yet you say you are not good at the strategic. Chen got the sense that Tyrathan had not wanted to return to the monastery. Out here, in the field, he had constant distractions. He didn't want time to think about Zouchin. Chen had no idea why, save for that haunting memory of the man's wide smile in its aftermath.

Though the man might have downplayed his ability to think on a strategic level, Chen had seen Vol'jin digest the sort of information they were gathering and weave it into exquisite battle plans. It was one thing to be able to estimate the size of an army but yet another to know what a good general could do with it. Vol'jin was the sort who could see all that and see that little flaw in planning that could make even the best plan fall to pieces.

Chen found Tyrathan most eager to share his thoughts about their mission in the evening, during those silent times when a possible change of subject could have led back to questions about the man's family. Chen would have pursued that line out of natural curiosity but suspected Tyrathan's counterattack would have been to ask about Yalia and then tease him about his plans.

The pandaren knew the teasing would be in good fun. Another time, over a mug of ale or steaming bowl of tea, Chen would give as good as he got. But he didn't want to spoil thinking about Yalia. He wanted to cherish his thoughts and memories. Even though he knew he was being fanciful in how he thought of her, he didn't want to be reminded of that fact.

So, the two of them let conversation lapse, each happy in the darkness for his own reasons. And then each morning, they would hide all signs of their camp and move on.

On the third day, they spied a croft built into a hillside. The hills around it had been terraced. They'd also once been well tended, but weeds had just sprouted, and some crops had been nibbled by wildlife. Dark clouds were slowly gathering to the north, pregnant with black rain. Without exchanging a word, and less than cautiously, they made their way to the croft just before the rain began to fall.

The farmhouse had been built solidly from stone,

with a wooden roof that kept the rain out. The farmer and his family must have evacuated when alerted by refugees or monks. Despite some things having been packed hastily, the house remained neat and clean. In fact, aside from squeaky floorboards, Chen found the place to be perfect.

Tyrathan had other ideas. He rapped a fist against the back wall, including a pantry next to the fireplace. It thumped hollowly. He felt around and found some sort of lever that, when he pulled it, slid the pantry in behind the fireplace. Beyond it lay a black hole, with steps leading down into a storage cellar.

The man went first, a drawn dagger in his right hand. Chen followed, carrying a small club in one paw and a glowing lantern in the other. He reached the middle of the stairs by the time Tyrathan hit the landing. One or the other of them stepped on a switch, for the pantry slid back behind them and clicked shut.

Tyrathan glanced up, then waved Chen down the rest of the way. "I think, my friend, we will wait out the storm in fine style."

Tiny though the storage cellar was, it had been built with shelves, each containing dozens of jars filled with pickled turnip and cabbage. Carrots had been gathered and stacked in baskets. Dried fish, clearly obtained in trade for vegetables, hung in long chains from rafters.

And, in the corner, a small oaken keg, just waiting to be tapped.

Chen looked at it, then at Tyrathan. "Just a taste?"

The man thought for a second, and was about to answer, when the wind howled above them. The door crashed open, which could have been due to the storm.

The tramp of heavy feet on the floor overhead, and

17

Vol'jin hunched over, one knee on the ground, his right forearm pressed to his side. He'd made it farther up the mountain than the spot where he'd spoken to Tyrathan, but not much beyond. It was steep going past that point. He wasn't unfamiliar with climbing, but the pain in his side wouldn't let him attack the mountain the way he wished.

He'd very much wanted to join Chen and Tyrathan on their scouting mission and was looking forward to their reports, but he was happy that Taran Zhu had agreed with the man's assessment that Vol'jin was needed to plan defenses. Not only had he more experience in that discipline, but, being a troll himself, he also knew trolls and their behavior better than anyone else.

"Do you not find it curious, Vol'jin, even after the poison has left your system, why you have not fully healed?"

The troll's head whipped around, his chest still heaving.

Taran Zhu stood there, a half dozen yards down the trail, looking as if he'd been out for a simple stroll.

Vol'jin decided that was because the monk was in far

better shape than most, not because Vol'jin was in much worse shape. "It be not unknown. Zul'jin lost an eye, cut off his own arm. They did not heal."

"Regrowing a severed limb or a complex organ is not the same as healing a cut." The pandaren slowly shook his head. "Your throat makes it difficult for you to speak. Your side, for you to run and endure in battle. We both know that had you gone with your friends, you would have slowed them down."

Vol'jin nodded. "Even with the man's leg."

"Yes. He's had more time here, granted, but he has recovered better than you have."

The troll's eyes tightened. "Why do you think that be?"

"On some level, he thinks he is worthy of recovering." The monk shook his head. "You, on some level, do not."

Vol'jin wanted to roar a denial, but his throat simply wouldn't allow it. *I be not having enough breath either.* "Go on."

The pandaren smiled in an infuriating way that could have justified the Zandalari invasion. "There is a species of crab that appropriates shells for a carapace. Once a pair of them, brothers, grew side by side. As they got bigger, one found a skull. The face had been smashed, and he made his way inside. The other found the helmet that had guarded the skull. The first loved the skull and grew into it perfectly. The second regarded the helmet as just another shell. But when it came time to move on, the first did not want to leave the skull. It had defined him, so he stopped growing. The second, though reluctant, had to leave the helmet and his brother behind. He could not stop growing."

"Which brother be I?"

"It would depend on your choice. Are you the skull-crab

who is content to have trapped himself?" Taran Zhu shrugged. "Or are you the crab who continues to grow, seeking a new home?"

Vol'jin scrubbed a hand over his face. "Be I a troll, or be I Vol'jin?"

"After a manner. I would reverse them. Are you the Vol'jin who nearly died in a cave, or are you a troll seeking a new home?"

"Home, that being an allegory."

"More and less."

Have I trapped myself in that cave? When he thought of how he'd been lured there, shame roared through him. Yes, the fact that he'd not died was a victory, but he never should have been in that battle anyway. Garrosh had tossed out bait and Vol'jin had swallowed it. Had Garrosh invited him to dinner, just the two of them, he'd have expected treachery and arrived with the entire Darkspear tribe.

The troll shivered.

I've trapped myself in that shame. As he looked at it, Vol'jin saw the terrible cycle. No self-respecting troll should have been taken in like that. Even a man like Tyrathan wouldn't have fallen for so transparent a ruse. His shame anchored him, and the fact that he couldn't remember how he'd gotten away meant he didn't have the tools to cut himself free. In that, Tyrathan had been right. Vol'jin feared what he didn't know.

Yet, in looking at the cycle, he noted the weakness in it. How he survived was immaterial. He could have been dragged from the cave by virmen to be washed up in the river and eaten, and it didn't matter. What mattered was that he was still alive. He could still grow. He could continue. He didn't have to be trapped.

And there it is. Because no troll should have been trapped the way he was, and because he had been, Vol'jin had mentally exiled himself from being a troll. He'd fought hard, as a troll would and could, but only to prove his trollness to the pandaren and the Zandalari. And a man. *How far gone be I?*

He shook his head. *Trapped like that be no place for a troll.* But only a troll could have survived being trapped like that. Garrosh had sent a pet orc assassin to kill him. Only one. Did not Garrosh know better? Had not Vol'jin threatened to send an arrow through him? *How dare he be sending anything less than trolls or titans against me?*

Taran Zhu raised a paw in caution. "You are at a critical juncture, Vol'jin, so listen to the rest of the crab's tale. That other brother, in searching for his new home, found a skull, a larger skull, and the helmet that had housed it. He had to choose. Skull or helmet."

The troll slowly nodded. "But those be not the only choices."

"For the Shado-pan, they are the most convenient to consider. You, on the other paw, have other choices available." The monk nodded. "If you wish more parables, I should be pleased to provide them. You will, I hope, be willing to continue to advise me on matters of military strategy."

"Yes. Skull-crab or not, it be part of me."

"Then I shall leave you to your considerations."

Vol'jin shifted from a crouch to sitting on the ground. In deciding that no troll should have been trapped as he had been, he'd convinced himself that he was not a troll. Proving that to be a lie to outsiders did nothing to change what he thought within. *But I be a troll. I survived. I be everything I was before. And wiser.*

He chuckled for his own benefit. *And wise enough to see how foolish I been.*

Vol'jin gathered himself and moved within, opening himself to the loa. He slipped into the gray landscape, noting shadows within shadows, dim silhouettes of plants and trees from the jungles of home. He took this as a good sign, then spun, finding Bwonsamdi looming up over him.

I be not taken blind again.

Not by orcs, anyway. The guardian of the dead laughed from behind his mask. *Who be this I see before me?*

A troll. That be enough for now. Vol'jin extended a hand toward him. *I be needing it back.*

What are you thinking I have?

My sense of being a troll.

Bwonsamdi laughed again and plucked a scintillating black pearl from within his belt. *When you came to me, you'd convinced yourself you be not a troll. I didn't think you'd be needing it.*

And you kept it safe for me. Vol'jin took it cupped in both hands. It lingered there, weightless, sending stinging sparks into his palms. Like the needles of a sleeping limb waking back up. *Thank you.*

And thank you for the ones you sent me. The loa looked back over his shoulder at a distant phalanx of Zandalari. *They hate being under my protection.*

I gonna send you more.

You gonna be a dutiful troll.

Vol'jin closed his left fist over the pearl. *The others, sending me visions. Why?*

To be reminding you of what it is to be a troll.

But the vision the Mother of Venom sent, it be working against her Zandalari.

They be doing the things they think please her, but that doesn't mean they know her mind. Bwonsamdi shrugged. *If it be not a real effort, be it a worthy offering?*

She be pitting me against her people to make them work?

And you gonna be a bit beholden to her if they fail.

When they fail.

Ha! This be why you were always one of my favorites, who-ever you are.

I gonna let you know when it be decided. Vol'jin smiled. *The lips of dead Zandalari be delivering the message.*

My wanting is vast, troll. And my favor great.

Vol'jin nodded as the gray world slowly melted back into the mountain peak. He opened his left hand, but the pearl had already sunk into his flesh. Vol'jin concentrated, looking within, and found the essence spreading through him, doing its work. Already pains eased and tissue renewed itself.

The troll took over the process in two areas. The stitch on his side he mended mostly. The lung he repaired so he could breathe, but he left a scar there. He wanted twinges. He wanted to be reminded of mistakes he had made.

Likewise he healed his throat, but not all the way. He let the wound steal the melodiousness because that had been Vol'jin's voice. That had been the voice that threatened Garrosh. That had been the voice that accepted the mission. Vol'jin didn't want to hear it again.

He didn't fully recognize his current voice, but he could live with that. As he had told Bwonsamdi, for now he was a troll. He didn't need to be more. *By the time I know who I be, I gonna know the sound of who I become.*

As he descended to the monastery, he realized that, in many ways, he had been the skull-crab. He'd let himself become defined by others. His father's dream had become his legacy, and it shaped him in one way. He almost thought *trapped*, but his father would have been horrified to think his son had felt trapped. Being a shadow hunter, leading the Darkspears, being among the leaders of the Horde, all of these things had been the bony plates that had created the skull.

And there was the real secret of the parable. The skull and the helmet that had once protected it had been created for two different purposes. Each crab needed protection, but only the crab that chose the helmet had chosen correctly. The other's choice, while being functional, did not allow him to continue to grow into his destiny.

Skull, helmet, or . . . what? For monks who were faced with the choice, they could turn completely inward and remain in the monastery like the crab in the skull. Others—and Vol'jin could see Yalia Sagewhisper in this latter class—could go beyond the monastery, grow into whomever they needed to be. And, in Pandaria, there was little need to look beyond two choices. If they wanted a third, then there was the turtle shell, and the life of adventuring Chen had chosen.

But, for me . . . The elements he'd used to describe the skull plates were not all bad. His father's dream had merit. Vol'jin agreed with it. Parallel to that was his leadership of the Darkspears. And his position in the Horde. Vol'jin had resisted Zandalari entreaties before, choosing the Horde as his allies for this new world. But now the Horde had turned on him.

The decisions he would have to make were not simple, and he accepted that. He realized that so often decisions had been made for him. That could have seemed malignant, but it wasn't. His father's encouragement and others' expectations of him made choosing to become a shadow hunter easy. Not that the actual doing of the thing had been, or that he regretted it, but he had never really considered an alternative.

Similarly, moving to the lead of the Darkspears and assuming responsibility for them had started a cascade of events. He regretted none of them either. Zalazane had to be stopped. Even supporting the Horde against the Zandalari king Rastakhan was a choice already made since Thrall and the Horde had helped him and his father save the Darkspears and build their home in the Echo Isles.

Withdrawing from the Horde be the hardest decision I ever made. It almost be my death.

Vol'jin returned to the monastery. He joined the monks in their exercises, not only to learn what they could do and to strengthen himself but also to show them what a troll could do. The monk he'd saved by beheading a Zandalari at Zouchin ratified Vol'jin's stories about the hardiness of trolls. The Shado-pan, by and large, then redoubled their efforts against him.

And left him hard-pressed to defend himself.

There were, no doubt about it, skull-crabs and helmet-crabs among the monks. This did not disturb Vol'jin on one level. For every warrior in the ranks of an army, there were five people left back to keep him fed, his kit in good repair, and to see to his other needs. Many of the Shado-pan, the old monks especially, contented themselves with these support roles, while the younger monks took more eagerly to learning how to fight trolls.

Vol'jin watched Taran Zhu as the elder monk observed the exercises. *Be you liking the shape of the helmet into which your monks are growing?* Even though their gazes met from time to time, the leader of the Shado-pan gave no sign of his thoughts one way or the other.

During the time when he was not training physically, Vol'jin bent himself to becoming a scholar of Pandaren geography and military history. He found the latter a frustrating subject. Everything had happened so long ago—at least for the pandaren—that it had taken on the status of myth and folklore. It could, in fact, be that a dozen monks had held a mountain pass for twelve years, each one defending it for a single month himself, then resting for the remainder of the year. Each monk was said to have pioneered a fighting style, from which all current styles were said to have descended.

Geography was easier. Ancient imperial charts had mapped the continent out in great detail. He still found some areas only vaguely described. This was especially true of the Vale of Eternal Blossoms, where one map had clearly been inked over in the south central area.

Vol'jin pointed it out as Taran Zhu entered the library. "I be not finding many references to this area."

"That is a problem we must take steps to remedy." The monk half turned as Chen and Tyrathan, haggard and just a little bloody, entered the library behind him. "As your friends have discovered, it would appear that's precisely where the invaders are headed."

18

Chen quickly blew out the lamp. Darkness filled the cellar. It amplified the sounds from above. As nearly as the pandaren could determine, an entire company of trolls had jammed themselves into the croft.

One of the trolls lit a candle. Thin slivers of light shot down through cracks in the floorboards. They striped both Chen and Tyrathan. The man had frozen in place, a finger raised to his lips. Chen nodded once and the man lowered his hand, but otherwise did not move.

Chen couldn't understand a single thing the Zandalari were saying, but he listened intently anyway. He was less hoping to pick up any Pandaren geographical references than he was to identify individual voices. He caught one that seemed to be giving a lot of short, sharp orders, and two others that replied wearily. One of those also made whispered comments.

He looked at Tyrathan and raised three fingers.

The man shook his head and added another. He pointed toward where the commander stood, then the two Chen had identified. His hand then indicated a fourth, in the corner, whose presence was marked by a slow drip of water on floorboards.

Chen shivered. This was not at all like the time ogres had captured him. Not only were trolls smarter in general, but the Zandalari prided themselves on being smart. And cruel. From what little he'd seen at Zouchin and heard about other battles the Zandalari had fought, he had no doubt that to be discovered was to be killed.

Because they'd been exploring the house, Chen and Tyrathan had not left their weapons or packs upstairs. They weren't unarmed, but the cellar was not really a good place for an archer to ply his trade. While Chen could defend himself with martial arts, close-in fighting like this generally favored people wielding short, stabbity-type weapons. Any battle in the cellar would be nasty, tight, and even the victors would get bloodied.

We have to hope they don't get curious and come down here. The storm will break, and they will go. The wind's shrieking intensified, mocking Chen's hope. *At least we won't go hungry.*

Tyrathan seated himself on the floor and selected eight arrows from his quiver. Each had a nasty, barbed head, half of them with two edges and the others with four. All the edges had a crescent cut back in toward the shaft so that once they went in, like a fishhook, they'd be tough to pull out.

He laid the arrows side by side, pairing a two edge with a four, and reversed the four. Using bandages, which he cut into short lengths with a skinning knife, he tied the arrows together, making them double-headed.

Though the partial light made reading his expression difficult, Chen could see Tyrathan's face had a grim determination. As he worked he would glance up at the low ceiling. He'd watch and listen, then nod to himself.

After an eternity, the trolls settled down. Heavy

thumps from above suggested they'd removed their armor for sleeping—three of them, anyway. The silent one didn't, but blotted out enough light to mark where he lay. The commander was the last to bed. He blew out their final candle before he stretched out.

Silent as a ghost, Tyrathan reached Chen's side. "On my signal—and you will know it—go up the stairs. Find the lever to open the pantry. Kill anything you find."

"They could leave in the morning."

The man pointed toward where the commander lay. "He's keeping a logbook. We need it."

Chen nodded, then moved to the base of the stairs. In the main part of the cellar, Tyrathan took his double-headed arrows and slid the double-edged heads into the floor cracks. He twisted, lodging an arrow beneath each of the sleeping trolls. He positioned things for the commander first, then the two talkers, and finally the silent one. Remaining in that last place, he looked at Chen. He pointed to the four arrows, ending with the commander, then pointed at Chen and signaled for him to go up the stairs.

The pandaren nodded and prepared himself.

The man shoved the first arrow up into a troll and twisted it. Even before his victim shouted, he leaped back to the middle two and drove them up, one with each hand. They yelped as he got to the last arrow and stabbed it up too.

Chen bounded up the stairs and didn't even bother to search for a lever. He barreled through the door. Wood cracked. Crockery and wooden bowls flew into the room a half second before he did. To his right, the silent troll lay on his left side. The arrow had run through his upper arm and into his chest. He reached for a knife with his right hand, but Chen lashed out with a foot. The Zandalari's head snapped back, smashing into the stone wall.

Chen spun and stopped. The two talkative trolls thrashed on the floor. An arrow had come up through one's belly. The other appeared pinned by the spine. As each tried to sit up, the four-edged arrowhead snagged in the crack, catching them firmly. Blood sprayed with their screams as their heels beat against wood and fingers clawed curled splinters from the floorboard.

The commander, a shaman, stood by the door. Dark, pulsing energy gathered in a ball between his hands. His dying comrades' cries had alerted him to his danger. The arrow meant for him had only sliced his ribs. He stared at Chen with black eyes boiling with venom and snarled something cruel in the troll tongue.

Chen, knowing what would happen if he did nothing—and knowing it would happen even if he did something—set himself and leaped. Not fast enough.

A heartbeat before his flying kick carried him to his target, and half a heartbeat before the shaman completed his spell, an arrow splintered the floor. It flashed past Chen's ankle, between the shaman's hands and his body. It caught the troll under the chin, popping up through his skull and pinning his tongue to the roof of his mouth.

Then Chen's kick landed, blasting the Zandalari back through the door and out into the storm's darkness.

Tyrathan, bow in hand with arrow nocked, appeared at the top of the stairs. "Lever stuck?"

The pandaren nodded as the trolls thrashed out the last moments of their lives. "Stuck. Yes."

The man checked the silent troll, then slit his throat. The two in the middle of the floor were obviously dead, but he checked them anyway. Then he moved to where the commander had laid his things, and located a satchel with a book and a small box with pens and inks. He flipped through the book for a second, then returned it to the satchel.

"I can't read Zandali, but I caught enough of their conversation to know they're scouting just like us." He looked around. "We'll drag the other one back in. Burn the place?"

Chen shook his head. "Probably best. I'll tap that keg in the cellar and use my breath of fire to light it. I'll also remember this place and will make it right for these people."

The man looked at him. "You're not responsible for them losing their farm."

"I may not be, but I feel I am." Chen took one last look in the farmhouse, tried to remember how it had been, then turned it into a pyre and followed the man into the storm.

They headed west, toward the monastery, and found a cave complex that curled down and around. They dared make a small fire. Chen welcomed the chance to make some tea. He needed the warmth and needed the time to think while Tyrathan studied the book.

Chen had never been a stranger to combat. As he had told his niece, he'd seen things he'd just as soon forget. That was one of the small miracles of life: the most painful things could be forgotten, or at least the memory of them would dull. *If you let it dull.*

He'd seen many things. He'd even done many things, bloody things, but never quite had seen what Tyrathan had done in the farmhouse. It wasn't the shot through the floorboard that would stick with him—even though that had probably saved his life. He'd seen enough soldiers with shields pinned to their arms by arrows to know wood offered inadequate defense against a good archer. Granted, the man was a spectacular archer, but what he had done there came as no surprise.

What Chen was uncertain that he'd ever forget was the calm and determined way in which the man had prepared the arrows he'd used from below. He'd designed them deliberately, not just to kill, but against the probability that they would not kill. He'd meant them to trap the trolls. He twisted the shafts after they went in to make sure the arrowheads would catch against ribs or other bones.

There was honor in combat, in fighting well. Even what Tyrathan and Vol'jin had done at Zouchin, in remaining behind to snipe at the Zandalari and slow them down, was honorable. It allowed monks to save villagers. The Zandalari might have thought it cowardly, but then using siege engines against a fishing village completely lacked honor.

Chen poured tea and handed a small bowl to Tyrathan. The man accepted it, closing the book. He breathed the steam in, then drank. "Thank you. It's perfect."

The pandaren forced a smile. "Anything useful in there?"

"The shaman was a good little artist. He drew maps well. He even had a few flowers pressed into the pages. He did sketches of local animals and rock features." Tyrathan tapped the book with a finger. "Some of the later pages are blank, save for a random series of dots in the four corners. There's that on pages he'd already written on, and he actually repeated the pattern on a couple that didn't have it. The blank pages had the symbols inscribed, I think, by someone else."

Chen sipped his tea, wishing it would warm him more. "What does that mean?"

"I think it was a means of navigation. Put the bottom edge of the page on the horizon and look for constellations matching the dots. That points you in your new direction." He frowned. "Can't see the night sky now, of course, and the constellations are different here, but I'm betting we can work out which way they were going when the weather clears."

"That would be good."

Tyrathan set his tea down on the book's leather cover. "Should we clear the air in here?"

"What do you mean?"

The man pointed back in the farm's general direction. "You've been uncharacteristically quiet since the farmhouse. What's the matter?"

Chen looked down into his tea bowl, but the steaming liquid revealed no answers. "The way you killed them. It wasn't combat. It wasn't . . ."

"Fair?" The man sighed. "I assessed the situation. There were four of them, and they were better suited to the fight we'd have than we were. I had to kill or incapacitate as many as I could as quickly as I could. Incapacitate meant making sure they couldn't attack us, not effectively."

Tyrathan looked up at Chen, his expression faintly haunted. "Can you imagine what would have happened had you burst in there and the two on the floor weren't stuck like that? The one in the corner also? They'd have cut you down and then they would have killed me."

"You could have shot them through the floor."

"That only worked because I was below him, and his spell was making a lovely light." Tyrathan sighed. "What

I did was cruel, yes, and I could tell you that war is always cruel, but I won't show you that disrespect. It's tha—I don't have the words for it. . . ."

Chen poured him a bit more tea. "Hunt for them. You're good at that."

"No, my friend, I'm not good at that. What I'm good at is killing." Tyrathan drank, then closed his eyes. "I'm good at killing at a long range, at not seeing the faces of those I kill. I don't want to. It's all about holding the enemy at bay, keeping them at a distance. I keep everyone at a distance. I'm sorry that what you saw disturbed you."

The anguish in the man's voice squeezed Chen's heart. "You're good at other things."

"No, actually, I'm not."

"Jihui."

"A hunter's game—at least the way I play." Tyrathan half laughed, then smiled. "This is why I envy you, Chen. I envy your ability to make people smile. You make them feel good about themselves. Were I to go out and kill enough beasts for a banquet and then turn them into the most exquisite food anyone there had ever tasted, it would be memorable. But if you came and told just one of your stories, you would be remembered. You have a way of touching hearts. The only way I touch them is with steel at the end of a cloth-yard shaft."

"Maybe that's who you were, but that isn't who you have to be now."

The man hesitated for a moment, then drank more tea. "You're right, though I fear that's who I am becoming again. You see, I am good at this killing bit, very good.

And I fear I come to like it far too much. Thing of it is, it obviously scares you. It scares me even more."

Chen nodded silently because there was nothing he could say that would touch the man's heart. He realized that this was the end of Huojin in the eyes of most pandaren. Giving way to impulsiveness meant giving too little value to anyone and anything. A faceless enemy at a distance was easier to kill than someone a sword's length away. Huojin, carried to the extreme, made all life valueless, and was simply the harbinger of evil.

But the reverse, Tushui, would logically lead to someone who spent so much time in consideration of everything that no action was possible. That would hardly be the antithesis of evil. Which was why the monks stressed balance. He looked at Tyrathan. *A balance my friend is finding elusive.*

The question of that balance remained on Chen's mind for the rest of their trip back to the monastery. Chen sought his own balance point, which seemed centered on whether he should raise a family or continue his exploring. He found it easy to imagine doing both with Yalia by his side, allowing him to have the best aspects of life.

As they traveled, Tyrathan took reckonings using the troll's journal. "It's a rough guess, but they're heading for the heart of Pandaria."

"The Vale of Eternal Blossoms." Chen looked to the south. "It's beautiful, and ancient."

"You've been?"

"I only know its splendor from attending my duties

19

"**U**nderstatement be overrated in a time of war, Lord Taran Zhu." Vol'jin nodded to Chen and Tyrathan. "I'm glad you both be back."

The man returned the nod. "Glad to have made it. And glad to hear your voice recovering."

"Yes, very glad, Vol'jin." The pandaren brewmaster smiled. "I can make some tea that could help further your recovery."

The troll shook his head. He noticed some distance between Chen and the man, but now was not the time to explore it. "This be as good as it gonna be getting. For now. With all due respect, Lord Taran Zhu, we be needing to know about this place."

"Do not judge the pandaren harshly, Vol'jin. Doubtless you will find flaws with how we have done things. You already believe our lack of a formal military, despite millennia without successful invasions, is a mistake. You may yet be proved correct." The Shado-pan leader gathered his paws behind his back. "From what Chen has told me of the world beyond the mists, you, too, have been faced with catastrophes that could not have been predicted. You could argue that our logic in this matter is flawed, but for millennia it has been valid, so much so that it has become as much a truth as the sun rising with dawn and setting at dusk."

"Your words be not terribly informative."

"Save that it alerts you to your prejudices, which could impair your judgment about what you will see." Taran Zhu nodded toward the map. "References are minimal, but the vale is not unknown. It is even populated, and refugees from recent incursions have been given sanctuary there. Still, we have no survey or tactical information of the sort that you desire."

"It is as if you hoped, by keeping the vale hidden, you could insulate Pandaria from what lurks within." Tyrathan looked at the map. "Hiding a problem does not eliminate it."

"It does, however, slow those who would unleash the problem." The elder pandaren drew in a deep breath and exhaled slowly. "What I will show you has been passed from Shado-pan lord to lord, extending back to a time before the Shado-pan existed. I can show you only what I have been shown. I do not know if the fears and biases of my predecessors have shaded things. I do not know what has been forgotten or embellished. What I will share with you I have done so with no monks."

His paws appeared again at his waist, then spread apart. Dark balls of energy crackled in the palm of each. He held one low and one high, both off to the side. A window radiating golden light appeared in the space between them. Within that window images began to move.

"This area is hidden within the Tu Shen Burial Ground. The Thunder King—the first mogu tyrant and the one with whom your Zandalari treated back in the dawn of time—had under him a circle of trusted retainers. His warlords were slain as their master was dying—perhaps to forestall their usurping his throne and plunging the empire into civil war. We do not know. What we do know is that there is a belief among the mogu that death is not always final and that the dead, or parts thereof, can be revivified for later use. I would guess this is the purpose for their invasion of the vale."

Vol'jin peered closely, catching sight for the first time of a mogu—instead of just sensing them as he had in the cave. His mouth went dry and his throat began to ache. Taller than even a Zandalari, thickly thewed and merciless of expression, the mogu warriors might have been carved from a basalt dolmen. Vol'jin granted, as Taran Zhu warned, that memory might have made them more fearsome than reality. Even so, to reduce them by half would still make them formidable.

In the vision, they strode across Pandaria, using sword and fire to extend their dominion over subject peoples. The pandaren were reduced to a race of slaves. The lucky ones clowned enough to entertain their mogu masters. Those pandaren lived in stone palaces, and their lives knew relative luxury. But that luxury ended when a joke offended and only the snapping of a spine or the popped removal of a head could inspire more mogu laughter.

The vision shifted for a moment, and Vol'jin's stomach knotted. He was back in the cave where he died, but it was more than a wet, moldy place covered in bat guano. Mogu sorcerers worked within. Clutches of lizard eggs, crocolisk, perhaps—Vol'jin couldn't tell, but it hardly mattered—were sorted and buried in sands warmed through magic to very precise temperatures. And then when the creatures hatched, they were conveyed to another part of what the troll now recognized to be a rookery.

There, in the chamber where he died, the mogu touched the magic he'd felt. Titan magic. The magic that had shaped the world. In that place, mortals worked with the stuff of divinity to take simple creatures and transform them into the saurok. They used the lizard people as surrogate troops to maintain their empire, allowing the mogu to enjoy the fruits of their conquest.

The process was terrible to watch, yet Vol'jin could not look away. Bones snapped and stretched. Joints reset themselves and muscles ripped. As they grew back together, angles reorganized to provide more power. The saurok stood tall. Fingers grew and thumbs shifted. From lizard to scaled warrior in a matter of minutes—a testament less to the skill of the mogu than to the sheer power of the magics with which they played.

The troll shivered. *Did the titan magic staining that place make it so I not be dying?* The moment the thought occurred to him, he wanted to laugh. It would be just like Garrosh to plan his murder in the one place it could not possibly happen.

Laughter caught in his throat as the scene shifted again, to one of fire and blood, much darker than the conquest. The skies darkened over. Red lightning flowed from above like lava and splashed over the landscape. Magic warped reality as monks cast down their mogu overlords. Monks led the fight for freedom and valiantly won the day.

In the aftermath of the mogu empire's fall, as the skies grew lighter and blood drained from rivers and streams, the pandaren took up their slain enemies and entombed them in the Tu Shen Burial Ground. The respect they showed the mogu warlords surprised him. Had Vol'jin met Tyrathan on a battlefield and slain him, he'd have mounted the man's head on a stick and posted it at a crossroads so travelers would know of his victory.

This be going back to their sense of balance. The fear and hatred be offset by respect. Vol'jin watched as the tombs were sealed, the clues were hidden, and the mists were raised to shroud Pandaria. *That, too, is balance. The peace of camouflage—invisibility—versus war's terror. Their kindness be for healing, just as the hiding be outta necessity.*

As the vision faded, the troll met Taran Zhu's gaze. "I be understanding, Lord Taran Zhu. I do not judge."

"But you wish things were otherwise."

"Things past counting. Wishing, however, be not winning battle." Vol'jin pressed a finger to the Tu Shen region on the map. "People be living there, you said. What can they tell us?"

"Scant little. They are largely content and do not explore, nor do they communicate with outsiders. They are happily hidden in their paradise." Taran Zhu smiled. "And those pandaren who were of the adventuring nature were encouraged to chase the turtle."

Chen's head came up. "So we would not disturb the tombs of mogu warlords and emperors."

"You understand, Master Stormstout. Though some mogu survived, they never presented much of a threat. What little we knew of the Zandalari came from the mogu viewpoint. They understated the power of the Zandalari. We labored under the belief that no one had the ability or desire to resurrect the mogu. It would appear that your Zandalari have taken steps to do so. They removed the Thunder King from his tomb, and . . ."

The man folded his arms over his chest. ". . . now they're going back for the Thunder King's warlords?"

"They amplify his will and his power."

The Thunder King be seeing them the same as Garrosh does the leaders of the Horde's other contingents. Vol'jin nodded. "So, then, it be logical to be thinking two things. The reestablishment of his reign be the first goal for the Thunder King."

Chen shook his head. "That would be bad for Pandaria."

"Yeah. Folks here may have forgotten him after putting him in the grave, but I doubt time in the tomb has dulled his memory." The man sighed. "The second thing is to stop a Zandalari invasion force from getting to the burial ground."

"No," said Vol'jin, "stop them from resurrecting the warlords. Likely there be only a few individuals strong enough for the summoning."

Tyrathan nodded curtly. "Got it. Kill them. . . ."

"Killing a portion of them gonna work, I be thinking." Vol'jin looked at Taran Zhu. "And your priorities gonna be to prepare Pandaria to resist the mogu. How many monks do you have for doing that?"

"A hundred, almost half of whom I have dispatched to the provinces to begin to organize. Logistics. Some training. But these are not the monks to whom you refer." The pandaren lifted his chin. "Of the sort you mean, of the lethal kind, including the three of you and myself, I have fifty."

"Half a hundred to be stopping a Zandalari invasion and sending a millennia-old mogu tyrant back to the grave." Vol'jin nodded slowly. "To be dealing with the burial ground, I'll need seven. Now let's be figuring out what you'll be doing with the rest while we're gone."

• • •

"This be not pleasing me, Captain Nir'zan." The fact that the troll lay prostrate on the ground before Khal'ak did not have the usual mollifying effect on her spirit. "I be believin' you wish praise for having determined dat the man who killed a party of scouts was da same who fought here in Zouchin. You might be understanding that I would prefer to know he be dead, not that he continues to fight."

"Yes, my lady."

"Losing the shaman's journal, that be deepenin' my displeasure. The man and his pandaren ally shoulda been captured. I should be having the journal here, now."

Had the troll attempted to protest the impossibility of her comment, she would have killed him herself as an example for the other officers watching. Khal'ak knew it was quite unreasonable to have expected that he, dispatched only after the scouting party had failed to report back, could have caught up with their murderers.

She toed his shoulder, prompting him to rise into a kneeling position. "It be doing you credit that you reported back yourself. Same with keeping your unit posted to the east. It be good you sketched the man's footprints in the fishing village and recognized his track here. You got more intelligence than I might otherwise be thinking."

Captain Nir'zan kept his gaze averted to the ground. "You be kind, my lady. I be lucky that the storm that extinguished the croft fire had not washed away the footprints."

She pressed her hands together before her lips for a moment, then lowered them and nodded. "Each of you gonna take your companies and fan out along our intended route. Assume the enemy knows you be coming.

You gonna set up at crossroads and appropriate places where you can delay any material opposition. If you or any of your soldiers retreat, well, do not. Better you die quickly at da hands of the enemy than you die slowly under my tender care.

"You will be takin' prisoners. You gonna wring from them information. If dey are individuals of political influence or office, you gonna convey them to me. Their families gonna be beheaded. Their bodies gonna be burned and their heads gonna be posted at crossroads. The deaths of our scouts be attributable in part to a pandaren, so I wish ten of dese beastly creatures slain for every one of our losses. Release one prisoner—someone young or old, not a combatant—to spread the story."

She leaned forward, lifting Nir'zan's pointy chin with a crooked finger. "And to you, Nir'zan, be going a great privilege. You identified the man's part in dis. You and your company gonna range farthest. You gonna find where the Alliance lines are drawn. You gonna, without revealing yourself, capture prisoners. Humans preferably, worgen even, elves if you must, two dwarves or three gnomes. I be wantin' a dozen equivalent in man weight to pay for our dead. With them, release no survivors. They gonna soon enough know why their people be missing."

"Yes, my lady."

"You gonna bring them to the warlords' tombs. I gonna find a use for them there." She straightened up. "Go now, all of you. Report back when you have success."

Sand flew as a dozen troll captains raced to their units. She watched them go, suppressing a laugh of satisfaction. They would not fail her, but only because the mission she'd given them was one at which they could not fail. Success was necessary to build their confidence, which they would need when later she demanded they do the impossible.

She turned, having felt the mogu's shadow fall over her before she saw it darken the sand. "Fair morning, Honored Chae-nan."

"You value your dead too little. I would slay a hundred pandaren for each of your dead."

"I considered dat, but we have located too few crossroads, and there be a shortage of sticks." She shrugged easily. "Besides, we can always be killin' more, and I would do so at your master's pleasure."

"I doubt dead pandaren would amuse him, but men, these might." The mogu smiled in a way that demonstrated why executioners often wore hoods. "The man you seek, the pandaren, and, I believe, a troll from before—these would greatly please my master."

"Den I gonna do all in my power to obtain them." She bowed to him. "I gonna deliver them myself, and da Thunder King can suck out their souls and sup on their agonies."

20

Vol'jin found himself trapped in a dream or a vision. He wasn't certain which. The dream he could have dismissed as his mind digesting what he had seen and been told. The vision—which had all the signs of being a gift from the Silk Dancer—had to be given weight, and that meant he had to see it through.

He hid his face behind a rush'kah mask. He was glad of that. It meant any chance reflection would hide whether or not he truly was within a Zandalari body. It wasn't like wearing Tyrathan's skin. Vol'jin felt very much a troll—more so than even when he was in his own skin. As he looked around, he realized he stood in a time before there were any trolls who were not Zandalari.

He stood farther back in time than he had ever been.

He recognized Pandaria but knew if he uttered that name, his host would not acknowledge it. Pandaria was the vulgar name for the place. The mogu so guarded its true name that even though he was an honored guest, it would not be shared with him.

Pandaren, though none of them as prosperously portly as Chen, ran and fetched and carried. His host, a mogu Spiritrender of equivalent societal rank, had suggested they climb a mountain to survey the land better. They'd stopped near the top to lay out a midday meal.

Vol'jin, though his body remained thousands of years in the future, recognized their stopping place as the monastery's eventual home. He sat, nibbling on sweet rice cakes beneath his mask, in the same spot where his body now slept. He almost wondered if, somehow, he was being allowed access to memories from a previous life.

The thought thrilled him and revolted him.

The thrill came, though he resisted it, simply because of the troll culture in which he was raised. The Zandalari looked down on the other trolls, and though trolls such as the Darkspears made jokes about how far the Zandalari had fallen, being denied Zandalari respect was like a child being denied a parent's love. It left a hole that, no matter how undeserving the parent might be, was easily filled by the least possible kindness. So, to find himself having once been a Zandalari, or to at least feel somewhat comfortable in a Zandalari's flesh, answered a longing he sought to deny.

Acknowledging its existence be not enslaving myself to it. The aspect that revolted him made it easier to remove himself from that longing. His mogu host, in not having had his cup filled quickly enough, gestured at a servant. Blue-black lightning struck the hunched pandaren. The creature stumbled, spilling wine from a golden pitcher. His mogu master blasted him again and again, then turned.

"I am a bad host. I deny you this pleasure."

Vol'jin's heart leaped at the invitation to torture the pandaren. It wasn't about being able to prove himself superior to the broken servant. No. It was to prove himself his host's equal in being able to inflict pain. They were arcane archers shooting at a target, each seeking to get closer to the bull's-eye. Only the contest mattered, not the target.

No one be mourning the target.

Mercifully, before Vol'jin discovered whether he would indulge in the sport, the scene shifted. He and his guest lounged atop a pyramid in the jungles now known as Stranglethorn. The city that spread out before them had covered a vast plain in stone, much of which had been hauled from afar, from throughout the world the trolls dominated. So ancient was the city that, in Vol'jin's time, no trace remained, save for those few stones that had been plundered from city after city and now were ground to rubble to fill walls overgrown with vines.

From his guest, Vol'jin caught the faintest hints of contempt. The pyramid was hardly as lofty a perch as the mountain had been—and they'd never made it to the top—but trolls did not need mountains to see their realms. When one could communicate with the loa, when one was graced with visions, the need for physical—mortal—height vanished. And trolls had not slave races to use as personal servants, but then what species was worthy enough to be allowed to touch a troll? They had their society ranked by caste, each with its role and purpose. All things were ordered under the heavens.

They were as they should be, and loa pity the mogu who failed to understand why this was the way of reality.

Vol'jin tried to sense any trace of the titan magic on his guest but could not. Perhaps they'd not discovered it yet. Perhaps they only used it to create the saurok late in their empire's life. Perhaps the Thunder King had been insane enough to order its use, or had been driven insane by its use. It hardly mattered.

What did matter was the rift between Zandalari and mogu. Therein lay the fertile ground that had allowed the mogu to fall. The hints of contempt Vol'jin felt would grow into polite indifference between the peoples. They trusted each other not to attack because they were confident that they could destroy their partner. While they stood back to back, they did not watch the other and did not see the other falter.

Curiously enough, each society did stumble. The slaves that the mogu cherished and relied upon were the creatures who rose up and overthrew them. The castes that maintained the Zandalari on top grew to be their own people. As they became diminished, the Zandalari were content to let them go away—abandoning unruly children until they saw the folly of the youthful rebellion and came back begging. . . .

Begging for Zandalari approval.

Vol'jin awoke with a snarl in his cell, surprised that he wore no mask but instead had a single strand of spider silk stretched over his eyes. The air was pregnant with the hint of snow. He sat up, hugging his knees to himself for a moment, then pulled on his clothes and headed out. He bypassed the courtyard in which monks exercised—each wearing silk or leather armor—and headed for the mountain.

While neither Zandalari nor mogu had felt the need to reach the summit, Vol'jin's heart demanded he attain the heights they had been too lazy to discover. It occurred to him that, by the pandaren way of thinking, their talking themselves into the belief that they didn't need to reach the top had convinced them they'd attained balance in their lives.

Their self-deception doomed them.

Three-quarters of the way up the mountain, he found the man waiting for him. "You're awfully damned quiet, even when you're lost in thought."

"But you be detecting my approach anyway."

"I've spent much time here. I'm used to the sounds. I didn't hear you. I just heard everything else reacting to the fact that they had." The man smiled. "Had a bad night of it?"

"Not until the end." Vol'jin stretched his back. "Have trouble sleeping?"

"I slept astonishingly well." Tyrathan rose from his rock and started up the narrow trail. "Surprising, since I've agreed with your plan, which is pretty much of a suicide mission."

"It would not be the first for you."

"That you can say that and be correct casts my sanity into serious doubt."

The troll loped along, pleased that he could neither detect any trace of Tyrathan's limp nor feel anything but the ghost of a twinge in his side. "It be testament to your survival skills."

"Not much of one." The man glanced back, his eyes tight. "You saw how I survived Serpent's Heart. I ran."

"You crawled." Vol'jin raised open hands. "You did what you had to for surviving."

"I was a coward."

"If it be cowardice to avoid dying with your men, then every general be a coward." The troll shook his head. "Besides, you be not that man. That man had no beard. He dyed his hair. He never be running while those who depended on him still lived."

"But I did, Vol'jin." Tyrathan laughed but did not share the joke. "As for the beard and letting my hair grow back in its natural color, I have found that my encounter with death leaves me unwilling to delude myself. I understand myself much better now. Who and what I am. And have no fear; I won't run."

"Be I fearing that, I would not allow you to come."

"Why are you letting Chen come?"

Anger simmered in Vol'jin's blood. "Chen not gonna run."

"I know that and did not mean to suggest it." The man sighed. "It's because he won't run that I don't think he should come. The monks, few have family beyond this place. I am alone. I don't know of you. . . ."

Vol'jin shook his head. "She gonna understand."

"Chen's got his niece and Yalia. And, frankly, he's got too big a heart to witness what we're going to do."

"What was it happened out there?"

As they climbed the rest of the way to the top, the man described in very precise detail exactly what had happened. Vol'jin understood perfectly. He'd chosen to kill the silent one first because he'd not removed his armor. That meant he'd be the hardest to eliminate. The other two soldiers were just that: soldiers. And conversation had indicated that their leader wasn't a warrior.

The man had made the same decisions Vol'jin would have made, and for the same reasons. Finding a way to trap the trolls had been critical. It took them out of the fight, and the pain and terror also rendered them useless.

And yet, as much as he understood what Tyrathan had done and why, he also now understood Chen's uncharacteristic taciturnity. Many people who went to war refused to look at what they were doing. War was defined by cultures in terms of heroic tales of bravery. Those stories skipped over the horror of it all in favor of praising courage and fortitude against overwhelming odds. A thousand songs were sung of the warrior who held off a thousand hated enemies, yet not a single one of the fallen merited even a memorial note.

Chen was one of those who had always been able to mythologize battles, primarily because he was at a distance from them. It wasn't that he was never threatened. He was, often, and acquitted himself well. But any fighter who allowed himself to dwell on his personal danger was one who went mad or threw himself at the enemy to end his madness.

Until now, Chen had fought for his friends, supporting them in their battles. But here, he was fighting for a place he could call home. Out there, he was the only pandaren. None of the dead looked like him. Or his niece or his friend.

When they reached the pinnacle, Vol'jin crouched. "I be understanding your questions about Chen. Neither of us be doubting his courage. Neither of us be wanting him hurt. But this be why he must come. It gonna hurt him more not to have acted, whether we fail or succeed, than to watch us slay thousands in ways that leave them screaming out their last. He be pandaren. Pandaria be his future. This be his fight. We cannot be protecting him from this, so it's better to have him with us so he can be saving us."

The man considered for a moment, then nodded. "Chen told me some stories of you, of your past. He said you were wise. Did you ever imagine, during those times, that the tables would be turned, and you'd be fighting for his home as he did for yours?"

"No." The troll looked out over Pandaria, studying mountains that nudged their way through clouds, and forests peeking out from gaps below. "This be a place worth fighting for. Worth dying for."

"A fight so we can stop others from doing here what they've done to our homes?"

"Yes."

Tyrathan scratched at his goatee. "How is it that a leader of the Horde and an Alliance soldier are united in fighting for a people who have no claim on our allegiance?"

"You be referring to the people we once were." Vol'jin shrugged. "My body survived assassination, but who I was did die in that cave. The Vol'jin they meant to kill be truly dead."

"You're no closer to deciding who you now are than I am."

"I be not a skull-crab." Vol'jin read a lack of comprehension in Tyrathan's eyes. "An allegory Taran Zhu told me."

"He used the Room of a Thousand Doors on me. Some I can squeeze through, but only one will be a perfect fit, and the one I entered through has vanished."

"Have you chosen your door?"

"No, but I think I am coming close to choosing. My choices have narrowed." The man smiled. "You know, of course, that once I do go through, I'll find myself in another room of a thousand doors."

"And I gonna be outgrowing whatever shell I find myself in." Vol'jin swept a hand over the expanse of Pandaria and the green valleys. "Promised yourself to be looking again on the valleys of your homeland before you died. Be these a worthy substitute?"

"Let me lie to you and tell you no." The man gave another smile. "If I say yes, then my oath would allow me to die."

"I gonna, as I promised, get the one who kills you."

"Then let that be a long time from now, when I'm too old to remember why but still young enough to be grateful."

The troll looked at him, then away. "Why be our races hating each other so much, when we be reasonable, the two of us?"

"Because finding the differences upon which we can hang hatred is much easier than discovering the common ground that can unite." Tyrathan chuckled quickly. "If I return to the Alliance and tell tales of what we have done together . . ."

"You gonna be thought a madman?"

"I'll be tried for treason and executed."

"More common ground between us. Execution be cleaner than assassination."

"And yet rooted in the ease of finding differences." The man shook his head. "You realize that if we do this—when we do this—were all the world to see and understand, they'd still never sing the songs or tell the stories of what we accomplished."

Vol'jin nodded. "But do we be doing this to have songs sung about us?"

"No. They won't fit through my door."

"Then, my friend, let the songs be sung as Zandalari lamentations." He stood and started down the mountain. "Let them be sung for a thousand generations and serenade us into eternity."

21

The Shado-pan monks prepared for war with laudable focus, though their actions lacked the hints of grim humor that Vol'jin had seen accompany the same preparations among other peoples. Four monks, two from the survivors of the blue squad and two from the red, were chosen by lottery to join Vol'jin, Tyrathan, and Chen. At least, their choice was supposed to be by chance, but Vol'jin suspected that the lottery was just to allow those who could not handle the mission to withdraw from it without any loss of esteem.

Assaulting the Vale of Eternal Blossoms would not be a simple thing. Shrouded in shadow and warded by impassible mountains, the place was a fortress that had remained unexplored for thousands of years. If he took any comfort in the difficulty in actually entering the place, it was only that the Zandalari, with their much larger force, would find passage that much more troublesome.

I be hoping.

Each of the seven set about the preparations in his or her own way. Tyrathan searched the monastery's armory, chose the best arrows, broke them down, and fletched them himself. He painted the shafts bright red and made the feathers blue—in honor of the red and blue monks, he said. When asked why he blackened the arrowheads with soot, he said it was to honor the Zandalari's black hearts.

Chen set himself on the task of victualing the expedition. To the monks, in their inexperience with the kind of war the Zandalari would bring, this might have seemed almost a frivolous pursuit, but Vol'jin understood his friend's twin purposes. Not only would having proper food, fluids, and bandages be critical for the mission's success, but it was also Chen's way of taking care of the others. No matter what war had shown him or would make him do, Chen would be true to his nature. Vol'jin was grateful for that.

Taran Zhu approached the battlement where the troll sat running a whetstone along the curved edge of the first of his glaive's blades. "You cannot make it sharper with any more strokes. It can already split night from day."

Vol'jin raised the blade and watched golden sunlight spark from the edge. "Sharpening the fighter who be wielding it wants more time than we have."

"I think he, too, is honed to a fine edge." The elder monk looked toward the south, where the vale's mountains trapped a lake of clouds. "Back when the last mogu emperor fell, monks led the rebellion. I doubt the monks then would recognize the Shado-pan as their heirs, and we might not recognize them as our inspiration. We revere their legends too much, and they would have hoped for much more from us."

The monk frowned. "In that rebellion, they had more than pandaren fighting with them. The jinyu, the hozen, even the grummles participated. It could be, though the Lorewalkers never mention it, that even men and trolls fought with the pandaren."

The troll smiled. "Hardly likely. Unrefined, men were at the time. The Zandalari would still be seeing the mogu as allies then, too."

"But there are always the exceptional among every population."

"You be thinking of the insane and the renegades."

"The point being that our fight for our freedom is a fight you could have understood then, and do understand now." Taran Zhu shook his head. "That war, and the time before, our time of enslavement, was so terrible that it scars our souls. Perhaps that wound only had the chance to fester, never to heal."

Vol'jin flipped his sword around and rasped the whetstone over the other curved edge. "Wounds that foul need cutting and draining."

"In our desire to forget our nightmare, we might have lost that knowledge. Not of how to do such things, but the why of their necessity." The elder monk nodded. "Your presence here and your conduct so far have contributed greatly to my seeing that."

A chill ran down Vol'jin's spine. "I be glad but also saddened. I've seen enough war not to like it. Not like some, who live for it."

"Like the man?"

"No, not even him. He be good at it, but were he the sort to need war, he'd have long since quit this place." Vol'jin's eyes became slits. "One thing he and I share be the willingness to shoulder responsibilities others are not. The same be true of the Shado-pan, and now you know why it be so important."

"Yes." The pandaren nodded. "As per our discussions, I have sent envoys to the jinyu and hozen. I hope they will stand with us."

"The grummles seem willing." A small knot of the tiny, long-armed creatures had gathered around Chen, each being fitted with sacks to haul. They would bring the team's gear to the vale, then head back to the monastery to let Taran Zhu know the team had gotten that far. Given the grummles' stamina and great strength, they would save the team's energy for the second half of the expedition, into the vale itself.

"They are compliant and wiser than they would seem." The monk smiled. "We, and I mean the peoples of Pandaria, will never be able to thank you for all you've done. I have sent my master carvers into the mountain to carve your likenesses into the bones. If you die . . ."

Vol'jin nodded. For him, the dropping of a statuette would be a matter of military intelligence, but clearly, for the Shado-pan, it was another matter entirely. "You be honoring me greatly."

"Yet inadequately memorializing what you are doing for us. Monks led the rebellion and now will write a new ending to it."

The troll lifted an eyebrow. "You know we just be buying time. We can slow them down. We can set them back, but seven, or forty-seven, won't be enough to be stopping the Zandalari or the mogu."

"But time is what we need." Taran Zhu smiled. "Almost no one will remember the time when we were slaves, but no one wishes to be enslaved. As the mogu rise, they bring with them the rebirth of the reason we threw them down. Time is what we need to organize. Time to remind people of their past and teach them the value of their future."

• • •

As they set off the next morning for the Vale of Eternal Blossoms, Vol'jin took a look back toward the Peak of Serenity. There the first monks had trained in secret, their privacy guaranteed because the mogu were too lazy to climb to the top. His memory of lounging farther down with a mogu comrade burst with his remembrance of climbing to the top with the man. Another ally, a comrade, but circumstances that felt so much different.

And so proper, despite how strange.

Vol'jin studied the group and smiled. For each one of them came two grummles bearing weapons and rations and other supplies. Five pandaren, a man, and a troll. Had Garrosh been there to see it, to see how easily Vol'jin got along with them, he'd have yet more charges of treason to lay against him.

And it wasn't as if this company replaced the Horde in his mind or heart. It was a company of necessity, and in that way, it reminded him of the Horde. A diverse company united to preserve freedom. It was that unity of purpose that defined the Horde he knew and loved, the Horde that had fought under Thrall.

The purpose of Garrosh's Horde came from him, from his need for conquest and power. His desires would fracture it, perhaps beyond repair. That would be as great a tragedy, in Vol'jin's mind, as the Zandalari-mogu alliance returning the mogu to power in Pandaria.

They headed south and, after several days, reached the heights above the Vale of Eternal Blossoms. The clouds seethed and curled like ocean waves heralding a coming storm. If the grummles felt any foreboding, they said nothing. They made camp as before and segregated themselves.

Though he knew better than to do it, he had made a

point of learning each pandaren's name, as had Chen. Tyrathan had adopted the wiser course, addressing each one as "brother" or "sister" or "my friend," keeping some distance between them. Not knowing their names, not knowing their hopes and dreams, would make it easier if . . . *If their statues drop from the mountain's bones.*

Vol'jin didn't want it to be easy. He never had, but in the past he had been fighting with and for his tribe. Here it would be easy to distance himself, since it wasn't his people, wasn't his home, wasn't his tribe. *But if the fight be worth fighting, then these be my people, this be my home, and they be my tribe.*

It occurred to him that the mogu might be thinking exactly the same thing, though rooted in the past. This was their land. These were their people. Even after centuries and tens of centuries—even after they'd all but been forgotten—they burned with a hunger to have rights wronged. It was one thing for trolls to desire to return to the past because they, at least, had explored a future. The mogu had done little to organize or reestablish their domain. They remained shut off from the future because they clung so tightly to the past they'd lost.

Despite having made their camp in a cave facing south and west, the group lit no fire. They supped on rice balls, dried berries, and smoked fish. Chen had managed to steep tea in a waterskin, which made it all more than palatable.

Tyrathan drained his small bowl and held it out for a refill. "I always wondered what my last meal would be."

Chen smiled with genuine joy. "It's a question you'll ponder for a long time yet, Tyrathan."

"Perhaps, but if this is it, I can't imagine a better meal."

The troll raised his cup. "It be the company, not the food."

● ● ●

Vol'jin slept solidly until just before dawn, having taken the first watch after supper. He suffered no visions or dreams—at least, none he could remember. For a heartbeat, he wondered if the loa had abandoned him again. He decided, quite to the contrary, that Bwonsamdi had kept the others distant so Vol'jin would be rested enough to send more trolls his way.

The seven bade farewell to their grummle bearers. Tyrathan gave each of them one of his arrows as a remembrance. When Vol'jin threw him a glance, he shrugged. "I'll replace them with Zandalari. Face it: my supply of arrows was bound to run out well before their supply of Zandalari did."

Not to be outdone, and feeling the same level of gratitude, Vol'jin shaved the sides of his head. He presented each grummle with a lock of his red hair. The grummles looked as if they'd been handed fistfuls of jewels, and then they melted back into the hills and mountains.

The seven made their descent through the mountains easily enough. Brother Shan led the way, finding footholds on sheer faces and having the strength to anchor ropes as others followed. He recounted a story that said monks had, at the time of the rebellion, rappelled down these very mountains to surprise the mogu. Vol'jin took some comfort from that legend and hoped they would be equally successful.

By the middle of the day, they got below the clouds. The sun had burned off none of the mist, but the clouds glowed with a subtle golden light, which came as much from the ground reflection as it did from the sun's rays. Vol'jin crouched at the edge of a clearing on a mountain's southern face and studied the valley below.

Had the troll been pressed before to pick a color to define Pandaria, it would have been green. So many shades of green, from the light buds of new grasses to the deep emerald of forests; the continent was green. But here, in the Vale of Eternal Blossoms, green gave way to gold and red. These were not the colors of autumn—though in places they came close—but the exploding hues of plants in full flower. They were in their glory, springtime frozen in a world that did not age. The diffuse light cast no sharp shadows, and what little moved below did so with a dreamlike, languid quality.

The vale looked the way it felt to stretch luxuriously and long upon waking.

From the heights they could see some buildings but had no clue as to who lived there or maintained them. Their antiquity could not be disputed, but vegetation had not risen up to consume them. The vale's timelessness preserved them. Vol'jin wondered if that quality would keep all of them alive.

Or keep us dying forever.

Sister Quan-li, a pandaren with liver-colored fur to contrast with the white, pointed southeast. "The invaders would approach from that direction. The mogu palace lay there, and Lord Taran Zhu says the emperor's warlords were buried directly south of our position."

Tyrathan nodded. "The journal would have had them seeking passage in the east part of the valley. I don't see any signs they've made it yet."

The troll chuckled. "What would you expect, my friend? That we be seeing a black stain pouring over the landscape? Smoke from villages being burned to the ground?"

"No. There should, however, be makeshift camps. So we can choose to wait here until dark and see if fires reveal the enemy to us . . ."

"Or be slipping down and looking more closely just in case they, too, are keeping cold camps." Vol'jin stood. "I be favoring the latter."

"Easier to shoot by daylight. Not impossible at night. Just easier."

"Good. We gonna come out on this little plateau above that road. Keep to the heights."

Tyrathan pointed with the end of his bow. "If we can head straight south and curl back around east, we could come in behind their line of march. They wouldn't be looking for us in ground they've already secured. Plus, those folks who are critical to accomplishing their ends are not likely to be at the front line but somewhere back, away from perceived danger."

"Yes. Identify them and kill them."

Chen glanced over, his eyes tight. "And slip away again."

The troll and the man exchanged looks. Then Vol'jin nodded. "Probably back south and west. We be going back out the way we came in."

"At least we'd know the terrain and know where to set traps." The man lowered his bow. "Given that we're pitting seven against the elite of two empires, that isn't the most stupid plan we could have come up with."

"Agreed." The troll shifted the pack strapped to his back. "That I can't be thinking of a better one disturbs me."

"That's not the point, is it, Vol'jin?" Chen tugged on his own pack's straps. "We're here to disturb them, and I think this plan will do just that."

22

Though they walked through a golden valley that few outsiders had seen for years uncounted, Vol'jin did not fear. He knew he should have and consciously took every precaution he could to avoid discovery. Still, he didn't have that little chill cutting at his spine. The fur at the base of his skull didn't rise. It felt as if he had on a rush'kah mask, insulating him from fear.

And yet . . . he had no dreams while he slept in the Vale of Eternal Blossoms, but that was because he needed none. Walking through the valley was walking through a living vision. Something about the reality of the place bled into him. An arrogance, in part, resonating with his troll heritage. He was touching a lingering bit of mogu magic, being caressed by the ghost of the mogu empire.

Here, in this place, where great races had wielded great power, he could not know fear. There, on the far distant steps of Mogu'shan Palace—where his enemies likely slept—proud mogu fathers had faced their sons west, sweeping a hand before them to take in the whole of the valley. This land was theirs, and all land that touched it, to do with as they pleased. They could make it over as they willed, shape it to their hearts' desires. There was nothing here that would hurt them, because everything here feared them.

It was that last bit that saved Vol'jin. He knew what it was to be feared. He liked that his enemies feared him, but their terror was born from what he had done. He had earned it, sword stroke by sword stroke, spell by spell, conquest by conquest. It was not something he'd inherited and not something he saw as his birthright.

It was something he understood, and this separated him from the young mogu princes who beheld their domain. Because he understood this concept, he could use it. He could feel it ebb and flow. But they remained above it, seeing what they wanted to see, hearing what they wanted to hear. And never feeling the need to climb to the heights to see the reality of the world.

When they made camp on the night they'd gotten halfway across the valley, Tyrathan looked at him. "You feel it, don't you?"

Vol'jin nodded.

Chen looked up from his tea bowl. "Feel what?"

The man smiled. "That answers my question."

The pandaren shook his head. "What question? What is it you feel?"

Tyrathan frowned. "A sense that this place is mine and that I belong here because the land is soaked in blood and I am steeped in killing. That's what you feel, yes, Vol'jin?"

"Close enough."

Chen smiled, pouring himself some tea. "Oh, that."

The man's frown deepened. "Then you do feel it?"

"No, but I know you do." The brewmaster looked at the man and the troll in turn, then shrugged. "I've seen that look in your eyes before. You, Vol'jin, more than Tyrathan, but I've not fought beside him nearly as much as I have beside you. In every battle, at that point when you are fighting your hardest, you get that expression. It's just hard. Implacable. I see it and I know you will win. That expression says that you are the best combatant on the field that day. Anyone who challenges you will die."

The troll cocked his head. "And that's the expression I be wearing now?"

"Well, no, maybe a little, around the eyes. The both of you. When you don't think anyone is looking. Or when you don't realize anyone is looking. It says this is your land, won by right, which you won't surrender." Chen shrugged once more. "Given our task, this is good."

The man extended his cup to the pandaren and nodded when it was refilled. "Then what do you feel here?"

Chen set his waterskin down and scratched his chin. "I feel the peace that is this place's promise. I think the two of you feel a bit of the mogu legacy. But, for me, the peace, the promise, it's what I want in a home. It tells me I can stop wandering—but it doesn't demand it. It's a welcome that will never be withdrawn."

He looked at the both of them, and for the first time Vol'jin could remember, Chen's big golden eyes filled with sorrow. "I wish you could feel that too."

Vol'jin gave his friend a smile. "It be enough for me that you do, Chen. I have a home, one you helped win. You secured a home for me. Impossible not to be pleased for you."

Without much inducement, Vol'jin managed to get Chen and the monks to elaborate on their sense of the place. They complied happily, and Vol'jin took some joy in their impressions. However, after the sun set, a cold, dark wave rippled out from the east. The monks fell silent, and Tyrathan, who had been standing watch at the crest of the hill beneath which they camped, pointed.

"They're here."

Vol'jin and the others scrambled up with him. There, to the east, Mogu'shan Palace had lit up. Silver and blue lightning played over its faces, defining the structure with ivy-like twists that sparked at the corners. The display of magic impressed Vol'jin, not because of any sense of power but because of the aimless and casual way in which it was being displayed.

Chen shivered. "The welcome is being blanketed."

"It being smothered." Vol'jin shook his head. "Buried deeply. No one be welcome here anymore."

Tyrathan looked at Vol'jin. "It's more than a bowshot, but we could make it by dawn. Well before any revelers are awake."

"No. They be baiting us with that display. That be where they want us to strike."

The man raised an eyebrow. "They know we're coming?"

"They have to assume we be, just as we have to assume they know we gonna react to the journal you captured." Vol'jin pointed toward the southern mountain range. "Likely Horde and Alliance scouts be on the ridges. They gonna spot this and react. It gonna just take a while to discuss plans before they be moving."

"Unless someone does it on his own initiative." Tyrathan chuckled. "Months ago, that would have been me. I wonder who'll play the hero?"

"It doesn't matter to our mission—as long as they don't be getting in the way."

"Agreed." The man ran a hand over his beard. "Still straight in and hook east?"

"Until something be making that plan impossible, yes."

Vol'jin passed another dreamless night, but it was not a wholly restful one. He considered reaching out to the loa, but as was true of all gods, they could be capricious. If they were bored or annoyed, they could let slip a word that would alert his enemies to his presence. As he'd said to Tyrathan, they had to assume their enemies knew they were coming. The fact that the Zandalari could not pinpoint where they were was an advantage. Given the nature of their mission, any advantage was to be cherished.

The next morning, if the sun dawned at all, Vol'jin had no real way of knowing. The clouds had thickened. The only light coming through, aside from a faint jaundiced glow, was the result of the stray thunderbolts rippling through their depths. The lightning never touched the ground, as if afraid of reprisals from those in Mogu'shan Palace.

The seven slowed their pace out of necessity. Dim light made missteps more common. A trickle of gravel sliding underfoot sounded like thunder. They'd all freeze in place, ears straining for reactions. And their scouts had to shorten their lead on the party simply because darkness made it harder to see. This contributed to more frequent stops.

Night after night, the lightning show repeated itself from Mogu'shan Palace. With it came an intensification of the sense of the vale. This was Vol'jin's place by right, and those in the palace were challenging him. The palace was a flame to the moth of opposition, but none of the seven were to allow themselves to be trapped.

What Vol'jin didn't like was the lack of any sign of

Zandalari scouts. Had he been in command of their force, he would have pushed light troops far forward, even to the western wall between the vale and the home of creatures called the mantid. The stories told of them were the sort that would have quieted unruly children—and Vol'jin meant trolls, not mere pandaren cubs. To not secure that border would be gross negligence, especially when the Zandalari knew they faced opposition.

Two days of no sun had passed before they found their first sign of the Zandalari. Brother Shan had been in the lead, pausing in a saddle between two higher hills early in the evening. They'd reached the south wall of mountains and were heading east through the foothills. The monk signaled. Vol'jin and Tyrathan came forward, and Shan retreated to where the others waited.

The view below made Vol'jin's blood run cold. A company of a dozen and a half Zandalari light warriors had created an outpost. They'd cut down a stand of golden-leaved trees and hacked off the limbs. They'd sharpened the trunks and stouter limbs, then sunk them into the ground around the perimeter. The stakes pointed outward in all directions save for a narrow gap toward the west. There the ring's ends overlapped, so any attackers would have to make a sharp turn before they got inside the camp.

The troll's nostrils flared, but he refrained from snorting angrily. To have reduced a stand of beautiful trees to a cruel fortress seemed to Vol'jin to be blasphemy itself. *A small crime, but there gonna be retribution.*

Two tree trunks had been sunk into the ground at the heart of the camp, just east of a large bonfire. Twenty feet tall, they stood half that apart. Ropes had been attached at the top of each post, and again to the wrists of a warrior.

His blue tabard had been torn from him down to the waist, held by an unseen belt. His flesh had been cut in numerous places, never deeply but enough to be painful and for blood to flow.

Vol'jin was certain he'd never seen the man before, yet he seemed familiar. Four other humans were there, wearing tattered tabards that, the troll guessed, would have matched the one worn by the torture victim. The four were roped together and cowered as Zandalari watched over them.

Two trolls warded the gap, and two others guarded the prisoners. The rest, including a junior officer holding a human sword, gathered around the hanging man. The officer said something that prompted the Zandalari to laugh, and then he cut the man again.

Vol'jin had seen enough and was ready to move on. Then he looked at his companion's face. "We cannot be intervening. You know that."

The man swallowed with great difficulty. "I cannot leave him to be tortured."

"You be having no choice."

"No, you have no choice."

The troll nodded and drew an arrow. "I understand. I gonna be killing him then."

Tyrathan's jaw dropped; then he closed his mouth and shook his head. He refused to meet Vol'jin's gaze. "I can't let him die."

"A rescue gonna be suicide."

"It can be done."

"Who be they that you would be risking our lives and mission?"

The man's shoulders slumped. "There's not enough time to explain, not so it would make sense."

"To me, or to you?"

"Vol'jin, please, I have an obligation." The hunter closed his eyes, pain flashing over his features. "But, you're right about the mission. Get everyone else clear. I think I can manage this myself. We have to be close to our goal, so I'll make this a distraction. Please, my friend."

Vol'jin listened to the anguish in the man's voice, then studied the situation again. He nodded. "Sneak down as close as you can. I gonna shoot their leader. They gonna follow me into an ambush. You be getting the captives clear. Go into the mountains."

Tyrathan rested a hand on Vol'jin's shoulder. "That plan, my friend, is even stupider than our being here in the first place. There's only one way this works. I work my way around to that group of rocks. You and the pandaren get down into that grove near the gap. When the arrows start falling, all the Zandalari must die."

Vol'jin looked at the two staging points the man had picked out and agreed. "You be leaving the shooting to me. Your people gonna follow you out. They won't be following a troll."

"The hanging man is here because they believe me dead. It's best they continue to think that. You roar at them, tell them to run. Have Sister Quan-li lead them, liaise with the Alliance." Tyrathan sighed. "It will be for the best."

Vol'jin measured the distances with his eyes and nodded. Regardless of the complications of human relationships, the troll knew he would be better fighting hand to hand with the Zandalari. Moreover, he wanted to do that. The way they had shifted what the vale should have meant made them deserving of death. He wanted them to read contempt from his face as they died.

"Agreed."

The man squeezed the troll's shoulder. "And I know you could have made the shots."

"You know I would have been better than you."

"That too." The hunter smiled. "When you're in place, you'll see my signal."

Tyrathan headed off to his staging point while Vol'jin returned to the pandaren. He briefed them quickly. That none of them protested the insanity of it all surprised him. Then he remembered that Chen had always been a loyal friend and that loyalty was highly prized among the pandaren. There was a difference between compliance to help a friend and blind adherence to duty—the former made doing the impossible actually possible. Moreover, the monks saw the rescue as a bid to restore balance to the world, which made it more of an imperative for them than it was for Tyrathan.

The rescue party slipped into place easily enough, hunkering down in a small grove twenty yards from the gap. Having failed to clear it was reason enough, in Vol'jin's mind, for the Zandalari officer to die. Vol'jin brought his glaive to hand and slowly smiled.

Four and a half inches.

Tyrathan's signal came in the form of a single arrow that punched through the officer's open mouth. The troll had just turned to face his victim again, so the blood splattered two warriors squatting behind him. Before the first could spring up, a second arrow sank into his chest and burst out through his back. He stumbled and, in falling, impaled another troll on the bloody point.

The other squatting troll just fell back, grunting, staring at the blue-and-red arrow quivering in his chest.

The guards at the gap turned to face the commotion around the bonfire. That mistake destroyed their night vision, not that it would have mattered much at all. Vol'jin came silent as death, and the Shado-pan were death's shadow. Even Chen, who lagged a bit behind, made little enough noise that it disappeared beneath the fire's crackle and the gurgling deaths of the guards nearest the other prisoners.

Vol'jin raced into battle, his glaive humming as it spun. His first slash opened a thigh; then he whirled away as the guard turned toward him. The Darkspear came around, his second stroke crushing the troll's head. Vol'jin recognized the delicious scent of hot blood misting in the air and turned, seeking other prey.

Around him the pandaren engaged Zandalari fearlessly, despite the trolls' larger size and fierce weaponry. Sister Quan-li ducked beneath the slash of an axe and stabbed a knife-bladed paw into a troll's throat. The Zandalari wheezed, trying to breathe around a crushed larynx. She then shattered his pointy jaw with a straight punch and dropped him with a roundhouse kick.

Brother Dao had appropriated a spear and engaged a similarly armed troll. The Shado-pan parried every thrust, giving ground with each parry. The Zandalari took this as both a sign of the pandaren's fear and proof that he was winning the fight. This illusion lasted for two more parries, and then Dao swept in, spinning. He snapped the spear's haft against the troll's knee, crumpling it. Another blow caught the troll over the temple. That likely killed him, or at least rendered him senseless, thereby saving him the humiliation of the final spear thrust that pinned him to the ground.

Chen boiled into battle, lacking the precision of the Shado-pan but making up for it through experience. Wielding a stout staff, he blocked an overhand blow with a maul and twisted to let the troll's weapon slide off toward the left. The troll, determined to overpower the smaller pandaren, shoved his maul back in the other direction.

Chen let him, ducking, then hooking a leg behind the troll's. He shoved, simply and easily, dumping the Zandalari on his back. The troll hit heavily. Chen's right foot flashed out, stamping hard on the male's throat. Bones broke, and the brewmaster sailed toward another foe.

Throughout the fight, arrows flew. One of the ropes suspending the prisoner parted with a snap. The man twisted and slammed into the opposite post, hitting the back of his head. A second arrow cut the remaining rope and dropped the man to the ground. The arrow quivered in the post.

The Zandalari recovered from their shock quickly enough. They counterattacked, and two of them snarled as they drove at Vol'jin. One slashed low with a sword. Vol'jin parried it with one blade, then thrust sharply with his glaive's other end. The weapon pierced the troll's chest. As the troll fell back, ribs trapped the blade and ripped it from Vol'jin's grasp.

The other Zandalari yelled in triumph. "You die now, traitor!"

Vol'jin, hands clawed, roared at him.

The Zandalari swung a barbed mace around waist-high. Instead of leaping back, Vol'jin stepped forward. He caught the troll's wrist against his rib cage, then brought his left forearm up and over the Zandalari's forearm. Then Vol'jin pivoted to the right quickly enough to lock the elbow and continued to spin until it snapped. Screaming, the Zandalari dropped to his back.

Vol'jin, reversing his spin, punched down into and through the troll's face.

And as quickly as that, the battle ended. Sister Quan-li cut the prisoners loose. Chen already had reached the tortured man's side. Vol'jin approached but slowed as Chen helped the man to his feet. The man felt the back of his head, and his hand came away bloody, but not terribly so.

The man looked at the pandaren. "Where is he? Where is Tyrathan Khort?"

Vol'jin interceded before Chen could answer. "There be no Tyrathan Khort."

The man faced Vol'jin, his eyes filled with fire. "I may be seeing stars, but I know that shooting. I know the hand that painted and fletched those arrows. Where is he?"

The troll snarled. "He may have prepared those arrows, but Tyrathan Khort be dead."

"I don't believe you."

Vol'jin flashed teeth. "He be dead by my hand. Vol'jin, leader of the Darkspears."

Blood drained from the man's face. "They say you're dead."

"Then we both be ghosts." Vol'jin pointed south with his bloody sword. "Go, before you join us."

Sister Quan-li came to get the man, and the other prisoners joined them. They quickly scavenged supplies from among the trolls' gear, armed themselves, and fled into the mountains.

Chen turned to Vol'jin. "Why did you say he was dead?"

"It be for the best. For them, and for him." Vol'jin wiped his glaive on a dead Zandalari. "Let's move."

Vol'jin, Chen, and the three monks slipped back out of the enclosure. Using some of the branches the Zandalari had cut, they erased signs of the escapees' path and then their own. They headed west, returning to the place where the pandaren had waited while Tyrathan and Vol'jin had spied out the enemy camp.

As they entered the small clearing, a pillar of fire split the night, blinding Vol'jin. Slowly his vision cleared. There, at the far side, a female Zandalari stood flanked by a half dozen archers, arrows nocked and bows drawn. Tyrathan, blindfolded, hands bound behind his back, knelt at her feet.

She grabbed Tyrathan's hair and jerked his head back. "Your pet, Vol'jin, has caused me great discomfort. However, I be in a charitable mood. Lay down your blade, and neither you nor your pandaren playmates need see what happens when my mood, it be souring."

23

nger flashed through Vol'jin at hearing his name on her lips. He stared at the man, who, though trussed up, hardly looked beaten or tortured enough to have given away his identity. Then shame for thinking he had done that followed mockingly. *Tyrathan would not have betrayed me.*

Vol'jin stabbed his glaive into the ground.

The Zandalari inclined her head in a salute. "I would be takin' your word, Darkspear, dat you gonna cause no trouble, but since you've already caused trouble, I gonna be forced to bind your pets. You should be knowing I bear the pandaren no ill will, but not so my hosts."

Vol'jin looked around. "I be seeing no one else."

"Such be our intention. You gonna accompany me, and your luggage gonna be brought along behind." She paused, her eyes tightening for the barest of moments. "You don' recall me, do you?"

He studied her for long enough that she'd think he was making an effort. "I not gonna lie. I do not."

"I didn't expect you would. And thank you for not lying." She led the way down to the outpost and around it. There, in the middle—along with a handful of Zandalari poking and prodding bodies, measuring bowshots with their eyes—were two tall, powerfully built figures. Vol'jin had seen their like before, in visions and nightmares.

"Your hosts."

"The mogu. Rulers of Pandaria." She smiled indulgently. "You do know dis was a trap, yes? Not for you, per se, but for your archer. He vexed me. Setting a trap for him was not difficult."

"And you thought once you had him, you had me?"

"I had my hopes."

They passed to the east, cutting across where the humans and Sister Quan-li would have gone. Vol'jin saw no signs of pursuit. "You're letting the bait go?"

"If they can stay ahead of what I sent after them, certainly." The Zandalari gave him a look. "You can't imagine I would let dem escape. It would suggest weakness to the mogu, and they already believe us weak. If your companions get away, it matters little to me. I'd welcome it, actually. The stories dey tell gonna sow fear among the enemy. That'll be more useful than some Amani army promising to hold our flank."

Vol'jin said nothing, hiding the flicker of surprise at her mentioning Amani allies. "Even if they do escape, they not gonna be believed."

"But it will make for a good tale, an Alliance nobleman rescued from trolls by Vol'jin. A Vol'jin returned from the grave, no less." She led him over to where two grooms held the reins for sleek raptors. Beyond the saddle beasts stood two carts, both clearly of pandaren manufacture but with mushan to draw them.

She pulled herself into the saddle of the red raptor and waited for him to join her on the green-striped one. "Dat beast belonged to the officer you killed. Annoying

I be finding him, hence my willingness to sacrifice him. Ride with me, Vol'jin. Feel what it be to race through this land."

Her raptor leaped forward and shot away rapidly. His responded to heels dug into ribs and set off eagerly in pursuit. At the moment when she had suggested they race, he could think of nothing he wished to do less. As the wind played through his hair, and his body remembered how to shift his weight as the raptor sprinted, old joys rekindled. The speed and the ferocious power of the beast beneath him, coupled with the sense of the land, were intoxicating.

Vol'jin kicked his beast once more in the ribs. The raptor responded, knowing that was a promise of worse if it did not go faster. Claws shredded golden ground cover. Vol'jin leaned forward over the beast's neck, laughing harshly, hoarsely, as he caught his hostess and passed her.

He raced on, giving the raptor its head. It knew where they were going, and Vol'jin didn't care where. Just for that short time in the saddle, he forgot everything: his mission, the Horde, Garrosh, the monastery. With those burdens still back in the bloody dust of the Zandalari outpost, Vol'jin was able to breathe free. He couldn't remember when it was that he'd last felt like that, only that it had been far too long ago.

"Dis way!"

Their course had been taking them toward Mogu'shan Palace, which was nearing the height of its nightly cycle. She reined her mount off to the east and down between two hills. Vol'jin followed, bringing his ride to an end at a long, low building with high-pitched roofs and wings that enclosed a courtyard in the back. He dismounted, tossing the reins to the groom who had taken the same from his hostess, then followed her through the front door.

Khal'ak clapped her hands loudly, and trolls scurried from doorways and halls, heads lowered. Gurubashi mostly, if the tattoos were correct, but clearly serving under a handful of Zandalari.

His hostess pointed at him. "This be Vol'jin of the Darkspears. If you be ignorant of who he be, I gonna break my fast with your heart at dawn. You gonna bathe him and then attire him appropriately."

The foremost of the servants sniffed as she looked at Vol'jin. "He be Darkspear, mistress. He should wallow with pigs and steal clothes from a swineherd."

Vol'jin's hostess moved so fast and struck her so hard that the backhanded slap couldn't have been avoided even if the servant had a week to prepare. "He be shadow hunter. He be revered of the loa. You gonna see to it dat he shines like a god. Tomorrow, when the sun reaches its zenith, if he does not make the mogu weep for his beauty and the Zandalari wail in envy, you all gonna feel my wrath. Go!"

Save for the insensible crone stretched out on the floor, the servants scattered. His hostess turned and smiled slightly. "I trust your pandaren be serving you more faithfully. There be times I think even men like your archer might be more suited to serving. We gonna discuss these things, and others, when you have completed your ablutions and be properly attired."

Vol'jin, though he had no love lost for the Zandalari as a general rule, found her intriguing. "And then you gonna help me remember your name."

"No, my dear Vol'jin." Her smile broadened. "You have no chance of rememberin' because you've never heard it. But later I gonna tell it to you and be giving you good cause never to forget."

Vol'jin would have refused to go along with her having him cleaned up, save that her minions so clearly hated tending to his needs that it tortured them far more than it ever would him. For Zandalari and Gurubashi to wash him, trim his hair and nails, rub unguents into his hands and feet, and then dress him in a fine silken kilt with a raptor-leather belt, their torment had to be all but unendurable. To make matters worse, they were forced to grant him the honor of wearing a small dagger, a ceremonial one, in a sheath bound to his upper-left arm. Such was his right as a shadow hunter. As much as they might like to dismiss him as being from an ill-begotten and disobedient tribe of fallen mongrels, the lowest of them knew they never could have won the honors they now bestowed upon him.

The magic of the place also played on him, convincing him that, indeed, he was due honors and accolades. A small part of him welcomed his hostess's attentions because he had earned consideration. The Gurubashi and Amani may have dismissed the Darkspear with a sneer, but when the Zandalari king Rastakhan had sought to unite all the trolls, Vol'jin had been summoned to represent the Darkspears. He had refused to join the other tribes, noting that the Horde was now his family, but the fact was that he'd still been invited.

Once he'd been prepared, a long-faced servant led him to the central courtyard. A fire blazed at its heart in a simple circle of stones. A small table with two golden goblets and a matching pitcher filled with dark wine stood beside it and back a bit. Two lounging mats had been placed between the table and fire, allowing easy access to refreshments.

She knelt on one mat, poking the fire with a stick, then stood as he entered. She'd changed from leather to silk, a darker blue that caught lighter tones from the Mogu'shan Palace display. A simple gold-linked belt gathered her sleeveless gown at the waist. It had been fashioned from coins minted throughout the known lands and in a variety of eras. The ends dangled as far down as her knees, and he assumed she would simply double-loop it when conquests added more links.

She pointed toward the wine with a hand. "I be offering you refreshment. You be choosing the cup. You pour. I gonna drink from whichever or both. I want you to be knowing I mean you no mischief or deception. You be my guest."

Vol'jin nodded but kept the fire between them. "You pour and choose. You have done me this honor. I gonna trust you."

She poured, but both cups remained untouched on the table. "I be Khal'ak, servant of Vilnak'dor. He be to King Rastakhan what you be to Thrall, and more. He sees to the pandaren situation. Though he be not wholly aware of it, he owes you a great debt."

"How would that be?"

Khal'ak smiled. "Some history first. I served Vilnak'dor and he served our king when Rastakhan allowed Zul to propose all trolls be uniting under one banner. Of all the leaders dere, only you, only Vol'jin of the Darkspears, refused the offer to be joining. As you turned away and stalked off, you walked right past me. I watched you leave. After you'd gone from sight, I be spending a long time studying your footprints in the sand. I wondered which would erode first: Zul's dreams or your footprints."

She glanced down into the fire for a moment. "So I found myself surprised, dere at Zouchin, when one of my warriors be showing me a footprint I recognized so easily. By that time, of course, our spies within the Horde had passed on stories of your disappearance. The rumors about you do you great credit. Most of the Horde believes dat you perished performin' a secret mission of ultimate importance for their benefit. You be widely mourned. And, yet, dere be those who claim you've been murdered."

Vol'jin raised an eyebrow. "No one be considering that I have survived?"

Khal'ak picked up the goblets and approached, offering him equal choice. "There be lunatics who suppose that, and the odd shaman who be claiming you have ascended to be one of the loa. A few pray to you, and some have had a tattoo of a dark spear inked into their flesh. Usually flank or inside of the biceps, since the orcs do not favor such displays."

He accepted one of the goblets. "And your master be enjoying himself a ghost story? This be why he should thank me?"

"Oh, no, he owes you far more greatly." She sipped her wine, then turned. She walked to her lounging mat casually, the muscles of her lean body fluid beneath the silk. She knelt, almost like a supplicant before a god, then drank. "Please, join me."

Vol'jin did, returning his wine to the table before sitting. "Your master?"

"One thing, Vol'jin. I do you the honor of supposing you are not a fool. You gonna learn many things in our conversation, many important things. Understand that I be fully aware I am sharing them with you. I do have a purpose. I gonna treat with you honestly. Ask, and if I be able, I will respond."

He took up his goblet again and drank. The dark wine tasted of fruit and spices, some from Kalimdor, but more from Pandaria. He liked it yet did not let it put him at ease. "You were saying . . ."

"The mogu be arrogant and disdainful. Their experience of trolls is based on stories from before their empire disintegrated. What dey have seen since be Zandalari who control a fraction of what we did before, and other trolls that they be viewing as degraded creatures. And those be the trolls who fight with us. The mogu's experience of the few dat be fighting with the Horde only confirms their biases.

"And then there be Zouchin and you." She sipped her wine, licking her lips after. "I didn't know it was you, of course, and little dared hope after hearin' of your death. I was assuming the more sinister rumors be true, given dat you refused Garrosh more robustly than you did my king. I was thinking only the Horde could kill you, and now I see dat I was wrong."

Vol'jin did not answer her with words, but lifted his chin enough for her to see the scar at his throat.

"Yes. I wondered. Your voice be not as I be remembering it." Khal'ak smiled. "Our Alliance guests have also heard of your death. Relieved they be, most of them. Many a nightmare of which you be the author be vanished. For now, at least.

"But, back to the mogu. For a troll and a man to have beset us, dis amused them greatly. And yet, your elusiveness be suggesting a power that impresses them. As I was settin' the trap for this evening—and they greatly enjoyed the display, though your pandaren underlings and their presence disturbed them—I hoped I might be catching you. If not with the group, then at least meeting you in exchange for the life of your pets."

"Because?"

"Because I be wishin' you to join us. This would be impressing the mogu and suggesting dat we have powerful influence within the rest of the world. In their view, all we have done be to awaken their sleeping king. They, in their arrogance, ignore the fact that this service be not one they'd managed in the millennia since their empire crumbled. To have a man and a troll beset us so reflected our weakness, the loss of vitality in our blood. For you to be joining us, this would be grand."

Vol'jin frowned. "You were there. I already refused the Zandalari offer."

"Dis be not the same offer, Shadow Hunter, nor be it the same world." She reached out, a finger caressing the scar at his throat and again the one on his side. "Then you claimed the Horde be your family. They have rejected you. Garrosh, small-spirited and smaller-minded, slew the one troll who could have advised him through the maelstrom that be coming. You owe him no allegiance. Your people be the Darkspears, and we be willin' to make them first among the tribes.

"Yes, the Gurubashi gonna moan. The Amani gonna wail. They gonna point to their histories, and I gonna point out their failures. For the Darkspears be the one tribe that has remained true to itself. That you have not risen to rule an empire be not because you could not but because you have not chosen dat course. Having strived and lost, as they have, does not sanctify the effort. Dey wish glory for work done centuries ago and work undone a short time later."

She lifted her chin, her gaze meeting his, her eyes ablaze with the future's promise. "So this be my offer to you, Vol'jin Darkspear of the Darkspears. Be to me what you were to Thrall. Assume your full power as the shadow hunter your people need. Your people: the Darkspears and the trolls. Together we gonna show the world their folly and again bring order to lands which have languished in its absence."

Vol'jin lifted his cup. "This be a great honor, and an offer that only a fool would refuse."

24

"And one only a fool would be acceptin' on my words alone," said Khal'ak.

"You be persuasive."

"And you be kind." She laughed easily. "I do have things I need to know, of course. How be it dat I be findin' you in the company of pandaren, with a man helping you oppose us?"

Vol'jin watched her face for a moment. "Chen Stormstout you know of. He be a friend of long standing. He found me after the Horde was done with me. The monks, who your mogu allies hate, took me in and healed me. They had done the same with the man."

He drank a bit more wine. "As for opposing you, when I saw an invasion, thinking on who be invading never occurred. I be just repaying a kindness to my benefactors."

Khal'ak cocked her head. "'When I saw,' you said. Then the Silk Dancer gave you visions as well."

Vol'jin nodded. "I thought it might be she."

"Yes. Ever our patron, she be not pleased with our renewing our ties with the mogu. There were, in the past, I gather, some of our warriors who came to favor the mogu magic, so dey abandoned her. That cultus be long since gone, but she be robust in her remembering." Khal'ak stared into her wine's dark depths. "It does not surprise me she be willing to stir up a little trouble now to avoid much trouble later."

"You get the same visions I do, and you ignore them?"

"I be finding solutions to dem."

"And I be such a solution?"

"You be more than a solution, Vol'jin." She leaned in, lowering her voice. "You offer much, and your reward will be equal to your service. For example, right now your brave little band has shown our troops that being Zandalari does not make us arrow-proof. More important, it has reminded the mogu how deadly their former slaves can be. Dat we captured them be goin' much to our credit. Again, thank you."

The Darkspear sat back. "If I prove to be such a benefit, do you not fear that your master will be eliminating you and raising me in your place?"

"No. He fears you. He be lacking the spine you showed in refusing the king's request. He gonna keep me to keep you under control." She smiled shyly. "And I do not fear you betraying me because the way I gonna keep you under control is to control your friends. Chen Stormstout I do be recognizing. The man, no, but your regard for him be evident."

"The need for coercion be undercutting your offer of trust."

"No, I just wish a brake on your actions until you have a full chance to be considerin' what I offer. I be mindful of your refusal to join us in the past and your rejecting of Garrosh's dictates. You be principled, which be a wonderful trait. It be one I value." She set her cup aside and knelt there with her hands open in her lap. "If you be joining us with your full and open cooperation, I will free your companions."

"And not be setting hunters after them as you did the others?"

"Had we bargained for their safety, no one would be pursuing them." She raised a hand. "But, again, dis be not a decision for you to make now. Your companions gonna be comfortable—not enjoyin' the luxuries I offer you, but comfortable." Khal'ak smiled. "And, tomorrow, you gonna see firsthand what the mogu bring to our partnership. Once you be having your eyes opened to dat, you gonna see why my offer be most generous and gonna be worth serious consideration."

Their conversation turned to things more banal. Vol'jin had no doubt that had he so inclined himself, she would have slept with him. She would have seen intimacy as a way to encourage his cooperation—but only in someone of inferior intellect. She had not taken him for a fool, so she'd know he was bedding her simply to make her believe he was easily manipulable. She would distrust that and him.

On the other hand, refraining gave Vol'jin some measure of power over her. Competent though she might be, she was also clearly infatuated with him. She'd not have remembered the impression of his foot in sand from years ago were that not so. She would want consummation of their relationship simply to justify her years of interest in him.

He could use that, no matter which way he replied to her offer.

They spoke for a while longer, then slept in the

courtyard under the open sky. Vol'jin woke with the first hints of dawn lightening the dark vault above. He hardly felt rested but wasn't fatigued. Nervous energy was making up for his lack of sleep.

After a simple breakfast of smoked golden carp and sweet rice cakes, the servants again tended to his and Khal'ak's bodily needs. Then they mounted raptors and headed back toward the southwest. Khal'ak said nothing. She sat on a raptor well and looked magnificent as the wind tugged at her hair and cloak. In that image Vol'jin saw the Zandalari as they saw themselves. This erased all doubt in his mind as to why they so often sought to reclaim what they had lost before. *To know how far you have fallen and to fear never to reach that point again would devour one from within.*

They headed for a tall, stoop-shouldered mountain and rode around it. Here things had gone to ruin, though not through natural aging. The area had been broken by war long ago. Though weather might have washed away blood and soot, and golden plants buried bones and detritus, the remains of arches marked the violence that had shattered them.

As they came up the road through the mountains, dim though the day was, Pandaria's majesty made the place beautiful despite the signs of destruction. Vol'jin felt he had been here before, though it could have been that he understood from his time in Orgrimmar the power that had once resided here. While the Darkspears were content with modest dwellings that served their purposes, he recognized the needs of others to prove their superiority through grand works. He'd heard of the tall statues at Ironforge and Stormwind, and knew this place would similarly memorialize the mogu past.

The mogu did not disappoint.

The road led to a rough-hewn opening in the mountainside, providing the glimpse of a massive gray statue on a bronze base. The statue depicted a mogu warrior standing tall, his hands on the haft of a huge mace. Reduced to normal proportions, the weapon would have defied Garrosh's ability to lift it. Though the statue's impassive mask provided no clue as to the personality of the mogu, the weapon spoke of power, cruelty, and the desire to crush all opposition.

Khal'ak and Vol'jin did not enter the tomb, for in the distance, proceeding toward them at a stately pace, came a parade. Zandalari troops with pennants flying from spears led the procession. Behind them, in an elegant pandaren coach drawn by kodos, a half dozen Zandalari flanked three mogu. Behind them came a smaller coach with a dozen Zandalari witch doctors. Fourth, right before the Zandalari troops bringing up the rear, came a rickety wagon bearing Chen, Tyrathan, the three monks, and four humans, all male. Wood creaked and draft beasts grunted as their hooves thunderously shook the ground.

When the procession stopped before the tomb, the witch doctors took possession of the prisoners and hustled them within. Zandalari and their mogu hosts followed. Khal'ak snapped commands to the captain leading the remaining troops. They fanned out to take up defensive positions as she and Vol'jin stepped into the tomb's dark precincts.

One of the mogu—a Spiritrender, if Vol'jin would have been forced to guess—pointed two fingers at the prisoners. The Zandalari witch doctors brought Dao and Shan forward, positioning them at the near-left and far-right corners of the statue's base. The mogu pointed again, and two men were hauled into position at the other two corners.

Vol'jin felt a wave of shame for Tyrathan. The pandaren monks held their heads high as their captors led them to their positions. They didn't have to be shoved or coerced. The monks had a quiet dignity about them, completely denying the reality of what they had to know would happen. The men, on the other hand, whether lacking balance or being possessed of an acute sense of their own mortality, wept and had to be dragged into place. One could not stand and had to be held upright by two Zandalari. The other blubbered and urinated on himself.

Khal'ak half turned to Vol'jin and whispered, "I tried convincin' the mogu dat all they needed were men, but when they saw the Shado-pan fighting, they insisted. I was able to make Chen and your man off-limits, but . . ."

Vol'jin nodded. "Leadership be demanding uneasy decisions."

The mogu Spiritrender approached Brother Dao at the near-left corner. With one hand, the Spiritrender yanked the monk's head back, exposing his throat. With the other, using a single talon, the mogu stabbed Dao's throat—not a killing blow, not anything more than annoying. The nail came away heavy with a droplet of pandaren blood.

The mogu touched the drop to the corner of the bronze pedestal. A tiny gout of flame shot up. It shrank again into a small blue guttering tongue.

The Spiritrender moved next to the man at the front. His blood drop, when deposited at the corner, caused a small geyser of water to spurt upward. It calmed down into a tiny puddle. Its surface rippled in time with the flame's dance.

The mogu then came around to the second man. His blood produced a small cyclone, red in hue. It became invisible after that, save for the slight flutter it introduced to the man's dirty robe. Again, the flutter matched the water's ripple.

Last the mogu came to Brother Shan. The monk lifted his own chin, exposing his throat. The mogu took his blood, and when it touched the bronze, Vol'jin interpreted the resulting volcanic eruption as being fueled by Shan's anger. The molten earth did not quiet but continued to flow. It extended in lines toward the water and the cyclone.

Air, fire, and water also expanded. Where they met, they warred. The power of their collisions rose straight up in semitransparent, opalescent walls of force. They shot to the roof, quartering the statue. Sharp thunder sounded. Cracks appeared in the stone, huge rents as keen as those that remained on the broken stones outside. They radiated out like roots from a tree, and as Vol'jin figured it, when that statue collapsed, the tomb itself would be filled to a depth of ten feet.

Enough to bury us all.

But the statue didn't collapse. The energy lines shrank back down and drew into the cracks. For a handful of heartbeats, they coalesced at the center, where the mogu's heart would have been. They pulsed twice, maybe four times; then energy pumped out through invisible veins. An opalescent blush suffused the entire statue, and beneath it the statue cracked and cracked again. It was as if the glow put the statue under incredible pressure, like a millstone grinding it into dust.

And yet the power let it retain its shape.

Then, from ankle and wrist, an ethereal tendril flicked

out. It looked like fog. It wrapped around Brother Dao's face. The monk had thrown his head back to scream, and the fog flowed into his body. In the blink of an eye, the glow had surrounded him. And crushed him like a grape.

The slurry of what Brother Dao had been flowed back up through the tendril. Only after his horror ended did Vol'jin notice that the other three had vanished as well. The glow returned to the statue and grew brighter. It pulsed and intensified. Two spots burned where the eyes had been.

Then the magic contracted in a rippling series of pops and cracks. As the glow blazed, heat flared, then dropped off abruptly. The outline began to shrink. At the same time, the statue's arms spread. Lifeless stone compressed itself into thick muscles sliding beneath black skin. The light drew itself into the statue, the flesh healing along the jagged lines where stone had broken. It left no scars, only a peerless mogu warrior, naked and invincible, standing on a bronze dais.

The other two mogu hurried forward. They both dropped to a knee before him. With bowed heads, one offered a thick golden cloak trimmed in black. The other held up a golden baton of office. The mogu took the baton first, then stepped to the floor and allowed the other mogu to dress him.

Vol'jin studied the mogu's face intensely. He assumed that were he dragged out of the grave after millennia, he might be unguarded in his first few moments as he assessed what had happened. He caught a flicker of contempt when the warlord saw Zandalari present, and pure fury at a pandaren presence.

The warlord took a step toward where Chen and Brother Cuo stood, but centuries of death had made him a bit slow. Khal'ak interposed herself between him and the prisoners. As Vol'jin stood beside her and back one step, he realized that she'd chosen their vantage point for the ceremony anticipating this eventuality.

She bowed but did not go to a knee. "Warlord Kao, I be welcoming you in the name of General Vilnak'dor. He awaits your pleasure at the Isle of Thunder, where he resides with your resurrected master."

The mogu looked her up and down. "Killing pandaren will honor my master and will not delay us."

Khal'ak gestured with an open hand toward Vol'jin. "But it would be spoiling the gift Shadow Hunter Vol'jin Darkspear wishes to make of these two to your master. If it be pandaren you wish to slay, I gonna arrange a hunt as we travel. But dese two be promised."

Kao and Vol'jin exchanged glances. The warlord understood what was happening but was not prepared to deal with it at the moment. The hatred flaring in his dark eyes, however, informed Vol'jin that his part in this play of manners would not be forgiven.

The mogu warlord nodded. "I wish to kill a pandaren for every year I have been in the grave, and two for every year my master has been dead. Arrange it, troll, unless your shadow hunter has promised more of them to my master."

Vol'jin's eyes narrowed. "Warlord Kao, you would be slaying thousands upon thousands. Your empire fell for the want of pandaren labor. What you want may be just. The result would be tragic. Much has changed, my lord."

Kao snorted and turned away, stalking off to where the other mogu stood with Zandalari officials.

Khal'ak cautiously exhaled. "Well played."

"And you, for anticipating him." Vol'jin shook his head. "He gonna demand the lives of Chen and Cuo."

"I know. The monk I gonna likely have to give him. The mogu be hatin' the Shado-pan to the depths of their dark souls. I gonna find another to replace Chen. To the mogu, they all be lookin' alike anyway."

"If he discovers the deception, you gonna be killed."

"As you and Chen and your human gonna be." Khal'ak smiled. "Like it or not, Vol'jin Darkspear, our fortunes now be hopelessly intertwined."

25

"Which means some discomfort for me. It be unavoidable," said Vol'jin.

Khal'ak turned to regard him as troops guided the prisoners out and loaded them back on their wagon. "Meaning?"

"Kao is angry at being defied. Your master fears me. If I be traveling to this Isle of Thunder unfettered, their feelings gonna be encouraged." Vol'jin shrugged. "You be needing to demonstrate control over me. I be still a prisoner. I must be treated as such."

She considered for a moment, then nodded. "Plus this gonna put you close to your friends, so you can see after dem."

"I would be hoping any generosity that extends to me might be shared."

"They gonna be in irons. I gonna find you shackles of gold."

"Acceptable."

She held out a hand. "Your dagger."

Vol'jin smiled. "Of course. After we have ridden back."

"Of course."

Vol'jin allowed himself to enjoy his freedom on the

return ride to Khal'ak's home. The clouds, as if embarrassed by their inability to match Kao for darkness, lightened. The vale again returned to its golden luster. *Were I trapped in a tomb for centuries, this be the place I'd welcome for resurrecting.*

Khal'ak kept him in her home. True to her word, she produced golden shackles with thick chains linking them. They proved heavier than iron, but she gave him enough chain that he could move freely. She also gave him great freedom, posting no guard, but then they both knew he'd not run while Chen and Tyrathan were being held with other prisoners.

Khal'ak and Vol'jin spent the time constructively, discussing the forthcoming conquest of Pandaria. The decision to refrain from using goblin cannons in taking Zouchin had been hers. Vilnak'dor had disagreed and ordered cannons and gunpowder for the invasion. She felt it was a sign of weakness, but the mogu had made good use of them in the past, so her master said their purpose would honor their allies.

The mogu, it appeared, had done a bit more than daydream since their empire fell. Khal'ak felt they'd done little that could be considered constructive, but despite being unorganized, they had been breeding. The plan for the invasion was straightforward enough. Zandalari troops would support mogu troops in securing the heart of Pandaria, at which point, the mogu apparently believed, everything would magically reset like jihui pieces at the start of a game.

She assumed that the Zandalari would defend the mogu holdings until they organized themselves. Then they would strike at the Alliance or Horde, eliminating it before crushing the remaining faction. The mantid to the west had always been a problem and would be saved for last. Then the mogu empire could use its magic to support the Zandalari in their reconquest of Kalimdor, then the other half of the sundered continent.

In the morning, they set out again, and early this time. The nightly festivities at Mogu'shan Palace had been muted, so everyone was up early for fear that any tardiness would displease Warlord Kao. Vol'jin was allowed to ride a raptor, with his golden chains on full display. Chen, Cuo, Tyrathan, and other prisoners came on in wagons. Vol'jin saw little of them until they reached Zouchin, where he found himself being loaded onto a smaller ship and placed belowdecks in a cabin that was locked from the outside.

His three companions, dirty from the road and bloody from abuses, smiled nonetheless when Vol'jin ducked his head to get through the hatch. Chen clapped his paws. "Just like you to be a prisoner and have chains of gold."

"They still be chains." Vol'jin bowed to Cuo. "I be sorry for the loss of your brothers."

The monk returned the bow. "I am happy for their courage."

Tyrathan looked up at him. "Who is the female? Why . . . ?"

"We gonna have time to discuss that, but I be having a question for you, my friend. The truth. It be important."

The man nodded. "Ask."

"Did Chen tell you what I said to the man we freed?"

"That I was dead. That you'd killed me? Yes." Tyrathan half smiled. "Nice to know that nothing less than the Horde's elite could kill me. But that wasn't the question you wanted me to answer."

"No." Vol'jin frowned. "The man was wanting to

know where you were. Fearing and hoping, that be what he was. He wanted you breathing, saving him, and was terrified that you were. Why?"

The man fell silent for a bit, picking at one dirty fingernail with another. He didn't look up before he began to speak. "You were in my skin at Serpent's Heart, when the Sha of Doubt's energy touched me. You saw the man who gave me my orders. The man you saved was Morelan Vanyst, his nephew. My father was a huntsman before me, his before him, and we've always been in service to the Vanyst family. Bolten Vanyst, my lord, is a vain man with a scheming harridan of a wife. This is why he is a great comfort to Stormwind—if there is a campaign, he is all for it since it takes him away. Not that he is not manipulative himself. He has only three daughters, each married to an ambitious man with the promise of his realm if they please him. Yet, when he leaves, it's Morelan who is regent."

Vol'jin watched emotions play over the man's face as he spoke. Pride shone brightly at his family's service, only to be swallowed by disgust for his master's family drama. Tyrathan had clearly served as best as he was able, but a master such as Bolten Vanyst could never truly be satisfied or trusted. Not unlike Garrosh.

"With anyone else, the Sha of Doubt would have ripped them wide open. They'd have doubted their worthiness to live. They would have doubted their own minds and memories. They would have unmade themselves in the blink of an eye, unable to make a decision because the sha would convince them each choice was wrong. Like a mule placed between two equally appetizing piles of hay, they'd starve amid plenty simply because they could not make a choice."

The man finally looked up, weariness softening his

shoulders and etching years onto his face. "To me, the Sha of Doubt came as a candle in the darkness of my life. I doubted everyone else and, in that instant, saw the truth of everything."

Vol'jin nodded encouragingly but remained silent.

"I have a daughter, just four years old. Last time I was home, she wanted to tell me a story at her bedtime. She told me of a shepherdess who had to deal with an evil huntsman and did so with the aid of a kindly wolf. I recognized the story and put the altering of roles down to the influence of some Gilnean refugees who have taken up residence in our town. But when the sha touched me, I saw the truth.

"My wife was that shepherdess, so kind and so gentle, so innocent and loving. Oddly enough, I met her when I went out to destroy a pack of wolves preying on her flock. What she saw in me, I am not certain. For me, she was perfection. I pursued her and won her. She is the greatest prize of my life.

"Unfortunately, I am a killer. I kill to provide for my family. I kill to keep my nation safe. I create nothing. I just destroy things. That fact ate at her soul. It terrified her, knowing that if killing came so easily to me, I could kill anything. My life and what I had become were slowly leaching away her love of life."

The man shook his head. "The truth, my friends, is that she was right. In my absences, as I attended to my duties, she and Morelan became close. His wife died in childbirth years ago. His son is friends with my children. My wife has been a caretaker. I suspected nothing or, perhaps, wanted to see nothing because if I did see, I'd know he'd been a better father to my children and a better husband to my wife than I was."

Tyrathan gnawed his lower lip for a moment. "When I saw him, I knew he'd decided, on hearing of my death, that he needed to prove he could be brave too. So he came to Pandaria, and his uncle used him like any other playing piece. His escape will prove all that needs proving. He will be a hero. He can go home and be with his family."

"But they be your family." Vol'jin studied the man's face. "You still be loving them?"

"Completely." The man ran his hands over his face. "The idea of never seeing them again will kill me by degrees."

"And yet you gonna surrender your happiness for theirs?"

"I've always done what I've done to give them a good life." He looked up. "This is perhaps for the best. You've seen me. You saw my shooting that night. Part of me was shooting better than I ever have just so Morelan would know it was me. Killing is what I do, Vol'jin, and I do it very well. Well enough to kill my family."

"This be a very difficult decision you've made."

"I question it every day, but I will not turn back." Tyrathan's green eyes narrowed. "Why this line of questioning?"

"I, too, have a very difficult decision to be making. Similar to yours but of a bit greater magnitude." The troll sighed heavily. "No matter my choice, nations gonna bleed and people gonna die."

Proving themselves to be better friends than he felt he deserved, Vol'jin's three companions contented themselves with the knowledge that he would share more with them when he was ready to do so. *They trust me to make the right decision. I gonna. And I gonna bear the consequences. But they are not mine alone to bear.*

The Zandalari crew took some delight in tormenting Vol'jin, but within limits. They served decent food for the four prisoners, coming out of the same pot, but they served the two pandaren and the man first. Vol'jin got the leavings, which were not much, burned to the bottom of the pot and cold by the time he ate. If his companions balked, no one would eat, so Vol'jin encouraged them to get their fill.

Likewise, they were taken up on deck for some fresh air at noon, whereas he was placed at the bow before dawn and the ship turned so crashing waves would soak him. Vol'jin endured the water and bitterly cold winds without complaint, secretly pleased that the time he'd taken to become accustomed to the chilliness in the monastery served him well.

It helped more that while he stood there, the Zandalari themselves retreated to warmer and drier places.

Vol'jin chanced to be on deck when the ship arrived at the Isle of Thunder. The harbor facilities looked newer than anything else and bore signs of Zandalari construction. To the left, crews appeared to be moving gunpowder and other supplies to warehouses. He couldn't tell if the low buildings were full or empty, but even half-full they would keep an army in good supply for a long time. He suspected, since they were arriving with Warlord Kao, that supplies just being off-loaded would soon be reloaded, preparatory to a trip to Zouchin.

Once their ship had docked, the four prisoners were hustled down the gangway and into a cart drawn by oxen. It was really little more than a hay rig, but sailcloth had been used to shroud it, so the prisoners lay together in close darkness. The canvas had a few worn spots that were enlarged into holes with a thumb. Vol'jin and the others studied the island as the wagon made its way along roads paved with more broken stones than whole.

To his frustration, Vol'jin could see far too little, which conveyed far too much. Given that he'd been on deck when they arrived, it should have been midmorning. Instead, it seemed an hour past midnight, with the only useful illumination coming through lightning flashes. The lightning revealed a soggy, swampy landscape in which every patch of dry ground featured a troop tent or pavilion. He could read some of the standards as they traveled and found them more varied than he liked.

It could have been that the Zandalari had arranged a charade by putting so many tents along the route for their wagon, but Vol'jin doubted it. The need for such deception wouldn't occur to the Zandalari. They'd never believe an enemy who had gotten this far would ever be able to escape with the false data, and they didn't think any enemy could stand against them. Deception under those conditions was simply a dishonorable waste of time.

A foolish thing to be thinking, but they might well be right. While what Vol'jin knew of the Horde presence in Pandaria was months old, and Tyrathan's information was even older, the sheer numbers of Zandalari and allied trolls might be enough to drive the others back into the sea. Played well, and Khal'ak would see to it that they were, the Horde and Alliance might even be induced to turn on each other—or intensify their efforts against each other—guaranteeing success for Zandalari plans.

And if they gonna succeed, this tips the balance of my decision.

The cart trundled on slowly to their destination. This turned out to be a hastily erected detention cage, with strap-iron bars on a lockable door that looked as if it had been salvaged from one of the ships and pressed into service. The cage had been placed on a small hillock in a swamp, the only virtue of which was that a stinking moat separated the prisoners from their nearest guards.

Before Vol'jin could be tossed in with his three comrades, a coach arrived and carried him swiftly along a high road snaking through the swamp. One soldier drove; the other stood on the groom's board at the rear. They quickly made their way to a stone building set near a low, dark complex to the northeast.

His guards conveyed him inside. There he reacquainted himself with Khal'ak's servants. They did their thorough job of making him presentable, including the removal of the gold chains and the return of his ceremonial dagger. Then back into the carriage and on to the larger building, with paired quilen statues warding the front door and Khal'ak waiting for him.

"Good, you be quite presentable." She gave him a quick embrace. "Kao be in talking to the Thunder King now. If there be saving to be done of you and your friends— again, my apologies over the monks—my master will be having to intercede."

Khal'ak guided him through twists and turns that defied his ability to catalog. He didn't feel any magic at work but couldn't discount it. He suspected the complex had been cunningly restored to welcome the Thunder King back from the grave. The layout likely had significance and resonance for the mogu emperor, feeling familiar to him. It would ease his transition back into a world that had forgotten him, a world that would be given cause to dread his return.

Two guards snapped to attention beside a portal as Khal'ak swept into the room. At the far end waited Vilnak'dor, attired in mogu-style robes clearly tailored to fit his expansive girth. The Zandalari general had gone so far as to bleach his hair white, then have it curled in the manner of the mogu. It looked to Vol'jin as if he'd even started growing his fingernails into talons.

Khal'ak paused and bowed. "My lord, may I present—"

"I know who dis be. I be smelling his stench before he got here." The Zandalari leader waved her introduction aside. "Tell me, Vol'jin Run-in-Fear, why I shouldn't be killin' you where you stand."

The Darkspear smiled. "In your position, I probably would be doing just that."

26

Vilnak'dor stared at him, his eyes as wide as if they'd been trapped behind some pilfered gnomish goggles. "You would?"

"Certainly. It would appease Warlord Kao." Vol'jin opened his hands. "Your dress. Your styling. Clearly keeping the mogu happy be your primary concern. Killing me would help." The Darkspear let the Zandalari's gasped disbelief hang in the air for a moment, then continued. "It would also be a gross error. It would be costing you victory."

"Would it?"

"Absolutely." Vol'jin kept his voice low and as ragged as it had first been during his recovery. "The Horde believes me dead. Murdered. People know I have survived. If you be killing me and claim it, the Darkspears gonna never join. Your king's dream of one pan-troll empire be dead. You also be setting the Horde against you. You be freeing Garrosh from internal dissent. While I live, he be fearing my telling the truth of what happened. Khal'ak knows. Rumors run rife. I be the arrow that can be shot into Garrosh's heart when the time comes."

"An arrow in his heart or a thorn in my side?"

"A thorn in many sides." The shadow hunter smiled carefully. "You use me and my position to be goading the Gurubashi and Amani to do more. You use me as a promise of advancement for the smaller tribes. Motivation through fear works, but only if hope be balancing it."

The old Zandalari general's eyes narrowed. "I would elevate the Darkspears as an example. That would be your price?"

"Not too steep. You would bring in the Darkspears when your king could not."

Temptation again widened the old troll's eyes. "But can I be trusting you?"

Khal'ak nodded. "He be motivated, my lord."

Vol'jin bowed his head solemnly. "Not just because you hold three companions of mine. My choices be narrowed. The leader of the Horde had me murdered. There be no power there for me. The Darkspears, while loyal, be too small to stand alone against the Horde or your efforts. I knew that before I saw the mogu. The pandaren been strong enough in the past, but now? They be requiring a man and me in opposing you."

"And yet, for you, personally, Vol'jin, what would you be wishing from dis?" Vilnak'dor spread his arms. "Would you be supplantin' me? Would you be rising to rule the Zandalari?"

"If I desired that much power, I would rule in Orgrimmar from a throne wet with orc blood. That path, that desire, be blocked from me." Vol'jin patted the dagger bound to his upper-left arm. "You be heir to the Zandalari heritage. Zandalari traditions be shaping you. They be defining your destiny. So I be heir to an ancient tradition. I be shadow hunter. The Zandalari were in their infancy while my tradition had matured for a long while.

"My choices be defined by the loa. The loa want what be best for their people. If Elortha no Shadra had told me that your death be best for trolls, this little dagger would already be pinning your eye to the inside of your skull."

Vilnak'dor tried to retain his composure, but crossing his arms over his chest betrayed him. "Be that what—"

"She be sending visions, expressing displeasure, General, but not demanding I kill you." Vol'jin pressed his hands together. "She be reminding me of my responsibility. My life, my desires, be hers to command. Trolls again dominant, a return to the older traditions, these be making her happy. Serving you serves her. If you gonna have me."

The sincere tone of Vol'jin's last statement gave the Zandalari pause. He smiled indulgently, his hands tugging on the loose ends of the knotted sash of gold silk. His expression contracted into one Vilnak'dor clearly considered to be reflective of sagacity and deliberation.

And yet he be doing this while dressed up like a child in mogu clothing, in a room built to mogu proportions. With the tall windows as a backdrop, thick casement carvings, and images chiseled into the walls, the very decor diminished Vilnak'dor. Why Rastakhan would have sent him, Vol'jin could not imagine, unless it was that this general was least likely to offend the mogu. He also had to imagine that Vilnak'dor was not the only high-ranking of the Zandalari involved in the invasion.

But he be the one I have to deal with.

"What you have said be demanding thought, Darkspear." Vilnak'dor nodded. "Your status as shadow hunter be considerable, and your political assessment valuable. I gonna think on dese things."

"As it be pleasing you, my lord." Vol'jin bowed in the

pandaren fashion, then withdrew behind Khal'ak. They paced through the darkened corridors, their footsteps but whispers echoed through the shadowed vaults. They remained silent until they reached the steps and stood between the stone quilen.

Vol'jin faced her with an open expression. "You be realizing we gonna have to kill him. You be right that he fears me. He be fearing a shadow hunter more."

"Which be why he gonna be forced to have you eliminated." She frowned. "Nothing so clumsy as Garrosh's attempt. He gonna want the Darkspears brought in first; then he can do away with you. A note you write before your death gonna commend him and name him, or his puppet, as your heir."

"I agree. This be giving us time."

"He'll be letting you languish in prison for several days, then free you so you'll be grateful."

Vol'jin nodded. "Giving you time to prepare."

Before she could say anything to that, Warlord Kao strode through the door. He still wore the cloak he'd been given but had added to it tall boots, gold silk pants, a black silk tunic, and a belt of gold. He stopped, not out of surprise but on purpose.

So he stalked us.

"My master has promised me that I may slay as many pandaren as I desire. They are flawed creatures, and we shall make better. Then they shall be eliminated." The mogu bared white teeth. "Including your companions, troll."

"Your master's wisdom deserves honoring." Vol'jin bowed, not deeply or long, but he did bow.

The mogu snorted. "I know you, troll. Your kind. You understand only power. Watch and learn to fear my master's power."

Warlord Kao spread his arms wide, but not in a gesture of someone gathering power. Instead, he was a host, a master of a faire, presenting the delights his guests would enjoy inside. As his hands opened, taking in the quilen, the beasts moved. The stone didn't crack as it had during his resurrection. That magic had been inferior, trivial stuff compared to this. The Thunder King's power instantly transmuted gray stone into living flesh, and hollow-eyed creatures into hungry monsters.

Kao laughed. The quilen, like hounds called to the huntsman, spun on their pedestals and came to sit flanking him. "Your pandaren did not build this. With all the time they have had, they never could have built anything this elegant. The Thunder King raised this himself, through his dreams. Now that he is returned to us, he will raise his empire again. There is no force on this world which can stop him, and no force which can deny him anything he desires."

"Then only a fool would be opposing him." Vol'jin bowed more respectfully. "And I be no fool."

Once Kao withdrew, Khal'ak sighed deeply. "He be not an enemy I would have wished to cultivate."

"My mistake."

"A temporary misstep, which can be remedied." She moved to Vol'jin and removed the ceremonial dagger. "I gonna convince Vilnak'dor that you are the key to success. He gonna free you. Until den . . ."

The Darkspear smiled and lifted his hands to be bound again in the golden chains. "I be troll. I can be very patient."

Khal'ak kissed his cheek before turning him over to the guards. "Soon, Shadow Hunter, very soon."

● ● ●

Vol'jin's companions drew back from the cage's door as per Zandalari command, then welcomed him once the guards had gone away. They asked him to tell them everything. He did, starting with Khal'ak's offer to him and continuing to his conversation with the Zandalari leader and Kao's display of power.

Cuo said nothing. Chen remained uncharacteristically quiet. The man reached up, gripping the cage's overhead bars. "I can't fault your reasoning."

Vol'jin regarded him closely. "You made your decision to remain dead because, no matter how painful, it be best for your family, yes?"

"Right."

"And you made that decision because you be looking at life as it truly be, not as you imagined it or wished it be, yes?"

Tyrathan nodded. "As I said, I can't fault your logic."

Vol'jin squatted, lowering his voice. "To be doing the best for family, one must be acting on the truth, not illusion. This be, this will ever be, the Zandalari problem."

Chen crept a bit closer. "I don't understand."

"You should be seeing, my friend. You've seen firsthand. You be knowing the Darkspears. You been among us. You have seen our heart. The Zandalari, the Gurubashi, and the Amani, they be looking down on us. They be thinking we have accomplished nothing while they be raising empires and losing them. The Gurubashi be thinking they could exterminate us. They failed. They failed to be seeing the truth.

"The Darkspears have survived. We have survived because we be living in the world that is, not in the world we lament having lost. They be measuring everything against a standard that be imagined. They do not know what the past empires were like, not truly. They only be knowing the romantic fantasy of those empires. Their standards be unrealistic, not only because they be based on lies but also because those standards have no place in the world of today."

Seeing Vilnak'dor in mogu clothing, dwarfed by mogu architecture, had crystallized in Vol'jin's mind a thought that had haunted him through dream and vision. If one looked at the whole history of trolls, it could only be seen as a descent from heights. The trolls had once been unified, but since those days, their society had fractured, and then the shards had tried to re-create the imagined glory of the whole. Not only was that impossible, but to make it happen, they preyed upon each other. Even now the Zandalari collected a unity of trolls less to re-form what trolls once had been than to confirm their place at the apex of troll civilization. Each shard, in its drive to shape an empire and dominate the world, did so to prove it was the best.

But all they do confirms they don't believe they be the best.

Vol'jin's father, Sen'jin, had never seen it that way. He'd wanted what was best for the Darkspears. That was for them to be given a home free from fear, where they could see to their wants and needs without stress. For those obsessed with power, the past, and dreams of empire, this seemed a very tiny ambition.

And yet, that ambition be the only seed for empires. Tyrathan had framed it in terms of his wife's fears that all he knew how to do was to kill and destroy. Vol'jin felt she underestimated him, but her assessment certainly applied to the Zandalari and the mogu. A need for revenge drove them, but once they had destroyed all their enemies, what then? Would they be driven to create an idyllic society, or just to find new enemies?

Tyrathan was ready to sacrifice himself for family. Chen would do it in a heartbeat for Li Li and Yalia. Cuo and the Shado-pan would do it for Pandaria. Vol'jin's father had, and Vol'jin himself would. *But who be my family?*

When King Rastakhan's agent, Zul, had tried to gather all the trolls together, Vol'jin had withdrawn and told him that "the Horde be my family." Garrosh's attempt to kill him seemed to put the lie to that statement, but then Vol'jin realized that this act was not in furtherance of the Horde's goals. The murder had been to further Garrosh's goals. That he could murder Vol'jin marked the point of divergence between what the orc wanted and what was good for the Horde.

The Horde be my family. It be my duty to give everything for my family. Vol'jin nodded. Just sitting back in Pandaria, licking his wounds, was letting the Horde suffer. To do that was a betrayal of his family and his responsibilities.

As a troll and as a shadow hunter.

He'd not lied when he told Vilnak'dor that his duty as a shadow hunter was to do what was best for trolls. Joining a bloody effort to attempt to reestablish centuries-old empires was not best for trolls. This was not because it would cost lives; it was because the project had nothing to do with the realities of the world. The Horde was his family. The Darkspears were part of the Horde. The Horde was part of the current reality. The fates of the Horde and of trolls were undeniably tangled together. To act as if that wasn't the truth would be complete folly.

Vol'jin took hold of the golden chain between his hands. "The past be important. We can and must be learning from it, but it cannot shackle us. Ancient empires built by legions would be vanishing if up against a single company of goblin cannoneers. The old ways be valuable, but only as a foundation for the future we choose to be building."

The troll pointed a finger at Tyrathan. "It be like you, my friend. You be good at killing. But you can learn to be good at building—though, I gonna admit, killing be of more use right now. And you, Chen, you desiring a home and family, that be very powerful. Many a warrior has died opposing a fighter who seeks to defend just that. And you, Cuo, and the Shado-pan with your desiring balance. You be the water that lets the ship sail, and the anchor that stops it going too far."

Tyrathan looked at him. "I know you value my skill at killing, but I'm not using it in the employ of the Zandalari."

"I be hoping, my friend, you would be using it in my employ." With a simple twist of his wrist, Vol'jin wrenched apart the soft gold link centering the chain. "They built this prison to hold Zandalari. I be more. I be Darkspear. I be shadow hunter. Time we be informing them just how bad a mistake they've made."

27

Relief came off the others in waves. A tightness in Vol'jin's chest eased. He'd surprised himself when he didn't reject Khal'ak's offer out of hand. He would have liked to believe that his hesitation was simply based on her having power over his friends, but that was no more true than his rejection being because accepting her offer wouldn't save them from Warlord Kao. Hers was an offer he couldn't dismiss without due consideration. Acceptance became impossible until he identified the family for whom he would be fighting.

The troll nodded, keeping his voice low. "Now, the first thing we need to be doing—"

"We have it covered." Tyrathan stared out over his head. "Twelve guards. Eight split into pairs at the four points of the compass. Gurubashi given this detail as punishment. Four more, Zandalari, very young and new, out by the road, where it's a bit warmer, a lot drier, and with fewer bugs."

Vol'jin arched an eyebrow.

"I understand Zandali, remember? Guards complain, and the slurs that pass between the groups are horrible."

Chen stretched. "The door has been set in posts that

are still green. Lock side is solid, but not the hinge side. Bottom screws are almost out, and top screws cracked the wood."

Vol'jin looked at the monk expectantly.

Brother Cuo nodded. "Inspections starting at north in fifteen minutes, with the circuit complete in twenty. Shifts change every eight hours. Next change at midnight, if what Tyrathan has overheard is true."

Vol'jin rested his hands on his thighs, then stood and bowed to them. "You gonna be escaped in two hours."

"Kao wants them dead, and I don't like the view." The man returned the bow. "We were off to find you, mind, maybe kill a Thunder King or two to pass the time."

"The Thunder King has mogu, saurok, and massive quilen for guardians. Magics too. It would be taking an army to be getting an audience with him."

Chen frowned. "Then we run?"

Vol'jin nodded. "If we be about stopping an invasion."

Brother Cuo raised an eyebrow. "Wouldn't killing the Thunder King be more likely to succeed?"

"Remember, emperors command armies, but they not be so good at taking or holding land." Vol'jin smiled coldly. "If we be killing those who would win back his empire, we be hobbling him worse than a return to the grave."

Midnight came and went, and with it the predicted change of guards. The new shift's soldiers settled in quickly enough, wrapping themselves in blankets and cursing duty that left them without a fire. Vol'jin had heard such complaints in every military camp. Complaining about the cold or the food or overweening officers constituted ninety percent of conversation, meant only to stave off boredom or fear. Soldiers fell easily into patterns, and their worlds closed down into a tiny space where nothing existed outside their conversation.

While Tyrathan and Cuo kept watch, Chen and Vol'jin dealt with the door. The pandaren grabbed the bars, intending to push, while the troll grasped the post to twist. They would apply steady pressure, hopefully keeping any irregular noise to a minimum.

When Vol'jin got his hands on the doorpost, he snorted with disgust. "This prison wouldn't be holding a gnome." The doorpost had not been set deep at all. Given that any hole in the swamp must have filled with water almost immediately, the diggers went at it until they hit a steady flow of mud and dropped the post in place.

The troll worried the post like a loose tooth, and it came out easily. Chen did the same with the other side, and they were able to quickly pull the door out. The bolt slipped from the lock plate noiselessly, and Vol'jin had one more reason not to regret his choice.

To die here in this swamp be better than to command morons.

Chen and Cuo slipped out of the cage and into the swamp. They made their way to the western watch post. They eliminated the guards there with no more noise than to be expected from a guard stomping through the brush to see to bodily needs. Tyrathan and Vol'jin joined them, and each took possession of a dagger. The trolls had also carried bludgeons, which the pandaren appropriated.

Over the next fifteen minutes they worked their way around south and east to north, eliminating the posts in turn. Vol'jin opted out of using magic, since he felt none of the guards were worthy of being slain through a shadow hunter's arts. Chen and Cuo returned to the eastern post just before two Zandalari were to walk the perimeter. At the north post, Vol'jin pulled on one of the Gurubashi's uniforms and huddled beneath a blanket. As with the other bodies, Tyrathan dragged them deeper into the swamp and left them for the island's dragon turtles.

On the hour, two Zandalari warriors started to the north post. One, the smaller of the two—which still made him taller than Vol'jin—kicked Vol'jin's hip. "Get up, lazy dog. Where be your partner?"

Vol'jin grunted and pointed farther out at the swamp. As both Zandalari turned to look, he rose and swept his blanket over the closest Zandalari's head. The warrior's hands naturally went to pull it away, which allowed Vol'jin to quickly thrust his dagger three times into the troll's guts. He must have cut an artery with the first or second thrust. Blood gushed hot and sticky.

The Zandalari collapsed thrashing at Vol'jin's feet.

His companion fell over him. The Zandalari had never known Tyrathan was there until the man grabbed a handful of his hair and yanked his head back. The Gurubashi dagger wasn't particularly sharp, so Tyrathan had to saw it back and forth across the throat. Luckily the first slash went deep enough to cut the windpipe, so cries for help just came out as hoarse whisperings of a night breeze. Blood jetted from severed arteries after that. The troll bled out before relative calm returned to the swamp.

Chen and Cuo, not dripping in gore like the man or the troll, joined them, dragging the last two Zandalari into the depths. Once the watch team had headed toward Vol'jin, the pandaren had handled the remaining trolls. One had his skull caved in; the other might have been sleeping. Tyrathan nodded and dragged them off where, out of the monk's sight, he slit throats to be sure. They, along with all the others, disappeared deep in the dark waters.

Despite wanting to gag on the stench, Vol'jin remained in his Gurubashi uniform. They'd agreed that there was no reason the others should try to disguise themselves. Even the most stupid troll wouldn't mistake a man or pandaren for one of his or her own kind.

The fact was that they weren't even looking. Vol'jin could understand it on one level. No one the Zandalari designated as an enemy knew where the Isle of Thunder was, nor did they have an invasion force that could possibly take it over. If the Alliance or the Horde had attacked, fighting at the harbor would slow the advance enough that troops would be able to organize and counterattack. Drawing attackers into the swamps and hitting them there would give the trolls a tactical advantage if only from their knowledge of the terrain.

Sentries dozed at their posts or quick marched their perimeters so they could return to be with friends. This made executing Vol'jin's plan to cripple the invasion far too easy. The group would have accomplished it even if they had to kill sentries, but they didn't. They were able to walk through camps like ghosts—rather fitting in the case of Tyrathan and Vol'jin.

The trolls laid out their camps with boring regularity. They posted standards in the middle to announce which unit they were, and put smaller ones before the tents housing their sleeping officers. Vol'jin moved through those camps, killing sergeants and captains, the two key positions in the command structure of any army. Without captains to interpret orders, and sergeants to make sure the common soldiers actually executed them, even the most brilliant strategy would fall to pieces.

Vol'jin tackled this work coldly and efficiently. A quick slash in the dark. A troll gasping, then just falling limp on his sleeping mat. Vol'jin didn't care and happily consigned them to Bwonsamdi's cold embrace. Their own stupidity sentenced them to death. Vol'jin merely collected a debt.

And, every so often, he made certain to leave a clean and clear footprint in his wake.

It became quickly apparent, as they worked their way toward the harbor, that they couldn't kill enough officers. Cuo and Chen kept watch at the swamp's edge, forward and back of the area where Vol'jin and the man struck. Tyrathan didn't stray very far from the swamps, but Vol'jin was able to kill targets farther in. Progress came slowly, but as dawn was coming on, the time demanded by each strike ate into the chances of their escape.

Vol'jin didn't keep count of their victims, but if 5 percent of the officers were slain, he would have been happily surprised.

It gonna help, but it be not enough.

Tyrathan rejoined them, with a powerful Zandalari recurve bow and a quiver full of arrows. "A sergeant. He isn't going to need them. I don't feel naked anymore."

They pushed on more quickly, directly toward the harbor, and emerged from the swamps into some low hills on the warehouse side of things. While workers still moved supplies from ship to shore and back again, the stream had been reduced to a trickle. From the banging of carpenters' hammers aboard many of the ships, Vol'jin assumed bulkheads were being shifted around to make the ships over into troop carriers.

But not all of them. He smiled and turned to Tyrathan. "I be thinking you'll be happy you taught me jihui."

Vol'jin pointed to a small but sturdy fishing boat

dragged up on the beach seaward of them. "Chen, to your thinking, can that boat make it to Pandaria?"

The brewmaster nodded. "As long as it doesn't have a hole in the bottom."

"Good. You and Tyrathan be getting it in the water and to a hundred yards aft of that three-masted ship in the middle of the harbor. Half hour. By dawn."

"Consider it done."

Vol'jin grabbed Tyrathan's forearm. "Be ready to shoot, if you have to."

"Of course."

"Go."

The monk looked at him as the other two slipped away. The troll pointed at a lone guard patrolling the end of a short mole protecting the entrance to the harbor. "I be needing him alive, Cuo, right there, and you with him. Shortly after dawn."

The monk bowed. "Thank you, Master Vol'jin."

"Go."

Vol'jin waited for the pandaren to disappear before he worked his own way down the hill and toward the warehouse. He wished dearly now that he'd taken a Zandalari uniform from one of those they'd killed. Had he done so, despite being a head shorter than most, he'd have been able to stroll brazenly along the dock to the ship he'd pointed out. He would have added an imperious swagger. Everyone would have cleared out of his way.

Since he lacked the disguise to play to that set of expectations, he suited himself to another. Damp with swamp muck to the waist, and with his uniform sleeves already crusting with blood, he hunched his shoulders and let his right leg drag a bit, as if the hip had once broken and healed poorly. He pulled his leather cap slightly askew, then tilted his head back in the other direction.

He made his way along the docks, hurrying and purposeful—the urgency wasn't his own, it would seem. And the guard at the gangway to the ship barely gave him a glance.

Not so the Zandalari officer on the upper gun deck. "What be you doin'?"

"My master be wantin' a bilge rat. Not too fat, not too skinny. White if I can find it. White one be makin' for da best eating, you know."

"A bilge rat? Who be your master?"

"Who knows a witch doctor's mind? One time I be gettin' kicked awake because he be wantin' three silent crickets." Vol'jin ducked his head and hunched his shoulders as if ready to take a beating. "Those be not good eatin', da noisy kind or silent. Rats, though, some be liking to skin dem first, but I don't. You just get a stick and be shovin' it right up through—"

"Yes, yes, fascinatin', of course." The Zandalari looked as if he'd already eaten his fill of rat and hadn't found it agreeable. "Get on with it, den."

Vol'jin ducked his head again. "Thank you, boss. Won't be no trouble to catch you a plump one."

"No, just be hurrying."

The Darkspear went into the ship's depths. Two decks down he straightened up and headed directly for the magazine. One sailor sat on watch at the door, but the ship's gentle rising and falling with the swells had lulled him to sleep. Vol'jin grabbed his chin and skullcap, then twisted sharply. The troll's neck snapped wetly but quietly. He found the magazine key on the dead sailor, which saved his having to go back up on deck to kill the officer on watch to retrieve it, and un-locked the hatch.

Vol'jin deposited the body inside the magazine. He set aside four sacks of gunpowder, each sufficient to load a cannon, then stove in the lid of a barrel with his elbow. He tipped the barrel over toward the hatch, then picked up the bags and closed the hatch again. The hatch's lower edge leveled the black powder to a height of a half inch out onto the deck. Vol'jin then used two of the sacks to lay a line of powder along the bulkhead, hiding it in the shadows there, and around to the aft cabin.

There he laid a trail to the middle of the floor and poured out the other two sacks in a great pile. The cabin, which apparently served as the ship's hospital, had two oil lamps hanging on chains from the deck above. Vol'jin lit both, then turned their wicks up and spread the gun-powder beneath them.

He barred the door, surveyed his handiwork, and smiled. Then he opened the aft window and slipped out. He let himself hang from his hands so his feet dangled only ten feet above the dark water. He pointed his toes and let go. He plunged straight down with very little splash, then pushed off from the hull and swam under-water toward where he hoped Chen had his fishing boat.

He surfaced halfway there and reached the boat quickly enough. Chen and Tyrathan hauled him aboard. He lay in the bottom of the boat and pointed back. "You see those two lights?"

Tyrathan nocked an arrow, smiling. "Jihui. The fire-ship." He drew and released.

The arrow disappeared in the fading night. Though he trusted Tyrathan, Vol'jin did have a moment of doubt. Then he heard something break. He assumed it was a pane of glass as the arrow passed through. Tyrathan maintained Vol'jin was imagining things, since his shot went through the open window.

Liquid fire splashed through the distant cabin. Light flared brilliantly, and thick smoke billowed as the gunpowder flashed in a muffled thump. Vol'jin could imagine the officer of the watch turning, seeing the smoke rising. He'd either raise the alarm or leap from the ship—and certainly give no thought to a ratcatcher below, or his fellow crew trolls.

Then the magazine blew. That first barrel's spilled contents had ignited. Flames jetted beneath planks, popping one or two here and there. Then bagged charges went, and they lit off the other barrels. Explosions cascaded, building in brilliance and speed until they merged into one massive roar that blew out the starboard hull.

The ship rolled violently toward the dock, crushing it. Pilings stove through the hull. Explosions continued, working forward, blasting lids off gunports. One cannon was actually blown through the breached hull, dropping onto and through the dock.

And, in Vol'jin's imagination, crushing the fleeing watch officer.

Then a thunderous explosion shot a pillar of fire into the air, utterly destroying the ship. The masts became black silhouettes, jetting high through the flames. They reached for the stars, then tumbled back down. One stabbed through a second ship, punching through the hull. Another splintered a dock.

Cannons whirled through the air, guns separating from carriages. One flew to the shore, spinning wildly. It bounced through two trolls, then collapsed a warehouse façade.

Wooden debris, much of it burning, sprayed out. It rained over other ships and roofs of distant warehouses. The embers mirrored the scattering of stars in the sky. Flames flickered and coals glowed, silhouetting trolls and mogu running in panic.

A wave washed out from where the bow and stern of the ship slowly sank, propelling their small boat toward the ocean. Chen got both paws on the tiller and steered clear of fiery debris, while Tyrathan and Vol'jin wrestled a triangle of canvas up the mast.

The troll smiled as they headed for where Cuo awaited them. "Nice shooting there."

"One arrow, a ship killed and a harbor wounded." The man shook his head. "Just as well Tyrathan Khort is dead. That's so tall a tale, no one would believe it no matter who told it."

28

Khal'ak would have pitied the Gurubashi kneeling before Vilnak'dor in a puddle of his own blubberings, but his explanation became even more pathetic with the second telling. *Dat, and the fact that a Darkspear humiliated him.* The troll looked up at the Zandalari general, tear-brimming eyes begging for mercy.

"Then they be wakin' me up by dumping a bucket of water over me, my lord. And dis troll, he be grabbing my chin, and he gave me the message for you. His face, fierce by the light of the burning ships, it was. He be sayin' he be a shadow hunter and took responsibility for all this. And dat with his man and the Shado-pan, he'd guarantee even more ruin if we be invading. Then he did dis!"

The Gurubashi pulled back the lock of auburn hair that had fallen over his forehead. A crude spear-shaped scar had been carved into the troll's flesh. "Said it be so no one would forget the Darkspears."

Vilnak'dor kicked the troll full in the stomach, then looked over at Khal'ak. "Dis be your fault, Khal'ak. All your fault. You be letting him deceive you."

She brought her chin up. "He did nothing of the sort,

my lord. We had Vol'jin, had his head and heart, until Warlord Kao here undercut my authority."

The mogu warlord, who had stood silent during the gasping troll's recitation, idly inspected a talon. "He was in league with the Shado-pan. He could never have been trusted."

She suppressed a snarl. "He gonna be dealt with."

"As he dealt with your officers and your ship?"

On an island where your master can raise buildings through dreams, and he never be noticin' Vol'jin's escape? She hesitated for a moment, wondering if the Thunder King had noticed and just decided to say nothing. *Possible. Foolish. Foolish enough to seem brilliant, maybe.*

She briefly shelved that idea and addressed her superior. "The damage done be insignificant, both in numbers and effect. Troops be already at much higher alert, which will carry over to operations in Pandaria. The loss of one ship be regrettable, but the fires were contained. Had the warehouse become involved, it might have been settin' the invasion back a season. As it be, we gonna lose a fortnight in havin' the quay repaired and harbor cleared of debris."

Vilnak'dor smiled. "You see, Warlord Kao, we be sailin' in two weeks. Your master gonna be pleased."

The mogu shook his head. "You sail in two weeks. I sail inside a week. The Shado-pan must be destroyed. I will see to it, along with my bodyguards."

Khal'ak frowned. Bodyguards? The only mogu with whom Kao had associated were the two who approached him with baton and cloak in the tomb. "How many do you have?"

"Two." He brought his head up. "I will not need more."

"You don't know how many monks there be, Warlord."

"It matters not. We will prevail."

The troll general raised an eyebrow. "Don't take dis as my being impolite, but you did not in the past."

"This is not the past, General Vilnak'dor."

No, it be the present. A present in which we pulled you from a tomb where your beloved master put you.

Vilnak'dor's face closed. "I had hoped, my friend, to be surprising you with good news—that news bein' of the elimination of the Shado-pan."

"By what means?"

The troll nodded toward Khal'ak. "I be dispatchin' my aide to deal with them. She gonna bring with her five hundred elite Zandalari warriors—over half from my own household troop. Upon your master's arrival in Pandaria, they gonna present him with the heads of every Shado-pan—plus those of the Darkspear and his companions."

The mogu's eyes widened as he looked from the general to her and back again. "Her? The one who let this Darkspear slip away and create havoc? Have the Zandalari become senile over the centuries?"

"You fail to ask yourself, my friend, why I would be trustin' her to bring Vol'jin here in the first place. A demonstration, if you don't mind."

Khal'ak nodded. She prodded the Gurubashi with a toe. "Get up." A second kick and a sharper command roused him enough to reach his feet unsteadily.

She cuffed him hard over the left ear. "Run for the door. If you be makin' it, you live. Now!"

His hand probing his ear, the troll spun and sprinted. Khal'ak brought her right hand up, filling it with a dagger that had lain hidden in her sleeve. She pulled her hand back, measuring the distance. The troll had picked up speed, urgency straightening his steps. He even reached out for the door.

She snapped her hand forward.

The troll staggered and clutched at his chest, gasping loudly. He crashed to his knees, then flopped heavily onto his side. His body shook with a spasmodic palsy, his palms squeaking against the polished stone floor. His back arched, and he cried out one last time. His eyes became almost instantly glassy.

The mogu stalked over, his footfalls vibrating through the floor. He stared hard but did not bend close for a thorough inspection. There could be no doubting the troll was dead, but no blade protruded from his chest, nor did he lie in a widening pool of blood.

Kao turned back, then nodded. "I shall still send my bodyguards. You will deal with the Shado-pan, but one caution."

Khal'ak smiled indulgently. "Yes?"

"It would please my master if their demise was considerably more messy than this."

Once the mogu had departed, Khal'ak bowed to Vilnak'dor. "Your confidence in me be heartening, my lord."

"Expedient, more like. You have an enemy in Kao, and he gonna poison the Thunder King against you. You gonna deliver the heads as promised, or I gonna deliver your head."

"Understood, my lord." Khal'ak cocked her head. "How did you come to decide on five hundred?"

"At five hundred, those chosen will consider it an honor. More, and dey would be thinkin' it a fool's mission, or a forlorn hope. That impression would be takin' the heart out of the entire force. But, really, a Darkspear, a man, and some pandaren trapped on a mountain? The monastery can't be supporting more than a dozen dozen. Could you possibly need more?"

"You be quite right, my lord; dey should more than suffice." She smiled. "I gonna take great pains that they do so."

"Of course you gonna." The general pointed at the dead Gurubashi. "I be commending your handiwork."

"You're welcome, my lord. I gonna send for him to be hauled away." She bowed, then headed to the door. She stepped over the body without adjusting her stride, as if it were as much of a phantom as the knife she'd thrown.

The Gurubashi's death had been a show for the mogu. The knife she'd drawn and feigned throwing had slipped back into the wrist sheath as Kao turned to watch its flight. The Gurubashi hadn't died because of an invisible knife but because of the poison needle in a ring on the hand with which she'd cuffed him. Once she'd struck him, he had the count of ten before he died, and she the count of eight to throw her knife. Without using magic, she appeared to have killed with magic, which would give the mogu pause to wonder if the Zandalari had uncovered some new power while the mogu slept.

That sort of deception wasn't just for the mogu. Khal'ak had the feeling that it would take all that and more to destroy the Shado-pan. After all, Vol'jin had abandoned her and the Zandalari to cast his lot with the pandaren. She assumed that he knew something she did not and that her enlightenment would be bought with blood.

• • •

Under Chen's direction, Vol'jin and the others had put as much canvas on the ship's masts as they could hold. Though not the world's most accomplished sailor, the pandaren kept them running with the wind, south toward Pandaria. While tending to the ship and keeping watch for pursuit did demand attention, every so often one or another of them would laugh aloud, nervously, when thinking of their escape.

Vol'jin found himself amidships with Brother Cuo as the noon sun blazed overhead. The monk had been quiet, which was hardly uncharacteristic, but Vol'jin wondered if events during their escape further stilled his tongue.

"Brother Cuo, what I done with the Gurubashi soldier. . . . Cutting him that way be cruel, no denying, but I be not intending cruelty."

The pandaren nodded. "Please, Master Vol'jin, I understand why you did what you did. I also understand that balance is not a matter of abundance opposed by poverty. In theory, peace is the balance of war, but in practice, violence is balanced not by a lack but by violence of an equal nature, moving in the opposite direction."

Cuo opened his paws. "You think of the Shado-pan as isolated, perhaps provincial, because we have not seen what you have. But I do understand that violence is nuanced. What is the damage done by a sword stroke that cuts nothing? What you did in cutting that troll will distract the enemy so he strikes at nothing. Killing the soldiers means that the hand wielding the sword will be weak."

Vol'jin shook his head. "What I did means he not gonna strike at nothing; he gonna strike at us. He gonna strike at the Shado-pan. What we did gonna terrify the mogu and be forcing the Zandalari to eliminate the Shado-pan. And you saw the armies assembled on that island."

"They are formidable." The pandaren smiled. "But your Zandalari see us as a bright light. The mogu feel us as searing heat. What they fail to perceive is that we are fire. This will be a mistake they will very much regret."

Chen brought the small fishing boat into a tiny cove beneath the Peak of Serenity's stone spire. They hauled the boat up onto the beach at the high-water mark and moored it there. They knew they'd never use it again, but letting it drift off or scuttling it seemed unworthy payment for the service it had done them.

They made their way up the rocky slope, at times having to climb nearly sheer cliff faces. Vol'jin imagined Zandalari swarming over the same rocks. In his mind they became an undulating black wave cresting over the cliff. He indulged himself with the fantasy of an avalanche sending boulders tumbling down among them. Crushed trolls bled between rocks, while others were blasted back into the ocean and sank slowly as air bubbled out of their lungs.

But that be not how this gonna happen.

The best-case scenario for the Zandalari was not to attack the monastery at all. What they needed to do was surround the mountain with two or three cordons of troops. They could prevent the monks from descending to aid in Pandaria's defense. If the enemy included a company of pterrordax riders to counteract the cloud serpents, the Shado-pan would be helpless while the Zandalari and mogu occupied the Vale of Eternal Blossoms, the Jade Forest, and the Townlong Steppes. Once they had consolidated those areas, they could conquer the monastery at their leisure.

The problem for Vilnak'dor was that this strategy would not work. The mogu would demand the monks' destruction. The Zandalari would not allow the mogu to accomplish this because the mogu had not done well before against the pandaren. If they actually succeeded in killing the Shado-pan, the mogu might come to question their need for the Zandalari at all. If the mogu failed, the Zandalari would have to clean up after them and deal with an upset Thunder King.

Moreover, the troll troops would know just how lethal a shadow hunter and a man had been on the island. Given the way rumors flowed through military camps, Vol'jin was certain the soldiers believed that he was a shadow hunter trained by the monks or that the monks had been given special shadow hunter training by him. Either way, suddenly Pandaria had a new threat that could move unseen through enemy camps, which meant every soldier was vulnerable. This would not be good for morale.

Vol'jin explained his thoughts to Taran Zhu after the escapees reached the monastery. The elder monk had been only mildly surprised to see them. He'd known they weren't dead, since they'd not dropped from the mountain's bones. Neither had the image of Sister Quan-li, which gave the travelers heart.

The Shado-pan leader stood studying a map of the Kun-Lai district with Vol'jin and Tyrathan. "Your assessment, then, would be that the Zandalari must throw elite troops at us? Only that will raise morale and appease the mogu."

Vol'jin nodded. "I would be doing this along with a heavy push south from Zouchin. I would be sending one force straight south, and then one to the west, cutting you off from the Jade Forest and Townlong Steppes. Even if their elites did fail to kill you, you would be having no retreat."

Tyrathan tapped a finger on the map's southern edge. "If we move now and withdraw to the Valley of the Four Winds, we escape their trap. We leave a few people in place to make the monastery appear lived in, then have them escape at night by cloud serpent as the Zandalari close in."

The elder monk clasped his paws at the small of his back and nodded thoughtfully. "It is a wise plan. I shall arrange for you to evacuate."

Vol'jin's eyes tightened. "You sound as if you not gonna come."

"No Shado-pan will."

The troll stared at him. "I pointed the Zandalari here. I made you a target. I did that thinking you would move and be leading the opposition from elsewhere."

The pandaren slowly shook his head. "I appreciate your attempt to take responsibility for your actions, Vol'jin, but you did not make us a target. From this place pandaren planned the overthrow of the mogu. History is what made us a target. You may have provided more urgency, but they would have come for us. They must.

"And, for that same reason, we cannot leave." The monk pointed to the map with an open paw. "From here we secured the freedom of Pandaria. This is the only place from which we can keep Pandaria free. If the Peak of Serenity falls, peace will forever vanish from our home. But this is our home, not yours. I do not expect you or Chen to remain here. You should go south. Your people have the power to oppose the invasion. Warn them. Make them see sense."

Vol'jin shivered. "How many be you defending this place with?"

"With Brother Cuo's return, we are thirty."

"Thirty-one." Tyrathan hooked thumbs through his belt. "And I'll wager Chen's not leaving."

"Then I be thirty-three."

Taran Zhu bowed to both of them. "Your gesture humbles us and does you honor, but I shall not hold you to it. Return to your people. There is no reason for you to die here."

The troll lifted his chin. "Did you not carve us into this mountain's bones?"

The monk nodded solemnly.

"Then the Shado-pan be our people. They be family." Vol'jin smiled. "And I have no intention of dying here. That, my friends, be a job for the Zandalari."

29

Vol'jin felt his father's presence and dared not open his eyes. The shadow hunter had gone to his cell in the monastery and isolated himself despite the frenzy of activity going on in preparation for the coming assault. He firmly believed everything he'd said to Taran Zhu, about belonging there, about the monastery being a new home and the bond of his likeness having been carved into the mountain's bones.

So strong had been his conviction that he felt the need to immediately communicate with the loa. Though what he was doing was right—of that he had no doubt—he could imagine the loa turning their backs on him. They might view what the Zandalari were doing as harmful, but his commitment to the pandaren cause might also be seen as hurtful to trolls.

The sense of his father reassured him, at least in that he felt no hostility. Vol'jin forced himself to breathe in and out evenly. He combined what he had learned in the monastery with older practices. He came to the loa as a shadow hunter should—certain and resolute. And yet, as an adult who had revered and treasured his father and his father's dreams, he took youthful joy in Sen'jin having come first.

Vol'jin looked, seeing without opening his eyes. His father stood there, a bit more bent with age than Vol'jin liked to remember him but still bright of eye. His father wore a heavy, hooded cloak of blue wool, but the hood lay back against his shoulders. He appeared to be smiling.

The shadow hunter made no attempt at hiding his own smile, though it lasted for mere moments. *Be this what you expected of me?*

Opposing the Zandalari here, in a place where you must fall? Committing yourself to a battle that you cannot win, for the sake of a people who do not understand you and do not care to? Sen'jin, his shoulders slumping, shook his head. *No, my son.*

Vol'jin looked down, his heart aching. It felt as if a rusty chain, festooned with spikes, had been wrapped around his heart and pulled tight. If he had only one goal in life, it was to make his father proud. *And yet, if I must be disappointing him, so be it.*

His father's voice came softly, with a hint of mirth beneath its gravity. *This be not what I expected of you, Vol'jin, but what the loa be expecting of shadow hunters. While I did not expect it of you, I always knew you would be rising to this height when the time came.*

Vol'jin looked up, the pressure in his chest easing. *I don't think I be wholly understanding, Father.*

You, Vol'jin, be my son. I be enormously proud of you and all you have accomplished. His father's spirit raised a finger. *But when you became a shadow hunter, you transcended being my son. You became a father for all trolls. You bear responsibility for all of us, for what we gonna become. Our future be in your hands—and there be no one I can think of who can be more trusted with it.*

The world shifted around Vol'jin. Without moving, he found himself standing beside his father. He watched stars explode in a night sky rich with explosions. He watched Azeroth coalesce from nothing. The loa came and granted trolls their very nature, bargaining in return for eternal supplication and worship. Wars and calamities, good and joyful times, all flashed past, shining satin moments on the ribbon of history.

No matter what he saw, no matter how brief the glimpse, Vol'jin picked out a shadow hunter or two or five. Sometimes they had moved to the fore. Often they stood beside or behind a dynamic leader. Occasionally they huddled together as a council. Always was their endorsement sought and the wisdom of their decisions respected.

Until the Zandalari began to pull away. It made sense, really, as trolls became more sophisticated and built cities. They ceased wandering, acquired wealth, and began building. They created temples and shrines, and a class of surrogates arose to offer sacrifices and interpretations of the loa's messages. Vast populations meant that trolls were removed from occupations that brought them close to nature and the loa, and old precepts had to be revised and interpreted for a new time and civilization. The Zandalari found their full employment in this pursuit, which meant they had to reinforce the necessity of their role, else their caste would have no reason to exist.

This required, however, a redefining of the shadow hunter. Yes, to complete the training and testing was a great thing. A blessing everyone would celebrate. Shadow hunters were raised to be heroes of mythic proportion—respected but also feared, since they walked with the loa and, therefore, could not completely understand the needs of mortals.

Vol'jin shivered. The same innate desire for the approval of the Zandalari was not a failing that the other troll tribes enjoyed alone. Khal'ak was a victim of it too, but in another sense. She sought an alliance with a shadow hunter because of his status. Their working together gave her more legitimacy.

Until I went and ruined that.

History's parade slowed here and there, at key points. The displays had become more grand, the throngs larger, and the rhetoric more volcanic and vitriolic. Frenzy swept over vast hordes carpeting the landscape.

Yet, in these scenes, Vol'jin saw no shadow hunters. Or, if he did catch a glimpse, it was of a shadow hunter turning away. *As I did when asked to join Zul. As I did when breaking with Garrosh.*

All of a sudden the last piece slid into place. The Zandalari had set themselves up to be speakers for the loa. Perhaps they came to believe they were the equal of the loa themselves. Certainly they thought themselves a people apart from other trolls. They were better. They were more. And the Gurubashi and Amani, in attempting to emulate the Zandalari and revive their glories, suffered from that same vanity. That sense of self-importance bred hubris, which doomed their efforts.

In each case, a shadow hunter had turned away. The trolls interpreted that as a remnant of the past disapproving of the future. From their point of view, they had no other definition of that action. But their interpretation divorced them from their true nature.

A shadow hunter might counsel, might lead, but that was not his true purpose. This was not the reason the loa came to him and depended upon him. A shadow hunter was the true measure of what it was to be a troll. All trolls, and all of their actions, were measured against the shadow hunter. It was important to see the distinction of actions versus abilities or potential. Shadow hunters certainly were more able than most trolls, but there were no trolls who could not emulate shadow hunters, contributing their efforts to the community. That would be what confirmed them as being trolls.

Vol'jin visualized himself standing on a simple merchant's scale. Khal'ak and Vilnak'dor stepped on the opposite plate. The scale tipped in Vol'jin's favor, elevating the Zandalari. He could see how his adversaries, from their vantage point, justified believing he was less of a troll than they.

They vanished, and Chen replaced them. Then Taran Zhu and Brother Cuo stepped up. His old friend Rexxar appeared, and then even Tyrathan took to the scale. With each of them, the scale came to rest at even. Garrosh rose like a goblin rocket when his turn came.

Vol'jin puzzled over what he felt was the true nature of his companions in the monastery or Horde. Certainly the pandaren and the human were not his equal at being a troll, though their efforts on behalf of Pandaria would undoubtedly be equal to his. Their desire for freedom, their selflessness, and their willingness to sacrifice themselves matched those things in him without question. Measured on this scale, their character and heart were every bit as troll as his.

Rexxar, who loved the Horde as much as Vol'jin, likewise embraced those virtues. Vol'jin wished that his mok'náthal friend could be there with them. Not so he could die, but so he could help them destroy the Zandalari. Rexxar would have done so happily, no matter how sad the pre-ordained outcome.

And so would many others in the Horde. The majority, I be thinking.

The Horde, the Shado-pan, even Tyrathan were truer to the fundamental essence of being a troll than were the Zandalari. The Zandalari and their ilk were curl-tailed curs whining to the wolf that because they had once been like the wolves, but were now different, that they were better. True, their coats might be brighter; they might perform tasks better; they might live longer; but they had forgotten that none of those things meant anything to a wolf. A wolf's purpose was to be a wolf. Once that truth was forgotten, new truths had to be forged. No matter how clever the work, however, they would be but a shadow of the one truth.

Vol'jin cocked his head and looked at his father. *Being a troll has nothing to do with shape or bloodlines.*

Those things cannot be wholly discounted, my son, but the spirit which be making us trolls, which be making us worthy of gaining the notice of the loa, predates the forms we now wear. His father smiled more broadly. *And, as you have seen, the shadow hunter turns away from paths that shear us from that spirit. Since spirit be defining us, discovering that same spirit in others be a cause for celebration.*

Vol'jin laughed. *You would be allowing me to believe that the Horde be more troll than the Zandalari.*

There may be truth in that. Do you be knowing what we called ourselves before we called ourselves trolls?

I never . . . Vol'jin frowned. *I don't know, Father. What?*

Neither do I, my son. The troll spirit bobbed his head. *It be certain we were something before we became trolls, and likely gonna be something after. The Zandalari have always tried to shape what we be, and others have used circumstance to be reinforcing those ideas. However, I be not doubting that twenty millennia from now the question will be asked, "Do you know what they called us before we called ourselves Horde?"*

Be that your vision for trolls, Father?

Sen'jin slowly shook his head. *My vision for trolls was a simple one: for us to return to being a people following a shadow hunter. That required something special, however—a shadow hunter who could lead. Many shadow hunters be content to refuse a journey which leads to disaster. You, my son, be a shadow hunter who can lead away from disaster. If this means that you be leading us to a place where race matters less than the content of the heart, where deeds matter more than intent, then this be where we gonna thrive.*

But will the loa believe that?

Bwonsamdi's cold chuckle rippled through Vol'jin's chest as the troll spun to face the loa. *Have you not listened to your father, Shadow Hunter? The loa came before the troll. Your father be asking what trolls were called before they were called trolls. I be asking what they were called before that, or before that. What you are be a river. Some will say that means you be water. They would have you stagnate. You be more, as a river be more than water.*

And the Horde?

The loa spread his hands. *River be river. Wide and shallow, narrow, deep, and fast—it does not matter. We be spirits. Our concern be for your spirit. Abide by our compact, be true to your spirit and obligations, and you gonna prosper.*

You gonna have your fill of Zandalari souls soon.

The loa's laughter rang mirthlessly. *You never gonna sate my appetite.*

I gonna soon follow.

And I gonna welcome you. I be welcoming all trolls.

Vol'jin found that comment oddly comforting. Not because he had any desire to be dead, but because it meant he would not be separated from his friends. It didn't seem like much with death looming so large, but for the shadow hunter, it was, at the moment, enough.

hen felt sorry for the little bush behind which they'd hidden the pyramid of rocks. Each of the rocks—averaging the size of a troll's skull, though far rounder in shape—would have been enough to snap the bush in half. All of them combined would be an avalanche, would scour the land, uprooting the plant and, with any luck, mowing down a half dozen Zandalari climbing up toward the monastery.

Chen set his rock on top, then squatted and sighted down the slope. The stones would funnel into a narrow channel, where the trail got steep. Warriors would stack up there as they climbed, which made it a rather obvious point for an ambush. While the bush might screen the rocks from most watchful eyes, the Zandalari wouldn't miss them.

And we'd not want them to miss this, either. From a pouch on his belt, the pandaren pulled a pawful of small wooden disks. He inserted them into the gaps between stones. When the pile went rolling down the hill, the disks wouldn't travel far, but the Zandalari would discover them in the aftermath.

Farther up the trail, back behind where Chen stood,

Yalia knelt by a hole in the ground. She'd had to reach all the way down into it to firmly plant the sharpened bamboo stake that now pointed up at the sky. Chen had helped carve many of those stakes, first slashing the bamboo into a sharp point, then undercutting the edges to form solid barbs.

He trudged up the mountainside, being careful to stay off the trail. A tripwire had been stretched across it a foot in front of Yalia's pit. The thinking had been that the trolls would send one scout up past the steep point. He'd continue on, probably spotting the stones once he drew parallel to them. He'd then see the tripwire, which wasn't well hidden, and assume it would somehow trigger the stones to go crashing down. He'd cleverly step over the wire, plunging his foot into the pit. He'd scream, or his friends would see him go down, and they would rush to his aid.

At which time a small trebuchet farther up the mountain would launch rocks. They'd smash the area and trigger the avalanche, catching yet more trolls.

Chen offered Yalia his paw. She took one last glance at the thin slate shingle she'd placed over the pit, then accepted his aid and stood.

Chen liked it that she didn't immediately release her grip. "That looks great, Yalia. The way you blew that dust on it makes it look like it's been there forever. Tyrathan would be proud of that trap."

She smiled but too fast and too briefly. "We're not setting traps for dumb animals, are we, Chen?"

"No, the Zandalari are quite clever. That's why we're seeding them with the disks, too. But don't worry; your preparation will fool them."

She shook her head. "I have no concern over that. This will catch them, and catch them well."

"Then . . . ?"

"I asked because I must ask." Yalia sighed, partly weary but mostly something else. "I found myself being proud of my work, even though I know it will cause pain. And when I made that realization, I justified my feelings by seeing the Zandalari as animals. They were mindless killing machines. I transformed them into something unworthy of life, and that judgment of one is easily spread among the many. It can't be true of all of them, can it?"

"No." Chen gave her paw a squeeze. "You do well to think of that and remind me of it. Your willingness to see value in life, even of those who are opposed to you, is the mark of wisdom. It is one of the reasons I love you."

Yalia glanced down shyly, but only for a moment. "That you listen to me and think about what I say are among the reasons I love you, Chen. I wish that we had more time. Together, yes, but also for you. You have sought a home for so long. I have hoped that you found one here. For you to lose it so soon, this makes me sad."

He reached up and brushed away a brimming tear before it could dampen her silken fur. "Don't be sad. Finding a home is to be made whole. That is a pleasure so wonderful that more time can't increase it. I know all of it because I now have a sense for who I am and what I've been meant to be."

"How so?"

"All these brews and concoctions I made were my attempt to capture a place or a time. A bard might do that with a song, or a painter with a picture. They play to ear and eye, whereas I play to nose and palate and, perhaps, touch too. I always sought the perfect brew, hoping to find that one which would describe the emptiness in my life. It could fill it. But here, now, I know I am whole. And while I can capture a place and time in what I do, now I possess joy and happiness—both of which are compounded by your presence in my life."

Yalia moved to him, circling his neck with her arms. "Perhaps, then, I am the selfish one. I wish for more, Chen. I want eternity."

"We will have that, Yalia Sagewhisper." Chen pulled her close, holding her firmly. "We're already eternal. Our images may drop from the mountain's bones, but the mountain itself will fall before we are forgotten. Bards will sing of us. Painters will splash our images from here to Orgrimmar and back. Brewmasters will claim for eons that they have my secret recipe for the brew that sustained the Thirty-three. They'll probably just call it that: 'Thirty-three.'"

"And we will be united forever in their memories?"

"There won't be a boy in Pandaria who doesn't seek his Yalia, and count himself lucky when he's found her. Girls will be happy when they tame their wandering Chen."

Yalia pulled back, raising an eyebrow. "Is that what you think I think?"

Chen kissed the tip of her nose. "No. You have shared your peace with me. You are the anchor and the ocean. And any cub who finds his Yalia and is given the benefit of those things will be the most fortunate pandaren alive."

She kissed him full on the mouth, passionately, desperately. It took his breath away. He crushed her to him, hugging her fiercely, stroking the back of her head as they kissed. It was a moment he never wanted to end, and he hoped the artists and bards would do it true justice.

When they pulled back, Yalia laid her head on his shoulder. "I could only wish it would be our cubs doing that looking."

"I know." He stroked her fur. "I know. I take solace in knowing that many other cubs will do the searching."

She nodded wordlessly and kept her head there for just a bit longer. Then they parted and began the trek back up the mountain, laying more traps, adding more verses to the songs that would be sung of them, and preparing lessons for the Zandalari that they should have long since learned.

"The mogu could be searching forever, and they would still never be finding all the arrows you've hidden." Vol'jin folded his arms as the human straightened up. "You've got one for every soldier on the isle."

"And two each for the officers." Tyrathan shrugged. "And it's not just quivers I've been hiding. There are knives and swords and sticks and bows. Outside I have heavier bows, perfect for use with long arrows to hit targets at range. In here, compact bows, shorter arrows, easier to employ in close quarters."

Vol'jin looked around the White Tiger shrine. "If fighting ever gets in here . . ."

"You mean *when*. . . ." The man slapped the stone shoulder of a sitting tiger statue. "You'll be glad to know his tail's curled around a half dozen throwing knives."

"Or that there be a sword up there, where I could be reaching it but you could not."

"Remember, you promised to get the one that gets me. I just want to make sure you have the tools."

"I do." Vol'jin reached behind him and pulled around the new glaive, which had been strapped across his back. "Brother Cuo worked the forge hard. Chen described the weapon I normally be carrying. Cuo put together something suitable for fighting Zandalari."

"That's the way he said it, yes, as if fighting wasn't the same as killing?"

Vol'jin nodded. "It be giving him peace to make the distinction."

Tyrathan studied the weapon and smiled. "He's made the blades longer, with a nastier hook to them. They'll slash well, either end, and stab. But the center, the grip is a bit more stout, it seems."

"Yes. A single tang be running all the way through." Vol'jin freed it from the scabbard and spun it around so quickly it whistled. "Perfectly balanced. He says he sized it for my forearm. It suits me better than the one I lost."

"A pandaren monk creating a traditional troll weapon." The man gave a grin. "The world as we knew it has changed."

"His work be as remarkable as a man and a troll joining together to keep other people free."

"We're dead. Rules don't apply."

"I be thinking I appreciate human glibness now." Vol'jin slid the glaive back into the scabbard. "Being of a different temperament, trolls do not speak as quickly. We be giving things more time."

Tyrathan gave him a look. "So, your telling Garrosh you'd kill him, that wasn't glib?"

"Rash, no doubting. Thinking on it, though, be not changing what I said or meant." The troll opened his arms. "No changing, even if I'd been knowing the future. I won't be dying here without regrets, but they won't be consuming me."

The man smiled wryly. "I'm sorry I won't keep my oath to see my home one more time, but this is now my home. I'll happily haunt it forever."

Vol'jin looked around. "Not much of a tomb, really. Though the Zandalari won't bury us."

"Nor will the mogu allow this place to stand. They'll hurl all the stones into the ocean, let the vultures eat their fill, then grind our bones into dust and let the winds scatter us." Tyrathan shrugged. "Good enough gust, and I might make it back to my home mountains after all."

"I gonna hope for good winds, then." Vol'jin squatted, pulling a fingernail along a seam between stones in the floor. "Tyrathan Khort, I be wanting to say . . ."

"No." The man shook his head. "No good-byes. No fond farewells. I don't want things settled. I don't want to think I've said all there is to say. If I do that, I'll give up a little bit sooner. That desire to tell you one more thing, to laugh when you find one of my swords, or to see your face when one of my arrows kills someone fixing to slit your throat—those things will keep me going. We know we have no future. But, we can have one more minute, one more heartbeat, and that's enough time to kill one more of the enemy. They steal my future; I steal theirs. Fair trade, though I'll be buying in bulk."

"I understand. I concur." The troll nodded. "Did you do as others did? Chen wrote his niece. . . ."

The man looked down at his empty hands. "Write my family? No. Not directly. I did send a short note to Li Li. I asked her to befriend my children if their paths ever cross. She wouldn't need to say why or even tell them about me. Did you write anyone?"

"A few notes went out."

"Nothing for Garrosh?"

"A note in my hand might scare him, but he would be taking credit for my death. I gonna be denying him that pleasure."

Tyrathan frowned. "Did you set into motion a plan to avenge yourself?"

"I told no one what he'd done. He'd be claiming the notes be forged anyway, or coerced by the Zandalari." Vol'jin shook his head. "I just told people I be proud of their commitment to the Horde and the dream it represents. They gonna come to understand what I meant."

"Not as satisfying as killing Garrosh directly, but you'll rest well in the grave." Tyrathan smiled. "Though I did like the image of you shooting him. I always saw the arrow as being one I made for that purpose."

"It would have flown true, I have no doubt."

"If you survive, rescue a few of my arrows from dead Zandalari. They'll sting at least twice." The man clapped his hands. "If we were saying good-byes, I'd shake your hand and tell you that we need to get back to work."

"But no good-byes, so it be just back to work." The shadow hunter smiled and took one last look around. "We gonna haunt the mogu, shifting stones, and then the fish. And the fish gonna turn to poison and be killing all those we couldn't get ourselves. Not much of a plan, but it gonna make eternity interesting."

31

The Amani's scream tightened Khal'ak's flesh. She waited, listening for its repeat, for it to be abruptly cut off, or for the rumble of stones followed by other screams. The Amani did scream again, but it tailed into a pitiful mewing. Either he wasn't hurt as badly as he was frightened, or he'd fainted from the pain.

Khal'ak had not intended to press Amani or Gurubashi into combat roles. She'd brought sufficient of each along with her because her Zandalari couldn't be expected to cook and clean and carry for themselves. Unfortunately, her troops tended to stoicism when it came to the troll traps that had been laid out. They wouldn't scream or panic, which meant they didn't alert their companions to danger.

There had been dangers aplenty, and she knew they were mostly the shadow hunter's doing. Pit traps and deadfalls, rockslides and showers of darts from small siege machines, all had been arrayed to take maximum advantage of the terrain. The path forced troops to slow and bunch in places. The Zandalari learned to be on guard in such areas, minimizing the actual damage done to her troops.

Physical damage, anyway.

Because trolls healed quickly, that which did not kill them immediately allowed them to recover. While the Zandalari viewed their bandages as badges of courage and dismissed the meager efforts against them, Khal'ak could already see the psychological effect it was having on them. They moved more cautiously, which wasn't necessarily bad for an army, but her people became more tentative when she needed courage and decisiveness.

At places where there appeared a logical but difficult climb to work around a bottleneck, her troops would skillfully scale the sheer face. At the top they might find signs where a small siege engine had been set up, and then tracks leading back to the entrance to a warren of caves. The caves might be trapped, were always tight for the large Zandalari, and invariably sealed fifty or a hundred feet along a tortuous route.

As frustrating as that was, it wasn't until hours later that the climbers, who had scratched fingers or debris trapped beneath nails, suddenly found their extremities tingling. They began to swell. Handholds had been smeared with toxins that wouldn't kill anyone but incapacitated them by triggering hideous hallucinations. Thereafter, the presence of dampness or an oily residue gave them cause to hesitate. They'd concentrate on seeing if they had been poisoned, which meant they were distracted from their real task.

Vol'jin be attacking their minds, effectively killing them.

The shadow hunter also taunted them. Khal'ak flipped a small wooden token between her thumb and fingers. On one side had been burned the troll symbol for the number 33. On the other side, it had been rendered in mogu. They found the tokens scattered in the bottoms of pits or at sites where scouts had clearly been observing them. Rumor had it that one had even been found in her tent, hinting that the shadow hunter could have killed her as easily as he'd killed troops on the Isle of Thunder. The number, some determined, referred to the millennia since the fall of the Thunder King (through odd tricks of numerology), or to Vol'jin as the thirty-third shadow hunter of a particular tradition. None could actually state which tradition, and she'd been forced to kill an Amani to make an example of the perils of rumor mongering, but once the idea had taken root, there was no stopping it.

The theory she liked best was that every defender had pledged that they would slay thirty-three before they died, which meant her force faced less than twenty defenders. While such pledges had tactical value only in minstrels' songs, it did make her wary. *Intending me for one of your thirty-three, Vol'jin?*

She listened on the wind for an answer. She heard nothing.

Captain Nir'zan ran up and saluted. "An Amani cook strayed out of cleared areas to be relievin' himself. Found a likely spot. Ground crumbled beneath his feet. He fell forward on his knees, impaling his thighs, abdomen, and one hand. He will live."

"Has he been freed yet?"

"No."

"Can we be arranging for everyone to march past him as we proceed this morning?"

The troll warrior nodded. "As you desire, my lady."

"Good. If he has the fortitude to survive until all have passed, free him."

"Yes, mistress."

He did not move, so she raised an eyebrow. "And?"

"A runner brought signals from the fleet. They will be returnin' to Zouchin's shores. There's a severe storm coming in from the north. Heavy winds, ice, snow. It gonna delay the sailing from the Isle of Thunder too."

"Good. Dat be giving us more time to consolidate Pandaria after we destroy the monastery." Khal'ak glanced higher up the mountain at their destination, then down at her camp. The tents had been spread out and as often as not pitched on the backslope of hills to protect them from slides and assaults. They'd kept cold camps simply to make it difficult for the enemy to determine their numbers.

She tapped a finger against her lips for a moment, then nodded. "We have to be pressin' on, and quickly. We cannot weather a storm in the open, and we be closer to the monastery dan we be to shelter below. A day and a half to the top, yes?"

"At our present rate, yes. We should be arriving as the storm does."

"Send out two companies of our best, but have dem wear clothes they be exchangin' with our Gurubashi contingent. I want them ahead and flanking us. By midnight I want them to be clearin' any caves they find farther along. If the storm arrives fast, we gonna need shelter. Then, while the rest of us be pushing forward, I want them opening the monks' escape tunnels and working their way up. Leave the wounded to be picked up later. Their traps only work to delay us. We have to push through quickly.

"And tonight, we gonna be having fires, not a cold camp. Big fires, two per tent."

Her subordinate's eyes narrowed. "Mistress, that gonna consume most of our firewood."

"Most? Let it all go." She pointed at the monastery. "If our people ever want to be warm again, it gonna be in the glow of the Shado-pan pyre!"

Vol'jin could not help smiling as day surrendered to dusk and long shadows pointed toward dawn. Toward the Zandalari. His group's traps and attacks had not killed nearly as many of Khal'ak's forces as he desired, but she had been moved to acts of desperation because of them. She'd flung two companies wide, diluting her strength, and bulled on through a number of attacks. By the time they reached the monastery, they'd be angry, frustrated, and weary—three things no general likes in his soldiers.

Given that the Zandalari had stopped for the night exactly where the defenders planned for them to stop—save the flanking battalions that had found smaller places a bit higher—Taran Zhu had been willing to call together the Thirty-three. Actually it was only thirty-one. Brother Cuo and Tyrathan had agreed to take an early watch while the elder monk called his charges to the Temple of the White Tiger.

The monks stood before him in two rows of ten and a back row of eight. Chen and Vol'jin formed the rectangle's back two corners. Off to the sides, tables had been laden with food and a brew that Chen had put together quickly—though he maintained it was his best. Vol'jin didn't doubt him. He'd seldom seen his friend concentrate so on a task, and his claims came with sincerity, not hyperbole.

The old monk spread his paws. "You are all too young to recall when we overthrew the mogu. Despite speculation and joking, I am too young as well. Still, I have been given access to history and memories, tales passed down from a time before this monastery existed. Tales from a time when opposing the mogu was not only a high honor but a necessity.

"You are now part of that grand tradition. So are all our brothers and sisters. Many wished to be here, but our purpose demands they be elsewhere. Sister Quan-li, you will be happy to know, has not yet fallen from the bones. Yet one more of us lives to oppose our ancient masters."

Vol'jin nodded to himself, quite pleased. He felt confident that Quan-li would be able to reveal enough information to the Alliance that they would be moved to act. Horde spies would pass on that information to their superiors. While he dreaded what Garrosh might do with the news, for once Garrosh's affinity for war did not seem to be a great problem. Though the Thirty-three would die here, the Zandalari invasion would follow them quickly into the grave.

Taran Zhu pressed his palms together. "Though I was not present when the mogu fell, I am given assurances that this story of the last mogu emperor is true. He had climbed with a pandaren servant to the Peak of Serenity, high above us. He stood there, arms outstretched, turning round and round. He surveyed Pandaria and was pleased. He said to his servant, 'I wish to do something to make everyone in Pandaria smile.' And the servant said, 'You'll jump, then?'"

The monks laughed and the happy echo filled the room. Vol'jin hoped he would remember laughter when the screams of the wounded and dying dominated. There was no purpose in wondering if any of them would survive. None would, but he decided that were he the last to die, he would laugh and remind the room of that moment.

"The story does not tell what became of that servant, but it is said that the emperor, hurt and angry, let it be known that he considered this part of the mountain tainted. No mogu would visit, leaving the way open for us to gather and plan and train to overthrow them. Here we were unseen because they never thought to look for us."

Taran Zhu bowed solemnly to Chen and Vol'jin before he continued. "Months ago I, like the mogu, had not thought to look for those we needed. Master Stormstout brought me first the man and then the shadow hunter. While I allowed them to stay, I told him to bring me no more. That is a decision I regret. In this very room, I spoke with Master Stormstout on this matter, speaking of anchors and ocean, of Huojin and Tushui. I asked him which was most important, and he said it was neither; it was the crew. I have thought long and hard on this, and now, here before me, you stand, the crew."

He gathered his paws at the small of his back. "You all came here for different reasons. You have learned lessons as one. Yet it is this crisis, this noble cause, which makes you one."

Taran Zhu held up one of the wooden tokens. "Master Stormstout has prepared a brew to share. He calls it 'Thirty-three' in our honor. And, as the Thirty-three, we shall forever be known. While people will think of us and remember us with pride, I wish you to know I have never been prouder than to be one among you."

He bowed deeply and held it as long as respect demanded. The monks, as well as Vol'jin and Chen, returned the salute. Vol'jin's throat became thick. Part of him found it remarkable that he was bowing so to a creature he would have once considered beneath him, and yet his heart swelled at being numbered in the same company with them all.

They were the Thirty-three, what he had always imagined the Horde to be. Their strength came from diversity united by common vision. Their spirits—the kind of spirit Bwonsamdi would see as troll—had fused through their purpose. Yes, Vol'jin still saw himself as a troll, but that was no longer the whole of his being, just an important part of it.

The monks straightened, and then the assembly broke and headed over to feast. Providing food and drink on the eve of battle made good sense, and Chen's brew ran light on alcohol simply to prevent any disasters. The monks had laid out a great deal of food, and the idea of eating enough that the enemy would find the larder bare was the source of grim humor for all.

Chen, accompanied by Yalia, brought Vol'jin a foaming tankard of his brew. "I have truly saved my best for last."

Vol'jin raised his tankard, then drank. Berry and spice scents tickled his nose. The brew, warmer than it was cold, felt full yet had the bite of a hard cider. Odd tastes, some soft and sweet, others tart and piercing, danced over his tongue. He would have been hard-pressed to identify even half of them, but they fit together so well he was inclined to do no analysis at all.

Vol'jin wiped his mouth on his sleeve. "It be reminding me of the first night I slept in the Echo Isles after we'd retaken them. Warm evening, soft breeze, tang of the ocean. I had no fear because that was the place I was meant to be. Thank you, Chen."

"I owe you thanks, Vol'jin."

"Because?"

"Because you have told me that my best did all I intended."

"Then you be the greatest among us, for you have given us all heart. This be the place we be home. Without fear." Vol'jin nodded and drank again. "At least until the Zandalari be arriving, hauling their fear, at which time we gonna load them down with more."

32

It occurred to Vol'jin that this moment, that infinitesimally short pause before violence erupted, might be the very last one he remembered as he died. His heart leaped at that idea. The Zandalari had made their approach into the Grove of Falling Blossoms even as dark clouds brought the day to an early end. The first snowflakes fell like ash, slowly drifting, driven by capricious breezes. The trees, full of pink blossoms, hid the enemy, but not to their benefit.

On his right, a dozen yards farther along, Tyrathan's bow groaned as the man drew it. He shot. Time slowed enough for Vol'jin to see the arrow itself bend a split second before it sped from the bow. Red shaft, blue feathers and stripes, with a barbed head designed to punch through ring mail, the arrow disappeared into the pink curtain of blossoms. Only two small petals drifted down with snowflakes, marking its passage.

Farther out, something coughed wetly in the twilight's gloaming. A body thudded to the ground. And then, shrieking war cries and curses ancient and vile, the Zandalari dashed forward in a massive wave assault.

Some fell as they moved through the grove. Feet again plunged into hidden pits. Even if there hadn't been upward-pointing spikes to wound them, or downward-pointed spikes to trap them, the speed and force of the trolls' sprint would have snapped legs and twisted knees. The Zandalari did not pause for the fallen but instead sailed over them in great bounds.

Because of the seriousness of their situation, Taran Zhu had exhorted his monks to push their skills to their utmost. He had selected a half dozen of his best archers and, in conjunction with Vol'jin, had devised a strategy that would allow any single arrow to kill a handful of the enemy. At Vol'jin's solemn nod, as the invaders filtered through the trees, the monks loosed arrows.

Preparations for the grove had included more than just digging pits. Branches had been trimmed and sharpened into spikes. Some had scythe blades bound to them. A few had chain nets fixed with barbs furled along their lengths. All of them, well hidden within the pink canopy, had been drawn back and bound with ceremonial knots.

The monks shot arrows with a V-shaped head. The interior had been sharpened. The blades cut the cords quickly, letting the branches spring back into place.

Chain netting wrapped one Zandalari in a lover's metal embrace. He shook himself to pieces trying to wriggle free. Scythe blades swept through necks or stabbed deep, lifting their victims from the ground. One slashed a troll midface, ruining his eyes, clipping an ear, and leaving him seated beneath the tree, trying to reassemble himself with bloody fingers.

From the north side, in front of the Sealed Chambers, small siege machines clacked. Tens of dozens of tiny earthenware jars tumbled through the sky. They shattered all along the approach to the narrow rope-and-plank bridge leading to the island at the monastery's heart. Some reeked of the toxins that had been smeared on stones. Others had been filled with oil, making footing slick. Others burst, splashing fluids that mixed with the residue of other jars, producing bitter vapors of white, purple, and green.

Vol'jin hoped that the scent might slow the trolls. Unfortunately the rising wind thinned the vapor. The sheeting snowflakes that came to replace it still gave Vol'jin far too easy a view of the Zandalari pouring through the grove. The bridge did lead to an island, and he waited there in the open pavilion at its heart, but the gully the bridge spanned wouldn't slow the Zandalari.

"Tyrathan, pull back. They not gonna stop unless I be stopping them." The troll shook his glaive free of its scabbard. "Retreat, everyone, as planned. And thank you."

The monks and human withdrew from the island along another bridge to where the siege machines waited. They looped back around to the Snowdrift Dojo to the south, meeting Brother Cuo and his command there.

Across from Vol'jin, the Zandalari reached the edge of the gully. They hesitated, either wanting a moment's rest before charging on or surprised to see him, a Darkspear, a shadow hunter, waiting alone on the island. He told himself it was the latter, since Zandalari would never hesitate otherwise.

He raised the glaive in both hands over his head and shouted above the rising wind. "I be Vol'jin of the Darkspears, son of Sen'jin of the Darkspears! I be shadow hunter! Any of you believes his blood and courage and skill can best me, I invite here to duel! If you have any honor, or believe you be brave, you will be accepting my challenge!"

The trolls looked at one another, surprised and astounded. Jostling on the line pitched one down into the gully. He landed in a heap, fully dusted with snow, and looked up at Vol'jin. He scrabbled at the gully wall, and his compatriots just laughed at him. It seemed rather odd behavior for a Zandalari, but Vol'jin had no time to think about what that might portend.

Fools be not believing me. Vol'jin looked at the troll in the pit. Snow had covered him, but the spell Vol'jin cast wreathed him in frost. The troll collapsed, shivering, slothfully clawing at the pit's wall to escape.

A mogu bearing a stabbing spear shouldered his way to the far end of the bridge. "I am Deng-Tai, son of Deng-Chon. My family has served the immortal emperor since before the Darkspears existed. I know my blood makes me superior. I do not fear you. My skill will leave you weeping blood from a thousand cuts."

Vol'jin nodded, stepping back to invite the mogu forward. The bridge's ropes drew taut as Deng-Tai advanced. Boards creaked. Vol'jin wished for cord-cutting arrows to part the cables, but the short fall would only anger the mogu and dishonor Vol'jin.

Had the drop been sufficiently lethal, Vol'jin could have survived the dishonor. He wasn't so certain about the spear, which had a fairly short haft with a long blade that curved at the tip and appeared to be sharpened all around. A single, casual blow with that weapon could easily decapitate an ox.

Fortunately, I be not an ox.

The mogu, a foot taller than Vol'jin, half again as wide, and encased in ring and plate, did not slow when he hit the small island. He drove straight at Vol'jin, coming with surprising speed. His armor, though clearly heavy, encumbered him not at all.

Deng-Tai thrust. Vol'jin twisted to the left. The spear's blade struck sparks off a stone column on the island's pavilion. Vol'jin whipped the glaive down and around. One blade's tip clawed the mogu's right wrist. It punched down through the mail, connecting bracer to gauntlet. Black blood spurted.

Any joy the troll might have taken at drawing first blood vanished as the mogu thrust back with the spear. The blunt end, which had been capped with a steel ball, slammed into Vol'jin's ribs. The blow lifted him from his feet. He bounced back and landed in a crouch, bracing to parry a slashing blow as the mogu spun.

And vanished as wind-whipped snow snaked in a curtain between them.

Vol'jin flattened and slashed with his sword. The mogu's blade sliced air bare inches above him. The glaive hit something—an ankle most likely—but not solidly. It skipped off armor.

Vol'jin tucked his right arm under and rolled right. He stayed low, fearing another sweeping slash with the spear. Instead, as he'd hoped, the mogu loomed large through the snow and stabbed down where Vol'jin had previously lain. The spearhead plunged into the rock, cracking it, burying itself five inches deep.

Seeing his chance, Vol'jin rose and spun. He slashed his glaive upward, from low left to high right. The curved blade struck through the mogu's left armpit. Mail rings pinged as they parted. Blood gushed, but neither rings nor drops came away in a flood sufficient to signify true damage.

Vol'jin's slash brought him around in a half circle, facing him back toward the grove and the trolls waiting on the gully lip. A Zandalari officer appeared, gesticulating wildly. Though Vol'jin saw him only in brief flashes between whiteouts, and the wind snatched his commands away, there was no doubt he was exhorting his soldiers to attack.

Into the gully the wave descended.

Vol'jin would have shouted a warning, but the mogu spun. He'd not freed the spearhead from the ground. Instead, he'd twisted the haft, splintering it, and swung it around. The blow caught Vol'jin across the belly, smashing him back into the pavilion's column. Stars burst before his eyes as his head hit. The shadow hunter, stunned, slumped to his knees.

Deng-Tai rose above him, the haft reversed, the steel cap poised for an overhand blow that would crush his skull. The mogu smiled. "Why they fear you, I do not understand."

Vol'jin grinned. "Because they be knowing a shadow hunter be always lethal."

Deng-Tai stared at him, non-comprehending. Snow whirled around the island, hiding the combatants as well as the mists of Pandaria had hidden the continent. Despite that, a blackened arrow pierced the storm. Had Tyrathan intended to kill the mogu, he missed. Still, the arrow passed as a veil before Deng-Tai's eyes, causing a moment's hesitation.

And that be all I need.

The spear haft descended.

The distraction bought Vol'jin time to shift to his right. The steel cap missed his head but caught his left shoulder. Vol'jin heard bones shatter more than he felt them. His left arm went dead. Another time that would have concerned him, but now he felt disconnected from the pain and had no worries about the future.

In fact, the only connection he felt was to the monastery and the monks and the training he'd been given. Nothing else mattered. Nothing else could matter. *The Zandalari be unworthy of this place and be fools for thinking they can destroy me.*

Spinning on his knees, he came around and scythed the glaive through the inside of the mogu's own left knee. Blackness gushed fluidly. More important, the knee buckled.

Deng-Tai stumbled to the left and went down. He landed heavily on his wounded knee. Pain laced his grunt. He caught himself with his left hand and straightened his right leg for balance. He swept the spear haft around, trying to catch Vol'jin pressing his advantage.

That trick hadn't worked on Vol'jin since before he'd been entrusted with herding small raptors as a child. He leaned back, the steel cap whistling past his chin, then darted in. With a savage kick, he crumpled the mogu's right knee from the side, then stomped down to crush the ankle as well.

Deng-Tai's reverse blow snapped the spear haft against Vol'jin's hip. The troll had anticipated it and braced himself. The mogu's right hand swept past; then a flick of the glaive took it off at the wrist. It, and the broken fragments of spear, spun off into the blizzard.

The mogu stared at the steaming blood pulsing from the stump. Then Vol'jin whipped the glaive around in a forehand cut that sliced cleanly through the mogu's neck.

One of the loa—for only the loa could have made it happen—stopped the storm for a heartbeat. The winds died. The air cleared. And remained silent and clear for as long as it took for the mogu's head to slowly slide forward, tip, and bounce off his breastplate. It rolled to a stop in a snowdrift, sightless eyes staring at headless body with the intensity of a spurned lover staring at an unfaithful spouse.

The battle had ceased for just that handful of heartbeats. The trolls and monks all stared at the island. The mogu knelt before the shadow hunter. The mogu's head appeared to nod; then the body thumped forward in a full and formal bow.

Then the troll captain pointed his sword toward Vol'jin. "He be alone and broken. Kill him. Kill them all!"

Peace shattered along with the silence, and the Zandalari force surged.

33

As he engaged the trolls coming along the bridge and swarming up the edges of the island, Vol'jin consciously realized what he'd unconsciously discovered previously: he wasn't facing Zandalari. Not all of them, anyway. The tall ones certainly were. Their height—and the fact that more than one sprouted a red-shafted arrow from eye or throat as they came—gave them away. The others, though wearing Zandalari armor, had to be Gurubashi and Amani.

Vol'jin understood the tactic of driving lesser forces before the best, overwhelming defenders. Khal'ak would think herself brilliant for coming up with it. Vol'jin felt compelled to convince her that it wasn't a workable idea. Since he could not see her in the horde pouring into the monastery, he contented himself with destroying her troops.

Destruction it had to be, because it wasn't truly a fight. Sheer weight of meat guaranteed her forces would over-whelm him. In addition to the warriors closing in, priests and witch doctors appeared from the grove. Black energy sizzled between their hands. Spells launched, arcing out toward the monks defending the Sealed Chambers. Some of them fell, but the handful of Shado-pan stormcallers responded. Their spells exploded amid the trolls, setting some on fire, opening the chest of at least one other.

His left shoulder already having recovered a minimal amount of utility, Vol'jin swept into the trolls. He considered himself a sharp and vengeful part of the winds swirling blinding snow blankets over the battlefield. Just as the cold wind could cut through clothing to chill the flesh, his glaive sliced deep. It plunged into groins, ripping open femoral arteries. It caressed necks, hot blood spurting to darken falling snow. The blade point punched through the backs of knees, cut heel tendons, and plucked out eyes.

He left his enemies' throats intact so they could give voice to fear and pain.

Some opposed him bravely, but others came at him slowly and tentatively. They looked for openings and weaknesses. He just made openings. He'd long since counted himself dead, so their little cuts, their thrusts, mattered not at all. If a blow didn't kill him outright, it was as good as a miss.

Deep down inside, Vol'jin knew he wouldn't always prevail, but the snarl on his lips, the glint in his eyes, and the eagerness with which he attacked hinted at just the opposite. His enemies saw him as a troll who, despite wearing tattered armor and being bathed in blood, would keep coming. If they weren't sure they could stop him or kill him, fear froze their guts.

And then Vol'jin opened them.

He spun away from one troll madly trying to stuff ropy intestines back into a ruined belly and found himself completely surrounded. The battle had turned him around, so he faced it as the invaders had. The arcane exchange of spells lit the battlefield to his right. Through sheets of snow, arrows came from off to the left. Half-visible trolls crested over the far gully edge, engaging the monks defending the Sealed Chambers. In that direction lay sanctuary, and Vol'jin knew he'd never make it.

Then, in a burst of light and licking flame, Chen exploded onto the island. As one of the true Zandalari turned toward him, Chen again breathed fire. The troll's face ran like melting wax, his hair a torch and his flesh sizzling sweetly.

Behind him, Yalia, Cuo, and three other Shado-pan monks raced along the bridge to the island. The crack Chen had burned open was expanded with staves and swords. Yalia's staff moved so quickly it would have been invisible even if there were no snow. Her blows dented armor and crushed bones beneath. Every thump produced a clank and a curse; every uppercut launched teeth from shattered jaws.

Chen extended a paw. "Hurry!"

Vol'jin, surprised, hesitated. The Zandalari circle might have closed around him again, but the monks drove forward. They surrounded him with their own cordon. Paws and feet blurred. Swords clanged. The monks proved excellent on defense, turning thrusts and blocking slashes. Even though their speed left their enemies open, they didn't press their advantage. They didn't seem to think their mission to rescue Vol'jin meant also killing as many of the enemy as they could.

Vol'jin took Chen's paw and sprinted over the bridge. He had no desire to be leaving the fight, but the island was no place to be fighting. Had he stayed, they all would have stayed. And died. In fact, the monks withdrew in good order, all of them reaching the landing before the Sealed Chambers.

Even as he contemplated stepping up to defend the bridge, the Snowdrift Dojo's alarm bell pealed loudly. It rang a half dozen times with urgency, then abruptly stopped. He looked over and trolls poured from it—obviously Zandalari despite the shabby clothes they wore.

And there, with them, stood a mogu and Khal'ak.

Taran Zhu appeared at the Sealed Chambers' main entrance. "Fall back now!" The command contained no panic, nor did it allow for refusal. The monks pulled back immediately, with Chen and Vol'jin the last to retreat.

The Zandalari, confident of their victory, seemed happy to let them go.

Vol'jin paused in the doorway, looking toward the Snowdrift Dojo. Snow stole his sight of it, with the last thing he saw being Zandalari tossing dead monks into the gully. He looked for any sign of Tyrathan, but blood dripped into his eyes.

Two monks closed the ornate bronze doors behind him and dropped a heavy bar into place. Vol'jin went to a knee to catch his breath. He swiped at the blood on his face, then looked up again.

The Thirty-three had become fourteen. All but Taran Zhu showed signs of the fighting. Blood stained many robes. Magic had scorched others. At least two of the survivors had broken bones, and Vol'jin suspected others were hiding injuries. Yalia was definitely favoring broken ribs. The blood dripping from Chen's right paw did so too fluidly to be anything but his own.

The troll glanced at the Shado-pan leader. "How did they get into the Snowdrift Dojo?"

"I believe they worked their way up through the

tunnels." Taran Zhu examined a fingernail rather distractedly. "Others tried coming up from below here, but were discouraged." He glanced at a half-open alcove behind the statue of a tiger, and Vol'jin wondered what manner of mayhem lay beyond it.

The shadow hunter winced as he straightened up and worked his left shoulder around. "Khal'ak sent some of her elite troops out in those flanking parties. She be forcing the others into being the brunt of the attackers. We've done well. We've killed many."

"But not enough." The elder monk nodded. The winds howled and he smiled. "Perhaps the winter will kill them for us."

Vol'jin shook his head. "I doubt they will wait that long."

The Sealed Chambers had been laid out in the shape of a T. The main door opened onto a circular depression. Three wings spread out from it, opposite him and at right angles. To his left, in the longer of the wings, stood another pair of doors. A heavy fist pounded on them, demanding entrance.

Chen laughed. "I don't think we should answer that."

"Agreed." Vol'jin looked from one door to the other. "I be suspecting Khal'ak gonna concentrate her attacks there, to the far side, to attract our attention. She gonna then hit this door, quickly and hard. Chen, if you wanted to be preparing her a warm welcome . . ."

The pandaren nodded. "My pleasure."

"Brother Cuo, the far door be yours." Vol'jin crossed over to where Tyrathan had hidden a quiver and a compact horse bow. He strung it and tested the draw. "I gonna position myself here, in the middle, to see what I can do."

Taran Zhu nodded, then ascended the stair and seated himself at the heart of the wing opposite the door Chen would defend. He composed himself, serene and pristine, the antithesis of the other thirteen. Vol'jin would have protested, but Taran Zhu's apparent peace and lack of concern buoyed the troll's heart. *If he be not worried, why should I be?*

The Zandalari began their assault on the west-wing door. Spells pounded it with the relentless monotony of a blacksmith hammering a horseshoe. The metal opposite the wooden bar soon glowed a dull red. The wood smoked. Monks fingered their weapons. Chen and Yalia hugged.

Then came a heavy explosion. Molten metal sprayed out into the room. One of the doors sagged in; the other twisted outward. The oaken bar had been reduced to smoke and glowing cinders that created a red carpet for the invaders.

Vol'jin drew and shot as quickly as he could. Tyrathan had been right. The short bow sped arrows with enough power to pierce armor at such close range. So thick was the mass of Zandalari that he couldn't help but hit a target. The difficulty was that they moved so quickly that wounding was as likely as a kill shot, and were packed so close that wounded or dead, they took their time falling to the floor.

The monks fought valiantly. Blades flashed silver and gold in the building's warm lamplight, drinking deeply of troll blood. The same overwhelming rush of bodies that made it impossible for him to miss also restricted the monks' movement. On a more open battlefield, they could have carved great swaths through the Zandalari. The carnage made apparent that trolls had died in droves outside not because they had been Gurubashi and Amani, but because they had dared attack the Shado-pan.

Spears and swords hungrily sought them and, one by one, the monks fell. Brother Cuo was one of the last. He spun, his face cleaved in half. Others just vanished in a sea of troll flesh, dying perhaps content in the knowledge that they had taken many trolls with them.

A second explosion blasted the main doors open. Chen breathed fire, wreathing Zandalari in flame. More elite warriors poured through, engaging Chen and Yalia. The captain who had led the attack outside darted forward. Behind him, Khal'ak stood with the other mogu. She surveyed the place as if the fighting were finished and she were only there to count bodies.

Vol'jin cast aside the bow, downed a troll in a blistering burst of dark magic, then brought his glaive to hand. He intercepted the Zandalari officer, turning a cut meant for Yalia, then nodding and beckoning the Zandalari forward. "You be not fearing me now, would you be?"

The Zandalari snarled and went for him. Whereas the mogu had relied on power, the troll fought with speed and skill. His saber whistled past Vol'jin's ducking head. The shadow hunter slashed at his midsection, but the Zandalari leaped back. Before Vol'jin could press him, he circled, then came in again, slashing sinisterly across the Darkspear's body.

Vol'jin turned the slashes, deflecting them high or wide. Saber rang against glaive; metal hissed on metal through parries. The blades themselves seemed alive, striking with the speed of vipers, vanishing as quickly as ghosts. Feints and dodges, leaps and strikes, had each troll circling with and through and around the other in lethally fluid motions. The pace of their fight increased, sparks flying.

Vol'jin thrust and the Zandalari leaped back, but only barely in time and with the leeway of an inch. He glanced down. Joy chased disbelief off his face. His belly should have been opened, his entrails spilling out. But, somehow, luckily, he'd avoided that thrust.

Then Vol'jin pushed with his left hand and raked back with his right. The motion hooked the glaive's curved blade around, ripping into the Zandalari's back. Vol'jin twisted his hands upward. The blade carved neatly around a kidney, severing the artery feeding it as well as the one going to the Zandalari's legs. He yanked the blade free in an explosion of crimson. His enemy fell in a limp tangle of limbs, splashing blood over the floor.

"Vol'jin, look out!"

Hands shoved the troll aside. Vol'jin tripped over his dead foe's legs, landing hard and rolling. He came up as the mogu's spear, which would have taken him full in the back, caught a battle-worn Tyrathan Khort in the belly. It hit him with enough force to carry him back to the wall. The spearhead embedded itself there, and the man, suspended grotesquely, stared down at the spear buried in his guts.

The mogu rushed forward, hands raised, making for Vol'jin. He didn't even glance at his spear. The fury in his eyes and the twitching of his fingers betrayed his intention to tear Vol'jin limb from limb.

And that might have happened, had not Taran Zhu launched himself in a flying kick. The Shado-pan lord caught the mogu in his left flank, denting armor. He struck with sufficient force that the mogu stumbled to the right, crashing into Zandalari surrounding Yalia and Chen. He landed heavily on one, but thrust himself to his feet quickly. The fact that he'd crushed a troll's skull in doing so appeared to be beneath his notice.

Vol'jin scooped up his glaive as he regained his feet, then stood and watched as the mogu hurled himself at the pandaren. Heavy blows pounded the ground where Taran Zhu had stood but a heartbeat before. They cracked stone and shook the earth. Fists flew. Feet swept and scythed and snapped. The mogu, though clearly skilled in unarmed combat and bigger than his enemy, simply couldn't touch the pandaren.

Taran Zhu ducked or danced back or tumbled and rolled. He leaped over leg sweeps, then slid away from combinations. The mogu shifted forms—Vol'jin recognized a few from his training—yet the pandaren did not adopt the opposing form. He just remained elusive, a phantom. The harder the mogu pressed him, the more easily he escaped, until the mogu finally paused to gather himself.

Then Taran Zhu attacked. Almost playfully he bounded forward, then snapped a kick up and around to the right. It caught the mogu in the middle of his left thigh, breaking it crisply. No sooner had the pandaren landed than he kicked again, this time with his left foot. The mogu's other thigh parted with a thunder-crack.

As the mogu fell forward, Taran Zhu punched up and out. His spear-pawed strike pierced the mogu's breastplate with a high-pitched pop. His arm disappeared to the elbow in the mogu's chest. Stiffened fingers dented the backplate from the inside out.

The elder monk slid his paw free and slipped back as

34

Khal'ak's right hand came up and whipped forward before Vol'jin could shout a warning. A slender knife spun through the air at the eldest monk. As it sped toward its target, she scooped a sword up from the ground and charged for Taran Zhu.

The pandaren monk's right paw came up in a circular parry, from inside toward out. He batted the dagger away with the back of his paw, redirecting it. In the blink of an eye, it quivered in a Zandalari, lodging in his throat before the victim or his companions had consciously realized their leader had thrown it, and well before any of them had taken the chance to heed the monk's warning. Stunned by unfolding events, they remained rooted in place.

Vol'jin interposed himself between her and the monk. "I be knowing better than to offer you mercy."

Her eyes blazed. "You be betraying your betters."

"Shadow hunters have no betters."

Khal'ak attacked, as skillfully as the troll he'd just killed and perhaps a bit quicker. Her blade flashed through serpentine twists and cuts. He didn't block many blows, just parried them or twisted aside. She gave him no openings to attack, but it would not have mattered if she had. His muscles already burned with fatigue. He wasn't certain he'd be fast enough to get past her guard. And she seemed to be waiting for something, having had the benefit of watching him fight.

What has she seen?

As if she'd read his mind, Khal'ak pressed him. She slashed high and low, circling to the right, to his strong side. She might have noticed his favoring of his left shoulder, but he'd recovered from that damage. If it wasn't that, what was she seeking to exploit?

Then he realized that it didn't matter what she had seen, because he knew what she had *not* seen. As she slashed at him with a cut aimed at his belly, he shifted his weapon to his left hand. He didn't turn the cut with his glaive; he just slowed it and stepped forward. Her sword still caught him over the hip, right where Deng-Tai had hit him with the spear haft. He felt the pain, but it seemed incredibly far away.

His left arm came down, trapping her wrist against his side. She looked up, fury in her eyes threatening to arc out and burn him. He met it with contempt, not because she was an enemy, but because she was the corruption that would destroy Pandaria and all trolls. He held her gaze for just long enough that he could believe she understood, and then he killed her.

Quickly.

Remorselessly.

Every time she'd seen him fight, he'd used a glaive and fought in a traditional manner. The only thing she hadn't seen and didn't know about was the training he'd had at the paws of the Shado-pan. *Fitting I kill her with my bare hands.*

His spear-handed thrust crushed her larynx and windpipe. His fingers drove deeper. Her vertebrae popped, going from hard to porridge-soft against his fingertips. Bone fragments shredded her spinal cord.

Khal'ak staggered back from the force of the blow alone. Her legs no longer worked. She collapsed at the dead mogu's feet. She stared venomously at him, her face purpling as she tried to take that one last breath.

She failed.

The Zandalari troops stood there, astonishment stark on their faces. Khal'ak dead. Their captain dead. Two mogu dead, and far too many of their comrades dead or moaning and dying inside and out. Already Gurubashi and Amani had begun to pull away. The back ranks thinned.

Vol'jin shifted the glaive to his right hand again. "Bwonsamdi, he be waiting to greet you."

His statement sent shudders through many. They joined their lesser companions in flight into the blizzard. A few of the remaining rushed forward. Taran Zhu scattered them as if they were flies he was shooing away. Bones snapped, bodies thumped, and trolls writhed on the floor.

Taran Zhu stepped back and gently waved a paw. "Tend to them. Far from here. You may go."

As if his grant of permission was a command, the last of the Zandalari melted away. A few hauled off their wounded, leaving the far wing awash in blood and corpses. Chen and Yalia limped forward, keeping an eye on the enemy, as Taran Zhu and Vol'jin crossed to Tyrathan.

Bright blood flecked the man's lips. He smiled weakly. "I'm stuck."

Vol'jin looked at the spear. The head had clearly pierced his spine and ruptured his bowels. To make things worse, it had a broad cross guard. They couldn't slide him off the spear, and it had lodged too deep in the wall to pull it free. "Hold still. I be knowing a spell. . . ."

The man shook his head and hissed as the elder monk felt around the exit wound. "No. I'm done. We did good. I can die happy."

The troll swallowed hard. "Foolish humans. You be not supposed to die happy."

"Telling me I'm wrong guarantees I won't." Tyrathan sighed. "Let me go. It's okay."

The man stiffened as the spear wavered. Something behind him snapped. He fell forward, and Taran Zhu caught him. Vol'jin helped the monk lower him to the floor. Tyrathan had closed his eyes, so Vol'jin didn't know if he could hear, but he spoke anyway. "I not gonna let you die. I didn't get the one that killed you, and you be owing me an arrow for Garrosh."

Vol'jin pressed his hands around the wound, tight to the spear blade. He nodded to Taran Zhu. The pandaren wiggled the haft gently, then slid the blade free. A good four inches of the spearhead had remained in the wall. The bloody edge looked as if it had been worried so much it had parted for metal fatigue. How the monk had broken the blade off, Vol'jin had no clue, and he had no time to think on it.

His hands closed over the wound, the man's blood seeping up between his fingers. Vol'jin invoked a spell. Golden energy gathered in his palms and pulsed down through Tyrathan. The magic hit the floor, then bounced up. It struck Yalia and Chen in turn. It even flew into the mass of bodies and pounced on a monk buried beneath enemy dead.

He waited to feel Tyrathan stir but was not content to leave things to magic alone. He closed his eyes and searched. He didn't have to work hard or go far, because Bwonsamdi's presence blanketed the monastery.

This one be not yours for the taking.

Be you so bold, Shadow Hunter, to tell the loa what we can and cannot be doing?

Sen'jin's voice rang in Vol'jin's ear. *Perhaps he means that the man be not yours to take yet.*

Yes. There be oaths. There be obligations.

The god of the dead laughed. *If that be sufficient to bar me, my realm would be empty and no one would ever be dying.*

A shadow hunter's oath. Vol'jin lifted his chin. *Perhaps that be sufficient to influence you.*

The spectral loa shrugged. *You have given me many to harvest.*

He did too.

True. And many more gonna be dying in the cold. If any survive to report what happened, they gonna be deemed mad and executed for cowardice. Bwonsamdi smiled. *Silk Dancer gonna rejoice in the web you've woven for her. So, yes, have your man. For now.*

Thank you, Bwonsamdi.

But not forever, Vol'jin. The loa faded with his whisper. *Nothing be forever.*

Tyrathan's body shook, his muscles twitching; then he relaxed and his breathing became more regular.

Vol'jin sat back on his heels and wiped the blood on his thighs. "I've healed what I can."

Taran Zhu smiled. "I think we have the facilities to nurse him back to health."

Vol'jin stood. Flesh littered the floor, but nothing moved save for snow playfully swirling in and blood slowly dripping downstairs. It thickened as the cold hit it, freezing into what could be mistaken for red candle wax. So benign, denying reality.

But the dead didn't matter. As Chen and Yalia moved to free the other surviving monk from beneath the slain, Vol'jin stooped and gathered the man into his arms. "Lead on, Lord Taran Zhu. It be time for healing to begin."

Chen inserted the final stick of lit incense into the sand-filled bronze pot, and bowed toward the shelving.

Yalia finished adjusting the last of the carven figures, then joined him and bowed. As they held the bows, white smoke, redolent of pines and the sea, drifted over the stone effigies they'd recovered from deep inside the mountain.

They straightened up, and somehow her left paw had found his right.

"You have been my strength in the last several days, Chen Stormstout." Yalia glanced down shyly. "So much grim work to be done. I could not have borne doing it alone."

He tipped her face up toward his with his free paw. "I could not have left, Yalia."

"No, of course not. The fallen were your comrades too."

He shook his head. "You know that isn't what I mean."

"I know you are anxious to see after your niece."

"And your family." Chen nodded toward the stone figures. "The Zandalari invasion did not end here. The mogu emperor still exists, and Zandalari troops are still an army on the march."

She nodded. "Is it selfish for me to wish it were over?"

"Wishing for peace is never selfish, I think." Chen

smiled. "At least, I hope not. I want it too. I want it because it means that fear doesn't rule my home and that I don't have to be away from you."

Yalia Sagewhisper leaned in and kissed him. "I want those same things." Moving forward, she slipped her arms around him and hugged him fiercely. "I would go with you . . ."

"You're needed here." Chen hugged her tightly, not wanting to let her go. "And I will return, you know. Have no doubt of that."

Yalia pulled back, smiling despite tears beginning to glisten in her eyes. "I have no doubt and no fear."

"Good." Chen stroked her cheek, then kissed her lips and forehead. She felt perfect in the circle of his arms. He breathed deeply of her scent and drank in her warmth. "And know this: we have many, many years before we drop from the mountain's bones. I mean for us to spend as much of that time as possible together. With you I am, for once and truly, at home."

Vol'jin found Tyrathan seated on the edge of his bed, his middle still swathed in bandages. The man had managed to stuff his feet into slippers, which the troll took as a good sign—two days earlier that same effort had met with failure.

"The mountain gonna wait for you."

The man laughed. "I'll let it wait. I left my best dagger in a Zandalari in the tunnels. I was hoping to get it back."

"I be wishing you needed to recover two dozen."

Tyrathan nodded. "So do I. When I went down there, I never thought I'd see the light of day again."

Khal'ak's elite troops had broken through into the tunnels beneath the monastery and overwhelmed the monks in the Snowdrift Dojo. Their initial drive into the building had bypassed Tyrathan. He'd entered the tunnels, and Vol'jin had seen his handiwork. The man had gone after the Zandalari who were meant to get into the Sealed Chambers and had stopped many of them. Arrows were useless down in the dark, so the man had killed with sword and dagger and rocks as big as his head. The troll was certain that some of his victims were yet to be found because they'd crawled off to die.

"I be very glad you made it out. You saved my life."

"And you, mine." Tyrathan glanced down, the ghost of a smile twisting his lips. "What I said, about letting me go . . ."

"That be the pain talking."

"It was, but not the physical pain." The man looked at his own hands lying open and benign against his thighs. "I think I liked the idea of being dead because it meant I could run from pain—the pain of my family situation. What you said about family, however, in making your decision to refuse the Zandalari, that has stuck with me. Our decision to stay and to fight was born out of courage and honor and a sense of family."

"A lot of foolishness too, many would be saying."

"They'd be right, but for the wrong reasons." Tyrathan sighed. "My willingness to die wasn't courageous. And no matter who I am, I don't want to live without courage or honor."

Vol'jin nodded. "I agree. There be much work to be done that will require both of those qualities—and more. Including a marksman's eye."

"I know. And I will be fletching you that arrow for Garrosh."

"But you have things you have to be doing before then."

"You learned too much of me when you were in my mind."

Vol'jin shook his head, then rested both hands on the man's shoulders. "I be learning more while in your company."

Tyrathan smiled. "I'll stay here for a bit, recovering, helping out. Then I honor that oath to see the valleys of my homeland again. While my vanishing might have been best for me, I'm lying to myself if I think it is best for my family. My children need to know me. My wife needs to know I understand. I may not be able to fix things, but to let a lie suggest things are not broken isn't good. Not for them. Not for me. It's not a door I want to travel through."

"I understand. You be braver than most in doing this." Vol'jin stepped back, folding his arms over his chest. "And I trust you gonna be there with that arrow when I be ready to use it."

"Just as I trust you'll get the one who gets me." The man levered himself unsteadily to his feet. "And I am hoping your discharge of that obligation will yet be many years coming."

Vol'jin stood on the island where he'd slain the mogu, and looked out toward the Grove of Falling Blossoms. Snow blanketed everything. He couldn't be certain if lumps were rocks or frozen corpses. It didn't matter. The white flakes, some of which rose on swirling winds, hid everything with their innocence.

Vol'jin willingly let them seduce him into believing the world, at least for a moment, was at peace.

Taran Zhu appeared at his side. "Peace is a natural state. You may enjoy it here for as long as you wish."

"You be very kind, Lord Taran Zhu."

The pandaren smiled. "But you will not enjoy it for as long as you should."

"To be doing so would be selfish." Vol'jin turned toward him. "The peace you be offering me, though welcome be it, would be as much a trap as a skull or a helmet."

Taran Zhu's head came up. "Do you really understand?"

"Yes. The parable be not about skulls or helmets; it be about the limitations one accepts when you define yourself. A crab that sees itself as a crab be defined not by the shelter it seeks but by its very need to seek shelter. I be not a crab. My future be not depending on what I can find to act as a shell. I have many more choices."

"And many more obligations."

"Very true." The troll drew in a deep breath and let it out slowly. Garrosh had betrayed the Horde and would continue to do so. That was in his nature. He allowed himself to be defined by his selfish desires and fears. He would never change, and would resort to many things, terrible things, to solidify his position. In doing so, he would shed rivers of blood and get washed away in the resulting flood.

"You, Lord Taran Zhu, have your family to care for here. So does Chen. Tyrathan gonna return to his family." Vol'jin's eyes tightened. "The Horde be my family. Just as Tyrathan can't let his family believe he be dead, nor can I do that to the Horde. They deserve peace, too, and my accepting it here would deny it to them."

"This a shadow hunter cannot do?"

"Can or cannot doesn't matter. Shadow hunter or troll doesn't matter." Vol'jin slowly nodded. "Vol'jin Darkspear not gonna do it. That be not who I am. Time come that I be reminding my enemies of that fact and making them pay for the evil they've wrought."

ACKNOWLEDGMENTS

The author would like to thank the following people for their contributions to this book. Without them, this never would have been done. Paul Arena, for suggesting I do a *World of Warcraft* novel; Scott Gaeta of Cryptozoic, for making introductions; Jerry Chu of Blizzard, for asking Scott to make the introduction; Micky Neilson, Dave Kosak, Cameron Dayton, Joshua Horst, Justin Parker, and Cate Gary of Blizzard, for working so hard to keep my coloring within the lines; Ed Schlesinger, my editor, who has the patience of a saint; Howard Morhaim, my agent, for making the deal work; and my friends Kat Klaybourne, Paul Garabedian, and Jami Kupperman, who conspired to keep me sane through the process of writing. (Which wasn't that bad. After all, when I needed a break, I could drop into Azeroth and consider it research.)

NOTES

The story you've just read is based in part on characters, situations, and locations from Blizzard Entertainment's computer game *World of Warcraft*, an online role-playing experience set in the award-winning Warcraft universe. In *World of Warcraft*, players create their own heroes and explore, adventure in, and quest across a vast world shared with thousands of other players. This rich and evolving game also allows them to interact with and fight against (or alongside) many of the powerful and intriguing characters featured in this novel.

Since launching in November 2004, *World of Warcraft* has become the world's most popular subscription-based massively multiplayer online role-playing game. The latest expansion, *Mists of Pandaria*, takes players to a never-before-seen continent filled with new quests and adventures. More information about *Mists of Pandaria*, upcoming content, and previous expansions can be found on WorldofWarcraft.com.

FURTHER READING

If you'd like to read more about the characters, situations, and settings featured in this novel, the sources listed below offer additional information.

- Through war and hardship, Vol'jin has led the Darkspear tribe with unparalleled courage. Details of the troll leader's life before he and his people joined the Horde can be found in the short story "The Judgment" by Brian Kindregan (on www.WorldofWarcraft.com). Vol'jin's more recent adventures, including his tense relationship with Garrosh Hellscream, are depicted in *World of Warcraft: Jaina Proudmoore: Tides of War* by Christie Golden.

- Famed brewmaster Chen Stormstout has traversed the world of Azeroth and beyond, braving forgotten dungeons and other perilous locales (often in search of the perfect brewing ingredients). A window into his thrilling life is offered in the graphic novel *World of Warcraft: Pearl of Pandaria* by Micky Neilson and Sean "Cheeks" Galloway. His journey to the mysterious continent of Pandaria is chronicled in the online four-part novella *Quest for Pandaria* by Sarah Pine (on www.WorldofWarcraft.com).

- For millennia, the Shado-pan order has stood watch over the wondrous lands of Pandaria. You can learn more about this mysterious organization and its closely guarded secrets in the short story "Trial of the Red Blossoms" by Cameron Dayton (on www.WorldofWarcraft.com).

- Further insight into Warchief Garrosh Hellscream and his previous exploits can be found in issues #15–20 of the monthly *World of Warcraft* comic book by Walter and Louise Simonson, Jon Buran, Mike Bowden, Phil Moy, Walden Wong, and Pop Mhan; *World of Warcraft: Jaina Proudmoore: Tides of War* and *World of Warcraft: The Shattering: Prelude to Cataclysm* by Christie Golden; *World of Warcraft: Beyond the Dark Portal* by Aaron Rosenberg and Christie Golden; *World of Warcraft: Wolfheart* by Richard A. Knaak; and the short stories "Heart of War" by Sarah Pine, "As Our Fathers Before Us" by Steven Nix, and "Edge of Night" by Dave Kosak (on www.WorldofWarcraft.com).

- Chen Stormstout's precocious niece, Li Li, has always dreamed of following her uncle's footsteps and wandering the diverse lands of Azeroth. More information about this curious pandaren is presented in the graphic novel *World of Warcraft: Pearl of Pandaria* by Micky Neilson and Sean "Cheeks" Galloway, the online four-part novella *Quest for Pandaria* by Sarah Pine, and the eleven-part journal series "Li Li's Travel Journal" (on www.WorldofWarcraft.com).

THE BATTLE RAGES ON

Shadows of the Horde offers a chilling glimpse of the ruthless measures Warchief Garrosh Hellscream is employing to silence his detractors. Yet these savage tactics have only stoked the fires of discontent among his proud faction, driving many of its members to the brink of open rebellion.

World of Warcraft's fourth expansion, *Mists of Pandaria*, chronicles Hellscream's brutal assassination attempt against Vol'jin and the mounting unrest that threatens to tear the Horde apart. *You* can take part in these historic events as you adventure through Pandaria, a never-before-seen continent filled with new allies, enemies, and thrilling quests. *Mists of Pandaria* also allows you to play as a noble pandaren (*WoW's* latest playable race) and join the Horde or the Alliance, depending on which faction aligns more with your ideals. Regardless of the side you choose, your adventures will impact the destinies of both the Horde and Azeroth itself.

To discover the ever-expanding realm that has entertained millions around the globe, go to WorldofWarcraft.com and download the free trial version. Live the story.